Chris started his career working on the floor in residential care as a night staffer, social worker, and supervisor. He formed a lifelong passion for the work.

After ten years he moved to the Public Prison Service, managing education, health and therapeutic programmes for the Wellington region's three prisons, eventually managing Mount Crawford Prison.

Chris returned to the Welfare System to become Manager of Operations for the country's Youth Justice Residences. He progressed to other senior roles in Youth Justice, eventually becoming the General Manager.

For my family, Debra, Amelia, Mat and Heather whose support and tolerance enabled me to have an interesting and successful career, and to write this book.

And for the staff and young people everywhere who spend time in residential care.

Chris Polaschek

THE NIGHT STAFFER

AUSTIN MACAULEY PUBLISHERS™

LONDON • CAMBRIDGE • NEW YORK • SHARJAH

A CIP catalogue record for this title is available from the British Library.

ISBN 9781398461956 (Paperback)
ISBN 9781398461963 (ePub e-book)

www.austinmacauley.com

First Published 2023
Austin Macauley Publishers Ltd®
1 Canada Square
Canary Wharf
London
E14 5AA

I want to thank Amelia and Debra for the considerable time spent helping me with editing this book.

Mat for his contribution to the cover design.

Heather for her ever-present interest and support over the two years I worked on this.

Part 1
New Beginnings: July 1987

Chapter 1
Wyatt's First Night

We ascend a dimly illuminated stairwell. Dark stained rimu wooden panelling on the walls contributes to the gloom. It smells of varnish and age. There's a faint hum coming from the floor above. It increases as we turn the last corner, becoming identifiable as a mixture of movement and chatter. John Land, senior social worker and my new boss is leading the way. We emerge onto a brightly lit landing and I catch my first glimpse of the boys I will be working with through an open doorway to my right, a mass of blue and white pyjamas. Before I can see more, we turn sharply left and I'm ushered into a small office. A young man dressed in a brown tracksuit with yellow striped edging is seated at a desk writing furiously. He is hunched over concentrating and all I can see is the back of his head and his long black ponytail which hangs down below the top of the chair. He does not look up as we enter but continues with his task.

John says to him, 'Gwynne, this is Wyatt Novak. He's the new night staffer. First night!'

Gwynne mutters something I can't hear, it may have been a greeting. 'Hi Gwynne,' I say, just in case.

'This is the night staff kingdom!' John waves his arm in an expansive semi-circle identifying the pokey untidy little room barely big enough to swing a cat in.

'Welcome, welcome, welcome! Brian Greene, we all call him Ted, will be here shortly. I know he's somewhere on the premises, probably doing his checks. How's that paperwork going, Gwynne, are you nearly finished?'

'Just about. What will I say about Aaron Lamas?' Gwynne is of Welch stock from the sounds of his accent.

'Settled shift and no problems!' says John. Short and sweet.

Gwynne makes a note, slams the book shut, gets up, flicks his ponytail with his hand and then indicates he is leaving.

'OK Wyatt, Ted will be here any minute. Things are pretty quiet up here, so we'll leave you to it. I'm sure you'll have a good first night!' With that John departs and I am standing in the office on my own.

The hum I heard when I first arrived seems to have dissipated. No point in mucking about, I think to myself, I might as well get out and meet the boys. I can't see anyone from in here. I step out of the office, left or, right? Left, I take a couple of steps down a short corridor and turn right.

The dormitory is murky, the only light is coming from the doorway where I stand and another at the far end of the room. I notice there are no actual doors, just the frames which they once occupied. I can make out three petitioned areas on both sides of the room. At the end of each are side by side wardrobes. This creates a nook for the bed and a pseudo corridor up the middle. In the first of the alcoves, there are two beds, both with obviously disturbed bedding and both without boys. I look across the aisle and see the same is true in the alcove opposite. Beds but no boys. Even a newbie can work out that something is wrong with this picture.

I'm about to move on to the next partition when all of a sudden there's a loud bang. It is magnified by the silence of a moment before. I nearly jump out of my skin. The door of the wardrobe nearest me bursts open and a diminutive figure leaps out in front of me.

'Heyaaaaah' he screams, adopting a karate-like stance with his hands and arms ready to strike a new and somewhat bewildered night staffer. He advances at pace towards me. He would almost be in my face, that is if he were a head taller.

'Heyaaaaaaaah…ah…ah…aaaah.' He gives it a little more emphasis and enthusiasm now. Over my initial shock which I hope none of the boys saw, I suppress an immediate thought that I might have to defend myself against this midget attacker. More banging and crashing. Other boys are leaping out of wardrobes and emerging from behind the partitions. Now the room is filled with a cacophony of noise, karate grunts, raucous laughter and other sounds I am unable to distinguish in the moment. I sense there are kids in the doorway behind me and I see some peering through the other entrance at the end of the dorm. Surprise party! They have been waiting for me to come into the room. Surrounded now, I am acutely mindful of my isolation. I keep my eyes focused on the midget ninja while retaining an awareness of the others in my peripheral vision, and follow my instincts.

'Who are you?' I ask a bit lamely. It's as if I have flicked a switch and turned off the party. Everything becomes still and silence now reigns again. The room is filled with anticipation.

'I'm Hatch, who are you?' says the karate kid.

'Hello, Hatch. I'm Wyatt, the new night attendant. Aren't you all supposed to be in bed?' I'm measured in my response, polite and quiet, but also trying to exude an air of confidence and authority.

'Oh hear that?' he asks the assembled multitude, waving a limp wrist in my direction, 'Very la... de... dah... de... dah. Oh and look, he's got a girlie earring in his ear. We know what you're here for... Wyatt.' He spits out my name. 'Wyatt... that's like a cowboy name, right? You don't look much like a cowboy to me, where's yah hat? You sound more like a nob, a gaybo nob. Are you a gaybo cowboy nob Wyatt?' The boys, who have gathered around now, chortle and snigger and a couple of other voices chime in, repeating the question. Hatch appears pleased with his challenge and the support from the other boys. He seems to grow a bit taller.

'Well Hatch, I can't help sounding educated, something that's worth a try when you get the chance.' I am aware I am being sarcastic, I better watch that. Right at this moment, I'm Wyatt the night attendant. Anything else I might be shouldn't matter to you.' I say bluntly. 'Although... I have got a horse tethered up out the front' I add trying to take a more conciliatory tone.

Silence. Not the response I'd hoped to engender.

As I stand caught in the moment and wondering what to do next, a rather large fellow approximately my height but more solidly built, steps towards me, 'You on your own?' he asks although it may be more of a statement.

I can see he's missing one of his front teeth. His face is sufficiently pale that I can tell it's covered in pimples even in the relative darkness. Perhaps a stranger to facial cleaning products.

I feel a twinge of vulnerability because he's not wrong, I am on my own. 'And you are?'

'Bentley Breezer. I'm in charge around here.' This causes a bit of guffawing from some of the boys. I guess this is another challenge, slightly more concerning than the one from the midget ninja.

'I'm sorry Bentley, they didn't mention that when I arrived. I'll be sure to check with my colleague Brian when he gets up here, should be any minute now.'

'Brian? You mean Ted. He isn't coming in today, that's what I heard. No worries, I'll help you out tonight. I know how to keep this bunch of dickheads in shape.' He reaches over and cuffs Hatch around the back of his head. Hatch gives him the finger.

'Thanks, Bentley, I appreciate the generous offer, but I don't think I'll be taking you up on it. Now if you don't mind…or even if you do, I think it's time all of you got back into your beds.'

'Now if you don't mind, la… de… da…de… dah…ah…ah!' Hatch has come back to life but no one seems interested in his attempt to stir things further.

As quickly as they gathered, the boys move away and the chatter starts up again. A few go back to running around, doing karate kicks, some pushing and shoving each other. Thank god for short attention spans! But I have not exerted any control. Bentley remains standing there looking at me with a strange grin on his face. He's not going anywhere.

Impasse. What to do next?

I am saved from answering the question when we are all taken by surprise. A booming voice fills the room, 'What's going on in here then!'

Most of the boys shoot off to, what I assume, are their allotted dorms. However several resume shoving each other and I'm distracted watching them.

'That'll be enough of that' says the voice. One of the boys looks up and steps out of the tussle. 'Into your dorm Hoani, you know you shouldn't be in here. Aaron, you shouldn't be in here either, get back to your dorm.' The voice is not as loud now but it still has presence and authority. As the boys disperse I turn to see the source. It's a tall, solidly built man who nearly fills the whole of the doorway. I can't see much else apart from the outline of a baseball cap and the silhouette of his bulky frame which further reduces the minimal light coming into the room.

'Can you go down the hall behind you and check the boys are in their rooms and their beds!' he directs me. 'I'll get the other lot in Rata settled. Meet you back in the office. I'm Brian by the way but everyone here calls me Ted.'

I do as I'm told, exit the dorm, make a couple of short turns and enter a narrow hallway. It's about fourteen metres long, the walls are punctuated with doorways. All are shut and there's no sign of anybody. I zigzag along opening each door as I go. The first two lead into shower and toilet areas respectively.

The others, four on each side, are bedrooms. I knock before entering. Seven of the eight bedrooms have an occupant in their bed, seemingly asleep. Surprising, given only a few moments ago they were running amuck. Although I greet each one, none acknowledge me. The eighth room is empty and the bed is not made up. Blankets are folded and piled at the foot, topped with a couple of brownish stained pillows without their slips. I head back to the office passing through the partitioned dorm. I say goodnight to the kung fu boys. Everyone's in bed and no one responds.

Ted is sitting at the desk writing in a large black book. It feels like he fills half the room. Now I can see him better, I pick him to be about my age. He has a jovial face, a slight smile lingers about it as he glances up and greets me. The baseball cap is gone, now sitting on the desk. Its absence reveals close-cropped blond hair, receding on each side of his forehead. He has a beard, also blonde, short and with a tailored point below his chin. His face is ruddy, possibly from being out in tonight's winter coolness. He's wearing a blue and brown checked swan dry, green corduroy pants and I can just make out the heels of burgundy coloured sneakers.

I deposit myself on a metal-framed wooden chair nestled beside the desk. Ted continues to write for a minute so I look around. There's junk cluttered everywhere and the room smells of age, decay, socks, dampness, perspiration, and something else I can't quite put my finger on. I'll get used to it. The walls are covered in notices and signs. The notices are busy so I will read most of those later. I read a few of the bigger signs.

'No boys in the office'

'All timesheets in by Tuesday night'

'All boys to be in bed and settled by 9.30 pm.'

'No boys to make phone calls after 7.30 pm.'

'Keep this room tidy!'

Two discoloured red couches form an 'L' shape against the back walls. Tucked between them I recognise the neck of an electric guitar. There is barely room to squeeze between the seated Ted and the couches but I do so and lift it out. It's a Fender Stratocaster copy. The black body is scratched and marked. Well used and a little abused, but it has all its strings, a good start. I put it back and return to my chair. Ted slams the book shut, sweeps it away from him across the desk and tosses the pen down next to it.

'That bloody guitar! Some staff let the boys have it at night. Pacifies them, does no harm that's what they say, but I'll tell you what, it's more about buying a bit of peace than anything else. And the Kung Fu movie, another brainwave, always has the same result. All the boys think they're Bruce Lee. Great for the day team because the boys love them and it keeps them occupied all evening. Bad for the night staff, they're all stirred up and don't settle. Sometimes I think the staff deliberately put them on for a laugh because they know what happens afterwards,' he muses.

Moving on without pause 'I see you've had the full induction into the job'. He has a wry smile on his face and I detect a little cynicism in his tone. After a brief pause, he asks, his tone more serious, 'Have you been shown around at all?'

'I saw what I passed on the way up to this office; a dining room, the office downstairs, and now I've been to all the dorms.'

'That's it! The full induction! The rest is learning on the job!' He's reverted to being frivolous, but not for long. 'Seriously, let's make sure the boys are truly settled then I'll give you a tour of the place. Who brought you up here?'

'John Land. He passed on a few things about some kids, a bit about the diary and then he said you would tell me the rest.'

I repeat the messages John passed on about the boys. He'd suggested we might need to keep an eye on a new admission who might be feeling a bit intimidated. Another is a boy released from the secure area who potentially could have been a bit difficult once he returned to the main house. He's settled so should be ok tonight. And there is a new guy admitted to the secure area who they don't know much about. John indicated he seemed settled too but who knows what might happen during the night. I'd managed to forget all the names. Mental note to self, write names down.

'Actually, I know about them' Ted says. 'There are notes in the diary.' He points to the black book. 'That's where all that sort of information is kept. Well, I'll tell you what, you've been lucky and have managed to get yourself into a pretty good team, yeah, Sarge, Gwynne and Abigail. They're solid and, out of all three teams, they're the best to follow from our perspective. One thing about us night staff, the way the roster works, we follow them all.' Not a perfect team obviously, I think to myself, what with the guitar and the Kung Fu movies. I wonder what the others are like, I guess I'll find out. He continues, 'And John Land, he's the best of the bunch of senior social workers, so lucky for you to have got him. Was it him who interviewed you? I'd heard they did interviews a couple of weeks ago that went on for a whole day, was that you?'

'Yeah he did, and yes it was.' Six of us were interviewed by a five-member panel in a convoluted process that included workshops, head to head forums and playing out scenarios.' At the time I thought it was a lot for a domestic services job that didn't require qualifications or experience. I hadn't even finished the whole process as I'd rushed off early to meet my childcare commitments, right in the middle of the final interview with the site manager, Mike Michelson, so I was pretty sure I'd missed my opportunity. History now, I got the job. John Land stood out from the rest of the panel because he seemed to take a particular interest in me. Now I know why, the vacant position was in his team. Also, I'd noted how he looked the most like a musician and possible kindred spirit, as opposed to the others who appeared more sporty or academic, or a combination of both. Well over six feet tall, thin in the frame, he has long shoulder-length hair, greying a little at the temples. On the day he was wearing black jeans, a brownish-green paisley shirt and pointed black boots. Tonight he's similarly dressed, a bit of a dated look but familiar to me from my days playing music out on the local circuits. He has small round glasses too, the John Lennon sixties flower power type so often seen on posters. These days I'd have to say I'm more into black, the John Lee Hooker or George Thorogood look, although I'm still a bit of a hippie at heart.

I tell Ted I met Sarge and Abigail in the office downstairs when I arrived tonight. Abigail is a short, stocky woman who looks to be in her early thirties. She was wearing track pants and a burnt orange polo shirt. Her brown hair is short-cropped and barely reaches the collar of her shirt and she has a fringe cut just above her eyebrows. Although I wouldn't describe her as beautiful, she is not unattractive. She was wearing no obvious makeup. The thing I noticed most was the twinkle in her eye, suggesting someone with a sense of fun. The other thing I remember noticing was the disproportionately large brown leather belt she was wearing which didn't seem to sit naturally on her hip. From it hung a long chain drooping and looping before disappearing back into a leather pouch. A key protruded from the pouch at right angles like it might have been resisting its confinement.

Sarge was also dressed in a tracksuit, this one was blue and white. He has short hair, grey flecked throughout. My guess is he's in his early forties. I got the vibe he's ex-military, it was written all over him, in his bearing and the direct

17

way he spoke. When he greeted me I almost felt I had to salute. His handshake was strong enough that I was concerned he might crush my fingers.

Gwynne, I met upstairs in the office.

Ted interrupts my brief reflections, confirming my feelings about Sarge. His real name is Terry. 'We've got a few ex-military on staff and some ex-league players. They've been the traditional recruiting grounds since before I arrived here. Recently we're started getting more social worker types like Abigail and Gwynne. I think the 'powers that be' want the residences to be more professionally focused. So far so good from what I can see, particularly if you're mainly measuring team performance. But someone needs to tell the boys we're here to help, not to just contain them!' I wonder what he means but before I can ask he goes on.

'Wyatt, where did that name come from? Are you American? You don't sound it.'

'Nah, It's a family name, my second name. My first name is Charles.'

'Oh yeah, what happened to Charles, didn't you like it?'

I explain how I was named after my father but kept getting called little Charles when I was growing up until I was bigger than him. Then they called me big Charles, or big Charlie which was worse, I didn't go for that. The old man didn't like being little Charlie or old Charles much either, so he started calling me Wyatt, my second name. Worked for me and him, so in the end, everyone picked up on it and it stuck.

'All good Wyatt. Everybody calls me Ted so I get it.' I am about to enquire about the back story regarding his name but he leaves no gap.

'It's been quiet for fifteen minutes, which generally means the boys are asleep. Let's go for a walk through the dorms. Regular walkabouts are an important tool in our kitbag. You have to keep an eye on what's going on and you're more likely to keep the kids in their beds if they poke their heads out and you're just there, or they hear you coming. Nip the problem in the bud I say.'

I'm not sure what it is about Ted but I take an immediate liking to him. Maybe it's his confidence or his easy manner… something connects.

Chapter 2
Wyatt Takes a Tour

Ted gets up from the desk and manoeuvres past me out of the office. I follow and as I step outside he pulls the door shut, sorts a key from the bunch attached to his belt, and locks up.

'We never, ever leave the office unlocked, even in an emergency' he says in a matter of fact tone. 'That's what you've got the large bunch of keys for, locking things and unlocking things.'

Before I came upstairs John made me sign for mine. Now secured in a pouch and belt around my waist, they feel cumbersome and a little foreign but hopefully look more at home than Abigail's did.

'Someone will almost certainly go in there. When they do, something will be pilfered or broken. This time it was a couple of marker pens. Fortunately, I got them. Aaron Finch took the opportunity to grab them while you were otherwise occupied by the ninja warriors. He was just coming out of the office as I came up the stairs. Caught him red-handed. Waste of time and energy for a few pens, but he's not in here because he makes good decisions. It could have been worse. If he had the time he could have looked at the diary or ripped out a couple of pages. These kids can get up to anything and sometimes for no obvious reason. It's not always silly stuff like that, some boys are cunning. Word of warning for you, be careful with them all… and more careful with some than others.'

'Lesson one for me' I acknowledge Ted's experience.

'Yeah, well actually, it's lesson three. Lesson one is don't let the day staff go off and leave you alone. You need to stand your ground on that or they'll do it all the time. At the end of their shift, they just want to get out of here. It's understandable but not the agreed process. You shouldn't be left on your own… period!… even more so on your first day. Lesson two is 'settled' should mean in bed, if not asleep, at a minimum the place should be quiet...' I sense a little weariness in his tone like this is a battle he has fought before.

'Any rate let's get on with what does happen and not spend too much time on what doesn't... for now.' He explains that for sleeping purposes the kids are split into three dorms, all named after native trees. The younger ones, twelve and thirteen-year-olds mainly, the most vulnerable, are down in Kauri. The older ones, in Rata, are mostly sixteen-year-olds, although the number of older boys is trending upward at the moment. Tonight there's only one, Johnny Remus. 'He'll be gone soon, off to Corrective Training, everyone refers to it as C.T., a programme for juveniles run by the Prison Service,' Ted says, 'He's done his chips in our system and he appears in the District Court on Wednesday for sentencing. He'll probably try and take off before then. He's not a 'bad apple' just a persistent offender. Burgs and stealing cars mainly. His brother's here too, younger but he's going the same way. There's another brother as well, currently in prison. Lovely family, all following in dad's footsteps doing the family business.'

As we wander Ted continues to talk. We re-enter the dorm where I encountered the Kung Fu kids. Ted picks up immediately. 'This dormitory is named Rimu and it holds all those who are not in Kauri or Rata.' The boys, if they're awake, ignore us as we pass through.

Once through Rimu, we enter a short hallway. Ted points out a door at the end of the landing and then to a small red box with a glass front covering a round red button positioned halfway along the hallway. 'Fire door and fire alarm! Fire doors are always locked so we need to open them in the event of a fire. Dumb putting the alarm there, too accessible, it should be in the office.' I wonder at this comment but there's a lot of information coming my way. I don't dwell on it. We turn left again.

We are now in Kauri, home of the younger boys. This is the only area where there are separate bedrooms. Ted is blunt, 'This is a safety move, it keeps these young ones away from the older boys at night and all the risks that can come with mixing them.' He doesn't elaborate but I get the picture.

He tells me some of the younger boys are transitioning to or from Hokio Beach in Levin, one of the county's residences that take younger children. There's another residence in Levin too, Kohitere, which takes the older kids. Stanmore houses boys going to both these and transitioning back into the South Island. Sometimes boys from other residences around the country are admitted here if they're full. This residence is supposed to be for short term placements however Ted indicates there seem to be increasing numbers of 'regulars' getting stuck here for longer. A couple of boys are long-termers and have been here for over six months.

He shows me the showers and the toilets. There are three of each. 'That's all the showers we have in this building but there are other toilets downstairs.' I am enlightened. Now we are at the end of the hall next to a second fire door. Looking through it I can see a house next to the property. There is an 'L' shaped fence separating the residence from the house, the second part of which extends along the back of the Stanmore Road supermarket.

'The supermarket is a hub of activity at night, especially around the food waste bins. You'll see for yourself. It accounts for some of the noise we hear at night, just so you know for future reference.'

I see all the fire doors are reinforced glass. Ted continues, 'we're required to have two fire exits up here under the fire regulations. Good thing too because this place is a fire hazard, wood everywhere, has been drying out for years. I'm surprised it hasn't burnt down already. The boys are always smuggling cigarettes into the place... and lighters or matches. They added a sprinkler system up here when they built the Special Needs Unit a few years ago. But I'll tell you what, the Fire Service, who come here quite a bit one way or another... as you'll see...' He gives me what I assume is a 'watch this space' nod, 'told me it's not much good, more like a temporary set-up than a real solution. That's why we get pretty excited about matches and lighters. Now let's have a look at Rata.' He's ramming as much information as he can into the conversation. I feel a bit overwhelmed but still appreciate it.

We walked back past the office and into an open dorm Rata, the one I caught a brief glimpse of when I arrived. Twelve boys in twelve beds, six on each side of the room. On one side there are two large sash windows which I see have been permanently screwed shut ... not additional fire exits then! They match a similar window I noticed in the stairwell.

'This is the big boy's area. Not a great arrangement because there are no partitions and the older boys are much harder to settle. And of course, bedtime here is mostly way before they'd go to sleep normally out in the real world. Some are used to living more at night than during the day, for obvious reasons. As you can see though, they're bye-byes for the night except for Aaron over there.

Goodnight Aaron.' A boy lifts his head and gives a little nod of acknowledgement.

'Rata's right next to our office so at least we can easily keep an ear on them, although as you have probably worked out already, you can't see into any of the dorms from there. Some genius thought through the surveillance part!' he scoffs. 'Obviously, no one asked the night staff what they needed. Water under the bridge now.'

We head back to the office and sit down, him at the desk, me on the chair next to it. He makes a couple of notes in the black book.

'First point, everything gets recorded in here. This is the Daily Log. Every time I do a check, I write down what I see and the time I made it. A check, by the way, means spot the real body, an arm, a leg, their head, and not just a lump in the bed.'

'That must disturb the boys. Does it cause problems?' I ask.

'Can do, although most of the time it's pretty easy to see something. It's worse for the boys in Kauri because you have to open the door and let the light in. Normally I just shine my torch on the end of the bed and work up from there, or on the wall above the boy's head. It can still disturb them. However, it has to be done. We're supposed to do checks on or about every twenty minutes. Most often we can manage to, not all the time though because things happen, but I try to keep to schedule as best I can.'

Ted indicates the diary is like a running log of events. As well as the client checks, all incoming and outgoing phone calls, perimeter checks, any movements by the boys, and even toilet stops. Everything, basically if it happened, or even if you think it happened, write it down! There are other books as well but they're not upstairs. Ted says he will take me through these later but he highlights the most important ones. There is an Admissions Register, a comprehensive guide to information about the boy including demographics, key contacts and reason for their admission to a residence including the legal status. It's essential for night staffers because there are often night admissions. Same story with the Special Needs Unit Admissions Register or S.N.U. The abbreviated letters are euphemistically clumped and pronounced as 'snoo'. Most of the recorded information sounds like a repeat of the Admissions register, except in this book the reasons why the secure placement is being made are specified.

'The special 'need' is that you need to be put into a locked area so you don't run away or so your aberrant behaviour can be controlled,' explains Ted 'It's a lock-up, that's how the boys see it!' He goes back to the books,' We also have an Incident Register, that's for more detailed accounts of some events...oh, and there's a maintenance book, where anything that needs fixing is recorded. Night staff often see things on their checks that others don't. You name it, there's a form for it. Bureaucracy in all its glory! Too much to take in at one time but you'll have plenty of time to learn all of that. Time...on nights it's one thing we have in abundance.'

I get the point. Now Ted starts to talk about the more interesting aspect, the boys.

Chapter 3
The Boys

'We get all sorts of boys. We call them 'clients'.' He illustrates an ambiguity about this title by using air parenthesis. 'In my view, a client seeks a service, these kids don't, more like they seek to avoid it! We offer a service but it's more for the State or the community, or the Police'. Ted explains, 'The Police, well, they don't like having kids in their cells, clogs them up and some of the kids are lippy. That's hardly a surprise because they are lippy here, including to the Police whenever they come ...which is pretty frequently. Pisses them off big time.'

Ted seems to be ruminating with himself as he says, 'I suppose we do provide something for the boys. We feed them and give them some safe time to sort their stuff out. And for everybody else involved to sort their stuff out too, which is probably just as important. It's supposed to be a crisis placement although sometimes the resolution takes a while.'

However, he also indicates that for increasing numbers of boys, the residence is becoming a second home. They're in and out until they are too old to be here. In the last couple of years, they have begun to receive older boys more often, and they are staying longer too. It has something to do with changes in the Criminal Justice Act. Ted admits he doesn't take much interest in what he describes as the 'legal mumbo jumbo'. He believes a big part of what they do at Stanmore is pure containment while the 'clients', air parenthesis again, are stabilised. He adds 'If it wasn't for the work of some of the more dedicated staff at Stanmore, there would be a few who spent their whole adolescence here.' The biggest grizzle residential social workers have is once a boy comes in, the field social worker breathes a sigh of relief and turns off the phone for a month or so. He sums it up, 'I'll tell you what, out of sight out of mind for a lot of these boys. And not just from social workers, ... everybody!'

He describes the incumbent population as a 'mixed bunch.' Different age groups are just one thing. There are offenders, some who have done serious stuff like aggravated robberies and assaults, although mostly it's 'burgs and knicking cars'. But there are a few he refers to in more colourful terms. The 'real nasty ones', boys who are dangerous and big, and can be a real handful for other clients and staff. And then there are the 'head cases' who have mental health issues, the odd one who talks to themselves or say they hear voices all the time. There's a group he describes 'as young fellows who just can't behave,' they won't stay at home or where they're placed and end up living on the streets, 'waifs and strays', street kids, a lot are wards of the State. Another group he refers to as 'glue bags', a derogatory term for glue sniffers, some of whom are so bad they have fried their brains. Interestingly, a few come from what seem to be good family homes but for some reason, they won't stay there. Ted believes plenty of violence and abuse happens in 'better off' families but they have the means to hide it so it's less visible.

'Of course,' he points out, 'lots of the boys have a bunch of these problems so I'm just generalising about the major 'presenting issues' that's the appropriate social work jargon!' Good for me to know. The language of the job is important.

There are a few kids with special needs or who have a very low IQ. He illustrates the point with a smile and a graphic example, 'We had one boy who had an IQ of sixty-five. I'll tell you what, he was hard to deal with, a bit like dealing with a four-year-old, but you know, biggish build and going through adolescence and all its mysteries. And believe me, they seemed to be mysterious to him. He got the masturbating bit though, just not the where and when. The other boys keep winding him up for laughs. That wasn't good for anyone.' He adds 'If I were to sum it up, the common theme is most of the boys who come through here have had crappy lives one way or the other. You'll see that when you read the files.' He pauses for a breath. I am fascinated but I can't think of anything to say now even though the opportunity has presented itself, so I wait and Ted pushes on.

Stanmore is supposed to be for regional kids, but in reality, the boys can come from anywhere on the South Island. Normally the place should only take thirty boys but it's not uncommon for there to be thirty-five or thirty-six.

'One night we had thirty-seven, although seven of those were in SNU. A couple were on mattresses in the dining room. It was an accident waiting to happen I tell you! Typical of this place, Disneyland, not the people here, but the system. I'll take you down to SNU shortly and you can have a look. At times you will be working there throughout the night, you down there, me up here or vice versa. Having said all that, thank god most of the time it is quiet! Generally, there's a bit of buzz early on, then nothing until the morning apart from the odd bladder call. We do get a few admissions at night though. I don't mind that, it helps break up the long lags of sitting about!'

So I ask what he does to fill in the time.

'I read quite a lot. And I do the odd job around here although we're not encouraged to despite me having offered many, many times. It'd help fill our time, keep us occupied and you know, make a contribution to the place. Some nights it can be a struggle just to get through but you do get used to it. I potter around, read everything I can lay my hands on and still average a novel a week.'

My induction moves on to the policies and procedures. The most important vehicle seems to be the Department's 'Yellow Book' which contains all the relevant information.

'As you can see it's a big volume so most things are in here but if it ain't, make it up. I do. You'll find you have to from time to time, but always make a record of what you've done. It's the safest way.' Ted's synopsis will do for now. There's plenty of reading in there. I'll look later on when I have a few quiet hours!

We go through the routines and the expectations of the night staff. He covers the rosters and it is pretty clear from the outset that these are a favoured topic of conversation for him. Too much information, I'm beginning to feel overloaded, mainly with the technical stuff, but I'm also fascinated. It's a different world, like the dark side of the moon. If you stop and consider it, you know it's out there, but, because mostly you don't see or experience it, you don't have cause to think about it.

I'm curious about the staffing arrangements. He points out it's both simple and complicated, an impression I am getting about the whole place. There are three members of the permanent night staff team. However, the way the shifts are set up, with all the leave and sickness, there is an unavoidably high usage of relieving staff. Ted reckons it's probably about a quarter of the time on nights. Most relievers are pretty good, a couple not so. He doesn't rely on them anyway because he always feels responsible as the permanent staff member. Our other team member is Johnny Rogers.

'He makes the boys call him Mr Rogers and he's adamant that we all do too. Not sure why but it was happening before I joined and he was clear on the day I started, call him Mr Rogers. You'll meet him on Saturday night. Mr Rogers, what can I say about him? He's been here more than seven years so back when the role was a sole charge position. He has a different view about this job than I do. All I'll say about that is I believe in being awake and vigilant all night. You never know what the boys might get up to and at what time. Hell! All sorts of things happen at night, in here and out on the property. People hang around the place, sometimes it will be boys, but other times I've bumped into more dubious types nosing around, especially around the SNU. We've had kids doing drugs, joyriders in cars, suspicious-looking adults hanging about, and even had the odd couple doing the 'dirty' out in the backfield next to the school. You name it we've encountered it!' He pauses for a moment as if contemplating whether to say more. It seems the mention of SNU reminds him we need to go down and have a look.

There's a couple of boys in tonight, one a newbie and the other, an old hand. They were asleep when he checked earlier. As part of his nightly routine, he visits SNU first thing when he comes on-site as he walks past it anyway. He likes to know how closely he might need to keep an eye on the place before he gets up to the main dorm area. 'Be prepared' is his motto, like a good boy scout. Sometimes there may be an extra staff member on at night because the kids are playing up or the numbers in SNU are high. A reliever is a useful addition as they can float between upstairs and SNU as needed. Ted's clear, once there are double-ups, two in a cell which happens quite often, the risks increase significantly. It doesn't mean a reliever is engaged. Normally it's one of the regulars who need to be down there if it needs staffing.

The phone rings, interrupting the conversation. Ted snaps up the receiver, 'Christchurch Boys Home. Yes… Ok…When?…Bye.'

'Police, we have incoming, Rowan Harding, nabbed in a stolen car. He's a regular, not a bad kid really, educated and well-spoken, just a persistent nuisance offender. No violence so we'll bring him up here.' Then he adds, 'Handy, I'll be able to take you through the admissions process when he comes. I don't know when they'll arrive but they say to expect them any time before midnight. In reality, that means anytime between now and six in the morning. They either ring and come straight away because they're already on their way or much later when they have nothing else to do. Quite often it will be four or five in the morning.

That's one of the differences between me and Mr Rogers. He hates doing admissions so when we're on shift together I pretty much do them all. I prefer to anyway, so it works for me. I like to talk to the boys when they arrive and see where they're at.' Ted explains that generally, the morning teams don't have much time to closely interview the new admissions so it's useful if we can pass something on. It might be about someone they've seen on the street, such as an absconder, or maybe a potential place to stay after court, or even something about their health or family. It's the 'one to one' thing. Boys will sometimes talk to us because they don't see us the same way as the day staff. At night you see their vulnerabilities, their worries, or fears because they can talk to you without others seeing or hearing what they have to say. You'll see when you walk around.'

He says there will be boys crying or upset about being stuck in here, or something that's happened to them during the day, or a phone call that went bad, someone who failed to visit, threats from bullies, that sort of thing. Others just seem to want to talk to an adult on their own. They will be worried about their placement, or court, … any number of reasons. Ted likes to talk with them, and especially, to listen. He feels this doesn't happen as often as it should during the day. 'Too many needy kids, too busy, and not enough staff' is his view.

However, when it comes to talking to groups of young people, he's not so keen. He had a bad experience one night early in his tenure. It started when he joined a conversation about girls and women. Some of the boys were very derogatory in their views, especially about their mums. Some mentioned girlfriends. Then there were comments about how hot some of the visiting girlfriends were. That didn't go down well with the boyfriends. Then it was how 'stink' being in here was. It got out of hand with boys threatening each other and this led to several hours of disruptions. He was just lucky that it all settled down eventually. Mr Rogers, his colleague that night, was none too pleased. He was pretty quick to point out that there are enough challenges on shift without the night staff causing more. Mr Rogers generally doesn't like talking to the boys much at all, never the less Ted says there are a few he seems to have a relationship with and he will go out of his way to talk to them.

He goes back to our new admission, 'Rowan will be in Court on Friday so he will probably only be here for a few days so the time for information gathering is short.'

The phone rings again. Ted grabs it, 'Christchurch Boys Home…yeah thanks John, they've rung already to say they're coming. I will put him into Kauri for the night, that way no one will be disturbed. Everything else is quiet here, just filling Wyatt in on the place…Yes, he's still here… Ha! Ha! Ha!… Ok bye.' He hangs up.

'That was John. The Police rang him earlier about admitting Rowan and he didn't pass it on so he's catching up. I think he also might have been checking on what's happening with you. There have been guys who start work here, mainly as relievers, and who just do not turn up after a couple of days. He might have thought you'd do a runner, be a staff absconder!' He has a big grin on his face as he says this.

'Really? Am I missing something? Is it that bad here?' I inquire, a bit tongue in cheek.

'No, no! not often. It has its moments that's for sure as you will no doubt find out. Most of the time though it's quiet and we just potter around, bored and trying to stay awake. As I said I get through heaps of books, nothing technical though. It can be hard work reading during the 'death hours' between about 3.30 to 5 am. It's when your body just wants to shut down, screaming for sleep, by far the hardest time on shift. I can't even read. That's partly why I'd like to do something manually, you know like tidy up the office because it helps keep me awake!' He offers to bring in some stuff he has on how hard night shifts are on the body. He collects material about it. Maybe at a later time, I think. He continues, 'Mr Rogers has the view that you should just sleep because that's what the kids are doing and it's what your body wants to do. He puts his feet up at midnight and doesn't do anything until about 5.30 am … if he can't avoid it, and he can get a bit grumpy if he has to. He has been doing this type of work for a long time and I think when he was a sole charge here, it's what they did. You slept and got up every three or four hours and did a check. Anyway, he was clear with me about his views on my first day and he'll probably say the same to you. Frankly, I think it puts it on your partner to stay awake. And I'll tell you what, it's not something he wants to be discussed with the day teams, you know, what happens on nights stays on nights! I guess what you choose to do in the end is your business. I have to admit, it's hard to stay awake all the time, every night, and you will find out for yourself. I've conked out a few times without even knowing it, but it's the exception, not the rule. The bottom line for me, I don't deliberately sleep.'

I get the message. I don't bother saying anything. I haven't taken this job because I thought I could sleep the time away. I have plans, I want to study and this type of job will support me to do so, although from the sounds of it, not between 4–5 am! I want to get on with finishing the degree I left behind when I dropped out of university back in the day when I didn't understand the value of a qualification. But I'm glad to be warned about what might happen when I do my first shift with my 'yet to meet' colleague Mr Rogers. I think it's odd about the name though, but whatever…up to him what he wants to be called.

'Any questions come out of what I've told you? It's a bit to take in and you'll get more over the first few days. I'm not too bright, he says with a grin 'and I got it in a couple of weeks!'

'Yeah, probably lots,' I can't even think where to start so I say the only thing that comes to mind. 'Mr Rogers, it seems to be odd to address him like that, why not John or Johnny?'

'I'll tell you what, you'll get used to it, we all have. Anyway, tell me a bit about you. What brought you to this place on this day?'

Chapter 4

Wyatt Meets Ted

It looks like we have a bit of time on our hands before the Police arrive so I get into it.

I'd been off work for six months with an injury and when my wife Rose got a full-time job, we decided it might be good if I found something at night. My previous job was contracting work that didn't pay regularly. Accident Compensation, although regular, was less money so we needed to restore the coffers which had taken a bit of a hit. And I've got three children, all under the age of seven, they like to be fed and clothed, goes with the territory. This job was serendipitous for sure. I started looking and literally, it came up within a few days. It was a bonus that it was social work linked, an area I have an interest in. He seems genuinely engaged so I forge on in more detail.

In my late teens, I did a bit of youth work at Arohata Borstal which was in my hometown of Tawa. For a while, I visited weekly to play basketball with the girls. There was not a heap of skill on show. They were pretty rough, tougher than most of the men I played against over the years. I got a few elbows in the head and the guts for my trouble, and my feet stomped on. It was all a bit of fun though and it was worth it. The sport was a great connection point and I got pretty friendly with a few of the girls over time. There were lots of Māori, a few Pacifica and the odd spattering of Pakeha. The warders told me many of the girls had been abused and had terrible experiences growing up. On the few occasions the girls talked to me about their lives, the mention of abuse or violence was treated as if it was just part of life. The subtext of their conversations was more about poverty, and why they were in Arohata. It seemed to be much of it was more about surviving than offending.

I'd known kids who got up to all sorts of things when I was growing up. Any one of them could have ended up in a place like that, but they had supportive parents, could get lawyers, pay compensation, the sort of things that can make trouble go away. My brother and I weren't angels either. We did a lot of silly adolescent stuff for the fun of it. Harmless or so we thought at the time. We never got caught so we were lucky. 'Model citizens now of course!' I proffer.

Right from the start, I found Arohata really fascinating, not so much the prison-like environment, although it was an eye-opener to a middle-class boy, but the way the whole Justice System worked. It happened at a time in my life when I was experiencing a political awakening, in part through listening to my favourite artist of the time, Bob Dylan with his protest songs focused on social justice like 'The Chimes of Freedom' and 'The Lonesome Death of Hattie Carrol'. It coincided with the end of the nineteen sixties movement, love peace, protests, anti-establishment feelings and great music. While the visits were happening I also started University studying Sociology, gathering intellectual frameworks that further challenged the way I viewed the world.

I discussed the possibility of becoming a social worker with my old man and he said to me 'If you can't live with eighty per cent failure, then you shouldn't get into social work. Do something useful with your life, build bridges or be a lawyer.' It put me off at the time. I dropped out of university after the first year, although not specifically because of his views. They contributed, but other things were going on at the time as well.

Over the years I was engaged with various factors that kept my social justice interest alive. How best to describe it? Probably experiencing the darker side, living a lifestyle where I frequented the edges of society. Young people doing hair raising things, families struggling to make ends meet, music, drugs, alcohol and rock 'n roll. None of it was criminal in the sense that I thought about criminal behaviour, that is, didn't warrant being locked up or taken away from your family or job, but definitely on the fringe.

A year before my accident I engaged a young fellow through an employment scheme who had been in and out of trouble all his life from what I could gather. He wasn't a bad kid, just not very bright and he kept doing stupid stuff. He didn't have even the basic skills needed to get by. I fished him out of Addington Prison a couple of times, always for petty opportunistic offending. In the end, he went too far and I couldn't do any more for him. But I couldn't see how sitting in prison was going to make his life better, and if it didn't help him then it didn't help society. That was my thinking at the time and remains so.

At any rate, I could have gone on all night but it's simple really, I took the job because I needed one, not necessarily because I think I can make a big difference to anything or anyone. It's a bonus it might lead me into a social work career, 'a foot in the door' was how Mike Michelsen from the panel described it. While it feels a little like I've gone full circle after the old man's observations, for now, I'm just focused on being a good night staffer and learning what I can. And working nights suits me, suits the family, and supports my future goals.

'A bit of a lefty eh, and you sound like you're educated. You'll fit in here then!' Ted says with a mild chuckle and a sprinkling of cynicism.

'What about you Ted? What brought you here? And what's the story about the name Ted?'

Ted gets started as we continue to wait for the admission. At thirty-four years of age, Brian 'Ted' Greene is a year older than me. He's been at Stanmore Road for nearly seven years. He's a family man with two children, a girl and a boy both under five years old. A Cantabrian through and through, he grew up and schooled in Linwood and now resides near his old family home with Jean, his wife of nine years. He left school after the fifth form having barely scraped through his School Certificate. That was enough schooling for him, he's not done any further study and doesn't intend to. He spent a short time labouring at a building site but working in the elements didn't do it for him and he got a job at the local tyre factory where he spent the next six years. Eventually, he ended up working a few nights which he enjoyed. He liked having part of his day free. He couldn't get a permanent role doing night work where he was, so he looked elsewhere. An opportunity to work part-time as a relieving night staffer came up at the Christchurch Boys Home. He hadn't thought about working with kids but it was nightwork. For a while, he continued working days at the factory and nights as they came up in the Boys Home. He started being asked to work more nights than he could cope with. The relieving work began to pay more than his daytime job. At the time they didn't have children so he took a gamble, tossed in the factory work and went into relieving as his main earner. After a couple of months, he was offered the job full time. It hadn't been a surprise because most of his work was covering the night staffer who'd been taking a lot of sick leave.

Ted revisits his deeply researched concerns about the impact of working nights on the physiology of the body and quality of life. I listen to a lengthy monologue without interrupting. I note however he's been doing it for seven years and intends to keep doing it into the future. I suspect the extra pay for working nights makes a difference. It does to me!

He's had a few requests to work on days as a reliever but it didn't work for him. He didn't like the way the place was run for too many reasons to be discussed now, but he tells me I'll see them for myself. He reiterates he's not a 'lefty' but he hastens to add that he isn't a 'righty' either, just nicely balanced in the middle is his self-evaluation.

I ask him what he reads. Thrillers, mysteries, action, nothing too intellectually challenging. In the 'death hour,' he goes walkabout up and down the dorms and outside around the perimeter to get a bit of the fresh evening air on his face.

He talks about the Welfare System, the Departments of Social Welfare and Justice, the Courts, and social work. In a nutshell; the bad kids are treated too soft and the sad kids are treated too hard. Most of what he says about the staff members doesn't mean much to me. It won't until I've met more people. It's good to hear his perspective on things though. We'll see how it aligns with mine once I've got more experience under my belt.

Finally, he says 'The big bunch of keys you have, they're your best tool, they take you everywhere in this place. I go into pretty much every room when I do my checks. Not the school though, that's the Ministry of Education, not us. It's how I find out what's going on. When I check admin, I pop into all the offices and see what's new, memos, policies, and announcements. One of the problems with being on nights is you miss out on the official briefings, the policy releases and news. Well, we don't! I find out for myself. There can be other little titbits you unearth as well. You'd be surprised what's lying about when it should be in locked desks or cabinets. It's legit for us to be in there,' he hastens to add, 'for security. Windows get left open, lights left on, things we routinely take care of. The info is the icing on the cake. Mr Rogers and I share that stuff, we both like to be up to speed.' I guess I will too.

My first impressions of Ted are reinforced as I talk to him. He seems like a genuinely nice guy, friendly and clear in his views about things. He's sceptical about the bureaucracy, how it works and whether the system will make any real difference to the boy's behaviour. He wouldn't be the first person I've met with low regard for Government agencies. Despite a bit of bluster about the boys, I get the sense he has a real interest and concern for most. I saw him interact with them tonight. He was clear and direct in an easy, engaging manner. There's an earnestness about him too that I like. I can learn things from him, and that works for me.

'What about the name Ted, where'd that come from?'

'I've been called Ted for most of my time here.'

One night not long after he started, a couple of the boys started calling him 'The Bear' possibly a reflection on his not inconsiderable girth. For a while the name stuck until one day after a confrontation during an SNU admission, the boy involved said he was more like a 'Teddy Bear.' It was supposed to be an insult. As can happen in this type of environment, over time he started to be referred to as Teddy, then just Ted. He doesn't mind the nickname, it could have been a lot worse. Eventually, all the staff picked up on it and now everybody calls him Ted. He warns me that I will get one sooner or later.

'You can't control it, it's bestowed on you by the boys and then it becomes your history here.' I tell him about the 'nob, gaybo cowboy' comment made by Hatch Hitch. 'That's not too good' he says, 'but if you're lucky it might get shortened to 'Cowbo' or nob boy! Ha, ha!'

Yes, Ted. Very funny!

Chapter 5
The SNU

There are no further communications about the imminent admission so we eventually head on down to SNU. The place is bleak. Immediately I get a feeling this is not a place where hope blossoms. It may be called a Special Needs Unit but if it looks like a cell block, smells like a cell block, it's a cell block.

And the boys call it 'Secure.' It's a stand-alone building that appears to date from around the 1970s. It's of simple concrete block construction, painted a tasteless pale yellow and has thick glass windows reinforced by grey horizontal steel bars. Tonight it's illuminated by a plethora of bright external lights showing it off in all its grandeur. It's somewhat less noticeable during the day as it is nestled in between other buildings but at night it stands out in the surrounding darkness and is visible to people driving and walking past on Stanmore Rd.

We go up a concrete ramp and through a heavy steel door on the left side of the building, tucked around the corner and not visible from the street. Ted tells me this door is most frequently used when admitting young people directly from the residence. It is closest to the main building and less visible to the public walking down Stanmore Rd or visiting the administration block. Once inside, we pass by a couple of rooms used for dining and visits. We turn a corner and I see three cells down one side of the corridor with grey metal doors and a small viewing window in each. At the end of the corridor is an open doorway to a small gym. It's about the size of half a basketball court. I can just make out a basketball ring and a thick rope hanging from the ceiling. We head into an office on the left and I can see that it too, is as chaotic as the others I've visited so far.

'What gets a boy in here and how long are they in here for?' I inquire.

'How long's a piece of string? Depends on what happened to bring them here in the first place. You get violent kids, runners, self-harm and some who are disruptive in the residence.'

'So it's a 'one size fits all' approach to problem-solving,' I pseudo jest. He misses it or ignores it and explains, 'They are supposed to have a plan that mitigates whatever the issues are. More often than not there isn't one, or should I say, I can never find them anyway. It's not easy though because half the time the boys don't know why they do what they do, so that makes it pretty hard to address!' Ted brings to the fore his healthy scepticism.

'The reasons for admission and the decisions to discharge are a lot greyer than they appear on paper. Some frequent runners end up in SNU multiple times but it's pretty obvious, certainly from my perspective, that the intervention they've had hasn't changed their behaviour one iota because they are out of SNU and off they go the first chance they get. The same situation is true for some of the bullies and stirrers, they either replicate the behaviour in SNU or pull their heads in for a few days until they're discharged back to the open unit. The best that can be said is, in the interim, the day staff and the boys have temporary relief. And you might get an 'insurgency' ring leader, someone who stirs the residential pot for their amusement, ending up in SNU for a period. We call them 'king pins' or KP's. They're sort of the informal leaders of the boys. They have less of an audience in here so it tends to calm them down for a while. They might only be in here for half a day but it can be a lot longer. It depends on what the 'powers that be' decide. Frankly, I find it hard to know why they make the decisions they do about placements. Well, sometimes it's obvious but other times, who knows? It has an impact on us though. Disruptive kids who should be in here are left in the main residence at night or returned there just before bedtime, but you can't control those decisions so you just get on with it!'

'Do we admit boys?' I inquire.

'Oh yeah, not often because it's hard for us to do. There are only two of us so that's the difficulty, especially if the boy wants to put up a fight. It means we both have to be involved and then there's no one upstairs while we get them down here and do the admission, which causes other problems. Sometimes if things look like they might get physical some of the boys wind up and there's the potential for something really ugly to happen. Most of the time though they do as requested. But I'll tell you what, if it needs to happen, then we make it happen.'

Originally when it was first built, SNU had its own team but for quite a long time the unit was hardly used so they moved onto the floor in the main residence to bolster numbers. However, he says since he started the demand for residential placements has increased and so has the use of the SNU but the staff never came back to the unit. Hence the current situation.

Ted reckons there are boys in SNU about seventy per cent of the time. During the day it's either staffed by someone from the shift team or more commonly, one or more relievers. He thinks that's one of the reasons the planning for locked boys is less than it should be.

'There's a staffing logic that applies during the day but not at night!' Ted states with an element of annoyance. 'At night if there are three or fewer young people, the place is never staffed unless there are special circumstances, such as one of the young people is actively suicidal. But there are times it isn't staffed and there are six or seven boys in here. The logic seems to be they should be asleep, so no trouble, and anyway what can happen? They're locked in! Yeh right!'

The monologue rolls on. 'At the most hectic times, after a mass absconding or serious incident, the place can be full to overflowing. In the worst situations, all the cells will be occupied with double-ups and there might also be a young person sleeping in the visiting area. It's rare but it happens. On the worst occasion I've heard about, two young people were sleeping in the gym as well, ten all up in an area built for three. Folly! and we were very lucky nothing went wrong!'

'What happens if it's a bit rumpty upstairs and you need to admit someone here, which seems like a possible scenario, how does that work?'

'Exactly' is the reply. 'I'll tell you what, it does happen, will happen, and we'll just deal with it.'

'So just to be clear, one of us could be doing the admission on our own while the other manages a bunch of boys playing up? Bit risky!' I state the obvious.

'Between Mr Rogers and I, we've managed so far and so will you. We can call the 'on call' senior for additional staff but it's pretty much always a waste of time. It's hard to get a reliever at short notice and worse at night. The 'on call' only comes in when the sky is falling …or to cover their arse. Maybe I'm being a bit harsh, the odd time they will come. John Land, your senior, tends to be more responsive than the others. He's reasonably new so perhaps he hasn't learned anything different yet. Welcome to the night staff world!'

My face must have failed to mask whatever emotions I'm feeling because he adds quickly, 'Really, it's not as bad as it sounds. We ask the Police to help when they come with a new admission and they're pretty good … unless they're flat out. In my experience, they've nearly always helped, especially when we have multiple admissions. If we ring the senior social worker first, they can get the coppers in if things upstairs are looking a bit hairy. They come if they can, it depends on what's happening out in the real world. And occasionally we have asked them to help get a problem case to secure, or even to their cells if it's really serious. They're more reluctant about that but if they are here or nearby… So I wouldn't worry!'

He adds more generally about managing admissions, that even if a new admission is going to be brought into the main residence, the night staff might do the paperwork in SNU because it's safest and easiest to manage if something goes wrong. It's a case by case decision depending on who it is, what they know and what the situation is like in the house.

Ted seems more amused than concerned and I take a bit of heart from that. I find the casualness of it all under-whelming, to say the least. It's too casual to be a prison, like the one I visited as a youth, but at the same time, it doesn't seem only about providing care either, more like a hybrid of care and custody. Maybe after I have been around for a while and learned the ropes, I'll get a better understanding of how the two things work together.

Just then a voice calls out from one of the cells.

'Hey, mister!'

'Baden Jones, I wonder what on earth he wants.' Ted leans over to a small panel on the desk with several dials on it. 'This is how we turn up the red lights. They're mounted outside the cells and shine through the windows. They are on a dimmer and we keep them on all the time at a very low level. It's supposed to let us monitor without disturbing the boy's sleep. I usually turn these up before I go in the cells rather than use the brighter cell lights.' He rises and proceeds out of the office beckoning me to follow.

In a few steps, we are at the cell in the middle of three.

'What can I do for you Baden? By the way, this is the new night staffer, Wyatt.'

'Hello, sir.' The face peering out at me through the cell door window is round, pale, and covered with a fair splattering of acne. He is smiling, showing a couple of stained front teeth. He looks to be about sixteen years of age. I can't see much of him but he appears to be stooping to look out his window.

'Not sir, just Wyatt will do,' I say.

'Ok sir' he says either ignoring me or being a bit cheeky. 'Hey Ted, can I have my Walkman? I can't sleep and it always helps. It's in my 'personals' in the office.'

'You're not allowed it in your room at night, only during the day. You know the score!' Ted replies without a beat.

'Oh come on man, it's late, I can't sleep. It's the only thing that helps. Come on man, just this once, no one needs to know.' Baden is pleading. Ted looks at me.

'Normally I wouldn't but it's kind of up to us what we do at night.' Ted says to me quietly behind his hand presumably to prevent Baden from hearing. And then to Baden, 'Ok, I'll allow it this time given you're having problems and you say it will help. I'll come back later and take it back but you can have it until we leave... about fifteen minutes...ok?'

We go back to the office where he goes to a box that has several brown manilla paper bags shoved unceremoniously into it. He pulls out one with Baden written on it in large black letters, rifles around and pulls out the Walkman.

'I don't open up the cells at night if I can avoid it. I always try to get the other night staff down first if I have to. You're here so that condition is met...I am only being a bit flexible with Baden because he's been here before and I know him. He lost his folks early, his father died in a work accident when he was a baby and his mother died shortly after of cancer. No one in his wider family was able to take him. Since then he has been with a whole lot of different caregivers. All I'll say about that is the experience wasn't as good as it should have been.' Ted is being vague. No doubt I'll find out more when I go through the file myself. 'You know he never gets any visitors. Bit of a sorry fellow really...' he pauses. 'Mainly does drugs with a bit of other minor stuff, cars, selling stolen property. His files over there' he points to an 'in tray' that holds three manilla folders.

We walk to the cell, Ted opens the door and passes the Walkman to Baden. I can't see much of him except that he is tall, over six feet. The arms of his pyjama jacket sit midway between his wrists and his elbows. He grabs it, not even offering a cursory 'thanks' as he steps back into the red-tinged dimness of his cell and sits down on his bed.

We leave Baden to it and I take my seat in the office again. I'd been so absorbed in Ted's briefing I hadn't taken too much notice of the office itself although I didn't miss its chaotic state. While Ted makes a couple of notes in the Daily Log, I look around. It's like the other two I've been in so far. There is sporting equipment all over the place and the desk has several files and books on it. The three walls that don't have windows are covered in notices and posters, many the same as those in the other offices. There are two whiteboards, one with the names of the occupants and one with notes about the programme for the day. There are several arty pictures but there seems to be no rhyme or reason why they're there. Apart from the seat at the desk and the one I am on, there is only one other. All are indiscriminate shades of brown, tired and threadbare. The room smells and I see there is a cluster of sneakers positioned next to the open door. A bin beside the desk also seems to be a contributor. It is full to overflowing and I can see a half-eaten sandwich poking through a bunch of scrunched up wrappers and other papers, which in turn barely conceal a browned off half-eaten apple in a well-advanced state of decomposition.

It just comes out of me before I think, 'This place has seen better days. Someone needs to have a word with the cleaners'.

'No one does it…or should I say, the staff do when they feel like it. The boys aren't allowed in here. They clean everywhere else. And the reality is because no one is located in the office as a permanent job, no one actually 'owns' the space so no one takes responsibility for keeping it tidy. Now and then when I have to spend a night stuck in here, I'll clean up if I have nothing else to do. So does Mr Rogers. Generally, that's when we can't stand the mess anymore.'

'The whole building looks a bit run down.' I broaden my observational comments.

'It is, or should I say, they both are, this and the main house. The rumours are there could be a move from the site to somewhere else in the 'not-too-distant' future. No one's said anything to us but I'll tell you what, the lack of interest and investment in this place is a signal that something's going on. This whole residence is tired and not fit for purpose. Everyone knows it and no one is doing anything about it, so a change would not surprise me. They have a big campus out at Kingslea over in Shirley where they have the girl's programme. They only use one of their buildings now because the numbers of girls are way down. We might end up there if I had to make a guess but to date no communication with the plebs. I'm not worried about any of that, a change won't mean we don't have a job whatever happens. There will always be naughty boys who need to be looked after somewhere.'

'There was no mention of any future moves when I was interviewed. The job is permanent so I guess we'll deal with that if and when it happens.' I acknowledge.

'I'm all done here, let's go back upstairs. Better grab that Walkman before we leave.'

As we pass by Baden's cell, Ted stops and peers in the viewing window. 'What the hell, have a look at this!' he exclaims. Baden is sitting on his bed in the corner, in the shadow and barely illuminated in the faint red light. In a small square patch of light provided by the viewing window lies the Walkman in pieces on the floor.

'Come on, we better have a look. Wait by the door.' Ted goes back and winds the dimmer up. The cell lights up bright red enabling us to see everything more clearly. He fumbles with his bulky bunch of keys looking for the right one. As we open the door Baden looks up.

'What's going on here Baden?' Ted demands, 'what have you done to the Walkman?'

'Dropped it and it broke', Baden mumbles a reply. His voice sounds subdued.

'Rubbish. It's been pulled apart. What was in it? Are you high?'

'Ha man… I had a few of mothers' little helpers, you know pills in it. Much better now, thanks, man. Should be able to sleep now.'

'What sort of pills?'

'Valium… calms me down.'

'How many?'

'Three.'

'Why should I believe you? You've already lied to me. I did you a favour and you took advantage. We can't have that.' Ted turns to me. 'I think we should get the Police?' his voice stern but not threatening. He winks at me so I guess he might be playing Baden. I don't know if there are protocols or not for these situations.

Before I can reply Baden says, 'No man, just a couple of pills. I couldn't get to sleep. I said the Walkman would help. No need for the Police, you'd be wasting their time. It's just a couple of downers and they're gone now.'

I've seen a few druggies in my time and just looking at him, he doesn't seem too out of it to me and his words are only slightly slurred. There are no signs of agitation or aggression which would be more troubling.

'Well Baden, you've done your chips with me. I've known you for a while and I thought we treated each other with respect, but now I see I can't trust you. No second chances. I will pass on what has happened to the morning team and they might have something to say about it. We're going to keep a close eye on you for the rest of the night.'

'You wouldn't say anything anyway man, ha... you broke the rules so you'll get into trouble.'

'Nah, my decision at night. A mistake... true, only because you sucked me in, but it gets reported so no one else falls for your bullshit!' Ted bends down, gathers up the remains of the Walkman and steps out of the cell, locking it as he goes.

Back in the office, he is annoyed, huffing and puffing. He sits down at the desk and rubs his head. 'He doesn't look too out of it, not compared to some I've seen here. He could be lying about what he's taken so we better keep an eye on him, frequent checks for a while.'

Just then the phone rings. He picks it up, 'The Police are here. It's time to do your first admission. We'll do it in the dining area in the main house.'

'What about Baden?' I ask.

'One of us can come back and check after twenty minutes,' replies Ted.

As he gets up to leave he pauses and shuts the office door ensuring he can't be overheard by anyone. 'There you go, that's a lesson for you, for us both. When you bend the rules it can bite you on the butt. My other self said not to do it, but I was soft and let my feelings get in the way of safe decision making. Not against the rules but just against common sense. I'll tell you what, listen to those little voices when they happen because most of the time they're right!'

We head out of the SNU and meet the Police who are just pulling up in front of the main residence. They hand over a rather poshly dressed, handsome, fit-looking young fellow of medium build with dyed blond hair.

'Hello Rowan, it's not good to see you back.'

'And lovely to see your smiling face too Ted my man. I thought I'd just pop in for a couple of days and check out my favourite jailers. Now what's for dinner?' asks Rowan.

This lad has a bit of charm and obviously, an education as well. Not what I expected in my preconceived notions about the boys who end up here.

We go into the dining room and sit at one of the twelve tables that populate the area. Ted leaves me with Rowan while he gets the Admissions Register.

The dining area, a large open space, is brightly lit except for a big rectangular alcove on our right. It's a servery and through this, I can see another large room shrouded in relative darkness. The light from the dining area is enough to identify the faint outline of benches. It reflects off several large stainless steel machines. I make out a mixer and a steriliser. Other objects are less discernible in the gloom. There are some tiny glowing red dots. This is the kitchen, metallic and mechanised. It's faintly humming like a beehive.

The table we are sitting at, like the others, has a plastic cover adorned with an ugly, busy, floral design. Most of all I am struck by the cacophony of smells. I noticed it when I first arrived, but now sitting here, I can give it more texture. There's the smell of the institution's kitchen, lingering food stores and waste, cleaning products, and a touch of stainless steel. There's the linoleum, hinting at the thousands of feet, dirt and crushed food now ingrained. Then there are the plastic table cloths, wiped but stained. It smells of ... institution! What is it about this place and the way it smells? I don't like it and I wonder how long it will take before I no longer notice.

Chapter 6
Jai

The dog barks. Sounds like a vicious bastard.

'I'm coming out!' he shouts, scared about what might happen if he doesn't. He'd run down the road from the house where, in the middle of committing the burglary, he was unfortunately interrupted by the owner. He knew he was busted, so he bolted. He'd leapt a fence to get off the main road and he spotted the shed. There was just enough room to slide under and take a moment's respite. But he hadn't counted on the dog. The dog van must've been in the vicinity when the call went out to the cops. Now he can hear it sniffing and he hears a gruff command, 'Get in there!' Suddenly it's crawling under the shed, growling. It snaps and he feels a sharp pain in his thigh.

'I'm coming out, I'm coming out!' he screams in a panic, slithering on his stomach towards a torchlight dancing around the edge of the shed. The dog keeps snapping at him but it has let go.

Next thing he's grabbed by his leg and pulled unceremoniously backwards. He's out, face down on the ground, arms pinned behind him. Cuffs are snapped on and ratcheted tight. Before he knows it, he's half standing and being propelled towards a wrought iron gate.

'Did he get him?' a deep voice asks.

'Can't see anything,' is the reply.

'It bit my thigh, you asshole. I said I was coming out.' The boy says with a grimace, feeling a mixture of anger, indignation, fear, and pain.

'Shut up, you'll live,' is the retort. Then to his colleague, he says, 'Must have nipped him. It caught him in the act of fleeing and resisting arrest.' There's a touch of amusement in the voice.

On the street he sees two police vehicles, lights spinning red and blue. One is a dog van. The boy is frog-marched to the other, the back door is opened, and he is tossed onto the seat. He lands hard, his cuffed hands unable to prevent a face dive. Bang! The door is slammed closed behind him.

He eventually struggles into a sitting position. Now he can see a couple of the coppers through the window. They're chatting and laughing. He knows one, Constable Johnston. He'd been picked up by him two, no, three times before. This is the second time for burglary. He knows the drill, and what's coming next.

His thigh is aching, his pants damp. It's just a bit too dark inside the car to make out how much he is bleeding. After a few minutes, Constable Johnston jumps into the front seat and starts the engine. He drives around the nearest corner and there on the side of the road is another cop. The boy knows him too, Constable Mahia. They must have split up to find him.

'He didn't get far then' Constable Mahia laughs as he climbs into the front seat of the car, nodding to the boy.

'No. Wally got him. Easy with a fresh scent. Had him pretty much straight away. He's not too bright, is our lad. Found him hiding under a shed. He wouldn't come out. Jack let Wally get in there and sort him out. He hasn't got anything with him so he must have only just entered the property, stashed it, or thrown it away. Lucky thing for the owner, catching him red-handed but it could have gone badly wrong and someone might have been hurt. If it had been someone bigger, tougher or uglier...' A snigger from Constable Johnson.

'I'm hurt,' the boy says.

'Bullshit, I couldn't see anything,' says Constable Johnston, 'but we'll have a closer look when we hit the station.'

Five minutes later they drive into a basement underneath the police station. He is out of the car and into a lift before he can say 'Ouch my leg hurts'. The doors open into a busy lobby reception area. A hand on his back pushes him forward. He knows where he is going. The cuffs are removed, a further shove and he's in a bleak grey holding cell. At least, he thinks to himself, they couldn't put him in with the adult drunken shitheads with all their crap talk and threats.

'Someone will see you shortly,' says Constable Mahia and the door clanks shut. It's cold and the cell is lit up like a beacon. 'Elroy was here!' some wit has scratched into the grey paint. Next to it is another note, 'Tell Elroy I was here too.' That's what leaps out and catches his eye straight away from amongst all the other graffiti. He has nothing to do but wait, so he reads further. There are phone numbers, offers to do blow jobs, threats to kill, pleas for help, and 'I'm innocent' in big red crayoned letters.

He looks at his trouser leg. It's stained with a circle of blood. He drops his pants and has a closer look. There are several neat round puncture marks where the dog's teeth pierced his skin. Two are deep and purple coloured but they're no longer bleeding much. It hurts like hell.

He waits, head in hands. After what feels like hours, the door opens.

'Come with me.' It's Constable Johnston who extends his arm giving the boy direction. He stands up and he experiences a sharp and immediate increase in pain. His thigh is stiff and sore, made worse by being immobile for a while. He nearly topples but he's able to mask it, appearing to only take a slight dip. He tries to walk freely as he passes the copper and down the hall and into the interview room.

'Sit down!' He does so on the white plastic chair. Johnston sits down across from him. A white plastic table with several grey-black cigarette burn marks separates them.

'We got you red-handed, no point in denying it. The owner saw you, so he'll be able to identify you.' He says after a brief pause to let this sink in, maybe attempting to get a comment. No response.

'Jai Rehua I'm arresting you for unlawfully being in a dwelling, attempted burglary, resisting arrest and attempted assault.'

'What? Who got assaulted? That would be me when you set your freaking dog on me' Jai says.

'You were trying to run and resist, that's what happened! You know it. You've been around so don't act all aggrieved with me. This time, we're going to put you somewhere we can find you until you appear in front of a judge at kiddies court. I'm taking you down to Social Welfare for the night, Stanmore Rd, and they can keep you. You better get used to the idea because we'll be asking that you're kept there for at least a week. It'll keep you out of trouble for a while. It's time you lifted your game.'

'Can I ring my mum?' Jai asks 'I know she or one of my aunties will come and get me.'

'Not likely, you aren't going home or wherever else you'd go if I let you out this door. You can ring her from Stanmore Rd but I'll be telling the staff to keep an eye on you because I want you in court. You need to get real lad! Do you think you can just keep doing what you like and get away with it, that's not happening on my watch. It's not good for anyone, and that includes you, if you keep doing crime, end of story! You're gonna spend some time at Stanmore and learn a lesson about what your future will look like if you keep doing what you're doing. At any rate, it's about 2.30 in the morning. One thing's for sure, you aren't going home!' Johnston says with a smile.

Jai has been in trouble before but custody, that's a whole new ball game. He'd heard things about Stanmore, not nice things, like the boys assault you in the showers, stick stuff up your butt and that. He'd probably get a hiding from the gang bangers at a minimum. And the staff might give him a good kicking as well. It'd never occurred to him he'd end up in custody! That place is only for the real bad arses. Now it's too late. Suddenly a part of him regrets doing a burg on that bloody house. He saw a skylight window open and went to have a better look. It was a spur of the moment thing, just dumb but not a big deal. If he's honest, he regrets being caught more than anything.

Maybe he can run when he gets to Stanmore. He knows boys who've been there and managed to run away. One day when he was in Richmond he'd checked the place out after hearing so many stories so he knows what it looks like from the outside. It is right there where everyone can see it on Stanmore Road, like a big boarding house. The same boys told him other stories too about what happens to the new guys the first time you go there, you get an 'initiation.' I'll smash any fucker who tries to 'initiation' me, he mutters to himself.

'Let's go!' Constable Johnston stands up ignoring Jia's mumbling.

Chapter 7
Mr Rogers

It's Friday night. I've been through one set of shifts, four nights in a row, had a day off, and now I'm doing my first weekend. My colleague tonight is Mr Rogers. I've heard a fair bit about him already, some of it not too complimentary however I take the view I need to meet the man before I believe too much of what I've heard. I have to say though, two things, in particular, are hard to put aside. The first is his nickname, 'Rogers the Rogerer.' It sounds pretty bad. I'd rather be 'Ted The Bear!' Ted couldn't confirm the origins of Mr Rogers's awful moniker because it predates his time at Stanmore but it's rumoured to have come from an incident when Mr Rogers was a sole charge night staffer back in the day. Allegedly he was seen in one of the younger boys' bedrooms, the bed covers were drawn back and the boy had no pyjama trousers on. As the story goes, one of the boys wandering around the residence in the middle of the night saw him. Ted didn't know if it was a matter that had been reported, or managed, or even if it were true. He's sure any allegation like that would have been investigated. He says he's never seen Mr Rogers doing anything remotely untoward around any of the boys or even heard him talk in any way that would arouse his suspicions about him being a paedophile. He's a bit effeminate in his mannerisms and speech and dyes his hair, things the boys might react negatively to. It's more than likely it's just the boys being horrible. The unfortunate reality is most of the boys hate him so they're not looking for the good things in him. According to Ted, everyone knows the nickname and it comes up frequently. He warned me any impression you create or pet name you get in this place will stick with you forever and will become part of your history. I'd asked if Mr Rogers knows he's got this awful derogatory name. He says the boys toss it in his face from time to time just to get a reaction. So yes he does. Ted says he's never seen him react to it though, he just ignores it. Must be hard to do!

I realise the safest strategy is to always be careful with these kids, keep everything you do out in the open, and stick together with a colleague as much as possible so the risk of getting this type of label doesn't happen to me. It will be challenging because of the nature of working nights.

The other issue is Mr Rogers is known for sleeping on the job. Midnight and its feet up and the 'Do not disturb' sign comes out. There's a small caveat written underneath it saying 'unless you really, really, really have to.' Ah well, it's his business, not mine. All I'm worried about is my integrity. Ted did say that no matter what, if trouble goes down, Mr Rogers will be there and that's worth heaps.

I arrive early, my already established practice, and I'm in the night staff office. The boys are all in their dorms and it's relatively quiet although there's still the muffled sound of many whispered voices. Suddenly, the hum increases to a rumbling, mainly coming from Rata, the big boy's dorm. Ted had warned me that sometimes this happens when they sense Mr Rogers arrive. I get up from the desk about to go and check it out when I bump into a tall, skinny guy coming round the corner from the stairwell.

Mr Rogers introduces himself as he brushes past me. He dumps the bag he's carrying on the couch and promptly sits down at the desk, in the chair I've just vacated. He swivels around in the seat and looks at me with a smile partway between amusement and cynicism. He has a narrow face, thin with sharp angles, high cheekbones, a pointed nose and chiselled chin, leathery skin, and is handsome in an outdoorsy sort of way. His dyed jet black hair hangs straight down to his shoulders. He's wearing blue jeans and a thick blue puffer jacket. He looks to be in his mid-forties but it is hard to tell because he has one of those faces that doesn't seem to age. He looks me up and down, slowly and deliberately. I feel mildly uncomfortable!

'So you're the new guy eh.' It's more a statement than a question. I don't bother to confirm and he carries on without a pause anyway. 'We'll have to get to know each other. I suppose Ted's filled your head with all the important stuff and by now you're an old hand!' He half laughs, half sniggers when he says this.

'Well, I like to do things my way when I'm on shift. No doubt we'll work it out. Anything I need to know from the handover?'

So we begin our journey. Looks like I am to be the early arriver, collector and transferrer of information in this relationship. Then having done this, I have the opportunity to fit in around Mr Rogers and his way of doing things. We'll see about that! It's not a great start to the first five minutes but I'm mindful that despite any initial impressions, we going to be working together fifty per cent of the time so it is important I try to make a positive connection.

'Not much to pass over John' I respond amicably. Oops, forgot the name thing.

He's back like a shot, 'Not John, I prefer Mr Rogers. I'm used to it and it's what everybody calls me.' True, I think, but then you insist on it.

'I like the professional distance and lord knows we need some professionalism around here. OK?'

'OK by me.' Now I have it from the horse's mouth so to speak. I continue 'Hatch Hitch had a bad day and was admitted to SNU. Toby Wardley was admitted today and he's been here before. He's settled in the Kauri wing. He's going on leave for the weekend from tomorrow morning, a trial placement I think Sarge said. He thinks if all goes well Toby will be discharged next weekend. Jason Fisher came in today from Court. He's in SNU. Seems to be settled. He will probably come into the main building tomorrow…'

'Ah, Fish! An old hand,' interrupts Mr Rogers, 'and a nasty piece of work that boy. They should keep him down there a lot longer. Typical of Billy Berse. Don't know if you've bumped into him yet? He's one of the Senior Social Workers. He likes Fish, who knows it and is smart enough to behave himself when Berse is around. He can be a pain in the butt for the night staff though. Pity, but what can you do…' He breaks off mid-sentence. I don't say anymore. Mr Rogers gets up out of the chair.

'I'm going to walk the beat and stop in on Toby, see what's happening for him. He's a good kid, just had a smattering of bad luck in his life. We'll get to know each other a bit more when I come back!' Off he goes heading towards the Kauri wing.

In the short time, we have talked I can see that Mr Rogers is a strong personality, confident, someone, who might try to dominate our relationship, or at least he's testing the waters to see if I will fit in with his world, maybe be a minion. It's not really in my nature so that isn't going to happen. He presents as slightly effeminate in his manner, the way he holds his hands, the curl of his lip when he sneer-talks, the way he smiles and looks at you. It's not overt, but it's there.

I've already learned that little things can mean a lot here. Even the slight suggestion of homosexuality might be something the boys will latch on to. I've already heard the term 'homo' used frequently as a put-down in the boys' night conversations. I've noted from reading the files that a number of the boys are known to have had homosexual experiences, much of which was sexual violence, a few at a very early age. several have records of actively soliciting. I've heard some other fairly explicit sexual references in their chatter at night, sufficiently graphic to surprise me. What some of these kids know and have experienced just isn't right!

After about fifteen minutes, when Mr Rogers comes back, I'm sitting in the chair by the desk, reading the new admissions files.

'All good' Mr Rogers indicates with a wave of his hand, I can stay in the seat like somehow I was about to vacate it for him.

'Young Toby seems pretty good. He's been at Hokio Beach. Have you heard of that place? It's up in Levin for the younger boys. Anyway, it wasn't much to his liking from what he said, glad to be back here. He met his new foster folks a few weeks ago. They made the trip to Hokio and he's looking forward to staying with them for a while. I hope it works out for him but…umm, he's had a few of these placements before and he always says the same thing and then for some reason it doesn't last. He's a bit of a runner and when the going gets difficult, he bails. So we'll see what happens this time. Still, in this place he's one of the better ones. Putting that aside, here you are, voluntarily doing time at the Christchurch Boys Home, how did that happen?' He turns his attention back to me.

I fill him in. He's friendly and engaging to talk to and asks questions that show a genuine interest in me and my family. I get the impression he's keen to build rapport and I appreciate it. It doesn't feel as natural as when I first met Ted. I don't immediately warm to the guy, but I still feel it's a positive step. Goodwill goes a long way and it's not hard to reciprocate in those circumstances.

For nearly twenty years, Mr Rogers has been a night staffer, ten of them at the boy's home. Before coming to Stanmore Rd he worked in a home for disabled young people needing residential care. He worked on his own. It was a 'sleepover' arrangement where he slept at night and woke up twice in the course of the shift to check on the children. At times they would wake him up if they needed something. Very occasionally he was woken by an event that was sufficiently disruptive to interrupt his sleep. He says he would have stayed forever because he loved the work but the place closed. He did a bit of relieving at Stanmore and when the opportunity came up, he applied for a permanent job.

At the time it was a sole charge role but things changed a couple of years later when the current double night staffing was introduced. A good move in his view!

It turns out he's forty-eight years old and married. Bernice, or Bernie as he calls her, is a career teacher and they've been together for twenty-five years. He has two teenage daughters, both still at secondary school. John and Bernice met at Teachers Training College. Although fully trained he found teaching wasn't his calling. He didn't like kids much, well not enough to spend all day awake with them. This elicits a chortle from him in the telling. In the end, it seems he couldn't get away from kids and it's why he's a night staffer, a compromise. 'They're so much better when they're asleep! Even mine' he says with amusement.

His real passion is breeding and showing dogs, Chihuahuas. Working nights is just perfect for the dog breeder he tells me. I don't know much about it but he tells me it is a significant commitment and extremely time-consuming. I can see it, not the time-consuming thing, but the Chihuahuas, somehow they seem to fit. He takes me on a verbal journey into the world of Chihuahua breeding. I feel his passion, I understand the commitment, I love dogs but I'm bored beyond belief. He finishes by telling me how, just before he leaves the residence in the morning, he prepares the food for his dogs. He describes his special super mix, a balanced diet for growing the healthiest puppies into the healthiest dogs.

It is now nearly midnight as he finishes.

'Well, that was a lot of chat. Exhausting! I'm worn out now!' He gets up and wanders off downstairs returning a few minutes later carrying a blanket and pillow. He says nothing but goes to the couch, tosses the pillow down at one end, lies down and pulls the blanket up.

'Sleepytime!' is all he says, making no effort to explain, justify or otherwise engage over it. 'I'll only be resting so… I'm here if needed.'

Two seconds later the phone goes. 'Bloody typical! Get that will you?' 'Christchurch Boys Home' I answer knowing the most likely caller is either the senior checking in or the Police wanting to admit someone. It's the latter. Mr Rogers is watching me as I put down the phone.

'Police wanting an admission, Jai Rehua. Do we know him?'

'Never heard of him. What's the story?'

'Burglary and resisting arrest. They want to bring him here but can't indicate exactly when … soonish.'

'Have you done an admission yet?' he inquires.

'I sat with Ted when he did one on my first night. Then on Thursday night, we did another one and I took the lead.'

'Experienced hand then, I'll leave you to it. Meet the Police when they come. They'll ring again when they're on their way so you can head off downstairs. He can go into SNU for the night. Any problems call me from SNU. I'll keep an eye on things up here.'

Hard to do if they are closed, I think to myself. I'd been warned so while I may want to argue, there didn't seem to be much point. I feel confident enough to manage the admission on my own, and I probably will be doing a lot more when I'm on with Mr Rogers.

Chapter 8
Jai Comes to Stanmore

The place is lit up like a supermarket on a dark winter night. There's a big tree out the front casting a huge cone-shaped shadow and partly obscuring the two-storied colonial looking building they approach more rapidly than Jai would like. They drive past a long grey prefabricated construct, up to a green wooden door tucked into an alcove that only emerges as they get nearer. He is feeling something about his pending admission but he's finding it hard to identify what exactly. Agitation, annoyance, aggrievement, apprehension, a raft of things. Too many. It can't be fear though because he doesn't get frightened. Nothing here I can't handle! He reassures himself. I'm here now so I have to get on with it.

The squad car rolls to a stop. Constable Johnston gets out, opens the back door, grabs him by the arm and hauls him out onto the asphalt drive. He is 'frog marched' up the three stairs in the alcove. The copper bangs on the green door three times with his fist, loud enough to wake the dead…and the boys. Johnston stands back still holding onto Jai's arm. It feels like minutes but it is probably only seconds before the door opens. A figure appears, silhouetted against the light from the room inside. The only discernible thing to immediately catch Jai's eye is the big bunch of keys in his hand attached to a chain that cascades from his belt, hanging nearly to his knees. Their meaning is not lost, he's a jailer.

The guy steps back half a pace and he can see a little bit more of him. He looks pretty ordinary. He's about medium height, not young, not old, with curly hair and a close-cropped beard. He's wearing black jeans and a black jersey. He turns his head slightly, reaching for the door and the light glints briefly off an earring in his left ear. When he turns back Jai feels his eyes lock on him. It's intense, piercing, scrutinising, maybe judging. Before he can take in anymore the jailer guy steps out the door and points behind Jai towards another building.

'We're going in there,' he indicates. Constable Johnston, who till then had retained a firm grip, finally lets him go.

'I'll leave him with you then. He's taken up enough of my time tonight, I've got real work to do.' He gives Jai a shove in the direction of the staffer. The jailer guy asks Constable Johnston if he has the papers and the copper says he will get them from the car. In an instant almost before Jai can draw a breath, the jailer guy is there, grabs his arm, turns him around and falls in beside him. He's escorted up a ramp to another door at the side of a concrete block building he hadn't noticed on the way in. The jailer uses one of his bunch of keys to unlock the door and he's hustled through it into a narrow, brightly lit hallway, made more glaring by the glossy daffodil yellow painted walls. He sees three doors, two on his right are open and the one at the end is closed.

'In there, first on the right, sit on the chair, don't move, I'll be right back' a voice behind him says, not unfriendly, just business-like. The guy goes back to the door and Jai hears muffled voices and then the clank of the door and the click of the key. Locked in.

Jai steps into the room, it is empty apart from a grey Formica topped table and two steel-framed chairs with wooden seats. There are some non-descript posters on the wall, not many pictures and lots of words. 'Know your rights' one says and a whole bunch of scribble too small for Jai to read, not that he was going to bother. Reading is the last thing on his mind right now.

'Hi' says the curly-haired guy, papers in hand, 'Jai isn't it? I'm Wyatt. If you'll take a seat please.' He is pointing at the chair furthest from the door.

'I'll just get the Admissions Book. Now you're here I need to go through a few things with you. Don't go anywhere!' He smiles at Jai. Not funny mate. This place is a bloody cell block just like the ones at the cop shop. He takes his appointed seat feeling like he's sitting under a spotlight about to be interrogated. The room has a small, oblong, single window, curtainless and covered with a grey steel grill.

Wyatt returns and sits down opposite him, placing a big blue book and matching folder on the table. In the silence that follows while his jailor reads the papers the Police gave him, that stupid song by the Clash, '*I fought the Law and the Law Won*' goes round and round in his head. He always liked to sing that song, but not so much right at this minute. Eventually Wyatt speaks, severing the irritating loop.

'Breaking and Entering, Burglary, Resisting Arrest, you've been a busy boy haven't you?' Not a question he's going to bother responding to. Jai looks Wyatt squarely in the face for the first time. Wyatt is looking back at him intently, eye to eye. Jai drops his head.

What happens next is a bit of a blur. A whole lot of questions, much the same thing as the Police have already asked, a few more about family. Had his family been contacted by Police? Had he spoken to them? Would someone come to court in the morning? He just replies 'no' to everything. He doesn't feel like talking, and besides, his thigh is hurting like hell. He has a fleeting thought he might be able to knock 'old Wyatty boy' over and take his keys, but then he thinks better of it. Wyatt looks fit and like he's no pushover. Anyway, he doesn't really do violence. He knows he couldn't run far with his stiffened and sore thigh even if he could somehow get out. Wyatt continues to look at him attentively as if he's reading Jai's mind.

'I see you have some blood on your pants. What's that from?' asks Wyatt.

'Dog bite.' Jai replies, brief, subdued, and to the point.

'Has anyone had a look at it?'

'No!' Emphatic, pissed off.

'I better do it then. I'll need you to take a shower and then you can show me. This way.' Wyatt stands and heads to the door. Jai follows. As he leaves the room he glances back at the entrance. Solid steel door. No way out without keys.

They take a few steps before turning to the left. In front of them is another hallway but this one has multiple doors, three on each side. Those on the right are shut. They are steel and have small square viewing windows two-thirds of the way from the top. Jai's heart pings… Cells… On the left, in contrast, the doors are made of wood. Two are shut, and the third is open. It is located in the middle of a large floor to ceiling window latticed with reinforced steel mesh. At the end of the hall, Jai can see there's a small gym even though the area is unlit.

The jailer guy points to a room on the left. 'The shower's in there. I'll get you a towel. You need to toss your clothes, everything, out here. While you're showering I'll get you something to wear for the night then I'll have a look at that bite and see what we can do. I'm just going to shut this door and lock it while you shower but I'll need those clothes first.' Jai stands there doing nothing, waiting, not wanting to get naked in front of a stranger. From what he'd heard this place was full of kiddie fiddlers.

'I'm not getting changed in front of you,' he blurts out, his apprehension overtaking him. He's thinking 'This guy could be a homo or a pedo!'

The guy doesn't say anything. He steps along the hall, unlocks the door next to the showers, grabs a towel and some toiletries and hands them to him.

'In there and once you've got your clothes off, toss them out here.' The door shuts behind him. Jai stands there doing nothing. After a few minutes where there's no sign of anyone coming back, he does as asked, opening the door once he has his gear off and kicking the crumpled clothes out through a narrow gap. He keeps his foot against the door and a good hold of the handle just in case.

'Put the towel around you... Right, out here now and stand over by that wall' More pointing and Jai, reluctantly, goes where directed. The jailer walks into the area where he took his clothes off. Jai can see through the door he is searching the place. When he comes out he says to Jai, 'Hold your hand out, palm up!'

What the fuck! Jai thinks but he does it anyway. 'Now the other one.' He has to switch the hand holding the towel around his waist to make sure it doesn't fall.

'Just checking you're not holding anything. OK, good to go, shower time. The quicker the better.'

Jai is feeling a bit more comfortable now, the guy hasn't made any moves on him. He seems pretty harmless, just getting the job done. It will be good to wash his leg, he thinks choosing the middle cubicle of the three available. He closes the door and turns on the shower.

A moment later he hears a door open. Here we go, he thinks. This guy's a pervert, what's he up to? I'll kick him in the balls if he tries anything. But then he hears the door close again almost immediately. He breathes a little sigh of relief. Still, he hurries to finish his shower. When he exits the cubicle there's a set of blue and white striped pyjamas sitting on the bench seat opposite. He barely dries himself and puts them on. He opens the door and Wyatt is just standing there seemly lost in thought. He looks up when he hears Jai. The discarded clothes are stacked and sitting on the floor.

'I'm going to wash them, just in case you're wondering. Might be tough to get the blood off but we'll do our best.' Wyatt seems to have read his mind again. 'And they will be clean for tomorrow, so you'll look your best for the Judge! You're going to stay in here tonight but before you go to bed I better have a look at the dog bite.' He motions for Jai to come into the room next door.

It's an office with a desk and chair, another seat by the door. It's a mess, posters, books and folders everywhere and gym stuff all over the place, and it smells. His eye is immediately drawn to a funky old guitar leaning against the wall. It only has four strings and looks like it may have been used as a cricket bat at some point. It has several spiderwebs of scratches and a 'swastika' is carved into the soundbox as well as some other writing he can't read from where he's sitting. A guitar with four strings is better than nothing, he thinks.

Jai sits on the chair by the door.

'Did you lot get a package deal on that shitty yellow paint?' Jai asks. He's feeling slightly more relaxed now.

'You'd think so. If it was up to me I would have gone for pink or mauve, you know more soothing colours, but they didn't ask,' is the reply. 'We don't normally let young people in the office but I better have a look at the bite'. Jai leans back in the chair, enough to pull down one side of his pyjamas exposing his thigh. The wound has started weeping a bit of blood and other goo.

'Definitely, a couple of puncture marks there. Looks deep but it doesn't look too bad, could be worse. The bleeding will have helped to clean it out. Probably could use a bit of antiseptic and a bandage though, so if you want, we'll do that. I'll let the morning shift know and they can check it again when you get up. You might need a tetanus jab.'

Wyatt goes to a green cabinet fixed to the wall, gets a tube of something out, a gauze bandage and a roll of sticking plaster. 'You can do this yourself. My policy is I don't touch the boys and they don't touch me. That's how it works but if you can't manage, then I'll help,' says Wyatt.

'I'm all right, I'll do it myself.' Jai doesn't want this guy or anyone else touching him.

'You can do it in your room if you like but I will want to see the scissors back.' Wyatt chuckles. 'Once that's done, I'll answer any questions you have and we'll get you settled in for the rest of the night, what's left of it.'

Jai doesn't worry about going to his room. He administers the antibiotic and manages to get gauze in place with the plaster holding everything together. Finished. Now he has questions.

'How many other boys are in here?' he asks.

'Two, and now, you makes three.'

'What are they here for?'

'Same as you…breaking the law and doing it often enough that the Police or Courts want you held in custody.' Wyatt says this without malice and Jai doesn't feel like he is being judged.

'Will I see them?'

'Yes, when you get up in the morning.'

'Will I get out of here tomorrow?' Jai wants to know.

'If you mean this unit? Most likely, we only hold young people in here if there's a risk they might run away or they are violent. I only put you in here tonight because I thought you might want to run away. If you mean 'out of Stanmore', it's up to the Judge tomorrow. That's why I asked you about family because if they come to court it might help get you out. Depends on a few things, obviously what they reckon you've done, what your history of offending is, but no family, not much chance. Just being real about things.'

'I got family and they'll be there. They just weren't home tonight. I'll be out of here man, sweet!' Jai is not sure this is true but says it anyway.

'Well it's no guarantee but if anything will help, that will. As I say, it depends on the judge and what the Police have to say. Now it's pretty late—you should get some sleep so you can be in the best space for tomorrow. Your clothes will be outside your door in the morning. Clean and folded... but not ironed. If you want you can do it yourself in the morning. Anything else I can help you with?' Wyatt asks.

'What are the other boys like?'

'The two in here are a bit like you but you will see for yourself. If you're worried about them, we have staff in here in the morning and no one gets out of their room if there's a problem, so you'll be safe.'

'I'm not worried,' Jai blusters, but he is a little bit, 'I just don't like 'eggs' that's all'.

'Yeah, me either, but we have all kinds of boys here for all kinds of issues. Most of them are 'ok', keeping their heads down until things get sorted out for them. That'd be my advice to you. Now I think it's best you get some sleep. I'm on again tomorrow night so if you come back, I might see you then.'

Conversation over! Wyatt leads him to the middle cell and unlocks the door. Jai steps in. All of a sudden he feels tired. It's been a long night one way or the other. He is greeted by a bed, a grilled window and the now-familiar four yellow walls. However, these are decorated with graffiti. Jai walks to the bed and lays down gingerly on top, his thigh still sore.

'Good night and good luck in the morning' says Wyatt as the heavy metal door clangs shut.

'KILL ALL KFs'. The words burned black into the ceiling, probably by a lighter, is the last thing he sees before the light is switched off. Jai knows what a KF is, a 'kiddie fiddler', prison talk. The moment the light goes off the room fills with an eerie red light. He sees it comes from a spotlight outside. He thinks for an instant he can see a face peering in but he blinks and whatever it might have been, is gone.

Lying there, his mind ticks over. What the fuck have I done? I'm in prison. I've got to get hold of mum tomorrow and get the hell out of here.

For now, he is safe, at least till they open the door in the morning. He thinks about the dog. Had they set it on him for fun? He knows Constable Johnston and he'd seen the other one around the place, and they knew him. They'd caught him doing a burglary at a school. It'd seemed like a fun thing to do at the time. He was with a couple of other boys he'd known for a while. They were just hanging out, a bit bored and figured there might be some money in the school office. As it turned out there wasn't, but there was a silent alarm. The bastard 'pigs' didn't use their sirens so copped them almost before the boys could say 'Run for your lives!' They all got taken home and had to do some community work for the school. At the time it was a bit embarrassing but he wasn't worried. They only did half of the hours but got signed off for doing them all. His mother wasn't happy and she got into him good and hard, but once she'd had a couple of wines she let it go. No problems from his father wherever he was.

Jai's father disappeared one day and never came back. Jai was sure when he buggered off his mother had started to hit the bottle. Since then his mother had other guys in her life, some only for a few days and then they were gone never to be seen again. A couple lasted longer. Mostly they didn't bother him. One had been a bit off, something spooky about the guy, always watching him. He used to come into his bedroom at night, wanting to talk to him. He never did anything, but a weirdo for sure. There was another one who acted like he was his new father. Not likely, he'd given him the message good and proper and then he did everything he could do to get the guy out of his house and out of his life. He wasn't a bad guy, his mum seemed to like him, but Jai didn't want or need another dad. Or anyone who thought they might be, or who thought they could tell him what to do.

Jai did not think of himself as an 'offender.' There'd been plenty of other 'offending' if someone wanted to call it that. Jai just considered what he was doing as harmless fun. Most of the time he didn't get caught and he made a few bucks selling stuff to friends. It was all pretty minor, mainly burgs and a bit of thieving, and the insurance was bound to cover it, that's what it was there for. The way he sees it, everyone benefits from crime and it keeps the wheels turning, the shops working and the less well-off supplied with needed goodies. It'd been worth it…up until now. Here I am in this shithole, he mutters to himself. I'll ask to ring mum tomorrow, early, make sure she turns up at court, yeah I'll be out of here tomorrow.

He hears movement outside his cell and then shortly after a door opens and closes. Wyatt must have left the building he supposes.

'Hey new boy, who are you?' a whispered voice comes from somewhere out of the wall. It sounds familiar.

'Who are you?' Jai whispers back trying to pick where the voice is coming from.

'Aaron Baker man, I know you, Jai from Linwood… yeah don't you remember? I've seen you in The Square…'

Part 2
Getting into the Swim

Chapter 9
Wyatt Finds Time Is flying

It's August and I've been at Stanmore for just over six weeks. The time has flown. I've already devoured all the information I can from every source available, and I feel I'm coming to grips with the expectations of the job, and the bureaucracy, of which there is plenty.

Among all the oddness of the place, probably, the Special Needs Unit is the standout. It's like a tiny Arohata Prison, but one that sits inside a care system. It's there for the most difficult cases at a time when their behaviour is the most concerning. Usually, boys are in there for a day or two, but sometimes, boys will be in for a week, or even weeks on end in a few cases. Despite its high needs nature, it's not staffed with specialists. From what I've seen it's often relieving staff. There's no school, so whatever programme there is remains in the hands of the staff who happen to be on shift at the time. There are limited activities for the kids. Staff do what they can but they may be looking after several boys at any given time, all in an acute phase of difficult behaviour. However as Ted told me in my induction, the SNU was supposed to be rarely used, and for as short a time as possible. So the plan seems to be 'Make do when you have to use it.'

I've already noted the number of SNU inhabitants fluctuates significantly. One day there might be one person and the next day there are four or five. The number of occupants has a direct relationship to the vibes in the Residence. Things can be settled shift after shift, and bang, all of a sudden the collective mood changes. Then the SNU fills up. It almost seems the tension escalates until this happens and then the residence settles again…for a while.

I'm fully into coming on shift early and going for a walk around the premises and into the SNU, regardless of whom I am working with. Tonight the SNU is full. Too full. There are six boys in the cells, so double-ups in each. For some reason, unfathomable to me, the evening shift team has admitted a seventh boy,

Chevy Woken, who is domiciled on a mattress in the dining room. The most incomprehensible thing is that he's not in a locked room despite being known as troublesome, more so than all the others currently in the unit.

At the changeover, we're told there is no relieving staff available to help. I must confess I've already become a little cynical and wonder how hard they tried to find someone, but what can you do? We just have to get on with it. We are on our own.

Ted and I, the team tonight, know we'll need to keep a close eye on the SNU but we can't be down there first thing. Although all the offices and the gym area are locked off, which is helpful, there is also a sizable boy partially unsecured. Our initial checks found that the occupants appear to be settled. Chevy was snoring away loudly in the dining area when I went through.

Upstairs things are a bit rumpty and the outgoing team informed us it's been like that all shift, despite all the SNU admissions. We both need to be on the floor in the dorms for a while. Once all is quiet, one of us will relocate downstairs.

Today has been one of those days where the mood in residence hasn't been good. I read about the incidents that occurred over the day. In the first, two boys got into a fight and wouldn't settle afterwards. They kept threatening each other and so they ended up in SNU ... together. Go figure! But then what were the options? They had to be kept separate all day, one in his room and the other out in the gym, and subsequently swapped around every hour.

In the second incident, three boys attempted to do a runner from the school, two were successfully stopped and duly placed in the unit, added to another two young people admitted directly after Court. Then right at bedtime Chevy was admitted. He'd been running about the dorms being loud and disrupting the whole residence. There's no talking to him when he's in such a frame of mind, and threats from staff, and then from boys, made no difference. Eventually... SNU was the last option if anyone was going to get any relief. There was no room left at the inn so he was placed in the dining room on a mattress. I guess it may have meant we avoided having to admit him later in more difficult circumstances, so that was something despite the current risky arrangement.

It takes about an hour to get everyone settled in the main house after which I head out to do a further perimeter check and visit the SNU. All is quiet apart from Chevy who continues to sound like a foghorn, so I head back upstairs to confer with Ted. Experience is already telling me that what you see may not be real. At least the majority of boys are locked. Things have been sufficiently

66

disruptive in the main residence we decide to continue to let it ride in SNU for now, but also step up the frequency of our checks when we can.

We are supposed to view all the boys, regardless of where they are, every twenty minutes. Regular checks form a pattern that, once identified, can be planned around allowing the discerning young person to get up to all sorts of shenanigans in the gaps. To counter this we mix it up doing checks in an irregular pattern early on in the shift to create a sense of uncertainty. However, regardless of this approach upstairs, the checks in SNU cannot be done quietly because the nature of the building acts as an echo chamber, magnifying even the smallest of noises. The boys hear you coming and they will be back in their beds and quiet before you've had time to relock the entrance door. During my first week on the job Mr Rogers told me, 'It's a good idea to do the checks in the SNU, go through the admin area, and then go back and look into the cells through their outside windows. It's surprising what you see or hear.' Sometimes it's personal stuff and he feels a bit like he's intruding, but other times it's talking about offences or planning new ones, or doing a runner, or views about staff or other boys. Mr Rogers is very proud of the fact that information he overhead one night from a lad bragging to a mate in the cell next door, helped to solve a major warehouse burglary involving members of the young person's family. Needless to say, that boy wasn't popular at home when he was discharged.

The staff call it 'intelligence' and it can be passed on to the appropriate party. I can see the benefits but I feel a bit uncomfortable about it too. It's a fact that lots of the boys talk a good game without really doing any of it. Also, I'm wary about being caught up in giving evidence in a court case. I mean, no boy would ever trust you again. Though if we're talking about risk to life or limb, that has to be a different matter and there'd be no choice.

In the end, I can't ignore my obligations, we don't want boys assaulting each other or running away.

I come to an uneasy peace with it. I am responsible for anything that happens on my watch and, in particular, being forewarned is being forearmed. I decide that checking the cells from outside will become part of my routine.

While I was in SNU I turned up the external red security lights, just enough so I will be able to see clearly into the cells from outside. I head into admin and wander about checking offices. I see an incident report on a desk in one of the senior's offices so I check it out. I can't have been more than five minutes. I exit the building. As I walk down the external ramp I glance across at the adjacent windows. That's odd, from where I stand the first cell door appears to be open. I slide up closer to the window, yes indeed, it is! No bodies in the beds either. I check the next cell, same again, door open, with vacant beds. I don't bother with the third window. Part of our initial security checking process is to test each cell door handle to ensure they are locked. I'd done this. The only way to open the doors is from the hallway because there are no internal handles. I don't have to be a rocket scientist to work out that someone has somehow got hold of a set of keys… Chevy, he's the only possibility. So where are the boys?

There isn't a means to contact Ted short of running up to the night staff area so I make an instant decision to enter the building. I'm not worried that there might be an ambush waiting, after all, they have keys so they don't need mine. I clip my torch to my belt and enter through the senior's office, a second access door to the facility and not our usual pathway. Straight away I see the internal office door is wide open and the frame is splintered. Blunt force trauma, applied from the hall side. I'm surprised I didn't hear the noise it must have made when I was in the admin. The wooden cupboard containing staff keys is wide open, the door levered off its hinges and the lock smashed. I see an empty hook. A single set of keys is missing. No chance of securing either the key cupboard or the office door. I grab the three remaining sets of keys. They are too bulky to stuff in my pockets so I quickly stash them out of sight behind the senior's desk. I move out of the office and into the hall, torch bouncing on my thigh as I go. A glance tells me all the doors to the cells are open although the staff office is still closed. Not good. Seven boys are somewhere. The door to the gym, which I know was closed, is now open. It contains the only other external door in SNU, a fire exit. I'm at the gym door in a second. I pause. Inside it's dark apart from a strip of light that extends from the hallway. No time to unlock the office and turn on the lights. I unhitch my torch, as long as a baton and bright enough to light up most of the gym. I stand for a moment at the door and listen. I hear rustling and slight movements. I'm pretty sure they're in there, listening too. By now they will know I am somewhere nearby. I flick on the torch and enter. I see the boys, seven of them huddled around the fire exit, silent, looking at me. I have interrupted their escapade just in the nick of time. I don't think, I just do what comes naturally.

'What are you lot up to?' I demand in my most authoritative voice. Silence in response.

Chevy is holding a set of keys in his hand.

'Chevy, I'll have those keys thank you, and you guys need to go back to your units…now!'

There is a bit of milling about and rumbling, but no action. Chevy suddenly tosses the keys across the gym. I follow their progress with my torchlight and go after them. As I do Chevy makes a run for the hallway. I don't follow him, I know he can't get out of the building, I locked the external door when I entered. I turn my attention, and my torch, towards the other boys.

'Into your cells, I don't want to tell you again! Come on, get moving! Move! No one is going anywhere tonight except back to their beds.' In the back of my mind, I know the boys could easily overpower me if they choose to despite the fact none left are big enough to do so on their own. And I don't see a leader among them who might take an initiative. However, they don't move. A brief stalemate. Silence ensues.

It is interrupted by a loud banshee type scream. Chevy charges down the hall and back into the gym. He has a metal bar in his hand. It looks familiar, he has pulled the leg off one of the dining room chairs. He stops a couple of metres away from me. In that brief instant, we look each other in the eye. I see rage. I hope I don't project anything except alertness. He screams again and rushes at me, lifting his weapon as he comes. I step into him, closing the space between us and reducing the risk of being struck. I grab his wrist as it comes down towards my head and at the same time I sweep his legs, a martial arts move I retained from the couple of sessions I did way back in the past. I rip the chair leg out of his hand as he falls sprawling onto the floor. No one else is moving, silent spectators now. Chevy is uninjured, although he takes a few moments to his get to his feet. His mouth hangs open, appearing to be stunned at the speed and ease with which I disarmed him. He is staring at me, but without the malicious intent present only a minute ago. Now he looks more like a bewildered little boy.

I am aware there are boys behind me. I step to the side so I can see them all and command in a loud voice 'I said into your cells!' For a moment, nothing, they still seem to be thinking about it. Then the tension breaks, they begin to move past me and return to their cells.

'Chevy, get down on the floor over there where I can see you,' I direct him to sit in the beam of light from the hallway, far enough away so I will have plenty of warning if he decides to move. To my surprise he does as asked, appearing now to be as meek as a lamb. Meanwhile, the boys go back into their cells without further fuss, in silence.

The fun is over. The chance to escape is gone. I walk into the hall and start locking doors, all the while keeping a watchful eye on Chevy. He's volatile and impulsive, like many of the boys, and although he looks subdued I have already experienced once tonight that appearances can be deceptive, I remain wary of a further attack. I still hold the chair leg in one hand. I have tucked the torch under my arm so I can turn the keys to lock the doors.

Once it's done I call out to Chevy, 'OK, come here. What am I going to do with you?'

'I'll go back to my bed sir.' He has his head down as he speaks.

'Not likely, that's wishful thinking. And don't call me sir!'

I decide it's safest to lock him in one of the cells for now. I'll use the one which holds the two oldest boys.

'Let's get your mattress and bring it here.' I follow him down to the dining room and watch as he gathers up his bedding and drags it into the hall. I keep him in front of me the whole time. No point in taking risks. I inform the boys in the allotted cell about their new roommate. I can see their faces peering out so I ask them to step away from the door.

I open the door and point. 'In there for now, until I decide what to do next.'

'Don't put that egg in here man!' One of the boys moans.

'How come?' I say. 'You seemed to be happy to follow him out the door!'

'I wasn't gonna go, just seeing what would happen, seeing if he'd get away.'

'Well, now you know. He's going in here until I decide what is happening next. All actions have consequences, sometimes unseen, and this is one for you. In Chevy! Now settle down the lot of you and make the best of it.'

As I walk away and head to the office, I can hear sufficient disgruntled noises coming from the cell to make me think no one is happy with the current arrangement.

Time to update Ted on what's been happening. I ring the night staff office, Ted answers straight away and I give him a summary.

'I thought I heard a bang from down there but there was a bit of movement here so I stayed put. I knew you'd be on to it, I'll be down in a couple of minutes.'

I have a moment to catch my breath. I am still holding the chair leg so I discard it. Did that contribute to the compliant behaviour? Possibly. It wasn't intended to so I hope not. I observe my hand is shaking. I wonder if the boys noticed.

Now the action is over it dawns on me that things could have gone horribly wrong. I dodged a bullet. The luck of it all, going past when I did. Quite possibly there are so many keys on the ring that they couldn't find the right one quickly enough. What if they had the door open already? I might have been able to grab one but then the rest would be gone. What would I have done if they'd refused my directions? For a moment or two, it looked likely. All they needed was a leader but no one stood up, and Chevy, well, he couldn't lead down a one-way hall. He'd faked being asleep. It was a convincing performance but maybe I should have picked it up earlier. I suspect he'd been wandering about talking to the boys, possibly for most of the night. One of them will have put him up to it because I doubt he has the clues to think of it himself. When he heard me leave after my last check, he assumed I wouldn't be back for a while and did the deed. I'm not sure what the attack was about though, frustration, an attempt to be the leader, a dislike of me, just an impulse, brain dysfunction, who knows?

Thank the stars the only real damage done was to the office. Nevertheless, this could have been the worst breakout from SNU in the history of the residence.

I am musing on this when I hear Ted arrive. He comments to one of the boys on the way past who is standing at the window of his cell door. I don't hear exactly what the conversation is about but I do hear him say, 'Well suck it up.'

He comes into the office. 'We can't have all those boys in one cell. It is a recipe for disaster…and we don't need another opportunity for problems. It's bad enough having two boys together. If they decide to beat each other up or do anything else like that, you can't open the door unless there are two of us here. So three! That's no good, not safe for anyone. I'll call the Police and we'll get Chevy moved to their custody. I'm sure they'll take him, no love lost there! The rest can be sorted out in the morning.'

He makes the call and lets me know they'll be happy to accommodate us and will come by when they can.

'Whew! A lucky break you came down when you did. It could have been a massive…massive… calamity… but it wasn't.' He says with a grin. 'Imagine the fallout if all the boys had got out! The paperwork, the headlines, national office scrutiny, doesn't bear too much thinking about!' He sighs and shakes his head. After a moment he says, 'And I'll tell you what, this incident won't do you any harm. You managed it, took control, didn't flinch, showed them who's in charge. It's not a small thing you know. That Chevy is dangerous, he doesn't have the wit to know the consequences of his actions. He will probably kill someone sooner or later. He wouldn't be the first, and he won't be the last boy to go through here who does. And the rest, well they can act like a pack and could have easily turned on you. You know this incident will be all around the residence by lunchtime.' I'm a little surprised at how animated he is. I feel flat.

He waxes on about how the boys respect strength, and despite the way they behave a lot of the time, they want the adults to be in control. Especially when it is done by force of personality and not by bullying or threats. It may seem strange he says, but they feel safer when they know the boundaries.

I'm not sure I fully comprehend this feedback. It's just a situation that happened. It had a momentum of its own. All I did was get caught up in it and respond without thinking too much. And I forcibly removed the chair leg. That was more about self-preservation than anything else.

'Dumb luck man!' I tell Ted what I feel.

'Doesn't matter how it happened, all that matters is that it happened. You stopped seven boys from escaping and disarmed a violent attacker, one who half the staff are afraid of!... All the talk will be about how ... 'You've known the man, now meet the legend! Ha! ha! You've made your name around here...Yeah ...I don't want to pump you up too much though, you might get a big head! But I'll tell you what, you take what you can get in this place.'

Maybe I will, but right now, I just feel tired. I hadn't realised just how much the adrenaline rush has taken out of me.

Chapter 10
Jai Takes a Hike

He's on the run. It kind of just happened. Not that he hadn't intended to run. He had from the moment he arrived back at Stanmore, it was just the how and when that had to be sorted out. Then an opportunity came knocking.

After his first admission, his mother managed to get it together enough to come to Court and he was released by the judge. The court officer from Welfare and Jai agreed, as part of his placement home, that he'd have a curfew every night from eight in the evening to eight in the morning. He was supposed to go back to school and, it pretty much goes without saying, keep out of trouble. All this until his next court date which was nearly two months away.

He had lasted most of that time although he only went to school on the first day. He was so far behind as a result of spending so much of his school time on the streets, it was embarrassing. He felt like a dummy. When he didn't go back the next day nothing happened, so he didn't bother again. He thought the teachers secretly didn't want him there anyway.

At first, a few of his mates came round to his place and they'd spent the evening having a few J's and sometimes a few drinks, watching videos, and chewing the fat. Things had been OK for a while. As time went on he missed the odd curfew, not deliberately, just got caught out a bit late with no transport. And Saturday nights were hard from the start, with too much going on. Maybe the social worker expected his mother to 'dob' him in if he was late. That was never going to happen. Half the time she was out herself and the other half she was out of it, too cut to know or care. She tried to say something the first time she found out it had happened and he told her to get lost. That was the first and last time.

It was just a bit of bad luck he got caught. Jai should've known better but he was bored. And he didn't care about the bloody curfew! His mate Jet came and picked him up in a pretty flash car he said was his 'new ride'. Jai knew that was bulldust. Turns out it belonged to some rich dude who discovered it was missing almost before Jet put his foot to the pedal. There were cops in the area when the bulletin went out, and they were spotted only a few minutes after he'd been picked up. Jet thought he'd be able to outrun the cops so he put his foot down hard. Within thirty seconds he missed a corner and hit the curb hard. He overcorrected and they ended up going through a grill fence and stopped in a flower bed in somebody's front garden. The car was pretty dinged up but neither of them was hurt. Jet stayed with the cops but after a couple of calls, Jai was taken back to Stanmore. He didn't know what happened to Jet but he was too old for Stanmore. The cops said they were going to do Jai for 'Unlawfully taking a Motor vehicle' and 'Unlawfully being in a Motor Vehicle' and more charges were to come. Bit unfair Jai thought, cops taking two bites of the cherry and all he did was take a ride. He had to admit he knew Jet could never afford to own a 1985 Holden Statesman! He worked part-time in a supermarket after all. Flash car though, and a good ride even though it had been only for a short time. Live hard, die young, fuck the world! The only good thing about being back was the music, yeh he liked that and chatting with the night staff guy when he could. And the food was all right…and regular.

An indication there might be some action tonight came early in the day. There'd been talk about someone doing a runner but Jai had heard plenty of that before. This day was a little different. Bryce Whitehouse, one of the boys he had known from the streets for ages, approached him shortly after lunch while he was sitting on the couch waiting for the afternoon meeting. He picked up the guitar and had started picking away at a tune called *Walkin Blues* he'd heard the Paul Butterfield Blues Band play. He liked it, easy to play and a bit funky, and good for getting the fingers moving. He wasn't singing though because, although he could sing, he wasn't doing that in front of the guys. He'd picked up the guitar a few times in the last few days and was slowly getting back into playing. It helped fill in the time and the boys showed him respect because of it.

Bryce Whitehouse didn't have much interest in music and he plonked himself down next to Jai and interrupted him in mid tune.

Bryce wasn't a guy Jai liked although he'd known him for a while. He and a few of his mates were always hanging around the edge of the square in the city centre where Jai spent plenty of time. He was a scrawny guy with dirty long blond hair. He always dressed in black and wore Doc Martens. On the few occasions he'd talked to him, Jai found him to be distant like he couldn't be bothered. He knows Bryce has 'Boot Boy' mates, members of a local White Power gang. He's got a rep too, mean and dirty when it comes to fighting. Jai had seen him king hit a guy once. No, not Jai's type in any way at all.

'It's all set up, I'm doing a runner,' Bryce whispered.

'Oh yeah,' Jai replied with feigned disinterest, although wondering to himself why Bryce was so generously sharing with him. He also felt a distinct ping in his gut. He'd bragged to the boys about being able to go anytime, now it might happen. Bryce, however, wasn't his natural choice for a running mate. 'When?'

'Easy, there's only a couple of staff on at night and once everyone's asleep they'll be in the office. One of them even sleeps half the time. Any rate, you just be ready, and I will let you know when the time comes.'

'Why me?' asked Jai, still surprised that Bryce approached him.

'Simple, I need to hide out. The 'pigs' will be looking for me for sure.' Last time I ran they found me after a day even though I kept my head down. This time needs to be different. I need to go somewhere they won't know to look. I hear you can do that. You know Tommy Mudlark and I want an intro. So...you're coming, be ready.' Not a request, a direction and Jai didn't really want to mix it up with Bryce, he's got a rep for getting what he wants. And, he had to admit, his interest was tweaked, especially when Tommy was mentioned.

'Oh yeah, how's it gonna happen?'

The meeting was called. 'Settle down you lot!'

'Later man' Bryce says.

After that, it was all he could think about. Will I or won't I? He tossed it around and around in his head. It was distracting and he nearly gave the game away a couple of times. He found it hard to hide his excitement. The wound-up spring feeling in his stomach hung around all afternoon. It must have shown because he was approached by two staff members just before dinner to see if there was something wrong. He sensed they were on to him and tried to hide his agitation and act normal. It turned out to be easy to fool them. They seemed to be just going through the motions.

Somewhere deep down inside he knew he was going before he finally acknowledged it to himself. It would be a bit of fun ... an adventure. At any rate, what could they do to him when they got him, put him back in Stanmore probably, in the SNU. Ah well, he'd seen what that was like the first time he was admitted, it was no big deal, boring but easily doable. Been there done that, got the badge he thought.

As he headed upstairs to his bed in the dorm, Bryce sidled up to him and put it on him again. 'Be ready, we're on!' and he was gone.

The night staff turned up half an hour later and he saw it was the two younger guys, Mr Greene, the teddy bear, and Wyatty boy. That wasn't too good. They are the best team. He felt that familiar little ping again in his heart. If he was going to run, he wanted it to be successful. If he was caught attempting to escape he would be in SNU anyway but without having had the fun part. He wanted to talk to Bryce, maybe they should hold off until tomorrow or until the sleeper guy was on, it'd be easier then. He got up and attempted to go to Bryce's dorm but as he passed by the night staff office a voice demanded 'Where do you think you're going?'

He didn't turn around to answer because he thought his face might give something away.

'I just need to talk to Bryce for a minute.' His heart was pounding.

'Not happening, you've had all day to talk to him and anything else can wait until tomorrow! Back to bed!' So that didn't work. 'Dumb! Dumb! Dumb!' he castigated himself. He trundled back to his bed.

Once his alcove partner was asleep, and after listening out for the night staff, Jai took off his pyjamas and tucked them into the pillowslip. He quickly hauled on his jeans, which he had hidden under his mattress, hopped back in bed and pulled the covers up to his neck. It turned out old domestic Annie who ran the laundry, didn't look too closely at what clothes were handed in after showers. Too many boys to check, and always in a hurry to get everyone off to bed. He wore his PJ pants when he handed in his gear, a shirt he'd 'borrowed' off one of the other boys and a jacket, but he kept on his tee-shirt. She didn't ask about the jeans, too easy!

He lay in bed awake, heart-thumping, pretending to sleep whenever the night staff patrolled past his alcove. In his head, he sang *Casey Jones* the song about the train driver he'd heard Mississippi John Hurt play to distract himself and calm his nerves. He loved the hypnotic train rhythm and it was good for blanking other things out. But it was hard to keep it up. There seemed to be a lot going on, a constant rumble from Rata and lots of movement. Now and again he could pick out a staff voice telling boys to settle down.

This went on for a while and eventually, things quietened down with the few sporadic voices becoming less and less frequent. Just when he thought maybe it wasn't going to happen, he heard Bryce's voice say from out in the hall 'Just going to the toilet sir.'

'OK' came a grunt of acknowledgement. Everyone knew they had no choice, the staff couldn't stop you from going to the toilet. But they nearly always followed you to make sure you didn't get up to anything you shouldn't. Next thing Bryce walked past, followed by Ted the Bear, about four steps behind. After about thirty seconds there was a bang and loud voices from Rata, a pause…and then more crashing and agitated shouts. Two seconds later the Bear hurried back past Jai's bed towards the source of the noise. Then he heard an urgent whisper.

'Come on.' It was Bryce. Jai was on his feet in a flash. They quietly slipped off in the opposite direction from the continuing hubbub in Rata, out to the hallway and the fire escape door. Bryce gave it a push. It opened with a click.

'Go! Go! Go!' he urgently whispered. After Jai stepped through Bryce did something to the door, and then pulled it shut. Jai couldn't see what, he was too busy hopping from leg to leg, he just wanted to run.

'Let's go! Let's go!' hissed Bryce and lead the way down the fire escape stairs. In seconds they were over the fence beside the Supermarket and running down the lane. Once around the corner, they dashed across Stanmore Road into Richmond Park and the cover of darkness where the trees cut out the light from the streetlamps. Mature bushes obscured them further. They didn't slow, Bryce kept them moving south to the end of the park, through a couple of backyards and into the adjacent street.

So here they are, out! Easy! Going towards Woolston and sanctuary. They just had to keep their wits about them for a little while. Not far up Cashel St, a car pulls up next to them. Bryce grabs Jai's arm and shoves him towards the car.

'Ah, our ride. Get in, they're mates.' They jump into the back seat. There are two guys in the front. Jai doesn't recognise either. The driver doesn't turn around. He has his hoodie pulled up over his head. The other guy looks into the back seat with a grin on his face which shows two of his front teeth missing. He's a bit dishevelled, hair sticking up all over the place, unshaven, a hard face, and it smells like he's had a few beers. 'How are ya boys?'

Honky Jai thinks to himself, White Power probably.

'Nicked a car just for the occasion. Where to?' the hooded head asks in a gruff voice.

Bryce nudges Jai. 'Head to Woolston' Jai says. Now they can breathe a sigh of relief. They're safe. Sort of. At least they are out of sight of anyone who might be looking.

'I teed up Joe for a pick up when I rang mum the other night. He's my bro in law. What a laugh man, the staff dialled the number to make sure I didn't ring anyone I shouldn't but once you're on the phone, they wouldn't know who the hell you're talking to. How long have you been waiting Joe?'

'Only about ten. We sat behind a parked car so we didn't stand out…In…cog. neat…toe… man! The car's fresh, won't have been reported yet but no point in taking risks. Pretty good timing from you guys. So, yeah, no worries!'

After a few further directions from Jai, they arrive at their destination and jump out of the car. Bryce has a word with his bro in law that Jai doesn't catch. Then the two original occupants drive off.

The house is set back off the street. The front section is a mass of shrubs and bushes through which they can just make out lights from the windows. The boys move up the path. Jai knocks. The door opens and after a brief exchange, they're ushered in.

They're greeted by Tommy Mudlark. The Mudlark family lived three doors down from Jai's place and he's known Tommy ever since he can remember. The parents had heavy 'pommie' accents, so strong Jai struggled to understand half of what they said. Tommy didn't, he sounded like a kiwi bloke. They'd seen each other around at primary school. Tommy was a year ahead and almost two years older, but that didn't matter. From the first moment, a bond developed between them. Over the subsequent years, they spent almost all their spare time together. They biked all over the city, to Centennial Swimming Pool or Queen Elizabeth Park, to the footie, or just because they were bored and wanted to go exploring. They played in the same junior rugby team for the Wanderers Club. Jai only stayed with the club because Tommy was there. Tommy was a winger, slim and fast, and not so keen on the crunchy stuff that happened in the scrums. He wasn't a chicken, just smart. His view was he didn't need to be damaged to have fun, so why would he want to be mixing it up with the tubbies or doing all the tackling? And that's how he played, dancing here, sidestepping there, and dropping off tackles. Jai also wasn't a big guy so he'd naturally gravitated to the backline and played second five-eight. He couldn't avoid the tackling. For some reason that wasn't obvious, he was always the one left to tackle some oversized maniac who'd already crunched through half a dozen tackles. He did it. He was fit and determined, he wanted to get his guy, bring him down. He prided himself that no one could get past him. But when he turned fourteen he stopped playing as other things he wanted to do became more important.

All the biking around eventually contributed to their first burg together. They were riding down Marshlands Road on their way home after a game against Kaiapoi when they took an opportunity to check out a garage that appeared unused and unloved, standing in the middle of an overgrown field partially obscured by a hedge. They'd gone and had a look at it. They couldn't see inside because the windows were covered by white paint. They couldn't open them from the outside. The door had a large padlock. No way in, so they left. Eventually, curiosity got the better of them. On the way back from their next game against Kaipoi they rode up the driveway and stuck their bikes out of sight buried in the hedge. Tommy had come prepared and pulled a short blue crowbar from his backpack. He levered the screws holding the padlock out. It made a loud creaking noise. For an instant, Jai wondered if they could be heard, but he dismissed the thought, they were in the middle of nowhere. They were in.

Jai was blown away by what he was seeing. He'd always thought they might find an old car in there or other garage stuff.

'No wonder it had a lock, I always knew there'd be something good in here.' Tommy observed bringing Jai out of his temporary astonishment. Inside was a lot different than its rough exterior might have promised. It was tidy but still chocked full of all sorts of stuff. Opposite the door, most of the far wall was occupied by a bench covered with electrical gear. It looked like the control deck on the spaceship Enterprise with switches, nobs, sliders, and buttons. Most had numbers and letters underneath written on strips of paper. There were a couple of tape decks, stacked, with a record player on top. He recognised a guitar amp tucked under the bench and a couple of guitar cases. Two massive blue speakers occupied a corner each. Off to one side was a bookshelf, the top half of which was full of books and magazines. The bottom three tiers were records. In front of it there stood a couple of guitars on stands, one acoustic and one electric. Around the walls were shelves containing boxes and tins. Jai knew guitars, his father was a muso, but he didn't know what most of this gear was.

After spending a few minutes sliding sliders and twiddling nobs, the boys decided to have a look in the boxes. Some were full of electronic stuff, microphones, foot pedals, leads and plugs. In one Tommy found a little brass pipe, a couple of bags of 'weed', some papers and a lighter. Jai knew about weed, he'd seen plenty at home, weed and vodka, his old man's staples. There was a metal box, buried out of sight behind some other cardboard boxes. Jai popped it open. It contained money, at a glance over a hundred bucks in cash, fives and tens. Tommy grabbed a fist full of notes and waved them around, man he was excited. He was jumping up and down saying they were rich. Jai wondered why anyone would be keeping cash here.

Then they heard the sound of a car in the driveway, the roar of an engine and tyres sliding over the gravel. Tommy stopped still. Trouble. Looking a bit panicky he stated the obvious, they needed to get the hell out of there. There was a window above the workbench holding the control desk. The boys made a dash for it, jumping onto the bench but avoiding the electrics. It was an aluminium window, bracketed so it wouldn't open too far. But the boys squeezed through it pretty easily. Jai reached up and pushed the window shut. A car door slammed. Luckily they were near to their stashed bikes. As quietly as they could they grabbed their bikes out of the hedge and pushed through a gap to the other side. Now they couldn't be spotted from the garage. The hedge provided cover to the road. They walked quickly and quietly, daring not to breathe and resist the urge to run. As soon as they were clear they jumped on their bikes. Jai half expected to hear someone call out after them and maybe chase them in the car. But it never happened.

Once they'd gone a mile, they slowed. Jai hadn't been aware of how fast his heart was beating until now. He took a couple of deep breaths. Tommy also seemed to be catching his breath. 'Nearly got caught! It must have had an alarm or something. The guy got there real quick! How long were we there…maybe ten minutes. What a gas man!' Jai was buzzing too. Who would have thought all that stuff was in a derelict old garage. They couldn't stop talking about it all the way home.

When they got to Tommy's place he asked Jai to hang for a while as his 'olds' weren't coming back till later in the evening. Once inside Tommy pulled out a fist full of money from his jacket pocket, from another he pulled out the pipe, and then from inside his jacket, one of the bags of 'weed'.

'It's party time! And KFC for us tonight,' he laughed. Jai was eleven years old and Tommy was nearly thirteen.

They got up to more tricks, lots more, but all that stopped when Tommy turned fifteen and left school and home in the same week. Jai lost touch with him for a while after that. He was hanging with a different crowd, guys Jai didn't know. Eventually, they bumped into each other again. They still had a friendship although it wasn't quite the same as it used to be. The main thing was that he knew where Tommy lived.

Tommy seems surprised and pleased when he sees Jai at the door. He looks just the same as the last time they met except now he's grown a wispy moustache and a trimmed, pointed goatee beard. He's gotten taller too. He used to be short like Jai but not anymore. He's nearly six feet tall and he has filled out as well. The other glaring change is his dress sense. Tommy looks like money, flash designer gear, a diamond stud in his ear, and a sharp-looking wristwatch.

'Been a while,' he says, hugging Jai. 'Who's this then?' He looks less pleased to have a stranger in his place.

'Bryce Whitehouse. Did a runner with me from Stanmore. He needs your help so I brought him here. Hope that's cool man. We just need to hang for the night and then we're gone.'

Tommy gives Bryce the once up and down then he seems to relax, 'Any mate of yours is ok by me,' he says patting Bryce on the shoulder. 'I got a couple of things to do but meantime, celebrate your newfound freedom!'

Fifteen minutes later they get the chance to catch up. After the usual family stuff, Tommy tells him what he's been up to, mainly having fun and spending money. Jai fills him in on Stanmore and the escape. Bryce can tell Tommy what he wants. Jai doesn't need to know the details.

The flat is a pretty cool pad. It's got all the mod cons, good kitchen gear, a huge stereo system, and a film projector. It must cost a fair bit. He tells Jai he's got a Mustang parked out the back. Tommy hasn't got a formal police record despite all the criminal stuff he gets up to. He's almost certainly on their radar but they've never come to his place…at least so far. If they knew what happened in his flat they'd be round every second day, just for the drug-taking alone.

Tommy's a 'fence', he moves stolen items. It connects him to all sorts of people in the underworld. He says he's over doing burgs, it's a mug's game as far as he's concerned, too much risk, too little return. He never does 'the business' at home, that's his basic rule. Keep the two things, business and living apart. Jai is pretty sure he has a storage garage in an industrial area near Sockburn. Tommy does his money transactions during the day in public places with 'drop offs' of the goodies happening at night. Jai doesn't know all the details but he does know the arrangements seem to work. Tommy always has cash, he never seems to get ripped off, and there never seems to be any agitation around him. He has lots of friends and does lots of partying.

Not surprisingly then, there's a party going on in the lounge. A dozen people are in various states of 'smashed' lying on the floor, draped over one of the leather couches or sitting on one of the two chairs. Jai doesn't know any of them and no one takes much interest in the two new arrivals, even after they are introduced. They just carry on passing the joints, sharing a beer and listening to the Eagle's Greatest Hits on the stereo. The music is at a moderate volume, loud enough to mildly strain private conversations but not loud enough to upset the neighbours or draw any unwanted attention to the flat. Jai and Bryce find a place against the wall and sit down, side by side.

As the 'J's and beers start casting their spell, their conversation moves from laughter about getting away, the thrill of the run, to the technicalities of how Bryce set it up. He fills Jai in. It was simple.

During the morning Aaron Tomas grabbed a roll of cello tape from the school and passed it to Bryce at lunchtime. All the boys were allowed to go upstairs to their bedrooms to get anything they might need before the afternoon programme started. This was done in groups of two accompanied by a staff member. Bryce and Aaron were the first chosen. Although they slept in different dorms, the staff member kept them together. Standard practice so they expected it. They trouped around to Rata where Bryce picked up a jersey, then on to Kauri and Aaron's room. The staffer let him in while he and Bryce stood outside. Aaron put on a good show. Cursing loudly, he came out saying he'd accidentally knocked a model car off his windowsill and it'd fallen out onto the fire escape stairs. After some grumbling about clumsy sods and the inconsiderateness of making work for everyone, the staff member took the boys around to the fire escape door. He made the two stand on the landing where he could see them easily, opened it, and went down the half a dozen steps to retrieve the car. Bryce slipped a doubled piece of cello tape over the hole where the lug from the door latch fitted snugly into the frame. He pressed it with his thumb so it was slightly indented. When the staffer came back up the stairs, Bryce bowed, made a flourish with his arm and pulled the door closed. It latched just enough to hold in place. It's a self-locking mechanism, the staffer didn't double-check. Not smart, and a trap for new players although it gets experienced staff members if they're in a hurry or if they haven't come across it before.

Everything was set up for the night. The biggest risk to the plan was the night staff. They were pretty vigilant and routinely check the locks all around the building. But they sometimes didn't do this straight away depending on how busy or rumpty things were when they arrived. Bryce had planned to keep them very busy.

When bedtime came a couple of boys in Rata set up a distraction as soon as the day staff departed. It started with boys wandering about when they should be in bed, a bit of swearing and arguing, just enough to keep the staff on the move and break their routine. Bryce had been around for long enough to know unsettled behaviour is contagious and others will buy-in. That's what happened, it all worked like a charm. The night staff did not do their normal checks. The moment things quietened down they retreated to their office. He waited ten minutes and then asked to go to the toilet. As soon as he was gone his buddies started a serious rumble in Rata knowing the night staff would come running. That's when he came and got Jai. All the boys know it, distractions are your best friend, whether deliberate or by chance, they always provide opportunities. Bryce grabbed the cello tape on the way out, no point in leaving clues for the staff. That's what Jai had seen him do.

'What about Aaron, what was in it for him?' Jai asks.

'He thought he was going to come. Didn't happen, don't need any hangers-on.' Ruthless, Jai muses, but too bad.

So here they are, Bryce and him. Out of Stanmore… easy as! Plenty of boys said it was a piece of piss and they were right. Tomorrow Bryce wants to get to Ashburton. Jai doesn't want to. Bryce can go on his own. Tommy will help for sure. Jai needs to find somewhere else to stay. He turns to Bryce and puts out his hand.

'Ever heard that song from the movie Easy Rider, *Don't Bogart that joint,* Jai sings a few bars. "No?" My old man loved that movie so much he bought the video. Any rate, it means stop hogging the 'J' and hand it over man.' He's feeling mellow now, too mellow to think about tomorrow… tomorrow is tomorrow.

Chapter 11
Wyatt Catches His Breath

Ted said to me not long after I started, 'I'll tell you what, working nights, it's something different.' Talk about stating the obvious I thought at the time, given a large part of your awake time moved into the night. However, I didn't understand what the implications might be. After six weeks or so, I haven't made a full adjustment yet and now I guess, it might take months. Sleeping during the day is hard work. Although I can be exhausted when I get home, I may only sleep for a few hours and then I'm wide awake and my body is saying 'Daytime!' The weekends are the hardest because everyone is milling about, community and household. It's a challenge, still, you're paid for it, but you pay for it too is my point.

On the job, I'm committed to staying awake. Sometimes my body does not want to match my good intentions. When total exhaustion sets in, it feels like I've got crawling things on my skin. I'm almost itchy all over, but nothing that can be scratched for relief. Staying awake becomes the sole mission. There are some basic techniques like chatting with your partner, washing your face with cold water, and walking about, especially outside in the cool night air. I like that one and it generally works for me. But with the best will in the world, if you are exhausted, before you know it you're being jolted awake because your head has dropped, or you're banging it on a wall because you fell asleep on your feet. One thing I've learned is if you get through the 'death hour' between 4 and 5 am, the highest risk time, you tend to wake up a bit with the rising sun. I expect it to become easier. However, I note it still happens to Ted on rare occasions despite his commitment and years of practice. It's most important that it doesn't happen to both team members at the same time. That's the problem with Mr Rogers' approach. When it happens to Ted or me, you know there's the cover, but with Mr Rogers, you're on your own.

Outside the residence, there is plenty of nightlife going on too. Within a few shifts, I've come across the regular dumpster divers who frequent the bins behind the supermarket next door during the early hours of the morning. There are over a dozen patrons who show up two or three times a week, as well as the occasional hanger-on. The shoppers are of a variety of ages, genders and cultures. They are a little community and from the familiarity of the chatter, they know each other reasonably well. It's a social gathering too. A number bring their 'borrowed' shopping trolleys and two have little tartan covered trundler bags. It pays to be prepared.

Out of curiosity, I checked out the dumpster one night. It's surprising what it contained. All sorts of grocery items, all past their 'use by date', but discarded regardless of their condition. Meat, bread, veggies and fruit, lots of it well and truly good enough to consume. There were no soft drinks but there were milk cartons, cream and other dairy products. There was even a beer. Ted, that fountain of knowledge, tells me if a carton is damaged, or a bottle is broken, the whole pack gets thrown out. I confess for a moment I was tempted…but it's not appropriate, and the night shoppers have a far greater need.

On my second Saturday night on duty, the alarm in the local working men's club went off at about 3 am. I wandered out to take a look, just being nosey, although Mr Rogers did not raise himself. The police duly arrived and for a while I watched the torches moving from floor to floor as they searched the premises. It took a while so I went upstairs and did a round of checks. I had only just sat down when the alarm went off again.

'Happens from time to time. Someone breaks in and sets off the alarm. The police search and don't find them. Then they set off the alarm breaking back out. I don't even check anymore.' Mr Rogers does not bother to open his eyes as he imparts this information to me.

'Break ins' often happen at the local shops too and we hear the alarms go off. Some nights we watch a person walk along the road hugging the shop frontages like a schizophrenic musician I once knew, who thought if he did that he was invisible, sliding in and out of each alcove, hugging the building. We found it amusing to watch him, although in retrospect it wasn't. Sometimes it's just a drunk weaving their way along, but other times, someone is up to no good. The alarm confirms one way or the other.

Richmond Park, directly across from the residence is a continual source of late-night activity too. On their perimeter patrols, Ted and Mr Rogers tell me they have witnessed fights, drinking parties and cars doing wheelies on the grassed area. Occasionally they have been sufficiently concerned to ring the police. Ted was saying one night when he was checking admin early in the morning, he heard some sort of grunting and squealing coming from the park. He thought he may be might be witnessing an assault so he nipped across to check it out. He found a young couple half-naked hard at it in the middle of the park. To his surprise, they weren't even daunted or inhibited by his approach! His comment, 'At least get a bush if you can't get a room!' and he left them to it.

The residence also attracts unwelcome night visitors. At least once a week some type of vehicle, probably stolen, does wheelies around the front driveways. Mostly it's kids, easy to identify because they can be seen hanging out the windows, hooting and shouting all sorts of abuse. Mr Rogers reckons there are times when staff, under the influence of the amber fluid after a session at the local watering hole next door, have done a bit of a circuit too. So far neither Ted nor I have witnessed such a thing. Staff, however, do come on the property frequently if they want to use the flat for some reason. Ted says it is not uncommon to hear all sorts of noises through the walls if you are in Rata. He went into the flat one night and found Frank Thomas and a person, not his wife, preparing for a bit of amorous action. Frank wasn't pleased with the interruption and made it known. Ted wasn't very impressed right back because such acts didn't align with his staunch family values. Turns out Frank had split with his wife and had found a new girlfriend and needed a place to strut his stuff. He was so annoyed with Ted that he spoke to his supervisor. The night staff are no longer required to check the flat as part of their routine. Since then, both Ted and Mr Rogers said the flat can be busy with comings and goings at all times of the night. Just who exactly, well who would know? Not those on duty anyway. I hadn't heard or seen anything so far. Tonight it's so quiet everywhere you could hear a pin drop ... and it's only 11.30 pm. It's boring. I decide I'll try and write a song about the boys' home to fill in the time.

Chapter 12
On the Run

Jai has been out and about for two weeks. Stanmore has become a bit of a distant memory, although now and again it niggles away at him like a guitar riff that he just can't work out. He feels if anyone's looking for him they would have found him because despite being on the run, he isn't exactly hiding. Sure, he's being careful not to go to really high-risk places like the Square but he's spending plenty of time around his other favourite haunts, Linwood, Woolston, Cashel St, and the library. He's even gone to his home a couple of times. His main strategy is to keep moving around, never staying in one place too long.

After being at Tommy's place for a couple of days Jai' had known it was time to move on. There was always a slight chance the police could come around because of his business activities. But also, even though hardly anyone knew he was there, he didn't want to be the cause of trouble, especially for his mate. Bryce had gone the very next day. Tommy fixed him up with a lift to Ashburton. It was the last Jai heard about him, or wanted to for that matter.

It'd been easy to find somewhere else to stay. There were vacant houses all over town. All the street kids knew where and it hadn't taken him long to hook up. For the last five days, he has been staying at a place near Barrington Mall, an old rundown villa in Sugden St.

The house is set at the back of a large overgrown section behind Barrington Park. It's obviously been abandoned for a long time because it's a shambles, inside and out. The windows were boarded up to prevent them from being broken but too late in most cases. Inside there's glass on the floor throughout, although someone's cleaned up the lounge where he's sleeping. The beautiful solid wood doors are all in place although they are marked and scratched. There are holes in the lathe and plaster walls where bits have fallen or broken off and the scrim underneath is exposed. Cupboard doors in the kitchen have been pulled off and, from the look of the burned fittings still visible among the ashes in the lounge fireplace, used as fuel for warmth. Paint is peeling off everywhere and large patches of the external timber walls, windows and surfeits are now just bare wood, greyed with age and exposure to the elements.

The property is surrounded by trees and shrubs forming a dense perimeter so, to passers-by, it remains hidden. A person can sit out on the veranda, smoke a 'J' and no one can see them or smell what you're up to. There's no electricity but in the bigger scheme of things, it's a minor matter. There is cold water. Someone must have turned on or failed to turn off the main supply. The toilet works. When a squatter needs a hot shower, which in Jai's case is not often, they go over to the changing rooms at Linwood Park. Sometimes it means you have to scale the iron gate at the front which is closed and locked at night. But that isn't a problem, there's enough of a gap at the top so a slim person can slide through easily. Jai has a torch and he can find his way around once inside. He's discovered the hot water turns off at night. He needs to time things just right so he's there early enough to get a warm shower, but late enough so he can't be seen getting in. Sometimes he goes down with Eric Romas who is the other person living at the house.

It was Eric who hooked him up. He's been living there for about two months. Eric is a small weedy guy. He wears big thick glasses that partially obscure the pockmarks all over his lily-white face. He reckons they are from having the measles when he was young. He's a true street kid who's been living rough for over a year. Jai was curious about why Eric is out on the streets so he asked him one evening as they were sitting in front of the small fireplace in the lounge burning a few pinecones gathered from the backyard.

'I like it. I'm my own man out here. It was shit at home.' His story sounds familiar to Jai. His mother had all these stupid arsehole boyfriends. He never knew who was going to be there when he got home from school. They'd be on the piss, stoned out or shooting up. Most of the time his mother never had much money. He thinks she might have gotten a few bucks from dealing. He didn't know for sure because he'd gone through her stuff plenty of times looking for something he could steal or sell but never found anything that looked like drugs, or of any worth for that matter. She was doing something though, because now and then she'd be flush. They would be rich for a day and then poor the next.

'There was hardly ever anything to eat. If some food miraculously appeared in the fridge, I'd stash a bit around the house to make sure there was something left for the next day. Then she would be away for a couple of days, or a week and I wouldn't know where she was or when she was going to turn up. I was left to fend for myself heaps. Might as well be out here doing it…without the hassles, or the drongo boyfriends.'

'What about your old man, where's he? Could you have stayed with him?' Jai inquired.

'Never met the guy, don't know who he is or where he is. I asked mum and she wouldn't tell me. I reckon she didn't know. I don't care, I like it out here doing what I want, with no one to bother me. I got my mates and I got my girlfriend, Ellise'.

'Oh yeah, where's she then?' An obvious follow-up question since Jai hadn't ever seen her.

'She's gone to Auckland to see a friend, went about a month ago. Not sure when she's coming back. She got a ride up north and the plan was to jump on the Picton ferry and then hitch up the island. She wanted me to go too but I didn't want to. I'm better off here.'

Jai wondered if Eric had missed a message. It sounded to him like Elise may have done a runner. None of his business though, he just wanted a place to stay, the less complicated the better.

Other young people have come and gone over the days since he arrived, drifting around from house to house. It's a way of life. Jai has been there, done that too. They are all drifting, waiting for something to happen, making ends meet however they can, raiding the local veggie gardens, helping themselves from the supermarkets or dairies, or going to the dumpsters at night. That's how Jai bumped into Eric in the first place. He'd seen him around The Square a few times and at Linwood Park, so he had a nodding acquaintance. The first time they actually spoke was at a bin behind the Linwood supermarket. The bin had a big padlock on it to stop people from doing what Eric and Jai were trying to do. Eric had a bit of pipe he was using as a lever. They had a chat about the principles of leverage, a couple of regular little physicists. Once they had successfully applied their scientific knowledge, they sat down and had a feed. Since then they'd bumped into each other a few times.

Not long after leaving Tommy's place, Jai was at Barrington Mall scouting about looking for opportunities. He wasn't particular about what they might be, he had an open mind. Then he saw Eric in the car park, busy helping himself to stuff out of the back of a parked car. This was Eric's scam. He would wait until someone dropped off their shopping and then if they went back into the mall for some reason, he'd take his chance. It was surprising how often cars were left unlocked, but if not, he would break into them using his trusty bent coat hanger. He's practised at the art and can be in a car in a matter of seconds as long as it's the right type of car. He says he never takes a huge amount, just what he can carry. He avoids taking anything that needs a lot of cooking because it's a problem, not impossible though because he has the fireplace. Mainly, if he has to cook, it's cans of stuff like baked beans or spaghetti, he loves them both, soups or tinned fruit, things he can heat up or toast on the fire. Eric made Jai laugh when he'd said 'It's like being a boy scout without the dressing up and the dodgy scoutmasters!'

Milk and bread are staples, although things like butter are a problem because they go off. No fridge, unfortunately! Sometimes he puts stuff in a bucket of cold water and that helps preserve it for a while but it's not great and doesn't work for many things. It's a good day if he gets Coke or Fanta or cigarettes. On great days, beer, wine or a bottle of something stronger. Wine or spirits are best because they're easier to carry but beggars can't be choosers and if beer's there for the taking, he'll grab it and lug it off. He doesn't bother with personal hygiene products. Jai can tell and he's noticed Eric's teeth are knackered. He's even got a couple of plastic shopping bags so he would look like any other shopper leaving the car park. And he has a backpack, a most useful item in the circumstances.

On the day they hooked up, Eric had experienced a top day. He'd made two raids. On both occasions, he managed to get cigarettes. On his first excursion, he'd been obliged to take a whole bag of groceries, not his norm, but he'd needed to be extra quick because there were a lot of people around. The quick grab meant he got a mystery pack. There were cornflakes, ham, fruit and some cleaning products. Nothing drinkable or good to sniff. Eric liked his sniff. He's very knowledgeable about sniffable products. He had given Jai a few stoned raves about all the different things that come in an aerosol can, how they are used and what they do to you.

It was on his second excursion that Jai saw him. Jai had just come out of the mall where he'd had no success in finding anything to improve his day. He was walking through the carpark planning to try Linwood Mall next when he saw Eric leaning over an open car boot stuffing a bottle into his backpack and other unidentifiable things into a plastic bag. Jai decided to follow him until they were clear of the car park. He knew Eric lived on the streets and would be staying somewhere. It was a spur of the moment thing that paid off big time. Somewhere to stay, and as a bonus, Eric had scored a bottle of whiskey. Paaarteeeee time!

Tonight is late night shopping, probably the best day for picking up groceries from the local supermarket car park. Even better, because it's Friday it means people will be dropping in for the weekend supplies. And yet better still, a number will come after being in the pub somewhere for a couple of hours, half-cut and likely to have alcohol. Full boots, carelessness, booze, darkness, almost ideal conditions. On the negative side, it will be busy with lots of people coming and going. Jai and Eric haven't eaten all day. They ate the last of a bag of Corn Flakes, dry without milk, and a can of baked beans between them yesterday. They also polished off the last of the whiskey and were feeling a bit under the weather this morning. Eric was in the worst state because he'd sniffed from a can of fly spray. Jai had declined the aerosol experience, not his bag.

Eric is so fast at getting into the cars. It's a no brainer that he'll be doing that part while Jai acts as the lookout. They hit the car park at seven. It is already dark, and as expected, it's busy and full. The hope is they can be in and out quickly, get some basics, and then maybe do a second run where they can be more selective.

Almost immediately on arriving they see an elderly woman deposit her groceries in the boot of her car, an older model Holden. She seems in a hurry and heads back into the mall. Bingo, they are in, easy pickings. Eric 'coat-hangers' the driver's door and pops the boot while Jai stays about twenty metres away keeping watch. As soon as the boot is opened Eric starts to rifle through the groceries. There are heaps to be searched, too much for him alone and he waves Jai over to help. They are engrossed, their heads down working fast when a voice behind them shatters their concentration.

'What the hell do you think you're doing?' They freeze. They have been too absorbed, motivated by their hunger and careless because it had been so easy. Jai didn't see the man approach, falling down on his part of the job. Now he's behind them and only a couple of metres away. Every man for himself! Sometimes it might have been fight rather than flight, but not this time. Neither boy is a fighter in either temperament or physical capability, so running is the logical option. No need for any discussion about the choices.

Unfortunately, Eric is closest to the man and he's grabbed by his arm. Jai, already twenty metres away, briefly looks back. For a fleeting moment, he thinks again about helping. The two of them might have a chance of fighting the guy off. But he quickly decides against it. Now he can see him more fully, he's young and looks like he means business. Jai's already a master of quick survival analysis and decision making. He's off, no point in them both getting into trouble. Ah well, getting caught is a risk of the game.

There's now a real racket going on behind him. The man is yelling out, 'Stop that kid, stop thief!' That's me! Bloody hell, thinks Jai, time to run like a midfielder.

He can hear Eric shouting, 'Let me go! …Help! …Child molester I didn't do anything.' The voices are quickly subsumed into the general hubbub of the busy car park and the increasing distance Jai is creating as he runs. When he's far enough away he glances back again. No one appears to be in pursuit. He slows to a walk. He doesn't want to draw any unwanted attention, slinging his little shopping bag partially full of goodies over his back.

Just to be doubly safe, he takes the first side road off Barrington St. He spends the next half an hour wandering the streets. Now, when it feels like he is totally in the clear, he finally makes his way back to the house. It's dark and quiet. He lets himself in through the loosened board that covers a side window and goes into the lounge. There is no one else at the house. Eric's stuff is where he left it next to Jai's small bag of clothes and personals gathered from one of his brief visits home. He sits down. At least he has food now. Bad luck for Eric but he doesn't feel any sadness, just relief for himself. Lucky it wasn't him who got caught.

He doesn't move for half an hour, alone in the darkness.

Eventually, he decides to start a fire. Before long, once there is sufficient light from the flames, he checks out Eric's stuff just in case there's anything of interest. It is unlikely Eric will be back for it anytime soon he thinks. He has a Walkman, and a couple of T-shirts, no point in leaving those behind when he departs, as he surely will first thing tomorrow. In the meantime, he'll eat. He uses his knife to open a can of beans and sticks it on the fire.

What a life this is. Eric was here one minute and gone the next. He feels a bit disorientated, dislocated, agitated, it's hard to tell exactly, he's not good with identifying feelings. As he sits there staring into the tiny fire, the flame sputtering and dancing, his mind begins to wander. He realises he's never really stopped and thought about what he was doing or where he might be going, he just goes with the flow and acts in the moment. Now he's on the run, a fugitive. Most of his life lately was just about making it through each day. Not that long ago he'd been at school, playing sports with his mates. Then things went wrong. All the stuff he'd been up to, he'd told himself, was just a bit of harmless fun. But he'd made a few bad decisions and now the future looks like Boys Homes, with locked doors and barred windows. I'm an outlaw, he thinks. Us against the world. Fuck the World. 'F.T.W.' He says it out aloud.

Warmed by the glowing embers, he picks up Eric's Walkman, puts the earphones in and pushes play. He recognises the tune from the first few bars, *Wild World* Cat Stevens, not really his thing. He checks Eric's bag, no other tapes. Ah well, he thinks, it will have to do, nice guitar and a good voice.

Chapter 13
Jai Keeps Moving

Next thing he wakes with a start. It's morning, and pasty sunlight speckled with a cosmos of dust particles, is streaking through the lounge's boarded window. He still has the earphones in but the player is dead. It comes back to him in a flash, Eric is gone. He feels a sense of urgency, time to move. He can't put his finger on why he feels this unease, it's a sixth sense. Eric might dob him in, possible, although not likely, he can't take the chance. He grabs the food he has left and stuffs it into his bag, also collecting Eric's T-shirts and the Walkman. He climbs out through the boarded-up window and heads across the section and into Barrington Park. As he enters the park he can see a couple of 'blue and whites' driving along Barrington Street. They are too far away so he is not worried they might see him. Maybe I got out just in time, he thinks.

He wanders about for a while, aimless. What he feels like is getting out of it. He knows where to go and sets off towards Linwood, home territory. There are always kids he knows hanging out in Linwood Park. Lots are users of some sort, glue or other substances and the park is a gathering point. Jai isn't a 'glue bag' himself but he doesn't care what anyone else does for kicks. He'd tried it once but the fumes made him puke. The real baggers told him you just have to enjoy the rush and you will get over the fumes, but, no, not for him—one go, didn't like it, not doing it again. Jai thought it was desperate to be sniffing glue, paint, fly spray and all the other things people got up to. A few of the hard out sniffers he knows are out of it, permanently. The very worst seem to have mush for brains. He doesn't need that. He can always get dope and booze, they're more his thing. But he also knows, that where there is partaking of substances there will always be a few joints floating about as well. And if he goes to the park, he'll also probably be able to find a place to stay for a few days.

He arrives at about ten in the morning and straight away he picks out the group. They move about a bit but today they are gathered under an oak tree deep in the park, barely visible from the road. There look to be about fifteen or so young people, mainly boys but a few girls, sitting around talking. A couple of them seem to be asleep, maybe already out of it.

Everyone, the cops, the schools, the social workers, know the kids are here and now and again one of those nobs comes looking for runaways or kids wagging, or because something has happened to lift the group's public profile and 'The System' has to be seen to be doing something. Jai had heard there'd been a few articles in the local rag about the kids in the park although Jai hadn't read any because he didn't bother with the papers. 'Disgrace' was one headline he'd been told about and another titled, 'Linwood Residents Have Had Enough'…but whatever, the kids laughed about it, 'Look, man, we got 'the fame'!'

The kids generally stayed somewhere near the back of the park so they could keep an eye out for possible intruders. It's a big space so there's plenty of back area. When an undesirable is spotted everybody scatters. Sometimes the problem child will give themselves up to take the heat out of the situation. Once in a blue moon, the police and social workers combine forces to do a big round-up. It makes it harder to get away because they're devious and they try to surround the group. The kids scatter in all directions and some inevitably escape. Those who get nabbed are taken to the cop shop, families or caregivers are contacted, and they are sent home. Only a temporary arrangement until they take off again. For those without family willing to take them or whom the police want to be secured, it is a placement at a Family Home or into Stanmore Road, or Kingslea. The raids are a hazard of being out and about…sure… but they don't happen often so they aren't something Jai is immediately concerned about, At any rate, at the moment needs must. He wants a place to stay that isn't a bush or under a bridge, he's not the outdoor type.

Within a few seconds, he's able to pick out someone he knows, Jomo Paku. He's Māori although he's pretty light-skinned so if you didn't know him you might not pick it. Jai thinks he's about eighteen but he looks years older. Jomo's been on the streets forever and he's well known. He's a skilled survivor and he's acquainted with all the necessary tricks. Just the hook-up Jai needs.

Jai looks at him. It's been a few months since he last saw him and Jomo has changed. He's got a wispy beard that resembles the ones Jai's seen on old

Chinamen in martial arts films. His hair hangs down to his shoulders, black and limp. It's much longer than Jai remembers. He wears black jeans and a black jersey which has loose bits of wool fraying from the sleeves and elbows. There's a hole in the front. The most striking thing is how thin he appears. The last time Jai saw him he was a pretty solid guy, now he looks like a starved refugee. His exposed wrists are like sticks and his cheekbones protrude out of his face like shelves under his eyes. He smiles at Jai and greets him. His teeth are stained and yellow and his gums are black. The eyes, now bearing down on Jai, seem to look right through him. Jomo is either high or he's had a really, really big night. It doesn't matter to Jai, he's connected. Step one of his mission is completed.

Jomo introduces him to a couple of kids he doesn't know. Jai nods at them in a silent greeting. Most of them he's seen or met before so no need for intros. He pulls Jomo aside, he needs to do the business before any more niceties.

'I need somewhere to stay bro. I did a runner from Stanmore a couple of weeks ago. I've been moving about every few days so it's not for long. I reckon if I keep my head down for a couple more, they'll forget all about me. I plan to get together some coin and head up to Auckland.'

Jai is making this up on the spot. He hasn't thought too far ahead but he remembered Elise and her escape plan so he just uses it. He'd never been to Auckland, all he knows is it's a big city. But there are always street kids and they are generally easy to find. Someone would give him an 'in' for sure.

'No worries man. We're staying in a house off Ferry Road in Woolston. It's not far from here. About twenty people are dossing down, lots of action, parties, shit happening. Another body won't make any difference. Rents free, ha, ha.' He gives more of a snort than a laugh which shows off his stained choppers. 'You might have to bring a little something with you, most people bring something. It's like the price of admission.'

'I've got some food in my bag, happy to share.'

'You and I might head off there now. Bring your food with you, we'll eat some of it on the way. See yous' all,' he addresses the group with a wave, 'Back later!'

Jai isn't going to come back later, not if he's got somewhere to stay. No point in being visible if you don't have to, especially here in the park.

They set off and before long they arrive at the house. It doesn't look much different to the dilapidated place he just came from, except it is on a fenced back section. There is a gate at the front which has a large sign on it saying 'Keep Out' and another underneath saying 'Danger' both in big red letters.

'The gate keeps everyone out but us' laughs Jomo. 'We put the sign there… got it off a construction site. Smart eh? We've been here for over a month. I think the neighbours know but we don't bother them and they don't bother us. We have a rule… Don't shit on the neighbours! So no burgs or swiping their cars or anything. That way I think we can stay here for as long as we like.'

They go into the house through a space where the back door once stood. In the lounge, there are a couple of old chairs covered in faded floral patterns which exaggerate the threadbare parts, and a sofa on which there's a motley fawn sleeping bag, clearly with someone inside. It's pulled up shielding the occupant's head from the light. There is a girl who looks to Jai to be about fourteen at a pinch, sitting smoking on a white painted wicker chair.

'That's Lorrie,' Jomo waves his hand in the direction of the girl, 'And that's Benny in the bag, he's a late starter. This is Jai.'

Lorrie is a small girl with bright orange hair tied up in a knot above her head. After the hair, which catches the eye straight away, Jai notices her bare arms are covered in red and purple splotches of some kind. Sitting on the arm of the chair is an ashtray full of cigarette butts. She vaguely waves in reply but doesn't say anything, puffs on the fag and blows a big smoke ring.

'I'll show yah where yah can sleep. We've got four bedrooms here. The room by the back door has the most space, you can hang there. My room's over there, and me and my missus are the only ones who stay in that room.'

They are in a hallway off which there are half a dozen doors. Jomo's waving about left and then right. Jai doesn't care, he doesn't want detail, just point him in the right direction. 'We've got a working dunny. There shouldn't be any water but when I turned it on it worked. It's a real boon. No power so no hot water, so unless you like cold showers…It's down to the park or the railway station. In here!'

Jomo opens a door to reveal a large room. It has jaded floral wallpaper, stained brown and green below a leaking window. Jai sees the floor is almost entirely covered in motley looking mattresses.

'There was a whole lot of stuff still in this house when we came here so I guess someone else was here before. All the better for us. There's a spot,' he points to a green and white striped single mattress which has a large brown stain on one corner and whose insides are desperately trying to escape from a tear in the middle. Jai's not worried, it's a place to sleep and he has certainly slept on worse. He tosses his bag down on the ripped bit. It's ownership. There is so much bedding jammed into the room, it's sort of like being back at a Stanmore dorm. Jai thinks, funny the way things turn out.

'I'll show you the rest of the palace.' Jomo's a wit. They walk out back into the hall and Jomo sticks his head in a third bedroom. Jai follows and pokes his head around the door without entering. There are a couple of young people under a blanket and two others stretched out on mattresses. Jomo introduces Jai. He points to the other bedroom door which is shut.

'I'll introduce you later. I need a fag. Come on.'

They go into the kitchen. There are cups and plates everywhere. On top of the stove is a small gas cooker, the type used for camping. The sink is full of dishes and there is a bin in the corner which is full of rubbish. Jai can see pizza boxes sitting on top. So they eat well from time to time he thinks, another bonus.

Jomo leads Jai back to the lounge. Lorrie has a packet of 'roll-your-owns' and Jomo bums some tobacco. Lorrie still doesn't seem very talkative and Jai doesn't bother trying to engage her. After rolling his cigarette, Jomo enters into a lengthy description of who's living at the house now and who's been here in the past. There are a few names he recognises. Two have been in Stanmore with him, Aaron Brown and Hatch Hitch. Jai was beginning to zone out. He's feeling hungry again. His hasty exit from his last place meant that he skipped breakfast and he hadn't eaten much on the walk over here.

Jomo talks briefly about Julie, his girlfriend. She works at a local café near the railway station, bringing in legit money. She also gets the leftovers from the café most nights, all sorts of goodies. The owners know she's struggling and they're happy for her to take it. It just goes to waste anyway. They don't know she lives here like this though. She showers at the station each morning on the way to work. She keeps the few clothes she has in the bedroom which is part of the reason it's off-limits to everyone, a rule rigidly enforced by Jomo. Julie plays a big part in helping this group survive.

'Staying in the house means you contribute every day somehow, mainly food, grog or drugs. How you do so is your business but after a couple of days of freebies, you're expected to contribute. Oh, and another rule, whatever you do to get stuff, don't bring trouble back here.' It's Julie who makes their contribution, he boasts to Jai. 'You gotta get the right missus man!'

After a short while, the sleeping bag on the couch begins to wiggle like an unearthed huhu grub and a rather groggy looking brown face emerges. Benny is rising. Jai's immediate impression is that Benny looks to be about eighteen or nineteen years old. He has a dense, stubbly growth of black hair covering his upper body from his chest almost up to his eyes. His hair is standing up on end like he's just been electrocuted or been in a wind tunnel. The big rings under bleary, almost black, eyes are pronounced. Jai isn't sure whether he's recovering from having been punched in the nose or if that's just the way his face is. Benny blinks a couple of times and then rubs his half glued shut eyes, liberating them.

'Man, what a night. That was some strong shit…whew, yeah, right out of it.' He croaks, and then he gives a short series of raking coughs, disturbing something pretty rough in his chest.

'Dry as a bone man, I need water badly.' He leaps up all of a sudden like he's having an adrenaline burst, kicking off the sleeping bag and leaving it where it lands on the floor. Benny is fully dressed in black jeans and a black T-shirt with big red Mick Jagger lips on the front. He rushes out of the lounge like he's got a hell hound on his trail. In a few minutes, he's back, his face and hair are wet and he is carrying a glass of water.

'Got any papers man?'

Chapter 14
Things Take a Turn

What an afternoon it turned out to be. Now the sun is gone the main illumination in the lounge is the fire that is roaring away, and has become the focal point for all. There are about fifteen people jammed in the room. Most of them are out of it one way or the other. Jai's feeling tired and jaded. He's been tooting most of the day and now it's taking a toll on him. Benny has 'some good shit' indeed and Jomo, Benny and Jai have been giving it a substantial hammering since his arrival. Others in the room have been sniffing. Hatch Hitch did some 'shopping' at the local hardware store in the afternoon and brought back half a dozen tubes of glue and a few spray cans of gold paint. Jai has watched with mild distaste as the goop was squirted or scraped into plastic bags which are held up over the nose and mouth and 'huffed'. It made a sound like a steam train pulling out of the station. Train to nowhere as far as Jai was concerned. Now bags are littering the floor, spent glue tubes and cans are strewn about, and bodies lying all over the place. Jai can see Lorrie. She's lying on the couch with gold paint stains on her face and hands. She is staring with glazed red eyes at a spot on the ceiling, off in her own world.

There's very little noise, just a couple of quiet conversations and a transistor radio playing music, 'Greatest Hits Radio'. The sound is down because the owner believes it'll reduce the drain on the batteries. Even through his current foggy haze, Jai can smell the paint and glue fumes which are so thick you can almost see them. He has a bit of a headache and he feels he needs to go outside and get some fresh air. He drags himself up from the floor where he is sitting with his back against the wall and wanders across the lounge, stepping over the odd body on the way.

As he passes Jomo's room he hears voices being raised. There's a heated discussion underway.

Jai noticed Jomo and Julie head off to their room a short while ago. Jomo took a tube with him for a private party. Jai can't help wondering how their relationship works. Jomo is a big huffer, one of the biggest in the Linwood group, but from what he's been told, Julie doesn't do much in the way of drugs. She will have a few wines or beers most nights but her job is important to her and she won't do anything that's going to get in the way of keeping it. Jai can see why having a missus who brings in the dollars works well for him. It's hard to see what's in it for Julie though. The mysteries of being in love!

He doesn't have a regular girlfriend. He never even had one who lasted more than a few weeks. He'd had sex, plenty, but as far as he was concerned, it was just that, no ties. It's not that there hadn't been some girls he'd fancied, but it just never seemed to work out. He had a knack for liking ones that are already attached or who were never going to look at him twice, even on a good day. He tells himself his lifestyle doesn't suit being tied down anyway. He isn't sure what'll happen if he ever meets someone he really likes. It makes him a little nervous when he thinks about it, so he doesn't.

He's just about out the backdoor and can hear the volume of the argument going up a few notches. Then the bedroom door opens and Julie is standing there, shouting back into the room. 'It's giving me a fucking headache, I need some air!' the door slams, making the wall shudder. No one else seems to take any notice so Jai suspects this happens often enough not to be a novelty. Julie stomps off past him, head down, bumping him as she passes.

He's only met Julie once before. He can't remember exactly when but it was in Linwood somewhere. She has an attractive face, it's what stuck in his memory, round with big cheeks which bulge under bright blue eyes. Her hair is short, cut to her shoulders and blond, dyed because he can see the dark roots peeking out from the part in the middle. Tonight she's dressed in tight blue jeans and a black cardigan. Yeah man she's hot, Jai can't help thinking as he follows her. He exits the vacant doorway and sees Julie sitting on the edge of the veranda hugging herself against the chilly air. Her feet are bare.

'Aren't you cold?' he asks feeling a bit awkward because he heard the fight and he can't think of anything else to say.

'No!' She is sharp in her reply. Then, seeming to realise it's him, she softens her tone.

'Sorry. I just needed some air. The room was so stinky I can't stand it. And there's so much shit all over the room, it's like being in the tip. Jomo needs to clear it out.' She gives him a sheepish smile, 'I suppose you heard! I need to sleep. It's hard enough with all these people here, partying and coming and going at all times of the day and night. At least in the bedroom, I can get away from it.' Jai can feel her exasperation. 'And I've asked Jomo not to huff in there but when he's really out of it he doesn't care. Most of the time it doesn't bother me too much... but tonight...' She doesn't finish her sentence. It's interrupted by a thunderous boom from inside the house, followed instantaneously by a whooshing sound. A blast of hot air hits them in the back, very nearly knocking them off the veranda.

Almost immediately they feel a rush of cooler air heading the other way back into the house. For a fraction of a second, they're stunned, unmoving, locked in an eerie silence. Then the void is filled with screams from inside. They're on their feet in a shot. Julie leads the way. Smoke is billowing from the lounge area, cascading across the ceiling and beginning to enter the hallway. The shrieking and wailing are getting louder now. Julie disappears into their bedroom. Jai races into the lounge. He can see enough through the smoke to make out that the ceiling and one of the curtains is on fire. The heat is already intense. Bodies are everywhere. While some seem to be where they were before the explosion, others appear to have been blown about, off couches or chairs. Lorrie still lies where she was, unmoved, looking at the same place on the ceiling, now covered in smoke, seemingly oblivious to the chaos around her.

Jai takes all this in from a glance around. Some of the kids are starting to move now. He locates the source of the loudest screams. It's Benny who is sitting on the floor with his face in his hands. Jai can see the ruby red Jagger lips on his T-shirt are gone and only a frayed piece of material is left tangled across his shoulder. The exposed parts of his body are black and red and bleeding in places. The smoke and heat in the room is already oppressive and Jai is struggling to catch his breath.

'Let's get everyone out, quick, go! go! Come on, Help!' he shouts to no one in particular. He rushes over to Benny and grabs his arm. Benny screeches and jerks his arm away.

'Come on man, come on! We have to get out!'

Benny is sort of screaming and sobbing at the same time. He continues to baulk at Jai's touch. Some of the flesh on his arm looks like it's burned away completely. He has to get him out. Jai reaches under his armpit and lifts him, being super careful not to touch the raw parts. Benny's a big boy and it's hard to move him. But he has to… right now! Jai heaves him up with all the force he can muster. Benny finally starts to help himself making it a little easier. They stagger towards the back doorway. Jai takes him out into the middle of the backyard and slowly eases him onto the ground. Benny looks up and Jai can see his eyebrows and beard are gone, as is most of his abundant hair. His face is blackened and one eye is closed. Jai suspects he must have been right in the centre of the blast. Now free of the fire he seems to calm down a little and Jai leaves him sitting there quietly whimpering. He can do no more and he needs to see who else is still inside.

Most of the kids are starting to move and there's a steady flow of young people exiting the back door. Some are crying out and some are silent, mute in shock. Jai pushes his way past and heads back towards the lounge. The smoke in the hall is descending like a grey blanket, already so low he has to stoop from the waist to stay below it. The heat is suffocating. Jai feels the hairs on his arms sizzling. There is only one person left in the room now, Hatch Hitch. Lorrie is gone. Hatch isn't moving but he does not seem as damaged as Benny, no obvious burns. Jai pulls at him.

'Come on Hatch, move!' Hatch doesn't move. As he grabs his arm, Jai is overcome with a fit of coughing and he puts his other arm up over his mouth. He's beginning to feel panicky. He has to get out. He drags Hatch along the floor. Even though he isn't a big guy, he's a dead weight and it still takes all Jai's strength. He's starting to feel dizzy from the smoke. His throat is burning. Each breath is making it worse. The roar of the fire is punctuated by small explosions as spent glue tubes and paint cans explode. With an almighty tug, he gets Hatch to the door of the lounge, and then other arms reach out and help. He closes his eyes and lets whomever they are, drag him outside as well.

Now laying on the back lawn, Jai gasps for oxygen. His throat is raw but in the coolness of the night air, he regains himself quickly. He looks around. No sign of Julie or Jomo. Every fibre in his body resists but he feels driven to go back inside and see where they are. They must still be in the bedroom. At least it wasn't the centre of the fire so they might be all right. He pushes his way through the last of the exiters and heads back inside the house. He's vaguely aware there are sirens in the distance, he can just make them out above the roaring and crackling of the inferno.

The door to Jomo's bedroom is closed. Jai tries the door handle but it is so hot he burns his hand, so he kicks it. It doesn't budge. In a superhuman effort, driven by desperation, he puts his shoulder against the door and pushes with all his might. It opens just enough to let him slip in. As soon as he's inside he sees why it was so hard to open, Julie is slumped over, sitting with her back against it. She is conscious and looking at him, resigned. Jomo is lying beside her, face down on the floor.

'I can't wake him. I tried to get him out!' she shouts in a croaky, breaking voice, 'but he's too heavy!'

The room is hot but at this point, there isn't any visible fire. Jai grabs one of Jomo's legs. Julie struggles to get to her feet allowing Jai to open the door enough to ease Jomo through. Thick smoke pours in from the opening. By the time they both have hold of Jomo's legs the room is already over half full of thick acrid smoke.

'Bend over. Keep below the smoke or you won't be able to breathe. Let's go! Let's go!' He knows the drill because he's been in a fire before and it's all coming back to him. Julie does as she is told, staggering but keeping her head down near her knees. The two of them somehow manage to haul the unconscious Jomo into the hallway and towards the back doorway. There's a popping sound from inside Jomo's room, presumably as more substance containers explode in the heat. The flames are now billowing from the lounge. In the seconds used to help Jomo, the hallway has turned into a blazing inferno. The flames seem to be chasing them from the house. They manage to get Jomo to the middle of the yard, well away from the house, into what is now a cluster of bodies, a casualty scenario from a disaster movie, except it's real.

Julie and Jai are coughing hard, doubled over and struggling to breathe, wheezing and gasping.

The yard is illuminated now by the red flashing lights of the fire trucks. Everything seems to be happening in slow motion. He lifts his head, finally able to grab his breath. Looking around he can see most of the kids he recalls were inside, are now on the lawn, sitting or lying down. Some are still screaming hysterically, others are quietly crying. Scattered about, a few are sitting silently, rocking back and forward on their haunches. He can make out four bodies lying on the ground not moving. Hatch Hitch isn't one of them, Jai can't see him anywhere.

Julie is sitting on the ground with Jomo's head in her lap. Tears are streaming down her face. Jomo is stretched out, motionless.

There are two fire trucks and firemen running everywhere, unrolling hoses, shouting directions, attending to stunned and injured young people, and handing out blankets as they go. The noise is incredible, contributing to a sense of absolute chaos.

Jai hadn't noticed but the police have arrived too. Although he can't see the cars, he is aware of the flashing blue now adding to the rest of the lights and noise. He just sits there. He knows he should move but he can't. He's exhausted. Now he's stopped moving, he feels the pain in his hands. He looks down and sees that they are black, red and raw.

Chapter 15
Waiting for Jai

I am sitting in the office playing Muddy Waters' version of '*I can't be satisfied*'. Ted seems to be quite engaged, almost enthusiastic; I don't think he's ever seen slide guitar before. From my second shift on the job, I've played the guitar every night, usually for an hour or so when the boys are reasonably quiet. Sometimes I have found it helps to settle them as well. I punctuate it with sojourns out into the dorms to do the required checks. I've never asked my colleagues if this was a problem and they've never said. Given they're not backward in coming forward, I took this as tacit approval. I even suspect they like it. Ted volunteered one day that his favourite record is'*20 Greatest Country Hits from the 1970s*'. The only song he could name was '*The Gambler*' by Kenny Rogers. Not much scope for an in-depth musical discussion there! From time to time I toss him a version of the aforementioned tune and he invariably beams from ear to ear. Mr Rogers is a classical music buff, the only 'real' music he says. It's not my bag so limited chat options there too. I've seen him tap his foot to the odd tune so some of what I play catches his rhythm section. Occasionally I've even sung a song or two. I sense this makes them feel a bit uncomfortable but it's pretty natural for me, so I do it anyway.

The phone rings and I stop.

'Incoming.' Says Ted putting down the phone.

'That's the 'on-call' social worker. There's been a fire at a house in Woolston. It was full of street kids and squatters. Some kids have been injured. At this stage, possibly two are dead, and at least one is critical. The police picked up Jai Rehua at the property. He has a few burns but according to them, he's been medically examined and is ok to be brought back here. No new charges at this point so no court tomorrow. The on-call reckons it will be about half an hour... SNU?'

'Yeah. I'll do the honours if you like' I offer. 'I get along with him reasonably well. He's not a bad kid. I wonder what the story is? Anyone else we know involved?' There are a couple of other runners at the moment and some of the absconders may be together.

'No, they would have said.' Ted responds. 'Yeah, Jai's OK. The guy he took off with, Bryce, not so much. He's a piece of work. Wouldn't want to meet him in a dark alley. One of the few you don't want to turn your back on…' He leaves it hanging.

'Surely he isn't all bad, I mean he's just a kid. He didn't create himself,' I offer.

'Doesn't give him a right to go about visiting his problems on other people' replies Ted, bluntly. 'Some of our colleagues think that most, if not all of these boys, are victims one way or another. I don't really buy that. Plenty of kids who come through here have siblings who grew up in the same conditions but don't come near Stanmore or Kingslea. Some keep it in and others spread it about. He spreads it about… Big-time.'

I've read Bryce's file. His fathers a dedicated crim, in and out of Paparoa Prison all his life, violence, drugs, burglaries, the lot. There's mention of a brother too, Archie, who's been through Stanmore, last heard of doing five years for aggravated robbery. Ted continues 'You know there's another brother, younger one, he's in the system too, Hokio Beach, and Mr Rogers, who has contacts at Kingslea, tells me there's a sister in care as well. I don't know about the mother but the whole rest of the family is in the system Those kids were trained to be crims before they could walk. Yeah…ok…victims maybe, depending on how you look at it, but victim creators too. And Bryce could make better choices now, he's old enough to think for himself. I knew what I was doing when I was his age. And the community's got a right to be safe. I'm with the Judge, give him a shot and if he doesn't take it, then too bad, community first.' It's plain and simple, there's no mistaking how Ted sees it.

'Jai's offending is a bit different though, minor stuff…no violence. He's more of a likeable rogue.' I interject.

'You mean likeable because you like him! Are you sure that's not because he plays the guitar?'

It's a fair question, although it rankles, but not correct. 'I talk about music and guitar with any boy who wants…and I don't like them all.' I say a little defensively, adding 'In this game, you use what you've got to get through, make a connection. For me it's music and sport…although if they want to talk to me about anything at all, I do…like they matter, deserve to be heard, you know… respect the person, even when it's hard.'

However, I admit 'But some boys you're drawn to more than others. He's one for me. Same as in all walks of life, some people you warm to, others you don't.'

'Yeh well that's true, and the stuff about being respectful, didn't I tell you that? Respect the person, not the behaviour. But I'll tell you what, Jai's still visiting his crap on other people no matter how you want to dress it up.'

I shut up, not feeling this conversation is going anywhere productive.

Eventually, Ted speaks, drawing us back to the task at hand. 'Sounds like we should keep a close eye on him, especially if he's injured and potentially lost one of his mates in the fire. Yeah, SNU is the best option…for the night anyway.'

We sit in silence for a while, waiting for notification of the imminent arrival. Ted says out of the blue 'It always interests me how two boys like Bryce and Jai who are so different join up and take a hike. They didn't seem to be mates. Maybe Jai's a follower or he was bullied into it. Who would know, so much happens between these boys that we don't see.'

After a further five minutes of silence, Ted, who appears to still be mulling things over in his head, says 'It's wrong that the waifs and street kids are mixed with the dangerous and violent boys, the more dedicated criminal ones. I'm sure it makes things worse for them…and everyone.' He adds. 'Perhaps Jai and Bryce are not the best examples because Jai is already a prolific offender, even though he's more of a street kid.' He starts to talk about Hatch Hitch. I'm familiar with his case.

His folks were killed in a car accident when he was a baby. He was in the car too and there's a suspicion he received brain damage as a result. He came into care as a one-year-old. Since then he's been in more than twenty care placements, three in the first year! Nothing proved to be stable at home or school. He became a runner. Initially, there was no known offending. He went to Hokio Beach for six months, when he came back he took off with a guy called Bradley Hughson, a hard kid who had been in lots of trouble. That's when he did his first burg. The pair were confronted by the elderly occupant whom they gave the bash. She put up a bit of a fight and unfortunately she was injured quite seriously. It was unclear how much Hatch was involved but he was there, so he was culpable. Social workers believe it had an ongoing impact on his behaviour, 'repressed guilt' is how it was described in a report. He's been in and out of residence ever since, and lots more offending although none of it has been for further violence.

Ted goes on 'There are at least half a dozen others in the same situation, and those are just the ones I know about. 'Contagion' that's the word, yeah contagion! Spreading the offending like a disease. They should sue the State for not meeting their duty of care, not keeping them safe from bad influences!'

'I don't know about that.' I reply. 'There's always going to be a place like Stanmore, the end of the road when things don't work out. Gotta do something with these kids, and there's not that many of them.'

'I'll tell you what, it probably means spending lots more money and I can't see anyone wanting to, not on these kids. It's out of sight, out of mind'. Ted is getting quite agitated, 'I'm not so bothered about the nasty, violent fellows, most of them have done their chips, but the waifs and strays, something needs to be different for them, and big-time, or we're just feeding the prisons!'

Ted's not in the best frame of mind tonight and the conversations have become increasingly intense. I decide I'll try to lighten the mood a little. I grab the guitar and start singing a couple of bars from '*The Times They are a Changing*' I pause mid-song and say, 'Maybe 'a change is coming' like Bob predicted because, despite the incredible insights we have as night staffers sitting here in our little office in Stanmore, we probably aren't the only ones who see this' I chuckle at my depreciating comment, hoping it's achieved its intent.

'Who's Bob?' Ted asks and he seems genuinely mystified and totally either misses or dismisses my intent.

'Bob Dylan. Used to be a folk singer, mate, from the sixties.' I'm surprised he doesn't know the tune but then, it never made the greatest country hits of the 1970s. 'It's a famous song directed at politicians, writers, everyone really, urging them to lift their game to meet the challenges of progress and change or they'd be left behind, especially by the younger generation. The song is enduring in that it always applies no matter what times we are in, so the sentiment is right,' I leave it there, not bothering to sing anymore, all of a sudden feeling a little flat.

A short period of ensuing silence is interrupted by shuffling sounds and a shadow zipping past the office door.

'Andrew Sores, what's he up to?' Ted asks, slightly grumpy and raising his eyebrows. 'Let's go.' We exit the office and while I lock the door Ted heads off at pace. Although it's taken less than half a minute I can hear an altercation coming from Kauri. I up my pace. It is just one voice, Andrew, abusing another boy, Tony Wehi. The word, repeated frequently, rising above the rest is 'fag.'

Tony, who prefers to be called Antonia, is a new admission, transferred in from Wellington today as there was no room at the local boys' home. Although he's sixteen years old, he has been given his own room because he dresses and behaves like a female.

Transvestites aren't a big deal to me. I schooled in South Wellington up in Tory St where Carmen, the most well-known, and her entourage had their club. The girls were highly visible around town. At first, it had been a bit of a novelty and a source of humour and banter to young schoolboys, but after five years it was all just part of the colourful and vibrant environment.

At the changeover, the outgoing team indicated there'd been problems from the moment Antonia arrived, with some of the boys giving her a hard time. A few of the staff had also been concerned because they believed she should have been placed in a Girl's Home. The Court, however, despite the representations of her counsel to the contrary, picked the Boys Home. The placement presents a challenge in the residence, not only because of the impact on group dynamics but also from a practical management perspective. On first hearing about it I wondered why Antonia is not in the SNU as there are potential issues for her safety, but the 'powers that be' determined it isn't required. I guess it's the right decision, she should be able to be kept safe in the house, it just seems easier to do so in SNU.

Antonia is at Stanmore for the first time. She's one of a family of four boys and the only one with an interest in cross-dressing. It seems from early on her parents were accepting, accommodating and supportive of her choice. However, things went awry when she was sent to Wellington College. On the face of it, this seemed to be a strange decision for obvious reasons, however, her dad was an old boy and he wanted the 'Wellington Coll' education for his son. He tried to get her to split her life in two, at school and outside school. It didn't work out. Antonia accepted having to wear the uniform while she was at school, however, she did not attempt to hide who she was, resulting in unrelenting bullying and grief from her classmates. After a while, she chose to attend the school's extracurricular activities dressed more consistently with her natural inclinations. There were incidents, these escalated, and Antonia voted with her feet. After eighteen months of persisting, Antonia's parents moved her to Wellington High, a school they believed had a more adaptive and effective approach to managing kids who found mainstream schooling a challenge. But by then Antonia was well behind in her studies and continued to avoid college. She had established a group of people on the streets who were more accommodating and accepting of her. Her parents assumed she managed to live from petty crime and possibly prostitution.

The charges that led to her admission, her first ever, are one of shoplifting and one of assault. She was caught in one of the more upmarket women's clothing stores in Cuba Street stealing an expensive blouse. The shop attendant had noticed Antonia in the shop on previous occasions. She was suspicious and was subtly keeping a close eye on her. When Antonia was about to leave, the attendant, suspicious, tried to stop her by grabbing her arm. It was obvious from Antonia's response that somewhere along the way she had learned how to look after herself. She took a swing at the shop attendant, smacking her in the face for her troubles. The cops, who are a regular presence in the street, were alerted by an angry attendant standing outside of her shop screaming at the top of her voice 'Stop that bitch. She's a thief!' Antonia was apprehended a couple of hundred metres from the shop and the rather elegant blue satin top was retrieved. It looks like the police didn't know what to do with her and chose custody. For some unknown reason, at least to the night staffers, her case was transferred to Christchurch. She is expected in Court Friday, two days away.

I briefly saw Antonia when I did my initial rounds. She's tall and skinny with long, straight, jet black hair hanging half way down her back. Her face is not unattractive although she currently has a fair dose of acne, and a hint of whisker stubble. Apart from that, she was in the standard-issue blue and white striped pyjamas like all the boys.

It isn't clear why Andrew has decided to take it upon himself to put the heat on Antonia. He may have been egged on by the other boys in Rata, or he might be wanting to score brownie points with the boys by showing his, and their collective, displeasure. I've heard some of the staff speculate that he has sexual issues of his own. We couldn't tell and at this point, we didn't care, we just wanted him either back in his bed, or he was going someplace where he wouldn't continue to be a problem.

Andrew is well known to us. He and his brother Rowan are frequent fliers at Stanmore, habitual burglars. Rowan is one of the informal leaders, a kingpin. It's not that he's a tough guy. He has notoriety because he likes to challenge the staff, frequently, taking any opportunity he can during the daily community meetings.

He's good at it too. Most often he takes 'the mickey' but just up to the edge where it might be considered as inciting the group. It's all done with humour, making fun by mimicking staff voices, or other times by challenging a particular rule for its fairness or the way it's being applied. He's been in here so often he knows the rules and regulations backwards. His challenges put staff on the back foot, especially if they're not on their game. He also continually brags about how he gets more from his crime than the punishment hurts him. 'Yer man, crime pays! Play hard, die young,' that's his often espoused philosophy. He's also one of those boys who's acutely aware he needs to stop offending when he turns seventeen because the cost/benefit ratio won't be on the plus side. I guess time will tell whether he can turn off the crime switch magically on his seventeenth birthday. Not long to wait as he will do so in less than a month.

Andrew, while spawned from the same origins, is a very different person. He's not that bright, and definitely not a leader. He is physically bigger than his brother and this makes him useful as Rowan counts on Andrew to be there and do what he's told, no matter what it is. He tries to be a kingpin by tossing his weight around but he doesn't engender any respect from the other boys. Andrew doesn't have the right combination of assets. He has the threat, menace, and fear factor, but lacks the engagement, control, subtlety and social nous.

'Back to your bed Andrew.' Ted takes the lead. He's managed to put his not-inconsiderable bulk between Andrew and Antonia who is sitting on her bed. Surprisingly she's not looking too troubled by Andrew's behaviour. Guess she's heard it all before.

'This fag should be at Kingslea with the other girlies!' Andrew sneers and then spits at her.

'Get out now!' Ted has lost patience already. 'Back to your bed or you're going to SNU.'

Andrew hesitates and it looks as if he's going to comply. Ted turns to address Antonia. As soon as his back is turned, Andrew, obviously feigning compliance steps around him. As he passes he swings his elbow at Ted's head, who picks up the movement and ducks. Not quite quick enough, catching a significant blow on the side of his head. He staggers sideways and bangs into the wall. I step into the room. Andrew turns and comes at me, taking a swing as he does. I jerk my head back, banging it on the door frame as I do. This isn't going well. Andrew is lifting his arm, looking to have another whack at me. I duck down and push out with my arms as I straighten up, shoving him square in the midriff and taking him off his feet. As he tumbles backwards, Ted, who has recovered his balance, literally falls on him like a big-time wrestler, pinning him to the ground. They are both big people, but Ted is big both ways, up and out. Andrew has the wind knocked out of him and he's momentarily stunned. The room is small and Ted and Andrew occupy most of the available floor space, making it hard for me to do anything. Antonia is sitting, feet up on the bed and arms around her legs, watching and saying nothing. This is a dangerous time. Andrew is struggling now and Ted is talking quietly in his ear.

'You going to behave if I let you up?' He enquires.

'You fucking fat slug, get off me, it's assault!' Andrew yells back, his face contorted and red.

I'm back standing in the doorway. There's no way out of the room except over me or through me.

Ted continues attempting to use a calm non-threatening tone although he's puffing a bit from the exertions, 'I'm going to let you up and then we are quietly going to walk down to SNU. OK?' He eases himself off Andrew who remains on the floor. Once Ted is up and standing, Andrew slowly gets to his feet.

'Bye-bye! Andy Pandy!' it's the first thing Antonia has said during the whole proceedings. It has the desired effect of winding him up. He lunges towards her. 'You little que…' He doesn't finish his sentence. She lifts her foot and kicks him squarely in the solar plexus. Before he's fully doubled over from the blow Ted has him, arm around his shoulders and the other twisting his arm behind his back, simultaneously turning him towards the doorway. I clear out of the way as Andrew is frog marched towards the fire escape door and the stairway down to SNU.

Andrew, who is winded, has stopped struggling now but he continues to gasp out about how he is being assaulted. Fortunately, the time taken to get to the fire escape and get him out is short, and despite his raspy efforts to stir up the other boys, there is no significant reaction just the minor hum of restlessness.

That's how it happens, violence out of nothing. Andrew acts and we have to react. I recall a question at my interview about what I'd do if I was confronted by a violent young person. I remember saying I'd do whatever was necessary to keep people safe in the circumstances while also resolving the issue. No one indicated at the time whether that was the right answer. It was met with blank stares that gave nothing away. But I guess it was, here we are doing exactly that.

Interestingly my heart is pounding even though I am not afraid and have not been involved in the physical altercation, it's just anticipation and adrenaline.

We get to the bottom of the stairs, me opening doors and making the path easy, and Ted marching our lad who has quietened down now he is deprived of an audience. As we step out onto the driveway, a Police car is pulling up. Jai is back.

Chapter 16
Jai Gets a Fright

He has minor burns in a few places on his body but his hands are a mess. A medic at the scene checked him out, put on a thick white cream on everything and bandaged what he could. It helped soothe the pain a little at the time. The medic told the police he should be checked over more closely so he needed to see a doctor or come to the hospital tomorrow.

No one talks much as they drive to the Res, and it seems to Jai, that everyone, including the cops, have been blown away by the events of the night.

It hadn't looked good for Jomo, lying there as still as a stone. Julie was pretty upset but Jai hadn't been able to do anything to help. He hadn't had the time. Anyway, he didn't know what to say or do. He was just too sore, too exhausted, and stunned. That's why he hadn't run when he could have. It would have been easy to get away during the pandemonium. Hatch did. All the focus was on the kids with serious problems…naturally.

The only question he asked the coppers on the way was whether they knew anything about how the other kids were. It wasn't a specific question about Jomo although he was the person Jai was most interested in. But they didn't seem to know anything more than he did.

Now he's going back to Stanmore. Ah well, it didn't bother him too much. He knew this day would come sooner or later. Being on the run had been pretty cool but it was always borrowed time, he knew it in his heart. He wonders to himself who'll be there when he arrives. He assumes he'll be stuck in SNU. Hopefully, it won't be for long.

As they pull up to the front of the Boys' Home, he sees Ted and Wyatt bringing Andrew whatever-his-name-is down the fire escape stairs, obviously getting admitted to SNU. So, he is going to be in the lockup with Andrew tomorrow. He's such an egg, Jai silently sighs. He doesn't like him and knows that he will need to watch him all the time because he's always trying to prove how tough he is. But right at this moment, he doesn't care too much. All he wants is to sleep. He hopes they get on with the blah de blah admission stuff and bloody Andrew doesn't slow things down.

In the end, the process takes longer than he hoped. The night guys split up and Ted 'the bear' deals with Andrew first. Jai sits with Wyatt in the dining room. Wyatt says a few things to him but Jai isn't really listening and only responds with grunts trying to put off further conversation. However, he does ask Wyatt if he knows whether anyone died in the fire. He doesn't seem to know any more than anyone else. Wyatt gets the message after a while and stops talking. He leaves Jai in the dining room for a moment and goes and gets a guitar. When he comes back he picks a slow blues tune. It's not one Jai knows but the sound is soothing. For the first time, he hears Wyatt, singing albeit very softly. *'Rivers run to the ocean/ oceans to the seas, I'm going to let that water/ wash all over me.'* He doesn't know what it means but somehow it feels right.

After processing, Wyatt takes him to his cell and locks him in. Jai lies on the bed, he's physically numb now except for his hands which throb.

He's been lying there for half an hour, eyes closed but wide awake. Everything that's happened in the last few hours keeps rolling round and round in his head. He'd tried singing to himself, the same song over and over, because sometimes when he couldn't sleep that helped. He kept trying *'Let it Be'* by the Beatles but it wasn't working.

All of a sudden, plain as day, he hears Jomo's voice. He pleading 'Help me, man.' It's so clear and present, it's like he's there with Jai. He pulls the covers over his head and tries singing louder.

'Help me, man!' More urgent this time, interrupting and overriding everything else. No use even trying to sleep now, he gives in, sticks his head out and opens his eyes.

'Help me, man.' Jomo repeats. Jai sits bolt upright. There he is. Jomo sitting on the end of his bed.

'What are you doing here? How did you get in here?' Jai asks him, heart pounding like a bass drum.

'Help me, man! Help me, man!'

'What do you want? What can I do?' Jai says desperately. Jomo does not react to his question. He is not looking at Jai, but more through him. He's just sitting there, his face blue and black, flecks of foam gathered on the sides of his mouth.

'Help me man' repeated like a broken record, soft and resigned, and then louder and pleading.

Jai knows this isn't right. Jomo's there in the room but he's not really there. It's a ghost, a spook, an apparition. A chill runs up Jai's back. And then he's afraid. What's happening? The room seems to be closing in on him, it's getting hard to breathe. He drags air into his lungs in large gulps. His throat still feels raw. His heart is just about to jump out of his chest. In a blind panic, he jumps off the bed, rushes to the cell door and thumps on it, urgently, repeatedly.

'Get me the fuck out of here. There's a fucking spook in here!' he shouts, kicking the door to get attention.

A loud whispering voice comes back to him, 'Settle down, settle down! You'll wake half of Christchurch. I'm opening up. Stand back!'

Jai turns away from the door. Jomo isn't there in the room with him anymore. He didn't see him go. He just isn't there. Wyatt opens the door and Jai bolts past him into the hall. He's puffing like he's run a hundred-metre sprint. He bends over at the waist trying to get his breath back. He feels like he's going to puke.

'He was there...Jomo... in my cell... I saw him. He asked me to help him. It was a ghost. He must be dead.' Jai splutters.

'Woah... Woah...slow down... Breathe... There's no one there. You're seeing things. Come on! Come into the office.' Wyatt steps away from the open cell door and ushers Jai past him and into the office. 'Sit down, take a few really deep breaths, slowly... slowly. Helps you settle and will get that heart rate down.'

Jai slumps onto the chair by the desk. 'I saw him, he was so real man, but I know he wasn't there...It's like his ghost has come to haunt me...I got him out, that was all I could do...dragged him out. He wasn't moving though, just lying there ...with Julie.' He is talking in short sharp bites.

'Deep and slowly...slowly...and then we can talk.' Wyatt says calmly.

'I'm not going back in that room. You can't 'f'ing well make me!'

'Let's get this sorted before we talk about anything else. That's better.'

Jai is sucking air deeply and he feels he's calming down although his mind is still racing. What the hell is going on? Four hours ago he was toking on a joint...having a laugh. Now he's in this hellhole again...trapped. Jomo must be dead though. It has to be the explanation. Only ghosts can walk through walls.

Who else is dead? Benny was burned pretty badly. He didn't look good. What if Benny comes next? He becomes aware Wyatt is talking to him.

'Who's Jomo?' Wyatt asks.

'It was his house…the fire…I pulled him out of his room. He was lying on the ground when the cops took me. He looked real, real, bad.'

'Well look, I wouldn't jump to conclusions. We'll probably know a bit more tomorrow'. And then, in what seems to be an afterthought, Wyatt asks, 'Did they give you anything for those burns? Medication, I mean?'

'Yeah the medics gave me something when they bandaged up my hands, I don't know what it was. Something that helped because I don't feel too sore. And they put some cream on as well' He remembers now, they gave him painkillers. The medics talked to the cops about taking him to the hospital. There was a bit of a heated discussion but in the end, they fixed him up and gave him something for the pain on the agreement he was seen again by a doctor in the morning. But he knows what a hallucination is, he's taken enough drugs to know. This wasn't the same, it was so tangible.

'I know what I saw. It was like he was right there. I know he wasn't there, like in person, he couldn't be, but he looked real and he sounded real' Jai is adamant.

'I'm not saying you're seeing things.' Wyatt replies almost too quickly but it seems to Jai that's exactly what he was implying.

'Plenty of strange things happen in this world that can't be explained. I'm not judging, just asking. I had an Irish aunt who insisted she saw dead people. Those who knew her well believed her. But I'm just checking about the drugs. Sometimes it can lead to hallucinations depending on the type and the mix. And on top of that, you've been through a very traumatic event. A lot of emotions that might contribute too,' Wyatt explains.

'I'm not going back to that 'f'ing room!' Jai is emphatic. 'If you put me back in there, well I don't know what will happen man, but it won't be good.'

'I'm hearing you. For now, you can stay out here with me and then we'll see what happens. I don't think I'll be putting you upstairs no matter what. The bottom line is you've been on the run and you've been in a very stressful situation so I think you need to be in here where we can keep a close eye on you and make sure everything's all right.'

Jai isn't sure how Wyatt thinks everything is going to be all right. They aren't, and they aren't going to be for quite a while. However, there didn't seem to be any point in arguing, he doesn't get the sense Wyatt is going to change his view anytime soon. At least he's listening.

'What I'll do is call Ted and if I'm not needed upstairs then we can sit here and chew the fat for a while and see how things go. You might change your mind. If not, I might pull your mattress out and you can sleep in the gym, but I have to be down here all night if that happens. We can't have you roaming about the SNU and I am not locking you into the gym. Anyway, locking you in somewhere else might not be a solution to the problem if you're having visitations.' Wyatt is saying this and to Jai, he appears sincere and not like he is making fun of him. He picks up the phone and bangs in a few numbers.

'It's me… yer …everything's ok down here. How about up there?' A pause and Wyatt is listening and nodding his head. 'Jai is here in the office with me… yer I know he shouldn't be…But he can't sleep, says he's seen one of the other young people from the fire in his cell…yer could be, but I asked him and he's adamant it's not a result of any meds. For now, he needs to be up… I've got it under control…yer,' …a long pause while he listens intently, 'Ok I'll tell him that, it might help. Call if you need to.' Wyatt puts down the phone.

'Ok, everything's quiet upstairs so we can sit here for a while. Ted was telling me there's been another occasion when a boy in here saw a spirit or a ghost or whatever it was in his cell. A Kaumatua came in and blessed the cell. It seemed to do the trick. Apparently, Wiremu Tomas is a kaumatua and he's on tomorrow so we can ask him to do the same. But it won't be tonight. It will probably be done even if the day team decides they're going to put you back in the house tomorrow, just in case there's something residual, you know a spirit, presence, whatever, hanging about. I'm not sure what the full story is but, it's the culturally appropriate thing to do so we'll go with that approach. You learn something every day around here.' Wyatt seemed to make this last remark to himself.

They sit in silence.

Jai hadn't heard anything much about things Māori. There were the aunties, his mother's sisters, who sometimes talked about that sort of stuff on the few times they came round home. He hadn't taken much notice and Mona never raised the subject. He certainly hadn't heard about kaumatuas and what they might be able to do to get rid of spirits. Plenty happened, though, to remind him of his Māori heritage, *Whakapapa*. These were mainly crappy things like being called a 'nigger' or a 'Hori', or remarks about the colour of his skin. All the negative things you can think of lumped together, applied to you, dumb, dirty, criminal. People assume they know things about you just because of the colour of your skin. They put you in an f…ing box, their box. Sometimes he'd even wished he wasn't Māori.

But this Kaumatua thing seemed like the right thing to do, he doesn't know why, it's a feeling. He still wasn't going back in that cell, no way. It needed to be blessed first to get rid of that spirit. He'd sit here and talk to Wyatt all night if he needs to. He didn't feel very chatty, just totally drained but strangely, also wide awake. Wyatt seemed to catch his vibe.

'Hey Jai, I've got a couple of things I need to do so you can just sit here if you don't feel like talking. But if you do, I'm happy to listen.' Wyatt picked up one of the books and opened it at one of the pages but Jai could see he wasn't writing anything.

After twenty minutes or so, Wyatt asked him 'How come you took off? I can't understand why some of you boys do that when all it seems to do is to make things go on for longer. You know, now you're back here and it'll probably be for another few months until everything's sorted out for you. It seems to me if what you want is to be out of here then you should be doing things that'll help get you out, not things that'll keep you here.'

Jai thought about it, not because he didn't know the answer, he just wasn't sure he wanted to discuss it with Wyatt. He let the silence ride for a minute then he replied.

'It just happened. You know I had the *Walking Blues* man…woke up one morning with itchy feet. I felt it and I just went. I didn't think much about what it might mean. Anyway, I don't know what's happening with my case. Nothing! I was supposed to hear something weeks ago.'

'Yeah well I understand the '*Walking Blues*' but it's pretty hard to work with someone when they can't be found though, wouldn't you say.' Wyatt was putting it on him but Jai didn't care. He'd only heard from his field social worker, Doug Goodly, once since he'd come to Stanmore and that was when he first went to court. Since then he'd felt Goodly had forgotten he even existed or else he didn't give a crap about him.

'Well, I suspect you're going to hear something tomorrow after all this business. Happy to make a note in the diary about contacting your social worker, that'll help make it happen!' Wyatt says. Jai thinks he might be trying to be funny but he's not sure…

'Whatever!' He leans back in his chair, closes his eyes and lets his mind wander. It takes him straight back to the spirit world. He shudders and starts rolling over the lyrics from *'Let it Be'* like a mantra, crowding his head so there's no room for anything else.

Part 3
Business as Usual

Chapter 17
Wyatt Does Days

After a few months as a night staffer, my supervisor, John Land, asks me to cover for a couple of weeks while one of the day team takes annual leave. He tells me he's hearing good things about me from the boys and staff and points out this is an opportunity to 'try it out in the real social work world.' I'm keen and jump at the chance. I'm findings the nightwork fascinating but it's also a challenge because of the sleep deprivation, and the juxtaposition of living at night while having a young family who lives on a normal human time clock. And frankly, with little activity occurring after midnight, even reading, playing guitar and drawing aren't sufficient to alleviate periods of sheer boredom.

My first-day shift is the early one starting at 6.30 am on Friday. It's the first day of the weekend shift cycle. I know the basic drill starting with the briefing from the night staff. Mr Rogers, newly prepared super dog food mix in a paper bag under his arm, can't help but direct a few barbs at me about switching to the 'dark' side which is ironic given the reality. I also get a bit of ribbing from the day team about doing some real work rather than sleeping for a living.

I'm excited, and also a little apprehensive. It's a feeling similar to starting a new job. I enjoy my engagements with the boys at night but they're generally brief and now I'll be doing eight and a half hours of it. And, additionally, I'll be working with new teammates.

While all the ribbing and banter are a bit of fun, the underlying messages are not so positive. The perception of sleeping on the job needles me and it highlights the attitude of many of the day staff to the work of the night team, not helped by Mr Roger's known antics. But for now, those feelings have to be put aside.

The first order of business is to 'manage' Chevy Woken. The handover highlighted his incessant antics from the last twenty-four hours. The night staff felt he should have been placed in SNU well before bedtime based on his behaviour during the afternoon shift, but it didn't happen. So they had to put up with Chevy disrupting the dorms, refusing to stay in bed, wandering around being loud, and generally having a good time albeit at everyone else's expense. It went on for two hours. He probably could have been placed in SNU then but I can understand why the night staff hadn't done so. At least the oncoming team are going to deal with it now.

'Managing' Chevy in this instance means confronting him and then dealing with the fallout. It might mean he pulls his head in but if history is anything to go by, he won't. Almost inevitably he ends up in SNU after some level of physical intervention.

The phrase 'physical intervention' covers any time a staff member has to use force to keep a young person safe, either themselves or others, or to prevent property damage. There are obvious examples where boys are assaulting each other or trying to smash up the place but I'm finding there is a bit of 'greyness' around it too, especially when the young person is non-compliant but not putting anyone in danger. There are times when staff stepping in to 'guide' a young person leads to resistance, and then force has to be applied. As Sarge said to me this morning, 'It's about taking control of the situation and someone has to, otherwise, we could stand about all day looking at each other and we'd get nothing done!'

Planning to prevent incidents can be helpful but it relies on having the time to do so. Even if there is time, they are dynamic and their trajectory, unpredictable. At night, out of necessity, we're reasonably good at preventing problems from escalating, but sometimes they're unavoidable. I have already experienced the 'physical' side of the work on a few occasions.

My most notable experience of something getting out of hand occurred when Ted and I were in the process of receiving a young fellow named Erol. We decided to put him in SNU because his arrest was for assaulting police and they reported he was still pretty feisty. On this night the police were called away immediately so unable to help. We were walking him up the concrete ramp towards the SNU, each holding an arm. As Ted reached for his keys, Erol leaned over and head butted him. At the same time he ripped his arm free, spun around behind me and elbowed me in the side of the head, a move worthy of a Bruce Lee movie. This caused me to let go of his other arm. Now free, Erol was off, vaulting the guard rail and running towards Richmond Park. We both recovered quickly and took off after him. I was rubbing my head as I ran, trying to clear

126

bit of the fuzziness and get the blood circulating. Erol, who was about ten paces in front of us, made the fatal mistake of looking back. He tripped over the curb. We got to him as he got back to his feet. He put up a solid fight, swinging his fists, and elbows, and kicking out. He was bellowing at the top of his voice as well. At 12.30 a.m. it was surprising that someone didn't call the police! We finally managed to subdue him and return him to the SNU. He reminded me with a big grin when I saw him the next night how he gave me the bash. I said to him 'Mate, I've been hit harder by my sister!' He just laughed and said 'She must be one tough bitch then!' Sharp reply. I didn't let on but his elbow hurt leaving a bruise on my head, giving me a headache for the rest of the shift, and a sore arm where I must have tweaked something in the process. Ted wasn't that flash afterwards either!

So Chevy is the subject of our first plan of the day. He's well known to everyone, staff and boys alike. He's almost a fixture at Stanmore. His history is a familiar litany of tragic episodes.

Chevy lived with his mum and brothers until he was seven. His father is nowhere to be found, so absent he isn't even identified in the case notes. His mother struggled to cope with his behaviour and its impact on his brothers. His continual failure to attend school eventually led to a referral to Social Welfare and he was placed in foster care. He ran and when he was found, he ran again. The more he ran, the more he got involved in petty crime. As he got older and spent more time in care placements, the other boys learned he was not too bright and could easily be manipulated. He would do pretty much anything he was asked to, no matter how stupid, dangerous, or risky it was. It was entertaining to wind him up and then watch what unfolded. On the streets, he was both the perpetrator and victim of violence. According to his file on at least one occasion before he was ten years old he was raped by a vagrant while on the run. He became sexualised. He's now considered a risk to younger boys and when he runs it's often with boys who are low intellectual functioning or otherwise known to be very vulnerable. The accusations have never been proven however most are terrified of him when they are returned to Stanmore. Chevy, now fifteen years old, stands over six feet tall and is fit and strong. He has the mental age of an eight-year-old, a violent and frustrated child in a man's body.

Sarge, Gwynne and I are the staff upstairs. Gwynne has a great idea, Sarge and I should do it. Gwynne, who started at Stanmore shortly before me, did his social work training in Wales within their hospital system. It's well known he doesn't like doing physical stuff. Join the club! He believes it is only acceptable for the protection of life and limb. Today he's also reasoning that he has a good relationship with Chevy and doesn't want to put it at risk. I note he doesn't think it's strong enough to get Chevy to behave and save us the trouble of intervening. On the contrary, he seems quite happy for him to be moved.

Sarge suggests we get him up before the others to minimise any entertainment potential. Chevy is in Rata the most public of the three dorms so whatever happens, it needs to be quick. He takes it upon himself to lead in getting the proceedings underway. I'm back up and support. After attempting to whisper Chevy awake, he gives him a shake by the shoulder.

'Wake up Chevy, I need you to keep quiet and come with me.'

Chevy stirs and sticks out with his arm to brush the hand off his shoulder. 'Get out of it' he mumbles sleepily.

'Up Chevy. Now!' Sarge is now boom whispering and shakes him again, harder. Chevy strikes out again half-heartedly, making contact with thin air. Sarge, for whom patience is almost always in short supply, pulls back his blankets. Chevy protests and refuses to move so Sarge shakes him again. This time Chevy opens his eyes and slowly hoists himself upright on the bed. Other boys in the dorm are beginning to stir. This isn't what we want but Sarge has a loud voice and even his whisper is like a foghorn. It was always going to be problematic.

'Get up now Chevy and come with me. I want to talk to you about your behaviour last night at bedtime.'

Chevy is now fully awake and leaps to his feet. 'Fuck off ya dick, I didn't do anything! Fucking Sarge' He swings his fist, Sarge, for some reason unfathomable to me, didn't seem to be expecting this and manages to move his head back but not quick enough, catching a glancing blow on the ear. He loses his balance and stumbles backwards, ending up down on one knee. Chevy steps forward and looks like he's shaping up to put in the boot. I'm there in an instant. I grab his arm, pulling him forward and down, taking him off balance. I lean into him as he topples, taking him to the floor. I have his arm behind his back and he is face down with me leaning on him to stop him from moving. Sarge is up now, shaking his head like he has a bug in his ear. He quickly grabs Chevy's other arm just below the shoulder. We lever him to his feet holding onto his upper arms and wrists. He is bellowing like a bull about what he is going to do to us. Now he needs to be moved quickly to make sure the whole place doesn't blow up.

'Assault on a staff member, you're going to SNU.' Sarge has taken one for the team.

Chevy behaved as expected, the result is as anticipated. He's moved to the SNU where he will reside for the next day at least. Sarge and I return to the dorms. Abigail and Gwynne are getting the boys up and everything is happening in as orderly a fashion as it does most mornings, still, though, with an element of minor chaos.

Before we join the others Sarge pulls me aside and says in a voice trying to portray pragmatism, but sounding patronising, 'Removing Chevy was the right move. Things are already calmer in the house as you can see, and it's increased the likelihood we'll have a settled shift. I suspect from the pattern of his behaviour yesterday and last night, that he would have kept pushing until this happened anyway. All we did was create an environment to hasten the process. Most of the kids would rather Chevy isn't in the unit, he's a threat to them and while stirring him up may entertain some of them, he's so unpredictable anything can happen. Most of the time the older boys especially, just want to get on with the daily programme and Chevy's antics can put paid to it, maybe even mean activities are suspended while we devote all our time and energy to managing him. The bottom line ... they're not unhappy to see him go. Win, win, situation. And there's a side benefit for us because it reminds the boys who's in charge, or at least, supposed to be! And it's also probably good for you. Some of these boys won't know much about you because you work nights. They see you handling the situation, good for your reputation and standing. So actually win, win, win, win! Welcome to the day shift!'

Welcome to the day shift indeed!

Chapter 18
Wyatt Has an Adventure

My first morning is only an hour old and it's started with a bang. Breakfast time is more like what I expected... mayhem! It's like the worst mealtime at home with my young kids, loud, semi-organised bedlam, except by a factor of eight. Staff are distributed around the tables so they can maintain a degree of control although there are not enough to cover them all. They are barking out lots of directions with very few being followed. I see food being flicked from one table to the next and then return fire. At least they are all staying in their seats, except when allowed to go to the servery to grab their meal.

Several of the boys I've spoken to frequently at night ask me to join their table. I'm buzzed to get the invite as there's plenty of groaning going on about particular staff members as they take their seats. Maybe there's an ulterior motive, they prefer me to someone they deem less desirable. Three of the boys I know a little better than most. Jai Rehua, my first real admission, Bentley Breezer and Jason Fisher, all of whom are longer-term placements, so time has provided ample opportunities for me to get to know them a bit and vice versa. I wouldn't say I've connected with Bentley but at least he is a recognised quantity to me. Fish and Jai, they're also guitar players.

The other boy, Sherwin Faitia, is a new face and this is his fifth day in residence. I'd heard he is a talented guitarist, much respected by the other boys for his skills. I'll be interested to see him play sometime later today. He's fourteen years old, stands about five feet four, with a wispy thin physique. He is very dark-skinned and his curly black hair falls to his shoulders. I remember reading in his file that he comes from a 'Black Power' family, so here he's known to be connected. I note he is wearing a blue T-shirt with a ZZ Top emblem on it. I'm pretty sure the T is just a clever way to show his gang colours. A hard one for the staff to challenge!

As we chat over breakfast, I notice Sherwin is doing most of the talking. The other three are unusually quiet, chipping in only when there's a space in the conversation or when invited to comment. Sherwin likes his music all right. He is big on AC/DC and asks me if I play their stuff and if I can work out how to play and teach him 'Dirty Deeds Done Dirt Cheap.' I'm not a fan but I tell him I'm happy to work out the chords. Strange thing to request really as I'm confident he could play any of their three-chord efforts without my help. Maybe he's just testing whether I'm willing to do something for him. Who knows, I'll take the opportunity if it arises, as I'd do so for any boy who asks.

We talk about the programme for the day ahead. The younger boys under sixteen go to the school on site. The older boys participate in whatever activities the programme coordinators have dreamed up for the day. Today it's kayaking on the Waimakariri River. Sherwin informs me he'll be kayaking rather than going to school. I think this is unlikely however I'm a day shift 'newbie' and I don't know what discussions or agreements are in place between individual boys and the rest of the team or the programme coordinators. I let it ride.

When the meal finishes most of the boys are allocated tasks in the kitchen, the dining room, or cleaning the ablutions block upstairs. My role is to take the unoccupied boys and supervise them in the common room. I have a group of about fifteen, all playing pool or generally milling around in small groups chatting. After a couple of minutes, Sarge comes into the room.

'Sherwin, aren't you supposed to be in the kitchen doing your job?' he booms.

'Breese said he wanted to do it, you know, do his bit towards the running of this place, earn his keep, and who am I to stop him?' is the response delivered with a slight smile.

'Very commendable I'm sure, normally we don't swap. If you've got a job, you do it, no one else,' barks Sarge in his usual directive manner.

'Take it up with Bentley,' is the calm, quietly delivered reply.

'I'll check him out. I'll bring him back in here and then you can go and do it' insists Sarge, not happy with the retort.

Sarge doesn't come back.

Later, just before the programme kicks off, I ask Sarge what happened. He says he approached Bentley but he insisted on doing the job and indicated he wouldn't be happy if he was prevented from 'making his contribution'. Given

Bentley can be pretty aggressive, Sarge decided this was not a battle he wanted to fight. Then he says something which tweaks my interest.

'Sherwin's been here for five days and he hasn't lifted a finger to do anything. There is always a 'volunteer' who insists on doing it for him. I've even seen the boys collect his meal for him and clear away his dirty dishes. When he's in the group, no one speaks until after he's had his say, or been given the subtle nod that it's OK. He asks other kids to do things for him, like get the guitar and bring it over, and off they toddle. It seems all the boys want to curry favour with him. No one on staff has reported seeing him threaten anyone or even raise his voice. At any rate, he's not big enough to be a threat physically. Don't know what it is, but he's got clout, you know, mana with the group.'

When Sarge says this it strikes a chord with me. When I was supervising the boys in the recreation area I noticed Sherwin ask one of the older boys who was playing the guitar to give it to him. Normally the response would be a firm and clear direction to get lost however the boy stopped playing immediately and handed it over. Getting what he wants could be the reason he is going on the day programme rather than going to school. Maybe he has some sway with the staff as well.

I've seen this type of dominance by a young person over the group before. When I was a visitor to Arohata Borstal in Tawa, the singing by the girls was always a highlight and something they clearly loved doing and did well. However, on this one particular day, when the first hymn started, it was the pastor's lone voice that rattled about in the hall. We few visitors did our best to contribute but we were thin in volume and suspect in our now exposed harmonies. This happened all service and when it was over I asked one of the wardens what was going on. She pointed out this diminutive Māori girl and said she didn't feel like singing today, so nobody else did either. Interestingly, although she was small, she stood out in the group with a presence about her that was tangible. It left a lasting impression on me.

Sherwin, it appears, is a similar character.

Around 10 a.m. the programme coordinator Mike Jackson, myself, Sarge and Gwynne set off out to the Waimakariri to go kayaking with a group of fourteen boys, including Sherwin. This type of endeavour falls under the description of a 'compensatory activity' intended to open up potential new interests and help develop new skills. Such programmes provide a physical challenge and potentially a sense of achievement. It also encourages young people to work as

132

a team, learn to share, cooperate, and rely on each other. The theory behind this approach is that most of these young people have missed out on positive experiences in their lives and this deficit should be ameliorated while they are in custody. Not all staff buy into this, however, more than a few think it's really about keeping the kids busy and entertained. It probably achieves all those things. Lots of benefits!

Ted's not a big convert to the compensatory experience. 'They took them skiing up to Mount Hutt once because, we all know it, lots of these boys will be taking up skiing in the future. Staff brought their skis, so we know at least one group it worked for. State subsidised recreational trip!' I don't know enough about it to have a view one way or the other but I must admit a trip to the Waimakariri will be both challenging and entertaining for me, so bring it on!

While I'm excited I'm also apprehensive. I haven't kayaked before so it's going to be a learning experience. I know the Waimakariri well enough, it's a large river, deep and fast-moving in places, especially during the spring snow thaw from the Southern Alps, which just happens to be now! Any show of apprehension or fear will be picked up by the boys so I need to keep it to myself. Anyway, how hard can it be? We're taking boys some of whom may be novices too. Before we leave Stanmore we have a briefing about expectations. It's all about behaviour, not about paddling!

After a twenty-five-minute van ride, the group disembarks by the side of the river down near the bridge on the road to Kaiapoi. It's an overcast day, a little on the nippy side as a cool southwest wind blows in off the mountains. The water levels are high and the current flows strong and steady.

Some of the boys, who like me have never kayaked, have questions during a second briefing which is a little smarter than me as I continue to pretend I know what is going on, hoping to wing it. Programme coordinator Mike instructs us. 'Staff members front, back and in the middle of the group. In the event one of you feels you're in any trouble then someone will be close enough to help. No silly stuff, the river can be dangerous! Keep to the middle and follow instructions. And watch this, it's easy but important to know!' Mike, who happens to be the only person wearing a wetsuit, jumps in his kayak, paddles out about ten metres then flips the kayak over, disappears under the water, and then a few seconds later pops up like a cork. He tells us it's called the Eskimo roll, describing in detail the technique used under the water. That's it, one demonstration, no further questions, and then into our kayaks! Mike holds mine as I cram myself into the small space that contains the seat. I snap the skirt into place. It fits snugly around my body and covers the hole where I sit. It should keep most of the water out. Then we are ready and off we go.

I'm in the middle of the group which pleases me no end because it means if I get into trouble it should be noticed and someone will help.

We paddle up the river for just over an hour and a quarter. It's uneventful although physically tiring as we work hard to make headway against the oppositional current. There hasn't even been much chatter or skylarking. Everyone has been concentrating on the task at hand. Mike, who's in the lead, indicates to the group it's time to turn and head back to the van. Now it's an opportunity to relax and ride the current.

As we drift along in the fast-flowing river, we are moving at pace. The group begins to stretch out, extending over five hundred metres or so from front to back. I'm still in the middle. As we pass under a bridge and emerge out the other side, I notice Jai and Bentley are drifting off to the left. They're skylarking and splashing each other with their paddles, typical teenage boy stuff. They don't seem to be aware of how far they're straying towards the side of the river. Almost directly in their path, I see a couple of large steel girders extending out of the water, perhaps the remnants of an old jetty. The already swift flow seems to get much faster as it cascades around and between them, forming a swirling pool of torrid water on the other side. I shout out a warning but they don't respond. I get the paddles moving hard and fast, driving in their direction. Suddenly the boys become aware of the imminent danger although it's still some fifty metres away. Bentley looks like he knows what he's doing. He swings his kayak around and strikes out almost upriver against the current. I sweep past him. Jai, nearest to the danger, is struggling to get his kayak out of the swift-flowing current. He's being pulled towards the gap between the girders. I dig in harder and manage to get alongside him. I push on the left back edge of his kayak as he paddles frantically. The front of the kayak lifts and the back end drops down, acting as a rudder. Even a small change is sufficient to change its trajectory. The kayak turns sharply, he sweeps around the first girder and is catapulted back out towards the middle of the river.

A fraction of a second later I feel something hit the back of my kayak. I don't have time to register what it is. The kayak turns partially side on to the flow. Water sweeps over the bow. I'm in trouble and I know it. In an instant, I lose my balance and tip over, tossed like a leaf by the churning current. Upside down now, I slam against the steel girder and stop dead. I fear the kayak can't resist the forces which rush around me. It will surely snap like a twig. Jammed against the pillar I can see the sky through the surface of the water. Momentarily I feel panic rising, I'm frozen in time and powerless. It feels like invisible hands are trying to wrench me from the kayak but the skirt is preventing it. I want to rip it off myself and get out but the hole is so small and I am tucked in so tightly, I know it will be nearly impossible. I desperately try to 'Eskimo Roll' but the powerful current is making it hard to move my paddle which is pinned hard against the kayak. Seconds feel like minutes. Think, don't panic!

I must find a way to move the paddle. After an interminable struggle, I manage to twist the blade a fraction so the edge is cutting through the current. As it turns slightly I feel the water catch it, forcing it away from the side of the kayak. I struggle to hold on to it and keep it there while I throw the top half of my body violently forward… once… twice…three times. The momentum of the current against the face of the paddle, and my weight shift, move the whole kayak forward. It slides slowly along the girder. All of a sudden I feel like I am grabbed and tossed free. Travelling upside down in the current, I am finally able to perform the 'Eskimo roll'. I pop up out of the water gasping for breath, my heart racing. I lean forward and let the river take me for a few seconds, breathing hard, recovering.

Jai and Bentley are now around two hundred and fifty metres in front of me. They are facing in my direction. I can see others out in the middle of the river, merrily rolling along oblivious to what has happened. No one is near me. I am shaking from my head to my knees and it's more than just from the blasting cold of the wind and the icy water. I've been lucky, doing the right thing by instinct at the last moment. It could so easily have gone another way.

I get myself together and paddle hard and catch up with the others. We're almost at the rendezvous point and kayaks are making their way to the side of the river. I do the same and within a few moments, I'm wrapped in a towel and drinking a cup of hot coffee from a thermos, thanks to Mike who came prepared. There is plenty of animated chat going on around me. It all feels a little surreal. Sarge comes up to me, 'You look like a drowned rat, take a bit of a dip did we?' he laughs and slaps me on the shoulder. State the obvious Sarge!

'Yeah, I decided to practice my Eskimo Roll!' I don't say anything else. I assume my lack of experience may have contributed to what occurred but I'm sure I did the right thing by heading over to help Jai. However while I recognised he was in serious jeopardy, I didn't appreciate my lack of ability in the circumstances. But what choice was there anyway? He was in my care, my responsibility. At the time I didn't think about any of that.

On the trip back to the residence there's lots of banter and it's clear boys and staff alike have enjoyed their kayaking experience. Sarge is chatting away with Sherwin and I see Jai in close conversation with Fish. Bentley is sitting on his own. I notice he is staring at me but he looks away when I catch his eye. I'm pretty quiet and although I respond to the odd comment or question thrown my way, internally I'm lost in my thoughts.

We get back just in time for lunch. It's the same organised chaos as breakfast except the food has changed. It's open sandwiches. The boys I'm sitting with say it isn't top of their menu favourites. After the morning's exertions, everyone is hungry and the meal is consumed with a minimum of complaints. Spirits are high, the mood of the group is good, and the boys appear to be relating well with the staff. When things are like this you feel a degree of satisfaction, objectives achieved, a job well done. But I have a nagging feeling too, like the chill of the water has got into my bones. I want to go home and see my family.

Jai comes up to me as I'm about to go off shift. 'Out on the Waimak, thanks for giving me a shove, I thought I was going under for sure.'

'No worries Jai, glad I was there to help' I say genuinely. His acknowledgement lifts me from my foreboding ruminations.

Chapter 19
Jai Is Doing a Long Haul

It's now nearly two months since his weeks on the run. The escape had been an adventure. It has given Jai standing with his peers. While being on the run is hardly uncommon, where he'd been, who he'd been with, and the terrible fire, have been the subject of a lot of conversation. The risk and potential consequences are real to the bros. Many boys knew kids who'd been involved, and Hatch, who is back in Res now, had talked about what Jai did to get the others out.

After the fire service and police arrived at the burning house, it was only a matter of time before they worked out who he was. He was treated for smoke inhalation by the ambulance service. It hadn't been too serious but even so, his lungs felt raw for days. His burned hands took weeks to heal. He hadn't had to do any jobs around the Res, a bit of a bonus, but eating with a knife and fork proved a challenge. For the first week, one of the staff had to feed him like a baby. A few of the boys gave him jip for that. The worst thing was that he couldn't play the guitar for nearly a month.

Jomo, though, hadn't survived. He was dead or near dead when Jai and Julie pulled him out of the house, not because of the fire but because what he was sniffing caused his heart to stop. Jai was allowed to go to the funeral with one of the social workers. He saw Julie there and she told him about Jomo and what happened to some of the others. Jai didn't say anything about being visited by his ghost in the SNU. He thought it might upset her, or maybe she would think he was nuts.

It was a big funeral held in a Catholic Church at Burwood where Jomo grew up. The place was packed. His parents, two brothers and three sisters were there. Jai hadn't known much about him outside his street life. Jomo never talked about his family or early life. His father spoke at the funeral, filling in that large gap.

From the moment he was born, his father said, they thought Jomo had something special. He looked a lot like his grandfather when he was a boy, and seemed to have inherited some of his traits. He was a good talker and made friends easily. At an early age, he had shown a sense of humour and a liking for fun and practical jokes. Jomo was a promising student and in particular, he was very good at maths. His father hoped he would be an engineer or maybe even a scientist. He was sporty too and had been an age group rep in basketball and cricket. But when he turned fourteen, what his father described as 'the troubles', began. He fell in with a bad crowd, got into drugs and started skipping school. Somehow he still managed to pass his fifth form year. Within a week of turning sixteen, he left school and home. The family hadn't seen much of him since apart from now and again when he'd contact one of his sisters, or one of them would see him in the street. The family had always been hopeful it was just a phase and he would come through it. They had, and always would, love Jomo.

Benny was there, his head, face and one of his arms heavily bandaged. Jai thought he looked like someone from a zombie movie. They spoke briefly. Benny insisted on going to the funeral so the hospital staff brought him in an ambulance. He was in a wheelchair and still had a drip attached. He was struggling and uncomfortable but he told Jai, 'Jomo was my main man, we'd been mates for years.' He expected to be in hospital for a few more weeks yet. He had other burns on his body that were less visible. He needed skin grafts everywhere and that was proving to be a painful experience on top of everything else. He couldn't remember what happened but he said the Fire Service thought someone must have lit a cigarette too close to a paint or glue container and it exploded. Things were made worse because there were so many fumes in the room. He was one of the worst casualties. Jai saw a few others there who had bandages on various parts of their body. Some kids from the house that night weren't there though. Hatch, who was at Stanmore like Jai, wasn't allowed to come because he was currently in SNU. Lorrie wasn't there either. No one knew where she was.

Julie said almost everyone was treated for smoke inhalation. Some of the kids were placed in welfare homes and others disappeared afterwards and she hadn't seen them since. She'd lost all her possessions in the fire. She'd had to go back home while she got herself sorted out. Her mother welcomed her with open arms but her father was not so pleased and he was not talking to her. Julie was going to stick it out though until she had a few dollars together and could go back out flatting. Fortunately, she'd retained her job despite everything. The café owners had been good to her even though they found out about how she'd been living. Jai thought Julie sounded pretty good, like she had got herself together. He wondered if somehow Jomo's death had set her free.

There was a cost to absconding, or more accurately, a cost to being on the run. He'd faced new charges a week after the fire; burglary, theft and escaping lawful custody. His lawyer and social worker argued he'd been led on when he absconded and that the rest of what happened after was a result of being on the run and needing to survive, presenting him as a victim. The Judge didn't buy it. Jai let his lawyer say this stuff in court although he knew it was bullshit. Well, the 'needing to survive bit' was a little bit true. But he knew what was going on and he was a master of his own choices… whatever…it might have worked and he could have been back out on the streets, maybe even gone to Auckland. The cops didn't appear to know about his antics with Eric, no charges related to that. Good thing because it means Eric didn't nark. Big tick for him!

However, he was beginning to wonder now if doing a runner had been such a good idea. Nothing was happening in his case and he felt like he was rotting away in the Res. No one was telling him anything. He'd called his social worker twice and 'Not Much' Goodley, as Jai liked to refer to him, had only been in to see him once since the court hearing. Everyone was saying the plans they had went out the window because he ran. It was frustrating, not knowing anything, and constantly being fobbed off.

But it wasn't so bad being in Stanmore. He could live anywhere and most of the time there were things to do. Every day the programme guys have something planned. He'd been out a bit doing things like hiking on the Port Hills or going to the beach, normally Taylor's Mistake. All the boys knew they are taken to places where it's hard to run or where there aren't many members of the public. He doesn't care though, it was better to get out and about, even if it's limited and staff watch you all the time.

He'd been told by Sarge that once upon a time outings had been to places like the museum or the botanic gardens but it all stopped because boys were able to run away too easily, which they demonstrated frequently. It was nearly impossible to prevent it. There'd been incidents where staff trying to stop a runner were themselves restrained by well-meaning members of the public who thought a 'nasty' adult was trying to grab a kid or beat them up. There used to be outings to the Centennial or the QE 2 swimming pools but these had been stopped because the boys would come back to the Res with things they'd acquired while in the changing sheds. There had also been an incident when one of the staff was supervising some kids changing and one of them claimed he was perving. Jai thought it was probably Mr Rogers. They didn't call him Mr Rogers the Rogerer for nothing. After this, the staff didn't want to supervise the boys in the changing sheds. It's why they only go to the beach now when the weather is good and no changing sheds used, just a towel wrapped around the body or dry clothes on wet bodies, while they travel back.

One day Jai went on an outing to walk in the Port Hills. Two of the boys jumped out of the van and started running the moment they arrived before the staff realised what was happening. They just kept going. They could all see them miles away in the distance on the open hillsides. One of the staff took the van to the pickup point at the end of the track in the hope of nabbing them as they emerged. But it didn't happen, they never arrived. Because of that incident, all 'off sites' were cancelled for a fortnight. The whole group was punished because of those guys, although the staff called it a 'consequence.' It annoyed the staff and boys because everyone likes getting out. When the first of the boys was recaptured and returned to Stanmore he got a bit of the 'biff' in SNU. The SNU staff guy, Barry Mossie, was in there on his own. It happened at lunchtime and all the boys were in the dining area. Barry stepped out to get something and when he came back Tyson, the runner, had a red eye and a cut on the side of his head. He said he fell against the edge of a table. The whole Res knew what had happened. He didn't complain. When Jai asked him why he hadn't told the senior or someone else, especially that Barry may have let it happen, Tyson just shrugged his shoulders and said it was no big deal. Maybe he just accepted it as 'bush justice', or it was a can of worms no one wanted to open...or he was too frightened.

Regardless of whether you get the bash or not, decide to run, or chose to make a complaint, you do what you need to get by. It's the way of the natural world in the 'Res'. Survival of the fittest, he'd heard that phrase somewhere. That's Jai, he's a survivor.

Some people are leaders and some people are followers, and some are like him, independents.

Jai had known he needed to demonstrate that anyone who wanted to mess with him was going to find out real quick he could and would stand up for himself. Win or lose, they'd know they'd been in a fight. It was a bit like when he was on the rugby field when the big guy charged, he was going to take him down no matter what the cost.

He isn't a 'kingpin', or as they are referred to by staff and boys, a K.P. and he doesn't want to be, but he also isn't interested in being anyone's minion. Until he got to Stanmore he didn't even know what a K.P. was but now, as they are part of Res life, he has to deal with them one way or the other.

He has worked out that KPs generally get their power by being connected to the right people, being violent, or through force of personality. Maybe a combination of all these.

The best connection is to a gang or a well-known bunch of hoods. There are always gang affiliates in Res. Sometimes they make it obvious, others keep it to themselves, a lot of that depends on who's in at the time. The boys are mainly linked to the most well-known gangs, the Mongrel Mob and the Black Power. The Blacks tend to be more Māori whereas the Mongies, the 'doggies' as they call themselves, seem to take any bros in as long as they pass the initiation. Very occasionally there's a fully patched member in Res but mostly it's 'prospects' kids who hang out with a gang and are prepared to do what's required to get membership, namely serious crime! Drug running is a common thing because everyone knows kids get off more lightly than adults when it comes to the Courts.

There are other Christchurch gangs that all the locals know. There are the Headstone Riders, the Hassle Mob, and The Positively 4th St. Gang. The Headstones have been around for so long, they're like an institution. Jai doesn't know much about the Positively 4ths except they like roaring around town in large groups on their bikes. They must get their people from somewhere but he has never come across anyone prospecting for them, or the Headstones for that matter. He's sure the Hassle Mob are a 'white power' gang. They're high profile and seem to be keen to take over the city's crime scene. He's already come across several guys in Res who're relatives or try-hards wanting to get in. They like their black gear, and Doc Martin boots seem to be compulsory. They're definitely getting some 'fame'. They seem to get lots of trouble from the cops too because he's seen heaps of them hanging around the Courts, or maybe they aren't very good crims!

There are other White Power gangs as well. Generally, they're easy to pick because they tend to be baldies, skinned off, nude nuts. From what he's heard you can tell the different chapters by the colour of their boot laces. As far as he was concerned they're all chickens, hit you from behind when you aren't looking but too scared to front up in a fight. Pack animals as well. There needed to be a lot more of them than the opposition before they'd fight. Jai thinks skinheads are the biggest dick heads.

There's this one guy who'd come in last month, called himself Brutus, what a laugh of a name, his real one was probably Rodney or something. He was short and stocky with swastikas all over his neck. He was all 'fuck niggers' and 'I don't talk to niggers' and 'You nigger staff members can't tell me what to do.' He spent his time in SNU, for everyone's sake including his own. Both the 'Doggies' and the Blacks wanted to give him a bash in his big ugly mouth. Jai wouldn't have minded if that happened. After a couple of days, he disappeared and Jai found out he'd been transferred to a Res in Auckland. One of the staff told him it would broaden his education about different cultures. No doubt the brown bros in Auckland would sort him out all right. Jai laughed to himself, he'll probably come back as a member of the Mongrel Mob!

Some of the boys who get transferred from Auckland belong to new gangs not yet in the South Island, the 'Crips' and the 'Bloods.' All Jai knows is they're copying Los Angeles gangs. The Crips wear blue and the Bloods wear red. Strange though because those colours are already taken and everyone knows that. You think they'd get their own! There's been a kid from a new Auckland gang come in a month or so ago. He can't remember what they were called. He had a vague recollection it was after some sort of insect. He hadn't taken much notice because there were always 'try-hard' gangs out there but mostly they didn't get the fame like the bigger ones. At least he had different colours, yellow.

The staff try to squash any gang-related stuff. When he was admitted Jai was told, no gang paraphernalia, no gang talk, no gang signs, and nothing gang coloured. But the staff can't stop it. The kids make gang signs to each other all the time so everybody in Res knows who belongs to what. Sometimes, to annoy the staff, the 'Doggies' bark when the staff talk to them. Man, it gets them mad as hell. When the 'woofing' starts everything else stops. The staff let them go but no one gets to do the programme or go to the gym while it's happening…group consequence and unfair! Everyone just sits there and gets a lecture about all the bad things about being a gang banger. Sometimes this is shouted over the baying. Normally it doesn't last too long though because the other boys start showing their displeasure, especially the Blacks. Things can get edgy. Or sometimes somebody gets removed from the group and put in SNU. Jai was in SNU once when members of rival gangs were in lock-up. The staff talked to them about having to get along. It seemed to Jai they did, for at least as long as it took to get out of SNU and to get away from the blah, blah, blah about being in a gang!

Jai just laughed about not being able to wear colours, talk about daft! The kids always have a little bit of red or blue somewhere on them, a red hair tie or a handkerchief sticking out a little from their pocket. Most hilarious are the kids who have Mongrel Mob tattooed somewhere on their body, the worst case being a kid with Mongrel tattooed on his forehead. No hats allowed inside is the rule, hello!

Being connected to the gangs helps because it means you always have allies, protection and support. Lots of boys claim to be gang affiliated. It's even helpful to pretend because it might mean you're left alone, at least by the kids who aren't in gangs. Jai knows the juvie's from both main gangs and so most of them know him. Living on the streets and doing a bit of crime does that. He'd been under pressure a few times to pick a team. Although he has more friends in the Blacks than the Doggies, he's resisted. His decision seems to be respected, at least so far. The biggest challenge is when tensions get to boiling point. Since he'd been in Res there'd been one riot when the blacks and the mongrels sorted out their differences. It happened over lunch and the cops were called and a couple of boys got carted off to the cop shop.

However not all KPs are gang members or affiliates. Some are big enough, ugly enough, tough enough, and used to getting their way through the use of force. Nothing seems to frighten them, including gangs. They are generally bullies but they often use more than just violence. If threats or violence were enough then the Chevy's and the Bentleys would-be leaders, but they're not. The more effective leaders combine bullying with something else. It might be friendship, or let you be one of the 'in-crowd'. Jai wasn't interested in the pissy little bit of status with the other residents that might bring. From his perspective, it's just protection dressed up. He has never felt he needed protection and he associates with anyone he wants to. Independents!

He is always a bit wary of some new clown coming into Res, trying to push their weight around and establish themselves. He deals with them all in the same way. Treat with care is his view, avoid trouble, but always be prepared to stand up for yourself no matter the consequences…and let everyone know it.

Sometimes there's trouble between 'wannabe' KP's which ends in a clash. It might be 'the bash' out in the open so all the boys get the message, or not so visible when the staff are distracted. A lot of the time though, threats are made publicly, like right in front of staff. It might just be a hand signal, a pointed finger, a finger across the throat. The most menacing guys only have to look at someone and it's enough. You didn't want to be 'seen' by them. As for the staff, when they saw threats, and if they cared to show they'd seen something, most often all they do is tell the KP off, like a slap on the hand with a wet bus ticket.

Now and again something more drastic might happen. He was at a community meeting one morning when the KP at the time, Fish, was holding a court of his own. He was talking over the staff, interrupting them with smartass comments about the rules and the proposed programme. He was also making comments on whom he thought should be on the programme and indicated that he didn't want one of the boys that he called a 'KF', a 'kiddie fucker' out with them. The morning team were struggling to control the situation because, while even a blind man could have seen what was going on, it was all being done with a smile. No one seemed to have the courage to call it out for what it was. Next thing, the senior who was passing through to the office, stopped, looked at the group, and said, 'You, come here!' pointing at Fish and then pointing at a spot on the floor in front of where he was standing. All the chatter stopped. Fish sneered and started to say something 'What the 'f' are you…' but didn't have time to get it all out. In two steps the senior was beside him lifting him off his seat and marching him out of the room to SNU. Jai wasn't sorry to see him gone. Fish was the unpredictable kind of KP, one who had no sense of loyalty and would turn on anyone at any time depending on his mood.

The other type of KP has the personality and the confidence to take leadership, the types who would be leaders no matter what their role might be. They may have connections or be violent, but they didn't rely on these. A good leader, the sort Jai liked and one he might take some notice of, could get the boys on board without threats or that sort of bullshit. He'd seen a couple of boys in the Res who weren't big and strong but were still the recognised leader. There was one in at the moment, Sherwin.

Jai had heard about him on the street although the first time he'd met him was in Res. Sherwin's Black Power, his father's the Sergeant at Arms, so a senior guy in his chapter. There is a rumour he'd got into conflict with an older boy who was prospecting for the 'doggies' and Sherwin had done him over with a piece of pipe. Jai thought this was probably not true because he knew violence and Sherwin didn't fit the bill. No, the reason people were into Sherwin was mainly because of his personality…he has mana. It was obvious as a dog's balls. Right at the moment, there's only Sherwin in from the Blacks and there are five Doggies, so they've got the numbers and no reason to bow to him, but not even a sniff of trouble from any of them.

He's the sort of guy that Jai likes to be around, confident, funny, tells good yarns, and plays really good guitar. He's smart too. He manages the staff and the boys. It's all subtle stuff. In group meetings, he makes little comments and has those around him in stitches but if he is challenged about it, he immediately quietens things down and gets the other boys to pull their heads in, like he's in charge. He does that with his jobs as well, doesn't do any but meanders about like he's the supervisor. Yeh, he's a true master. But in the end, he's here now, tomorrow he might be gone, and Jai's not looking for any long term connections.

His avoidance strategy has stood him in good stead with the KPs and the gang bangers alike so far. He knows it won't always be enough to keep safe though because trying to dodge the 'nutters' is like trying to deny sunrise, impossible.

Chapter 20
Jai Goes on an Outing

Jai is looking forward to the day. The programme this morning is kayaking on the Waimak. While Jai isn't into kayaking, and water sports aren't his thing, it's a chance to get out and beat the boredom. He likes a bit of a physical challenge and it gives him a chance to show off a bit to the others, the unfit and the 'gumbies' who have two left feet.

When the group gets to the Waimak they receive the usual talk about water safety from the programme coordinator. The plan is to pair up the boys with a staff member. Jai had hoped to be with Sherwin but he ended up going with Sarge. His partner is the nut job, Bentley. He's less than happy about it. Who knows what that loose unit might do out on the water he thinks to himself. The staffer with them is Wyatt who for some reason is working during the day at the moment. That's good, he's easy to get on with. He's a muso, sort of a cool guy if any staff member can be that is. He loves his playing at night, you can hear it anywhere in Rata and Rimu. It makes you forget you're there in the Res. The music is soothing and because most of the boys seem to listen, things can be pretty settled, which means you're left alone, which is good too. The other thing he likes about Wyatt is that he talks to the boys. Mostly the night staff just tell you to shut up and go to sleep. But if you asked Wyatt anything he would talk to you about it, well nearly anything.

He wasn't sure Wyatt is always honest though. One time a boy had asked him if he smoked a bit of 'dak' and Wyatt fudged the answer when he replied, 'Drug taking puts you at risk, just like drinking alcohol can.' Sounded like a 'yes' to Jai and a 'but I am not going to confirm or deny it...' The boy, John King, himself a muso, had said to him, 'Common man, you play music and you look like a hippie. You must have seen plenty in your time. I can tell!' Wyatt seemed to avoid answering by saying, 'It doesn't matter what I think about it, drug-taking is illegal and that's the law.'

Kingi, that's what people called him, kept on pushing. 'Lots of the staff in here must smoke dope, everyone does. I bet you do too sir.'

'Don't call me sir, I haven't been knighted. People can make choices about what they do. I don't have to be a slave to the things other people might be doing around me. Make choices and live with the consequences. That's what you guys are doing, living with your choices, can't blame anyone else.' It started a conversation among the boys about who was to blame for what was happening to them. Maybe it was what Wyatt intended but Jai had a sneaking suspicion he was changing the subject, yeh a verbal distraction! It worked because some boys got quite animated about who was to blame for their current situation, the Police, their social worker, or their family. A few owned up and took responsibility but they didn't seem to care. Getting nabbed was just part of the deal. Us against them... F.T.W... The conversation had become too rowdy and the other night staffer, Mr Rogers the freakin' Rogerer came along and wanted to know what all the noise was about. He didn't even care that Wyatt was there. Time to shut up and sleep.

There'd been another night Jai remembered where Wyatt had a long chat with the boys in Rimu. One of the boys, a new lad, Jade Donavan said 'Sieg heil' to Wyatt when he asked the boys who were deep in conversation to quieten down. Wyatt wasn't too impressed and he challenged Jade.

'Why are you saying that?'

''Cause you're the 'Establishment' man. You and the pigs pick on us 'cause we're on the streets and we won't do what you want, you know man, won't play the game. And then you lock us up.'

'First off, let's get it straight, I'm not picking on you or anybody else. It's time for sleep and it's the best thing you can be doing right now. We need to keep it down so those who want to sleep can.' Jai was one of those, that's all he wanted to do. There was a bit of a rumble in the dorm and it was clear most of the others weren't asleep. Wyatt must have been aware of this because he started talking again.

'You guys are Seig Heil this and Seig Heil that, do you even know what it means? 'he asked.

'The brothers say it. It means 'up the establishment and fuck you.' It's a sign we're in the brotherhood,' Jade came back at him with a cocky reply.

'Well, it might mean that to you but if you knew what it stands for you wouldn't be saying it. Just like those swastikas some of you have tattooed on your bodies. Do you know where they come from? The Nazi regime in Germany in the 1930s and during the second world war. You must have seen something about them in movies or on TV'. No response but all the boys, brown and white, are listening.

'I never understand why you guys want to put that stuff on your body. It's ugly for a start, but on top of that, the Nazis didn't like anyone who wasn't white, Aryan, so more than just white, the whitest of the white. And they didn't tolerate criminal behaviour either. They considered coloured people, criminals, homosexuals and Jews as sub-humans, you know, like animals! So that's all of you, and some of you twice over! You'd have been rounded up and shot, or gassed to death, or put in their concentration camps. Do you know about the concentration camps? You don't like being in here, well I can tell you this is a summer holiday camp compared to those places.'

The conversation went on for a while, Jai remembered. Wyatt spent about twenty minutes talking about the Nazis, how they came to power, what they believed, what they did, and how it ended for them. It was really interesting and things he had never heard. Of course, he'd seen Nazis on TV, he liked the flash uniforms and the strongman stuff, the cool weapons and the planes, especially the Stukas. He had a swastika tattooed on the underside of his wrist, done at school using a makeshift tattoo gun. He didn't know what it stood for, he just knew when people saw it they reacted, generally not in a good way. But in the end, it was there now. Maybe one of the boys who had needles and ink could do something to cover it up. He'd see about it. He didn't want it anymore.

He can't wait to get started and he feels impatient when the programme guy wants to give them a lecture about water safety. He knows enough about it, all common sense, wasting time. But before too long the merry kayakers set out on the water. As he expected, almost straight away, Bentley is trying to tip him over, coming alongside Jai's kayak and pushing him with his arms or the paddle, trying to knock him off balance. A couple of times Bentley also runs his kayak into the back of Jai's. It nearly works but Jai is able to hold his balance. Wyatty doesn't seem to notice. He smacks out at Bentley with his paddle even though he isn't worried about tipping over. He'd been out on the river before with the programme and he knows how to Eskimo Roll if he has to, but he isn't interested in getting too wet because the water and the wind are freezing. It's bad enough with the spray from the paddles.

They get a bit ahead of Wyatt but he eventually catches up with them and finally, he tells Bentley to cut it out. Bentley just says he is having fun and tells him to lighten up man!

They paddle up the river for quite a while and when they eventually turn, Jai is really happy because ploughing against the current was hard work. It's worth it now though because the ride back to the pick-up point is easy as they go with the racing current. Man, are they moving, the fastest ride he's had on the river.

Bentley is nearby and they pass under a bridge. The water around the pillars holding up the bridge looks wild and he is careful to keep in the middle between them. Once they're passed, Bentley is behind him whacking the back of his kayak with his paddle and laughing like a hyena. He's distracted for a moment, then he notices a couple of iron girders sticking out of the river on his left. It would be a good idea to avoid those. The next thing he knows Bentley rams the back of his kayak again. It swerves, veering sharply to the left, Jai sways wildly trying to get control. He manages to regain his balance but the couple of seconds it takes is enough to drive the kayak into the fast-moving water towards the exposed girders. Jai paddles frantically but the current is too strong. He can see it funnel between the upright steel and swirl like a whirlpool on the other side. He senses the danger and he gives it everything he's got, trying to escape the relentless pull of the rushing torrent. The back of his kayak seems to lift, the paddles are flailing like a windmill no longer in the water, and then he can feel the nose starting to dip. He's in trouble. If the nose goes right under he will flip… it's like slow motion. Suddenly, above the roar of the churning water, he hears Wyatt calling out, 'I've got you' and feels the back of his kayak dip a bit. The nose lifts. He feels the paddles grip the water. At the last second, the kayak sweeps around the nearest girder and he is catapulted into clear water and on down the river.

In a few strokes, he has the kayak fully under control. He takes in a deep breath then back paddles slowing his progress and turns around to thank Wyatt but there's no sign of him, only Bentley. The water continues to drive him downstream. His arms are too tired to keep back paddling so he lets himself be taken. As soon as he reaches a spot of calm water he sticks his paddle in, the kayak spins around and he's facing the girders although he is now over a hundred metres away. Bentley is right there with him. There's still no sign of Wyatt.

'Where the fuck is Wyatt, man? He was right behind me. I think he's gone under those girders. We need to go back, man! Come on we need to get help, do something!' He shouts at Bentley.

'Nah! No fuckin way! My arms are too stuffed to go paddling back there' comes the reply. 'I may have given him an accidental little flick. Let's see what happens. Eskimo Roll dude, let's see him do the roll!' Bentley has a malicious look on his face, a hint of a grin, or is it a grimace. Whatever it is it sends a chill down Jai's spine, far deeper than the icy southerly wind.

Jai looks around frantically but there is no one else near them. The majority of the paddlers are way past them now and the remaining few are stretched out up the river, too far away. He sees Sherwin go past but he's also over the other side of the river.

'Come on man, he stopped me going under, I've got to get one of the other staff to help.' Jai gets his paddle into the water.

Bentley reaches out with his paddle and smacks it hard across the bow of Jai's kayak.

'He's a staffer, who gives a fuck? I said let's see him, Eskimo Roll!' The message is clear, leave it alone…or else.

It seems they sit becalmed, watching and waiting for ages. Jai can't get his head around what's happening. Thoughts are racing through his mind. He doesn't care about Wyatt that much but he has nothing against him. And he doesn't get into harming people unless it's self-defence. This guy Bentley, he's a 'nutter' all right but this is way over the top and he just seems amused by it all, he has a smile across his ugly face. It all feels like a macabre game in which Jai is only a spectator. At that moment he is more frightened of Bentley than anything else he's ever experienced. This guy could do anything to anyone, especially out here where probably no one would even notice.

His heart is racing. Just when he feels that all hope is gone, Wyatt pops up. He is gasping for air, spitting and coughing. His kayak is grabbed by the mainstream and is now moving towards the calmer waters. Wyatt isn't paddling, he is leaning over the front of his kayak and looks to be throwing up. Thank Christ for that, Jai is surprised at his overwhelming sense of relief.

'What the fuck man?' Jai finally gets some words out.

'Shut your fucking mouth' Bentley snarls at him. 'I just wanted to see what would happen. He's all right. I told you, it was an accident, I was coming to help you. He got in the way and went under. That's the way it is, and you better make sure that's your story if anyone asks or I'll fucking well fix you, you better believe it!'

Jai looks at Bentley and feels another wave of fear rush through him. At that moment he knows it's true. That's Bentley's record, violence, committed without fear of consequences, no matter who you are. He even frightens most of the staff. He's as dumb as a plank, there's no point in talking to him… or taking him on unless he has to defend himself. Sooner or later he'll get you sure as day follows night!

There's not much that rattles round in that guy's empty head but vengeance loves the space, Jai has heard Bentley's endless raves about it. He wonders if Wyatt knows what happened.

Wyatt arrives next to them. He is still blowing hard but at least he seems all right.

'You ok?' Jai asks. 'I saw you'd disappeared but we were already down here. We were just coming back' he lies.

'Yeah, I got caught in the current and went under. Bit hairy there for a moment or two but I got out of it! Thank the 'Eskimo Roll' eh. Let's go guys, it's time to get back to the van. I'm freezing'

'*River runs to the ocean, oceans to the sea, gonna let that water wash all over me,*' lyrics from Brownie McGee pop into Jai's head. No more to be said, he's all right, I'm all right, no damage done so let it go, he thinks.

'Race you back' he challenges them both and digs his paddle into the water.

In the van, on the way back he's sitting on his own watching the others, staff and boys chatting away. Sherwin who's been sitting with Gwynne comes over and plonks himself down. 'What's up my man?' he asks. 'You're looking like you sucked a lemon!'

'Nothing… I'm just sick of dealing with dickheads!' Jai replies.

'Yeah, you mean that guy Breezer? I saw him bash your kayak with his paddle. He looked pretty angry even from where I was. What was that all about?' Sherwin had seen their altercation then.

'I saw Wyatty go under near the girders and I thought we should go back but Bentley didn't want to. He was letting me know, that's all.' Sherwin looks him in the eye, but Jai can't maintain the contact. No more is said on that. Instead, the conversation moves to *Stairway to Heaven* which Sherwin had been playing this morning. Although Jai didn't much like Led Zep, he did like that particular tune and he played a version, not quite right but close. It filled in the time before they arrived back at Stanmore.

Later that night Jai's lying in bed. Sherwin is in Rimu too, in the alcove across from him. He looks like he's asleep. There are still boys milling about. Bentley is going past and he stops by Jai's bed. 'Hello,' Jai wonders 'what's the dickhead going to do now?'

'Hey man, sorry about today. No hard feelings. I was just mucking around, having a bit of fun, you know joking with yah. I knew he'd be all right. He can look after himself. No worries, man... we all good?'

'Yeah forget it, man,' he says in a resigned way, knowing that Bentley surely will.

As Bentley takes his leave, Jai sees Sherwin looking at him from across the alcove. He wasn't asleep. He gives Jai a wink.

Chapter 21
Wyatt Goes to Court

It's Friday morning and for some of the boys, that means an appearance in Court. I'm to be one of the escorts along with Sarge and a reliever, Ter. I'm looking forward to it as it will be a new experience for me, a chance to see a whole new part of the business.

We have a briefing before we leave. Each of us is given a role. I am to sit next to the sliding door in the van to prevent any attempts at jumping out. Ter will be doing the driving. Sarge will be stationed behind the driver just to make sure no one tries to interfere with him. Each of us will have the responsibility of keeping a close eye on one of the boys once we arrive at court.

Three boys are appearing today, Hatch Hitch, Jason Fisher and Jai Rehua. Just after 9.30 am we all get in the van and set off. The courthouse is in Armagh St in the city, about a fifteen-minute drive away.

Jai and Hatch are in the back seat. Fish is sitting in front of them, head down, brooding. The two younger boys are in high spirits, laughing and boisterous. Sarge tries to get them to settle down but it's a half-hearted attempt and he quickly gives up.

We head up London St and Hatch, who seems to be in the wildest frame of mind is busying himself giving the middle finger to anyone who looks at the van. Sarge admonishes him.

We hit road works and stop at the Fitzgerald Ave intersection. Hatch, quick as a flash, jumps up on the back seat, pulls down his pants and bears his buttocks to the car behind. Sarge moves swiftly and pulls him and his bare buttocks off the rear window. Hatch, whose pants are now round his ankles, loses his balance ending up face down on the floor, cursing as he does. I look through the now-vacated back window and see that the car behind us has a woman and two children in it. The woman does not look happy and is talking to the children. Just as Hatch manages to get to his feet and is hauling up his trousers, we get the 'go' sign and the van pulls forward making him totter like he's drunk. He loses his balance again and crashes into the back of a seat and then flops onto the floor. Sarge is laughing like he's enjoying a Charlie Chaplin slapstick comedy routine and pointing out that this is what you get for being disrespectful. Hatch loses it completely uttering a bunch of unrepeatable expletives at him. Sarge tries to calm him down but to no avail, he's lost it. Then the brooding Fish intervenes, 'Shut the fuck up, Hitch!' Silence follows for the rest of the trip.

We arrive at the Court and take the nearest car park Ter can find. We need to walk the boys a hundred metres to get where we are going. Hatch, who has a bit of blood on his face from his crash landing, is still smarting from his embarrassing moment. As he passes the foot traffic around the court he's muttering to the odd person who catches his eye, 'What the 'f' are you looking at?' I'm beside him and encourage him to keep moving but there is little else I can do.

I don't know what I was expecting but I am unprepared for the chaos that greets us as we walk through the front door. The large Court waiting room is full of people, most standing because there is only limited seating around the edges. The crowd is shoulder to shoulder. There are a variety of adults present, parents, caregivers, social workers, and others who must be the providers of therapeutic programmes or other services. There are so many kids that they can't possibly all have parents here. It looks more like a gathering for all the street kids in town to me.

Ter, who is looking after Fish, positions himself next to the door. Fish has wandered off. Sarge is somewhere with Jai. Hatch immediately moves into the crowd. I try to follow but he's swallowed up. Well, he can't go far so I head over to stand with Ter, by the exit. From our observation point, I eventually spot Hatch. He's with a group of dishevelled looking fellows and I can see he's smoking a cigarette, albeit that he is doing his best to keep it out of sight.

The noise, which can only be described as a racket, is occasionally interrupted when a door at the far end of the room opens and everyone looks up to see who is being called. The place quietens down for a few seconds. An elderly gent sticks his head out 'Jai Rehua, Jai Rehua!' I see Jai go in. Sarge is with him but no one else follows.

After about ten minutes I see them come out and Fish is called. He goes in on his own. Ter doesn't move. Sarge comes over to where we are standing. 'Jai's back with us, nothing is happening for him. His mother didn't come and neither did his social worker! Poor bastard, he's pretty unhappy about it. Judge Mentor's on the bench today and he wasn't impressed. He blew me up, me! There's not much I can I do?'

While we wait, I watch the crowd. All sorts of things are going on. I can see a couple of girls pushing and shoving each other, clearly a dispute in progress. I smell weed so someone is having a smoke. I see a woman clip a boy round the head, presumably her own child. There's obvious flirting going on and I see Jai working his charm on a young woman with bright purple hair.

The Court door opens, 'Hatch Hitch, Hatch Hitch'. I watch as he goes into the court, alone. A couple of minutes later the door opens and the old guy is there again 'Who's here from Social Welfare?' he shouts above the hubbub. I look at Sarge and he says, 'You go, it'll be good for you to have a look inside the court. Say as little as you can get away with. If the Judge asks you anything tell him who you are and say his caseworker isn't on duty today. That's all you'll need to do!'

I enter the courtroom feeling more than a little apprehensive. There are a set of benches in a 'U' shape. Hatch is standing in the dock near the door. I stand next to him. At the top end sits the judge in his black robe, an elderly man with a ruddy, round face. He has a bald plate and fuzzy hair sticking out over his ears. He looks to be a bit like Crusty the Clown, except he has a pair of glasses resting on the end of his bulbous nose. He's peering over these looking at me. There are a few other people in the court, the policeman, and the lawyer are easy to pick out, but who the others are, no idea.

Judge Mentor addresses me. 'Who are you?' His abrupt manner puts me on alert.

'Charles Novak sir, from Stanmore your honour,' I stammer.

'Well, Mr Novak, Hatch here tells me that on the way to Court you or one of your colleagues gave him, to use his words, 'the biff'. He won't say who, but I can see he has blood on his head so something has happened. I believe an explanation is in order!'

I'm momentarily stunned by Hatch's bald-faced lie. I don't know what to say. I catch him out of the corner of my eye. A smirk dances around his face. I open and shut my mouth like a goldfish in a bowl. No sound escapes.

'Well?' says the Judge, clearly losing patience, 'What have you got to say for yourself?'

'He fell sir, in the van, and hit his head.' I blurt out.

'Humm… a bit unfortunate, wasn't it? He's in your care. I don't call that care, I call that careless!' This comment elicits a chortle from the policeman present and a smile from Hatch's lawyer. Not from everyone though, one of the other people in court looks very stony-faced. I wonder who that person is, but not for long.

'How did he manage to fall and hit his head?' I want to know how it happened!' The Judge is going to chase this down so I tell him exactly what happened. This elicits a laugh from the policemen and the Judge. Even old Stony Face cracks a smile. I look at Hatch. If looks could kill, I'd be a dead man.

The Judge addresses Hatch 'Sounds like it would be wiser to keep your pants up when you're riding in a van!' More chuckles. Then he turns to Stony Face, 'What's happening for Master Hitch, what has the Department got in mind'. Ah, Stony Face is the Department's representative. 'Why isn't his caseworker here? This matter has been put off for a month or so already and it's about time there was some action.'

I'm relieved to see the attention is no longer on me. It's intimidating being scrutinised by the Judge. However, it didn't seem to trouble Hatch.

The court officer stands 'He keeps absconding your honour. We find placements and he doesn't stay. Frankly, we're having trouble finding something for him. The solution has not proved to be obvious. His caseworker is currently looking at a placement on the West Coast at Reefton, and we are hoping to send him there.'

'Hmmm…I'm not convinced that we should be sending him to Reefton. What about his schooling?' inquires the Judge.

'It's a farm, your honour. He'll do correspondence and he's also going to learn about farm work. We're hoping a change of scenery away from the city and the crowd he mixes with, some clean rural air, and hard work, will make the difference. They're good people where he'll be staying, properly vetted and very experienced caregivers. There are no other clients on the farm so Hatch will get their undivided attention.'

'Well,' the Judge addresses Hatch, 'that appears to be progress! What do you think of that?'

'I hate farms, I hate animals and I don't like doddery old people and I don't want to go to Reefton or anywhere else on the West Coast.' Hatch doesn't leave any room to misunderstand his feelings.

156

The Judge ponders for a moment. 'That's… er…not sounding too hopeful then. I suspect the Department has a little bit more work to do.' The Judge addresses all present. 'I'll stand this matter down for a month. I expect to see a robust solution next time Hatch appears. In the meantime, he will remain in the custody of the Department.' Then to Hatch, he says, 'If you don't want to spend a whole lot longer at the Christchurch Boys Home, I advise you to work with the Department on solutions, not set up roadblocks all the time…and keep your pants on during the ride back. Stand down!'

I'm not sure who wanted to be out of the court quicker, me or Hatch. We get in a crush both trying to get through the door at the same time.

The boys from Stanmore have finished with the court now. Sarge has ascertained if there is to be a new admission from court Stoney Face will deliver them. It's time for us to go back. Ter gets the van and double parks outside the courthouse. We walk the boys back to the van being extra careful that they are closely attended to. None seem very happy to be returning and the mood on the ride back is subdued.

We arrive in time for lunch. I sit with Jai and Fish. I don't like the look of the food so I eat a couple of pieces of bread and give everything else to the boys. The boys don't have much to say. Jai is disappointed that his mother never turned up but then he didn't think she would. His caseworker didn't come either. Fish, who is appearing on serious charges, was told that he is going to the District Court so that means Corrective Training or prison. He'd been hoping it wouldn't happen, but his caseworker who also didn't come to court wrote a report saying there was nothing more Social Welfare can do for him. I try to say the right things because I feel for them both. Jai is adrift and Fish, who comes from a criminal family, seems to be following an inevitable path. Still, it's hard to see how prison will make any difference for him apart from improving his range of criminal contacts.

While I listen, I survey the rest of the group. I seek out Hatch. He is sitting a couple of tables away with Sarge and Bentley. I can see him in an animated discussion, waving his arms about to illustrate whatever important point he is making. I wonder if the events of the morning are being retold with him as the hero, a stretch to credibility but I'm sure he's having a go.

Sarge gets up to take his plate back to the servery and I see Hatch pass something to Bentley under the table.

Chapter 22
Office Day

After the Friday court shift, I have a few days off. I return to work on the following Wednesday for 'Office day'. This occurs once every three weeks when the team work eight to five doing non-contact activities. For the residential social workers it's an opportunity to get their casework records up to date, write reports, and do any other outstanding paperwork. For the night staff it is a chance to get together with their day shift team colleagues, and to get updates on relevant organisational information such as new policies, local directions, and general news. It also provides an opportunity for professional supervision which, for practical and obvious reasons, doesn't happen at night. In addition, as the shifts changeover there's a window of an hour and a half where all three shifts are on-site together and specialised training is offered.

My very first training session was on managing physical interventions. It was pretty rudimentary and only marginally useful. It focused on prevention, which was beneficial, but not so much on what happened when it doesn't do the trick, which seems to be quite often. Subsequent sessions however have proved more helpful, in particular those focused on mental health issues for young people, including depression, anxiety, psychosis and other serious problems. Other topics have included youth suicide and the stages of child and adolescent development.

I soak it up but I also feel a degree of ambivalence. It highlights how much I need to know by emphasising how little I know. The sessions are relatively short so it's only snippets of information and not real training. But it's helped convince me I must return to studying when the next opportunity presents itself.

Professional supervision has proved to be an interesting beast indeed. I've had it twice in six months. I didn't know what to expect before my first session.

I'd heard it being disparaged by some residential social workers and dissed by my night staff colleagues, so I wasn't expecting much.

John Land, my supervisor, checked how things were going and how I was settling in. My first burning question was that I wanted to know what Stanmore was supposed to be, a prison? A mental institution? A doss house? The reply left me a bit in 'no mans' land.

'It's a bit of all. That's what you get in a place of last resort. Somewhere boys, and for that matter girls, go when there are no other obvious solutions to their current problems, at least until one is found. We do have boys with a variety of significant issues but you can't treat their mental health here, not really because there isn't the time, the resources, or the expertise that's what you've got an Adolescent Unit at Sunnyside Hospital for. We can fix their physical health though, and we do a lot of that, sickness, teeth, eyes and ears, sexual diseases and so on. And yes, we effectively contain young people, they can't come and go as they please but we try to be more like a home than a lock-up, except for SNU of course, which is what it is.'

I replied at the time that it seemed like a blunt instrument to me. John said that from his perspective it was all about getting the best bang for your bucks, and the State makes those decisions, not him. 'In the interim, we do the best we can with what we've got, that's why we don't want boys in here for longer than necessary.' I think that helped me get a perspective at the time although my views are still forming on whether this is the best approach.

I had lots of other questions. I didn't obtain many satisfactory answers, just a lot of 'time and experience will help with that,' said in various ways. I raised my feelings of isolation... dismissed! It goes with the job so get used to it. I reported that I noticed how a lack of consistency between the shift teams impacts which in turn affects group dynamics, especially for the night staff at bedtime. Too hard basket...answer, 'You'll always get that, it's the nature of shift work.' Perhaps, I suggested we could just all apply the rules in the same way. Apparently, the application of rigid rules was not amenable to the current approach of creating a homelike environment. To me it seemed wildly aspirational to think Stanmore could be homelike in any conceivable way. Too many boys, too few staff, too many problems, too little space. Its whole operation is institutional as a matter of necessity. 'It's not a perfect world and there will be variations. You need to focus on the night team and your consistency there.' OK,

John, message received loud and clear, shut up and worry about your own performance! Early on I learned what questions not to ask.

There were valuable conversations too. John is an experienced social work practitioner. He helped me understand how to manage group dynamics, identify and respond to early indicators a young person might be winding themselves up, and some of the intricacies and challenges of individual case management.

I withdrew a couple of books from the library on group therapy and read these at night. Fascinating stuff but none of it is particularly relevant to the group at Stanmore. Although the clients are referred to as a group, they aren't, they're a cluster. John acknowledged the therapeutic approach to groupwork did not apply but talked about trying to replicate some of the useful tips and tricks in the residential setting. 'It's the best we can do' he said, 'hence the group meetings, keeping everyone together as much as possible, and the benefits of stating clear expectations, processes and boundaries. There is plenty of room for progressive thinking about how this could be strengthened, maybe something you can study at night and contribute more guidance about in the future. Call it your professional development.' A challenge was tossed my way, and not an easy one. Sounds more like a PhD thesis to me!

Today, however, my supervision isn't happening, other things more important things have required John's attention. This afternoon we're all going to Kingslea Girls Home for a presentation from the national office boffins on proposed changes to the welfare system and the way residences will operate in the future. We're told it's big news but the team tell me the welfare service is restructured every five minutes so they have no expectations anything substantial is really in the wind. Ted confided to me that during one of his recent 'security' checks of the managers' office he saw a memo on major changes looming. We all do this, check the manager's office, it's our informal briefing process. After management, we tend to be the second most informed people in the place. Ted saw a proposal that Stanmore is to close and the boy's programme moved to Kingslea. Also, there are big changes to the law governing how young people will be dealt with in the Courts. It sounded fairly significant to me so I went and checked the information myself. If the size of the document was anything to go on, it will be huge. I have peace of mind though regarding the tenure of my job.

'There will still need to be night staff no matter what they do,' Ted says. 'So all the rest doesn't matter to me. Need to wait and see what happens. Half the time a new lot of changes arrive before the last lot are in place. Best to wait six months before doing anything, just in case, don't want to expend a whole lot of energy pointlessly.' He seems a bit more positive about the new legal provisions though, especially the proposal to separate the boys who offend from those who are more vulnerable. 'Good move and about time. Tell you what, I've been saying it for ages!' But apart from that, he doesn't think much will be different for those of us who dwell in the dark hours. We'll see.

So for now I'm at a loose end this morning, I head off into the main residence to see what's happening. Sarge tells me it'd be helpful if I could keep an eye on Jai who is in bed with an ailment of some sort. I make my way upstairs to Rata where Jai is convalescing.

He's in bed with the covers pulled up over his head. I let him know I'm here and enquire about the usual things, how's he feeling, is there is anything I can do? He tells me to get lost without even taking his head from under the covers, but I persist. After several more exchanges, mainly him giving me further directions about what I might do to myself and the unworthiness of my pedigree, he eventually peers out from under the covers. He looks unwell, with puffy eyes and pallid in colour.

'Has anyone offered to get you to a doctor?'

'I don't need a fucking doctor, I need to get out of this place, it's unhealthy!' Comes the emphatic reply. 'This place is full of sick bastards and I don't mean just the boys. That bastard Sarge was coughing and spluttering the other day at our tea table, no wonder I'm sick. And Fish is too. Same thing. He went to the programme today 'cause he hopes he can give it to everybody else... freaking egg!'

'Good thing you didn't go then, a good choice on your part. Now what can I do?' I ask.

'Get me the fuck out of this place. I've been here for months. Nothing's happening. Doug Goodley promised to find me a placement, but he didn't turn up at court the other day. No fucking Goodley, more like it! I've asked Sarge to chase him up but he hasn't told me a thing either, probably hasn't done anything. No one in this place gives a fuck! It's a black hole. Once we come in there's no way out' Jai laments.

He sounds depressed to me, and he may have reason to be. I learned a bit about this from one of the training sessions... get him talking... and then tell someone else who has the skills to know what to do with the information you find!

I don't bother admonishing Jai for the stream of foul language. Even though Mr Rogers would call this 'turning a blind eye to poor behaviour', which it is, I don't want to put up any unnecessary barriers. At any rate, the swearing is not a public event, so I let it go.

'I am happy to talk to Sarge and find out what he's done about follow up. I'd read a couple of weeks ago it was actually all teed up for you to go home. What happened there?'

'Mmmmm…mum happened. Yeah, I was supposed to and then Goodley made a time to go see her and when he got there, she wasn't home. No surprise, bloody hopeless and she couldn't keep an appointment unless it's happening in the next five minutes. So, he gave her another chance first thing the next morning and when he got there she was pissed. It was nine-thirty so she was either still cut from the day before or had a liquid breakfast. You think she could've held it together for one day to get me out of this hell hole, but no, and that was the end of going home. Goodley said he'd look for somewhere else and blah, blah, bloody blah, and I haven't heard anything since. The dick can't even use a phone!'

'Yeah, got it, you're not happy with Mr Goodley. What about your dad, is he an option? Tell me a bit about your folks.' I know from Jai's file that he hasn't been around for a long time but I ask anyway. Maybe he has had recent contact. He flares up like a candle in a draft.

'He's been gone for years. I don't know where he is. Mum doesn't know either. If she does, she's never said. Up and pissed off when I was nine. A useless prick! The only good thing he ever did was give me an old guitar of his! He didn't even show me much!' I need to take the conversation down the music track where he seemed to be more comfortable.

'I've seen you tickle the strings a bit when I've been doing day shifts. Looks to me like you've got a bit of a gift for it.' He has indeed.

'Eh?… Oh, you mean playing the guitar. Yeah. I love it. I've heard you play at night too man. You know we all listen. Most of the guys like it. Helps you sleep. Me, I like to stay awake and listen for as long as I can.'

'Any tune in particular that rings your bell?' I ask.

'I love that *Shuffle Rag*, man, that the one, sounds so hard to play,' Jai responds immediately.

'Surprised you've even heard it. Yeah, it's what they call a 'finger buster, where the artist gets to show off, you know, strut their stuff. That will be challenge!' A connecting door opens a little. I'd go get the guitar and show him a thing or two, but the boy is supposed to be sick.

'You play such a good guitar I thought you must've had a lot of tuition. You certainly seem to know some complicated pieces. I think I could talk to thousands of people, even those in the music scene, and not many of them would know about Big Bill Broonzy's '*Shuffle Rag.*' I only know about him because my brothers went through a big blues phase and they had some of his records. As a catchy tune can do, that particular one got in my head like an earworm, I loved it from the moment I heard it. Who introduced you to it? It might know him, or I might have seen him around the traps' I enquire, genuinely curious.

'Dad didn't play *Shuffle Rag* but one of his mates did, a guy from the folk club. He came round home a few times for a jam. The old man couldn't keep up with that one.'

So this tune means something to Jai, it's important in more ways than one.

I have time, I'm not doing anything else important until the briefing…and I like this boy, he's got things going for him and I feel for him too. I've met plenty of musicians who were fickle fathers over the years. This is the first time I've ever talked to someone who's been on the other end of that fickleness.

What the hell, I'll get the guitar. It won't be plugged in so nobody will hear it…

Chapter 23
Jai Has a Musical Cure

He's up in bed, lying there with his head under the blankets, trying to keep the light out…and the world. He isn't sick, just sick of this hell hole and he couldn't be bothered getting up so he'd faked a cough. He'd been to court a couple of days ago and he was placed back in the Res because no one showed up at the hearing. He feels like he's rotting away. The time is starting to really drag. Yeah Sonny Terry had captured it so well in *Walking Blues* when he talked about how the minutes can go on so much that they feel like hours. And he was thinking that the days seemed like months and the months felt like years. It's depressing. FTW!

At first, when Wyatt came up he hadn't wanted to talk to anyone, including him. But he'd been sucked in a bit because Wyatt kept at him and he seemed genuinely interested in how he was feeling. He was the first person who'd spent time listening to him for ages. Wyatt wanted to talk to him about his parents. It made him angry because they were so useless. But Wyatt's got something Jai wants so he's got a good reason to play him along a bit.

Jai didn't like thinking about his father and he tried not to but now Wyatt has stirred things up he can't avoid it. He remembered vividly the night his old man left. Denny came into his bedroom and told him that he loved him and his brother, but he had to leave. He didn't say why and to this day Jai still doesn't know. He wanted to go too. He thought because they both loved music, it was their thing, but in the end, it wasn't the bond he thought it was. After that, he wrote his father off in his head.

He was nothing like his father. For a start, his dad is Pakeha, fair skinned, fine-featured with a small pointed nose and a narrow face. He's a tall man and skinny. Jai has a larger fatter nose and a round flat face more like his mother Mona. He has her shorter and stouter build as well. Mona had told him his old

164

man was sporty when he was young, played first fifteen rugby and did athletics, running and high jump. Jai is also quite sporty but he's sure this comes more to Mona who was a very good netball and basketball player, representing Canterbury in both before Jai was born. The other memory he has of his father is that he was away a lot doing long haul driving and if he wasn't doing that, he was away doing gigs. But when he was home, there was always plenty of music going down.

When Denny left, Jai thinks he blanked it all out for a long time, but now in the Res waiting, waiting, waiting, he hasn't been able to prevent his head from going there no matter how hard he tries, thinking about his folks, especially at night.

All he says to Wyatt is he flat out hates them both. He believes Denny left because his mother is hopeless. She isn't interested in anything, and she doesn't do anything except getting high. Denny was more of a goer, always playing music, entertaining or working…doing something!

Through a misty emotional fog that seems to have descended as he thinks back, he hears Wyatt say, 'That seems a bit harsh. It must've been hard on her when your father left.'

'Nah she doesn't care about me,' he dismisses the suggestion. 'She never came to anything at school or any of my sports. You'd think she'd at least have been interested in those. She can't even make it to Court. She's a loser and I can't be fucked with either of them!' He knows he sounds bitter but he can't hide it coming through in his voice.

He wants to make the point about his indifference to them, or theirs to him, he's not totally sure which. All he says about it is that from early on he stopped doing anything Mona asked him. She gave him the biff and then when he got too big for that she tried emotional blackmail, pestering and pleading, but it made no difference. Mona was more interested in having a succession of losers, hangers-on, dickhead, and pisshead 'boyfriends' than him. He put up with them for a while but in the end, he was happier just to go out on the streets and get away from it all. After that home became like a doss house, a place to keep his things and get a meal when he was really hungry and had no other means to get one.

'You've got a brother, right? Do you get on with him?' Jai thinks to himself, this guy sounds a bit like my social worker, always digging. 'I don't have much to do with him, we're different.' He's sure his mother always liked Dean more than him, mainly because he doesn't challenge her. Mostly he chases after her like a little slave. He looks much more like Denny too, fair-skinned and fine-featured. But the jokes on Mona though, because behind her back Dean gets up to all sorts of fun and games, he just doesn't get caught as often as Jai. On the few occasions he has been nabbed, he runs around like a headless chicken, doing his mother's bidding, bowing and scraping to shut her up, and it works.

The only meaningful thread left linking him to his father is music. Denny played in bands around Christchurch as a guitarist and a bass player. This was how his mom and dad met, out on the circuits where Mona was doing backup vocals for various bands. She and her sister Janice joined up with one of his dad's bands and they worked together for a couple of years, in Canterbury, down in the deep South, and across on the West Coast. Mona told him all the band stuff stopped when she was heavily pregnant with him. That's when they got married too. For a while, Denny kept on banding but Mona wasn't happy about it. She told Jai that he was 'sowing his seeds all about' so she made a fuss and he stopped touring. He continued to entertain though, becoming a regular at many of the local venues. Mona never went to see him and never went back to singing publicly but she still did a bit at home from time to time. Jai liked her singing. He wished she'd done more but like everything else, she didn't stick with it.

The first and last time he ever saw his old man play in public was when he was about seven or eight, Denny took him to the folk club which was having an afternoon session at the Gresham Hotel. The place was crowded and buzzing. Jai wandered around the pub while his father played his set. He had a glass of cola but it didn't last long so he helped himself to abandoned glasses that looked like cola. People clapped and cheered, his old man was a big hit. Jai was proud. But before he could say anything to him, Denny left the stage and disappeared for a while. When he finally turned up Jai was feeling pretty crook. He'd puked up under one of the tables and was being comforted by some random woman he didn't know. It turns out most of the glasses that looked like cola were Jim Beam or rum. It was his first taste of alcohol. He didn't like it. Now he knows it was also the first time he ever got pissed. Funny how things change he thinks to himself, love that rum and coke now! At any rate, his old man wasn't too pleased and dragged him home. He never took him to another gig.

Jai was enthralled with music from before he can remember. Denny played all sorts on his acoustic guitar when he was home. Jai remembers heaps of Bob Dylan and Leonard Cohen. He played hits off the radio too, the Eagles, the Rolling Stones, the Beatles and David Bowie's 'Sorrow.' Music was every day and everywhere. But the music Jai liked most was the blues. He loved the fingerpicking and the way the songs sounded like a band even though it was only his dad playing on his guitar. The bass walked along while the high strings played a melody. He made the guitar sound like a drum when he strummed it as well. Jai was fascinated from the moment he heard it. He wanted Denny to teach him how to play that way but he hadn't seemed very interested. 'You're just a kid, maybe when you're older!'

But Jai kept at him and eventually, Denny did give him his first lessons, showing him the basic chords C, F and G. 'These are the hardest. If you learn these then all the rest is easy.' Maybe he thought that would test Jai's resolve. He worked his fingers till they were so sore he couldn't hold the guitar but in the end, he got those chords down. That's right he remembers, he'd also shown Jai how to 'Boom Chick', pluck a bass string and strum the other strings. It sounded like Johnny Cash, so cool! He didn't say anything about any of that to Wyatt.

Jai's persistence and resolve must have stirred something in Denny because he let Jai have one of his old guitars, a handmade Yamaha with the guitar maker's signature scrawled in black ink in Japanese on the woodwork inside the soundhole. Jai cherished everything about that guitar, the way it looked, the matched woodwork front and back, the machine heads used for tuning, gold and engraved with an elaborate 'S.' He loved the feel of the neck which was worn and slick from years of Denny working it over. Above all, he loved the smell. It smelt of wood and varnish, of usage and history. It was a bit worn with a few dents and marks where it'd been hit or dropped and it had a bare patch where the varnish had been worn away from years of being strummed vigorously. Jai didn't care, all the better from having a history! He thinks it's the only thing he loves that linked him to his father. He tells Wyatt about his guitar, he knows he will be interested.

'So your old man did do something pretty significant for you then,' Wyatt interjects.

'It was a spare, so no cost to him.' No concession to be given there and putting a stop to that line of questions. Wyatt changes tack.

'So' he asks, 'from the bits I've heard, your playing seems to be pretty advanced, especially for a young guy. How'd that happen? Did someone else give you lessons?' Jai doesn't answer straight away. He hadn't ever been asked before and now he thought about it, he had taught himself mostly. When Denny took a hike he took most of his records with him however he left behind a few blues LPs, one by Jesse Fuller the one-man band, one by Sonny Terry and Brownie McGee, and one by Big Bill Broonzy. Jai played those records until the groves just about wore out. He learned how to 'hear' the music so he could pick up a lot of what was happening straight off the record, like what the musician was doing with his fingers at both ends of the guitar. He loved the sound of Big Bill best of all. The first song he learned was 'K*eys to the Highwa*y'. He played it until he could change the chords seamlessly.

'Once I learned that one it made Big Bills' other stuff easier to learn. Most of it is in the key of C and the style is the same. And at some point, later on, I got shown some fingering by one of my mother's loser boyfriends. A few of them were musos, she seemed to go for those types of guys. It was all this guy was good for!' He'd shown Jai how to 'claw hammer' and 'ripple pick', ways of picking all six guitar strings. The guy hadn't lasted long but by then Jai was musically experienced enough to remember things after seeing them once or twice. He practised, practised, practised and eventually his fingers did what he asked of them, almost instantly.

Thinking about music and how he came to play has shifted his mood, he can feel it. He's feeling better and his passion is warming his heart.

'You're good enough to start playing in front of other people. That sounds like the next step for you. What about at school? You know guitar players like to strut their stuff, show off what they can do, and playing to other people can help make you a better entertainer.'

'Nah, I don't like playing in front of people. I don't want to make mistakes, you know, it's embarrassing!'

'All guitarists make mistakes and most of the time the punters don't even know, and if they do, they don't care.' Wyatt seems genuinely encouraging.

Jai is adamant, he's different from his dad who lived for entertaining. He's only playing for himself, no one else. He doesn't need an audience.

'Opportunity being missed' Wyatt chides him. 'Playing the guitar gets the chicks, everybody knows that.' Jai doesn't bother to react but he thinks to himself, 'Not much chance of getting chicks when you're stuck in this hell hole, man.' Wyatt seems to appreciate not to chase the point further. Instead, he asks more questions about his musical education. Jai tells him how he spent plenty of time at a record store on High Street that had new and second-hand records and tapes. It has been so long since he's been there he'd forgotten how much he loved the record store. It always playing music loud and he was fascinated by the pictures and designs on the record covers and the posters on the walls. The guy who owned the place played and people would come by from time to time and jam. And there was Sedley Wells the musical instruments shop. He'd go there and try the guitars. At first, they'd shoo him off but after they realised he played and always showed respect for the instruments, they let him fiddle about and try out guitars. The guys there all played and they were happy to talk music with him if they weren't busy. The place was also a meeting place for musicians and he saw, heard and learned stuff from all of them just by watching. Turns out Wyatt knows it well, that's where he brought his favourite guitar.

All the while Jai was building up a tape collection for his Walkman, mainly by borrowing records from friends and making copies of the ones he liked. It's not something he mentions to Wyatt, but he nicked the odd tape from the music shop… only when he was desperate for something new to learn. He was careful though, he didn't want to get banned and the guys were good to him. Over time he accumulated about twenty different blues players, not a bad collection for a fifteen-year-old. Pity about the tapes though, they're long gone now, disappeared along with the Walkman during his time on the streets. Fortunately, he left the guitar at home and it's still there. He feels a touch of sadness. All this talk reminds him that he misses playing it.

He feels it's important to make the point. 'And I never think about my old man when I play it!'

'Really?' Wyatt sounds like he doesn't believe him.

When he first came to the Res, Jai played the guitar to fill in time because it was so boring, boring, boring. He'd picked up one of the funky guitars the staff generally kept in the office, tuned it up, and had a couple of goes on it. Even though he was very rusty, and had fingers that found it hard to move about, he was surprised he could still clearly remember and play bits from most of the tunes he'd learned. He didn't like playing in front of anyone but you couldn't avoid it in the Res because you were always with the group. The first time was just after lunch before a group meeting. He'd sat at the back of the lounge picking quietly. Before long a few of the boys came and sat around him to listen. He was embarrassed so he stopped but they put it on him to keep going. Jai didn't seek out attention, not just guitar-wise, but in all things. He didn't like this turn of events much, but he was blown away by the response. Even some of the guys he thought he'd never connect with seemed impressed. Yeah, he got some real respect from the boys.

Jai had been out in the open unit at Stanmore for a couple of days after his second admission when he'd heard one of the night staff guys playing the guitar after everyone settled down. The first night it was interesting but not very exciting, soft finger-picked stuff, country-sounding but a little bit blue too. He recognised the guy could play but nothing stood out. It was like many of the musos who came to his home. Still much better listening to music than the snoring and farting of his dorm mates.

It didn't take too many nights until he heard a tune that made the hairs on the back of his neck stand up, '*Shuffle Rag*'. He'd got up out of bed, tiptoed to the night staff office and stood outside the door to listen better. The music stopped after a couple of seconds and he heard the scrape of a chair. He ran back to bed before anyone discovered him. Since then, he'd done the same thing many times, being super careful and quiet. He was sure that if he listened more closely he would hear enough to learn how to play the tune. He lay in bed trying to memorise the phrases and envision how his hands would work playing them. Now, out of the blue, he's sitting on his sickbed talking with Wyatt about the tune he loves most.

Wyatt keeps talking and Jai's fully zoned in listening. 'So you're a Big Bill fan eh. My brother was a fan too. He taught me how to play *Trouble in Mind* and *Shuffle Rag*. He had several books with music tabs that showed how to pick complicated tunes. I never really had the patience to learn them note for note, like him, but I did pick up the way the tunes worked. Oh, and he did show me the bass run for that particular rag.'

Next thing you know he's back asking about Denny. 'Where did you say your old man plays?' He asks.

'I don't know what he does and he hasn't been around for so long I don't even know if he still plays, but he used to play at the Blues Club and the Musicians Club and some of the pubs too, and the Folk Club' replies Jai.

'I've done my time at the Blues Club and Folk Clubs. I've even played the Musicians Club, very exclusive and invitation only. Your old man must've been pretty good. What was your father's name?'

'Denny. Denny Jackson.'

'I've probably seen him but I don't remember the name but there were lots of people who played there. I don't recall them all. Plenty of them were good too. Quite a few played tunes by the old bluesmen, that's what I liked best. I always preferred the acoustic blues and ragtime players. Those solo players were very clever, made their guitars sound like a band. That's because they played dances so the band sound was what they were competing with, keeping things swinging. Broonzy, John Lee Hooker, Lightning Hopkins, Howlin Wolf, all those guys. Have you ever heard of Robert Johnson?' Jai shakes his head indicating he hasn't. 'He's sometimes considered the father of modern rock and roll. I don't know about that myself but he certainly was very influential. Lots of bands still play his music too, like the Rolling Stones, yeah...*Love in Vain*...a great tune. The one I remember most is called '*Hell Hound on my Trail*'. Mind-blowing stuff, not something that anyone could play but Johnson. It might resonate with you, especially how you're feeling at the moment, like no matter how much you run, you can't escape whatever's chasing you. Good to listen to and so full of feeling. I'll make you a tape with that one and a few other guys we've talked about!'

A good hour passes since they started chatting. Who'd have guessed that in all the places in the world, he would encounter a Broonzy fan in Stanmore? Not that he wasn't enjoying the chat, but finally Wyatt gets the black electric guitar, which has been left in the night staff office and starts going through the changes in *Shuffle Rag*. Jai's over the moon. What took you so long he thinks but says nothing.

They've only really got started when Sarge turns up looking for Wyatt, wanting to know why he's been away so long. He isn't impressed when he sees the guitar and asks Jai if he's faking his sickness. Wyatt intervenes, saying this is 'music therapy.'

Jai feels a bit brighter even though they've only got so far before being interrupted. It's already given him something to think about and practice. He agrees to come down for lunch. Maybe we'll get another chance to play today he is hoping as he gets dressed.

'Can we have a look after lunch' he asks Wyatt.

'Let's see how the time goes, but if not we'll find another time to get it done, just make sure you stick around.'

Always a staff member first Jai thinks, but he hears the message.

Chapter 24
Wyatt Sees the Future

In the end, there was no further music because I become involved in readmitting Hatch. On the day following his Court appearance, he scarpered from an outing at Taylor's Mistake beach. He lasted out in the world for three days before he was picked up by the police after attempting a burglary. Hatch is in a pretty sad state and has just been released from the hospital. The policemen who escorted him took great delight in filling us in on the details of how he was apprehended.

It seems that late last night Hatch spotted an open louvre window in a house in St Albans. It was small, fixed, and high up. After getting onto the sill, he got his head, upper torso and arms through when he lost purchase. This moved his weight forward a short distance, just enough so his waistband and belt became snagged on the edge of the window. He wriggled around frantically and managed to free himself but in doing so lost the only constraint preventing him from plunging forward. It turned out his chosen point of entry was the toilet. When he fell, he hit his face on the ceramic cistern, knocking out his two front teeth and stunning himself into the bargain. His ankle and foot became caught in the narrow edge of the open window preventing him from falling any further. The crash bought the occupants to the source of the noise. There they found Hatch, upside down, semi-conscious, his face in the toilet bowl. Fortunately for him, he was short enough that his head hadn't managed to reach the water or things could have been worse.

When the cops arrived they were highly amused, to say the least. Hatch was still upside down and stuck, although he had revived somewhat and was busy holding onto the bowl trying to keep his head up dropping down into the depths. The toilet area was covered in blood, not so much from the wounds to his mouth and teeth, but Hatch's spitting and cursing about being trapped. He spent a few hours in the hospital where his facial injuries were treated and he was monitored for concussion. They strapped up his ankle, wrenched when it prevented him from a worse, and more ignominious, fate. Those of us admitting him couldn't miss the gap in the middle of his face because he abused us all roundly and endlessly, displaying it in its full glory. The police insisted on staying to help with the admission but seemed more interested in having a bit of fun at Hatch's expense, taking every opportunity they could find to have a dig. 'The dummy in the dunny.'

'Don't they teach you anything in Stanmore? Use a brush to clean the toilet Hatch, not your head.'

'You got a look at your future.'

'That's what happens when you're always talking crap!' Hatch, true to form, managed to give some of it back, 'I was looking for your mother.'

'I was just trying to get back to Stanmore!'

'Should be you in here mate 'cause you've got shit for brains.' All in all, mildly amusing, but also, very sad.

After the fun and games of the admission, it was time to leave for the meeting at Kingslea. Abigail offered to take me. It's the first time I've spoken to her in-depth. She is one of only two women working as residential social workers at Stanmore, and she was the first. I've heard unsupportive talk from a few male colleagues. Their big issue seems to be a concern that she isn't able to handle herself in a physical confrontation with the bigger stronger boys. I don't get a sense it's personal, more a problem with having mixed-gender staffing working in any of the boy's homes.

Most of us don't like the physical stuff. Some actively seek to avoid it if at all possible. They find a reason to get off the floor if they sense it's about to blow, such as urgent photocopying, or they just need to get something from the office, or a 'must make' phone call. All men in my experience so far. Abigail has worked at Stanmore for a while so there must have been times when she needed to be a part of a restraint. I might ask her about it if the opportunity presents itself.

As soon as I sit in the car she engages me. She's interested in what brought me to the night staff role. I tell her my story briefly. I'm more interested in her.

She's the only girl, and the youngest, in a family with four brothers. All her brothers went into private businesses. That wasn't for her, instead, she earned a degree in the social sciences. She worked in the community as a social worker

173

before coming to the Residence. That is a bit unusual as most often working in the Residence is a stepping stone to getting out into the field.

Abigail's very personable and chats away freely. I ask her why she chose Stanmore. 'My brothers were pretty easy to manage, even the two oldest ones, so I couldn't see why I shouldn't work here. Men, boys, they are all the same,' she says with a laugh. 'When the powers that be refused to let me, well that just made me more determined,' she adds.

'But,' I have to ask, 'aren't you a bit worried about these boys, some are pretty tough.'

'Well, I wanted to work with the boys. I went to work at Kingslea with the girls because it was the only residential option available to me at the time, but I kept applying to come here and eventually they relented…and so they should have! They put in a new manager a couple of years ago, he's very progressive and wants to try things. I'm sure not everyone is happy about it though. As far as I'm concerned I'd rather work with the boys any day. It's more straightforward. If there's a problem you see it or you hear about it. It flares up then it's usually all over. With the girls, I found they tended to be more underhanded and secretive. And they can be pretty awful to each other. So yes, I wanted to come and work at Stanmore. Jean joined later. It's good to have another woman to share the experience with.'

I can't help it, I put it out there. 'What about the physical stuff, aren't you worried about that?'

'Oh, that old chestnut, well the answer is 'yes', I don't like the physical interactions. Do you?'

'No, but if 'needs must', then I get involved, it's part of the role,' I reply.

'When I was growing up my brothers didn't give an inch because I was a girl! And that included a bit of rough and tumble. But more importantly, I'm confident in my ability to stop things from escalating, and if they do, to resolve things without having to use physical force. It's hard to measure how effective my approach is but if the number of physical confrontations a person gets involved with is any form of measure, then I have very few. And I still manage to get boys to do as they are asked!'

She goes on to say how, in her view, some of the staff are not the best role models for the boys because they are too quick to get physical. She calls it the 'bull's roar', a macho thing. 'It sends the wrong message to the boys, that 'might it right'. Frankly, I don't like to see physical interventions used as often as they

174

are! Partly that's a problem because of who has been recruited over the years and why. And there's no real training. The staff I admire the most are those who have other ways of dealing with physical aggression. I feel pretty strongly about this as you can hear in my voice. Most of the boys we deal with are damaged and have experienced physical violence. They only know one way of responding to problems, violence, and frankly, they don't care particularly what the outcome is. They're used to it. It's a 'dog eat dog' world they live in, better to stand, fight and be beaten. More than anything they don't want to lose face. They don't when they're dealing with a woman, being physical is more likely to be seen as weak. There are exceptions and she has had to get involved, and she admits when she has it's been a bit 'messy', but no worse than other restraints she's witnessed. 'Mostly I get plenty of lip about being a woman and not worth hitting, but it just creates an opportunity as far as I am concerned and I try to use it.'

Then she says something that I hadn't remotely considered as an issue, 'My biggest problem is when I get into a potentially threatening situation one of the male staff steps in and takes over. It reinforces the message in the boy's mind that I can't cope, or that women need rescuing'. One of the other things that rankles is she gets assigned the jobs like managing the younger boys in the domestic or homelike roles such as the kitchen or looking after them at school. It's rare for her to go on a 'compensatory' experience like the trip to the Waimak.

'It just reinforces all the old stereotypes about women and their roles. It annoys the hell out of me! I have tried to address it. I get lots of nods of acknowledgement when I raise it in meetings, but then the next day the same old same old.'

'What can you do about it? If it were me, I'd probably have left by now' I tell her.

'No way, I came to Stanmore because I wanted to. I think that women have a lot to offer in the environment and I'm going to work to see a change, including bringing more women onto the floor. It takes a team to deal with these kids and a variety of skills, some of which women demonstrate more effectively than men. And I think the place would be safer if there were more women on the floor. That's what I want to see! The sooner the better!'

Whew, opened a floodgate there and the passion has poured forth. Good points though. I sit in silence for a moment or two, processing and not knowing where to go next. Then Abigail says, 'Sorry, I get fired up about this stuff…but you did ask.'

'I did indeed,' I say. I'd heard the negative comments from my night staff colleagues and I hadn't challenged them. I wonder in the ensuing silence how it would work on nights with a female colleague. If Abigail has her way it is probably on the cards at some point in the future. My thoughts are interrupted.

'Here we are, Kingslea. We're off to the Marae. Have you been on a Marae before?'

'Yeh, back when I was an adolescent. Always happy to do so as long as I'm not asked to speak.'

'That's highly unlikely,' she says with a smile, 'we'll be filling the back rows.'

After the formal greetings and welcome, the subsequent meeting is an hour and a half long. It focuses on pending changes to welfare legislation and the subsequent impact on the way kids will be managed. The amalgamation of Stanmore and Kingslea onto one site is confirmed. The boy's programme will be smaller. Boys and girls in residence for care reasons rather than offending will be housed together in separate smaller units. The 'suits' from National Office make the changes sound pretty revolutionary. I find it interesting for the first hour. Eventually, because the seats are as hard as church pews, my butt goes numb and I begin jiggling around, distracted. Some of the legislative changes whistle over my head. The key message I want to hear is confirmation I still have a job. Once this happens, I'm a happy camper.

In the car riding back, Abigail asks me how I found it all. 'Hard on the brain, harder on the butt, but I'm still employed. What about you?'.

'Time will tell!' is all she offers.

Part 4
Still Learning

Chapter 25
Almost an Old Hand

The newness of the job is gone. It's taken six months. I'm at the point where very little surprises me anymore. I wouldn't say I've become immune to feelings about what I see, just that I'm somewhat 'blunted' to the harshness of it all, the tragic stories, the stuffed up lives, the appalling way some people treat others, especially in families. I think it's a survival mechanism.

Because I am now less distracted with the stories, some of what Ted referred to on my first night as my 'lefty' type attitudes are starting to emerge. There are plenty of examples but we can start with my questioning and consequent cynicism about why there are so many recording requirements. Mostly it seems to be because someone wants the information, the Minister, the Chief Executive or the General Manager, the Regional Manager, or the site manager, and they want it 'now!' Each time there's a new request that leads to a change in practice or policy, it's added to an ever-accumulating heap. Nothing is ever taken off. Even for the humble night staffer, it seems to be as much about keeping the system safe as the kids.

There's a significant disconnect between the Head Office policy wonks and the front-line workers. The H.O. guys don't trust the front-line guys to do the job properly, and the front-line guys don't trust the H.O. guys to know enough about the job to create practical, useful and informed guidance. The relationship is symbiotic, they need each other and they resent it.

My current sense of the way the 'Welfare System' responds to working with difficult kids can be summed up as low interest, low engagement, and low investment. However from what I see I don't think it is actually 'low cost' because these boys 'cost' the system plenty one way or the other.

In every way you consider the term 'dump' it applies to Stanmore. It's a tired building, not fit for purpose, filled with society's cast-offs, too difficult to contain anywhere else. The Courts and the Police seem to regard the residence as a 'custodial' holding pen and nothing else. And people I know on the outside, while interested in hearing about the residence, don't have much time for the kids, blaming them as 'bad apples'. Most of what they know comes from The Press, from which never a positive story about the kids or the work ensues. Shut the door and leave us all to it. Out of sight out of mind. The only time anyone is interested is when something bad happens.

Putting the many things I can't control aside, there's still plenty in the job to tip the satisfaction balance in a positive direction. I like most of the boys I've met so far, and those I have connected with, even more so. Most of the time they seem just like any kids you'd see in a boarding school. Sure, not all of them all of the time, or they wouldn't be here. But it feels like when the good stuff happens it's uplifting and when the bad stuff happens, it's really bad, with not much in between. I like the challenge, more so when working on days, although nights have their moments.

For whatever reason, some kids just don't like you. Maybe you remind them of someone or you're just not their type, or they see you as 'The System'. However, most boys in residence find someone to connect with even if it's not you. It's only a small number, boys like Bentley and Chevy, who don't connect with anyone and don't seem to be capable of it.

I like to think I'm personable and that I have this in my tool kit along with music and sports, my major 'ins' with the boys, but I'm realistic, it's helpful but not enough. I try to keep away from having favourites and treat all with empathy, clinical fairness and evenness. It can be hard though because some boys you just like. Jai is one for me. One thing I've recognised in myself is that the boys I am drawn to are the ones for whom I feel there is hope. I know we should feel hope for them all, but some make it very hard.

In the real world, I'm a night staffer, a domestic worker, not a trained social worker. Even so, I have also worked out that little things can make a difference. A word here, a gesture there, the right challenge made in the right way at the right time. You need those skills at night. It's not rocket science.

Things are different at home now as well. Adapting our lives to the 'graveyard shift' has proved to be a challenge for the whole family. I'm seeing less of Rose as we are both working. On the bright side, our economic circumstances are improving. My job doesn't pay a lot but the penal rates are good, very good, increasing the total value of the job. I see more of my children now as I'm around more often before and after school. However, I'm only around for one of three weekends to watch my kids' sports and it means Rose has to look after the children on her own at those times. Weekends are a nightmare sleep-wise. Even getting a basic few hours is challenging with kids being kids. And your social life, not just yours but your partners too, is nearly obliterated. But it's where the big penal loading is, so pain for gain.

Getting enough sleep is tough on any given day. I am lucky if I get more than four or five hours whether I am working or not. Despite how hard I try to catch up, it just doesn't happen. Although I haven't had a substantial leave period yet, I wonder how being off for a couple of weeks might muck up my sleep patterns during my holiday and subsequently, when I return to work.

I'm beginning to notice the physiological impacts of night work. It's not just on my body clock, it feels like I'm only operating at eighty per cent capacity. I have less energy than before, and I'm finding it harder to concentrate. I don't eat as much as I used to either. I skip breakfast because I'm often like a walking zombie in the morning after a shift. I fall asleep on the couch waiting to drop off my youngest at creche. Then it's a fitful sleep for as long as is possible, but often it's only through to lunchtime. I eat tea with the family but I don't eat during the night. Despite being on the job now for months I haven't gotten used to the smell of the kitchen. Most of the time I give the meal left for me to one of my colleagues who don't suffer my aversion, or I give it to a boy being admitted at night if it's still available, generally consumed with gusto.

In my role, there are two things that I fear most of all. The first is the prospect that someone dies on your watch, either by their own hand or at the hands of others. The second is a full-blown riot. At night the risk is exacerbated as there are fewer readily available resources on site or in the community to help manage the situation.

Suicide risk is always lurking in the dark recesses of residential life. It's not surprising given the nature of the clients. Keeping the boys under constant supervision, that is together as a group as much as possible, is the way it's normally mitigated. But sometimes it requires more, highlighted when a boy says or does something that causes concern, or a medical professional raises the risk. A staff member is designated to 'special' the boy in the group by tracking them closely one to one. Where there's an acute risk, the boy may be placed in SNU, where managing him can involve using suicide prevention garments and blankets. There is frequent periodic checking, and occasionally there needs to be full-time observation. While it is not a constant problem with the boys in residence, it is there under the surface as both Ted and Mr Rogers know of ex-residents who have committed suicide. Abigail tells me that self-harm of all forms is far more prevalent amongst girls at Kingslea.

To date, I've been involved with one serious attempt to cause self-harm. It occurred in the SNU. I found a boy bleeding and stretched out on the cell floor during one of my routine checks. He was newly admitted from Court and identified at changeover as being very agitated. I called Ted who came down and stayed with him while I contacted the senior, who in turn rang the emergency services. When the stunned boy was sufficiently revived, we sat him down on his bed. We talked to him but he was somewhat incoherent. All of a sudden before we had any appreciation of what was happening, he jumped up and ran into the block wall with his head down. It was a shock to witness. We picked him up and tried to get through to him that support was on the way but he was either unable or unwilling to listen. He looked like he was about to have another go so Ted sat on him until the psych services arrived thirty minutes later. Interestingly, he didn't struggle at all, although admittedly it wouldn't have been easy, he seemed to be ok with being restrained. Ultimately, he was taken away to the Adolescent Mental Health Unit. He absconded from it two days later and was found and returned to us. The staff at the clinic stated, 'He won't stay put so there's nothing we can do with him.' And we can? Go figure!

Overall, the likelihood of a successful suicide attempt is very low, but the consequences if it were to happen... stratospheric. The boy's family would be impacted foremost, and it would deeply affect the staff charged with keeping him safe. Those things go pretty much without saying however Ted and Mr Rogers tell me it would have a far broader impact as well. There would be inevitable systemic fallout including internal investigations by senior clinical staff, with subsequent reviews of procedures and practices. A police investigation would be triggered. Politicians would be asking questions in the Parliament. Later in the process, the matter would go before the Coroners Court. To go through the whole process would take several years. Then there are the media, adding their bit every step of the way.

The second risk is the riot. I learned early on that the word 'riot' does not actually exist in our vocabulary. 'Riot' implies the situation is out of control however the term 'collective disturbance' which we are encouraged to use, creates an impression there is some 'often unspecified' degree of control still in play. Regardless of the permissible descriptor, the 'collective disturbance' is a high-risk event in both likelihood and consequences. From what I have been told there are always many variables at play when one occurs. Who's instigating the event and why, what happened on the previous shift or recent shifts, how the boys react to the team that's going off or coming on, who's in the residence at the time, the KPs, gang tensions, to name but a few of the most important. Even the weather can be a factor. For example, on hot days kids find it harder to settle. When it's cold they hunker down, but if they're inside for too long because it's wet, like us all, they can go a little stir crazy. Most significant though, once started a 'collective disturbance' takes on a life of its own.

Tonight John Land collars me as I pass his office doing my pre-shift checks. Ordinarily, he's nowhere to be seen this late in the evening. He says he needs to let me know about an undercurrent his team sensed with the residents today. The team hasn't been able to put their finger on what the issues are, but something's percolating away. I ask him, 'What do you think the level of risk is?'

'Maybe two and a half out of ten. The team are working the floor pretty hard so we'll have the place settled in no time.'

I cut short my checks and head on upstairs. As I walk up to the office the door is open and the team is out in the dorms. Young people are running all over the place. I'm already thinking risk three and a half out of ten.

I dump my bag, lock the door and go out into the dorms starting in Rimu. Gwynne passes me heading the other way. 'A bit rumpty tonight but not to worry! Most are settled, it's just one or two taking a bit of time. Leave it in your capable hands!' And then he's gone. I'd heard Abigail's voice in Rata as I came up the stairs but I assume she's going too. Possibly Sarge is around but I don't know. So...I have no known colleague on deck yet and the boys are still obviously agitated. The risk now is around five.

It takes no time to see the source of the disruption, Bentley, up to his usual tricks, wandering around stirring boys up by pushing or shoving or just getting in their face. I find him in one of the cubicles play-fighting and tickling Danny Taylor.

Danny is slow intellectually, not to the same level as Chevy or Bentley, but still sufficient to be alerted on his file. It's his first time in and he's been here now for a couple of days. He's fourteen years old but small in height and weight for his age. He has spikey blond hair and his skin is so fair it's translucent. It's very rare for anyone to wear their own pyjamas while here but Danny does, and they're covered in little pictures of dinosaurs. Oh man, I think to myself, why not put a target on his back! At yesterday's changeover, Sarge indicated he comes from a 'well to do' family. He arrived with a suitcase full of designer clothes which made him stand out. Many of the boys arrive with little or nothing other than the clothes they are standing in. He's already been pressured to part with a few items. In some ways, it's fortunate that he's small so his gear won't fit most boys or probably all of it would be gone. He's here because it's alleged he inappropriately touched his younger sister. According to the day staff, his social worker didn't like boys who 'fiddled' with little girls and hadn't looked very hard for an alternative placement. He's a fish out of water, and is being 'specialed'. Unsurprisingly no 'specials' assigned for the nights though!

'Cut it out Bentley, back to your bed,' I'm sharp in tone and clear in my direction.

Bentley looks at me, or more accurately, through me. Oh dear, he has that all too familiar look in his eyes, no one home! More disturbingly I can see from the swell in his pyjama pants, that he's aroused. Risk level now seven.

Bentley laughs. Then he runs off towards Kauri, me following. As I exit Rimu I hear the boom of Sarge's voice. Thank god, at least we still have Sarge on deck. The risk diminishes a little.

'Bentley, what the hell are you doing down here, get back to your dorm.' He bellows.

On rounding the corner of the corridor, I see Sarge down at the far end of the hall.

'He went in there' he points, indicating the second bedroom on the right. On entering I see young Dawson James in bed. Bentley is hiding behind the door. I need to nip this in the bud or it will be a long, long night. He jumps on top of Dawson and then he bounces off. He reminds me of a puppy bounding about the place, though more your Great Dane than one of Mr Rogers' chihuahuas. He heals for a moment like he will follow me but then he's off again with me in pursuit. Sarge steps out of the room he is in. We have him boxed in. The threat of placing him in SNU stops him in his tracks.

However, once back in Rata he leaps about the room shouting that the staff are threatening to take him to SNU for going to the toilet. The other boys are none too pleased and tell him to shut up. Eventually, he gets into his bed but continues to be lippy, muttering under his breath.

Sometimes ignoring the behaviour works with Bentley. Take away the audience and the performance stops. I head back to the office. By this time my colleague Mr Rogers has arrived and Sarge has come into the office to do the changeover. Mr Rogers is straight onto it. 'These ratbags are not settled. What're you going to do about it?'

We all know he's right in theory but in practice tonight is not too different from many others.

'In your hands,' laughs Sarge indicating his are now empty by holding them up Pontius Pilate style, fobbing Mr Rogers off and walking out the door.

Mr Rogers tonight, risk back up to seven.

It's less than ten minutes before Bentley is up and at it again. I bump into him outside the toilets, he must have slipped past the night staff office on the way.

'Just going to the toilet sir,' he says with a smirk.

'You got a bladder problem?' I ask with more irony than sympathy and knowing it will whistle right over his head. 'Maybe we need to get you looked at by the doctor, see what's going on!'

'No need' replies Bentley, 'I just need to drink less tea before bedtime.' A sharper reply than I would have expected from him. Sometimes he surprises me.

Two minutes later he's up again. This time he stays in his dorm but he is jumping on Joe Harris's bed. Mr Rogers attends to him this time, hauling Bentley off Joe physically and shoving him back towards his bed.

'That's assault!' shouts Bentley in faux indignation, 'You can get done for that!'

'Not likely buddy. You're a ratbag who was assaulting Joe and I'm protecting him.' Mr Rogers snaps. It's apparent he's already had enough of the behaviour.

Bentley is agitated although not overly aggressive … more hyped up. He returns to his bed. Mr Rogers comes back into the office and says with a sigh of resignation. 'Nobody home at Bentley's place, looks like we're in for a night of it.' He has barely closed his mouth and there is a flash of movement past the office doorway. My turn to follow up. Bentley's back in Rimu and he's jumped onto Danny's bed again. Danny curses, 'Get off! You fucker.'

Bentley is laughing hysterically, loud and disturbing everyone. He jumps off the bed and runs off towards Kauri before I can get in his way to prevent it. I follow, he is back in Dawson's room, chanting 'Mr Rogers is an arsehole and he is trying to put me in secure!'

I, too, am fed up with the nonsense. I sense movement from the dorms as the boys inevitably react. As he passes he bumps me, not hard but knocking me off balance. He's quick and I'm a little behind. He's back to Rata going from young person to young person proclaiming that the staff are trying to assault him, especially Mr Rogers, who wants to get him down to secure, "You know what for..." He's woken Jarrod McLelland and he is not a very happy camper. He shoves Bentley forcefully and threatens him. Several other boys are already out of bed.

Risk level eight.

'Settle down guys,' I'm now just being hopeful, but before I finish Bentley's off again. This time I stay in Rata hoping to get an increasing number of agitated boys to quieten down and back into their beds. As I do so I hear Mr Rogers saying loudly above the now intensifying hubbub 'Blah blah blah SNU.' Bentley's now completely out of control, 'That KF, he wants to put me in SNU for going to the toilet. Let's show him.' There is a loud bang.

I exit Rata having failed to settle the boys. When I get to Rimu I see Jai's bed has been tipped up. It looks like all the boys are awake. Jai is lying on the floor. He picks himself up and before either Mr Rogers or I can do anything he launches himself at Bentley, hitting him in the stomach and sending him sprawling onto Hatch's bed. Meanwhile there's an increasing cacophony coming from Rata. I need to get to Kauri to make sure the younger guys are safe. If we keep them settled, we may still be able to contain a burgeoning problem. I check, there is no sign of anyone in the hall and the bedroom doors are all shut.

In Rimu we now have a significant problem. All the boys are out of bed and milling about. Several are throwing bedding and pillows. One is swinging on a wardrobe door. I can't see Bentley anywhere. Then I hear him in Rata encouraging the kids to get up saying there's a riot.

It's bedlam. I join Mr Rogers who has already retreated to the office.

'I need to ring the senior,' he shouts over the din, then mutters a barely audible 'For what it's worth'.

At that moment I realise the lunacy of having to ring someone for permission to do anything during a crisis. It's the policy though, most likely brought in as a reaction to something that happened in the past. This isn't a slow burn or escalating incident, it's full-blown. We need immediate and practical help.

Mr Rogers is on the line, he holds the phone out, I can't hear the ringing over the noise but he points at it and then at his head, indicating no sense or no response. He almost misses the pickup when it happens.

'John Rogers here, we've got a riot…uh…collective disturbance… going on,' he shouts without ceremony, raising his eyebrows and nodding at me.

'What? What!' … he pauses and puts his hand over the mouthpiece, incredulous, he says

'He's just gone outside to see what he can see from his place,. Can you believe it? It's Wayne North tonight. He lives just down the road…can see the place from there apparently, but this is madness and typical. We need action…right now… and the 'on call' is doing a long-distance scan. God help us!'

We wait. The noise level is now just short of an Lancaster Park test match crowd. Boys are running back and forward past the office door so frequently they're a blur.

We hover over the phone earpiece waiting for the response. No point in rushing out into the fray; it's way beyond anything we can manage now. Then the senior is back, his voice is faint but I can just make it out.

'Hello, are you there?' I can't see anything from here and I can't hear anything either. What sort of problem are we talking about, a few kids running around or what?'

'All the kids are out of bed and running amuck. Bentley's the prime instigator who's stirring them up. Someone is going to get hurt. I need to call the Police now!' Mr Rogers shouts into the phone. 'God almighty, can't you hear the racket over the phone?'

It appears the reply Mr Rogers receives is not what he hoped for. The next thing I hear him say 'Fuck you, I'm calling the Police before someone gets hurt.' He hangs up, slamming the phone down with such force that the receiver jumps back into his hand.

'He says if it's just Bentley, he'll probably settle down, he usually does, just give it a bit of time, if not, put him in SNU! No permission to call the cops but I'm doing it anyway.' He starts dialling but he's only managed the first digit when the whole building is filled with the deafening sound of the fire alarm going off.

Risk level ten has arrived.

'I bet you that fuckwit can hear that, half of bloody Christchurch will!' Mr Rogers' sneer smiles.

'No need to call the Police, they're automatically alerted by the alarm. So's the Fire Service. We need to get the kids out. Head to Kauri and start herding them towards the stairwell.' Mr Rogers is taking charge and I defer to him. He's surprisingly calm and confident. He appears more annoyed that his nightly routine has been disrupted, rather than the risk to life or limb. I know the evacuation procedure so I get on with it.

I go through the dorms. 'Everybody out, go to the stairwell, don't take anything, just move it.' This was not the first time this has happened in the life of the residence and some old hands know exactly what to do.

I get everyone down the stairs and Mr Rogers lets them through to the dining room. Before he opens the final door to the exterior yard, he stops.

'Headcount, let's make sure we've got everyone.' He starts numbering off. In a few seconds, he puts his hand up so it shields his mouth and he whispers to me, 'One short, must still be upstairs. Can you go back and check?'

I rush upstairs and check the dorms. No sign of anyone. That leaves the ablutions blocks. No one in the toilets. I go into the shower room calling out over the ongoing alarm, 'Evacuation! Evacuation!' The first cubicle door is partially open allowing me to see it's empty. I push the second, it doesn't move. Locked. It shouldn't be. I kneel and peer through the gap underneath the door. I can't see anything. I give the door an almighty heave but it doesn't budge. I step back and kick it hard right on the handle, once, twice. It gives with a crack and slams back against the cubicle wall. Danny is hanging from the shower fitting by a thick brown belt. His face is purple. One of his legs is spasming. I leap in and grab him around the waist, lifting him as I do so. The belt is snagged and I try manoeuvring him to get it free. It doesn't work. Although he's not a big lad, he is still a heavy dead weight. I'm beginning to feel panicky now, desperate to get him free. I jig him up and down frantically and unceremoniously hoping the belt will dislodge. All of a sudden it does. We fall backwards out of the shower and onto the linoleum floor. With fumbling hands, I loosen the still taught belt from around his neck. With a loud gasp, he sucks in air. Instant relief all around! I'm sucking in air too and my heart is racing from the physical exertion. It takes a few seconds and a lot of deep breaths to recover sufficiently so I can speak.

'Come on Danny, we have to get out of here right now.'

Danny looks up at me, he has a nasty red slash mark on his neck. His face is beginning to regain its pale colour although his breathing is still raspy. He manages to mumble.

'I'm sorry… I set off the alarm… there's no fire.'

'Doesn't matter whether there is or not, the alarm goes off and we have to evacuate. Come on, let's go!'

He gets to his feet. He's still very shaky. So am I, the adrenaline is running rampant. I put my arm on his back to both direct and support him as we walk to the stairwell. I say to him above the pulsing screech of the fire alarm.

'I will have to tell someone what happened, you know that don't you.'

'Yes,' he says although he is barely audible. He has his head down but he seems to be recovering.

When we get to the dining area the others are gone. I presume they're in the gymnasium, the designated emergency assembly area.

As we exit the main building I hear noise from the gym and see the bright light coming through the open door. Danny and I go in. Boys are milling about although they are away from the entrance. Mr Rogers comes up to me.

'What were you doing? Evacuate means evacuate, not muck around. I see you found the missing body. Good, I'll do another count but I know Bentley's gone, took off when I opened the door. Good riddance! But apart from him, I think the rest are all here. Danny, over by the wall!' he points to the back of the gym.' Danny moves off.

Mr Rogers is business-like, 'another-day-at-the-office' sort of thing. I'm starting to calm down but there's still plenty going on. I take an opportunity to say in his ear. 'I found Danny hanging by his belt in the shower. He looked like he'd stopped breathing, his face had gone blue. Good thing you spotted that someone was missing when you did! … I let out a sigh releasing my tension.

'The power of the headcount. Dodged a bullet there!' he replies from behind his hand although there is no need because the boys are metres away and it would be hard for them to hear anything over the ongoing alarm. 'We've never had anyone kill themselves in residence and I would hate for it to be on my watch.' Probably meant with the right intentions. Then he says 'He's safely back in the group now so we can keep an eye on him until we decide what to do after all this nonsense is over.'

'Danny confessed to setting off the alarm so there is no fire.' I inform him.

'There normally isn't! Doesn't matter who did what at the moment, we're here until given a clearance by the Fire Service boys. We can talk to him later and find out what that's all about.' And then almost as an afterthought, he says pointing at the open gym door, 'Stand over there so no one can leave. I'll do another headcount. I expect the Fire Service and the Police will be here any minute.' He didn't seem either particularly surprised or troubled by what Danny had done.

Risk level now, about three and a half.

I'm feeling discombobulated about everything that has happened but at the moment I don't have time to make sense of it. I have a job to do and I need to get my focus where it belongs for now. I go to the door and watch Mr Rogers do his count. There is plenty of comment from the boys who seem to fall into two camps, those entertained or those agitated by the evening's events.

Mr Rogers is getting his fair share of lip, some boys are reminding him of his lack of pedigree for waking them up. Jarrod proclaims loudly, 'There is no 'f'…ing fire and we want to go back to bed and what the 'F' are we waiting for?'

Mr Rogers replies with the sweetest of smiles, 'The 'F' we are waiting for Jarrod is the F…F…Fire Service. Now pull your head in will you!'

A couple of boys are shouting abuse at each other and fronting up as if they might get into fisty cuffs. Risk is re-escalating again to about four and a half. This remains a very volatile group. If they decide to do anything they want on mass, run, fight, whatever, there'll be next to nothing we can do.

Then I hear the sirens, volume increasing as they come. Within a minute the flash of red light fills the doorway, magnified by reflections off the buildings around the gym. Mr Rogers strides across to the door saying, 'Wait here. I'll meet the firemen' as he steps out.

The next moment about a dozen kids rush to the door. They just seem curious and stop without going outside. I guess a man in a fire suit will always hold an attraction for some boys so I don't blame them. A couple of the firemen come to the door of the gym. They seem to be pretty relaxed.

'Been a while since we've been here, at least a couple of months,' says one. 'Used to be something that happened every week. The lads will come back and see you once they have given 'all clear'. There isn't a fire, we know that, but we still need to check officially.' He briefly pauses then adds as an afterthought, 'To be frank, if this place did have a fire it would probably burn down by the time we got here. These old buildings are bone dry wood, they're an absolute fire disaster waiting to happen. The sprinklers you got here won't make much difference, just delay the inevitable. This place is underdone for everything fire safety-wise. We've told your boss. Lucky it's a false alarm. Mind you, we'll be charging you the cost of a call out I'm afraid, them's the rules.'

While he's talking two Police officers appear at the door, one with a dog. The boys retreat to the end of the gym. Their agitation and boisterousness diminish slightly.

'Been having a bit of fun', jokes the taller of the two, a solid middle-aged Māori guy. His bald hatless head shines in the bright lights of the gym.

'Not really,' I reply, not feeling the levity of the situation in any way. 'We've lost one, Bentley Breezer. He took the opportunity to do a runner. He probably instigated the trouble so he could, who knows at this point, but he's gone. And we have had one try and kill himself. There's a bit of damage upstairs. Apart from that…business as usual.' I present like the situation is under control although it's bravado, given I am surrounded by flashing lights, police and firemen.

'Not to worry, once we get the clearance we'll help you get the little sods settled. I haven't seen you before, are you new?'

'Yes, newish, this is my first experience of a collective disturbance.'

'You mean riot, don't you? You social workers… you'd call a spade a gardening apparatus for undertaking digging!' He laughs.

'I think we'll appreciate the help.' I ignore the jibe.

The policeman just nods. 'I'll just go and call in about Breezer. We know him well! It shouldn't take long to pick him up. He's not too sharp, always runs to one of three places, the girlfriend, his mother or the Square.' He leaves to report. His colleague, the dog handler remains silent, watching. The dog is showing considerable interest in the boys, his head is bobbing from side to side responding to voices and movements. The boys, in return, are showing considerable wariness towards the dog.

'How come you brought the dog,' I inquire since to me this does not seem like a situation requiring a canine intervention.

'I'm normally in town somewhere unless on a specific job, so yeah, in the area and first responder, just came when the call went out.' He replies without taking his eyes off the boys. 'Doesn't do any harm. Butch's good for crowd control and he'll certainly quieten this lot down pronto.'

On-call senior Wayne North arrives. It must have been the flashing lights and sirens that brought him. Or maybe it was the screaming alarm!

It takes about fifteen minutes but eventually the Fire Service give the official clearance. They pack up and in short order they are gone. Mr Rogers and I move everyone back upstairs. The damage is mainly superficial, with ripped bedding, the odd hole in the wall, and a few books that are now minus their pages. There are a few broken bits of wood from the partitions, a door frame has been splintered, a broken bed leg, and a bedroom door in Kauri is off its hinges. I finally appreciate why there are no doors in Rata and Rimu. With the support of the Police, we get the boys to clean up enough so they can get to bed, ensuring nothing remotely representing a potential weapon is left anywhere it could be used now or stashed for the future. The debris is put downstairs in the dining area for the morning shift team to dispense with.

Wayne comes over to me and I fill him in about Danny. We all agree that for his safety, he'll be moved to SNU for the rest of the night and watched closely. Wayne indicates he'll ring the Crisis Prevention Team, and see if someone will come out tonight.

I am designated to take him down, put him in the suicide gown and get him into a cell. He's subdued and shows no resistance going through the admission process. I replace his bedding with off white aged, suicide prevention blankets, thick and untearable, while he is showering. I take him into the SNU office before I lock him and make a cup of tea while we wait to see what is happening with the Crisis Prevention Team.

It's been a very traumatic event. Wayne had mentioned that maybe I could talk to Danny and find out what's going on. I'm dubious, the only rapport I have with him is based on being the one who pulled him down. Wayne hopes this will be sufficient to help me build a communication bridge. He suspects his behaviour was a cry for help, not a genuine suicide attempt. I am not so sure, that purple face with bulging eyes looked very real to me.

'That was a near thing, Danny. You had me worried for a minute. Lucky I came back when I did. What's happening? Is there something I can do?'

No problem getting him to talk, he blurts out straight away 'I didn't want to run with Bentley. He's been on at me all day. I don't like him but he won't leave me alone.' He has his head down but I can see from the rise and fall of his shoulders, that he's crying.

'Why didn't you just say something to one of the staff?' I ask.

'I'm not a nark' he replies without hesitation.

'Yeah I get that, but it's not about narking. You should have approached one of the staff you trust, who could deal with Bentley without letting on too much where the information came from?' I push the point because it's the sort of thing that could well happen again.

'You don't get it, do you? He's not all there. If he thought I'd narked on him, even a sniff of it, he'd kill me.' He looks up. His tear-stained face shows genuine fear. 'He killed someone already, everyone knows that.'

'Who says so? He'd be locked up if it was true. You just can't get away with killing someone, it's all talk' I say trying to minimise the fear. I know where this impression comes from. I recall there was an incident in Bentley's file involving a nasty assault outside a bar in Rangiora where he'd beaten and stomped on the head of an older guy he got into a confrontation with. Fortunately two other boys he was with restrained him or it might have turned out to be worse. No one died though, but the guy was seriously hurt. Bentley wasn't charged. A file note mentioned he was allegedly attacked first, outnumbered, and also only fourteen years old at the time. This information had been mythologised, and not in a good way.

Maybe I didn't sound convincing when I tried to dismiss Danny's fears. There's no doubt Bentley's dangerous, so much so that he does not need to play up his history to create fear. Things he does daily are a constant reminder to staff and boys of the threat he poses. Just in the last couple of weeks, I'd read an incident report where he'd knocked a staff member unconscious during a restraint. Took him out with a calculated knee to the head. The social worker did not help himself by trying to grab his legs and thereby putting his head within range, but even so, witnesses said they saw the cold hard intent in Bentley's eyes. No complaint was made to the Police and no charges were laid.

Danny remains terrified, the words are tumbling out of his mouth.

'The other boys say, you know, he's crazy, not all there! He kept saying he knew somewhere we could go and we'd have some fun. I told him I didn't want to because I'm getting out in a couple of days. He reckoned it wouldn't make any difference, we could just go for the night. Then later on when I said no again he said I better, or you know, something would happen.'

'Well in the end you didn't go and he did.' I'm not doing a very good job of getting him calmed down. I try again, 'As long as you don't run with anyone, and you make sure you stay in sight of the staff, you'll be safe while you are here.'

Danny continues to visibly shake and the tears have returned. 'When Bentley comes back will he be put in SNU?'

'I can't say what will happen to either you or him. It's a very serious thing to try and hurt yourself and we need to get the right people to help you. Hopefully, that can be done quickly. As for Bentley, he will come back at some point. It won't be tonight because the Police have said they'll hold him if they catch him. What I can say confidently is that I'll make sure I raise your concerns in my Incident Report. All the oncoming teams and the senior social workers see these and they will keep an eye out for any further problems, and they can do it without saying anything to anyone.' I can't control anything happening on day shifts but I know Wayne is still around upstairs and I'll have the chance to talk to him before he goes off. This is the best I can offer.

Just then the phone rings. It's Wayne.

'The Crisis Team isn't coming. They'll send someone out tomorrow if we still think there's still a need.' No cavalry on the horizon then.

'You will need to stay down in SNU for the next few hours and keep an eye on Danny. Is all the suicide gear in place?' I confirm that it is. 'I'll stay up here with Mr Rogers and make sure this lot is settled before I leave. All the excitement seems to have tired everyone out. There is no chance of getting any additional cover because it's so late, but you should be right'.

'Wayne I need to see you before you go!' I emphasise in reply.

Chapter 26
Jai Hates 'Eggs'

Bloody Bentley is being a real egg tonight, worse than usual. Jai is getting sick of his behaviour and he's not the only one. His stupid antics are annoying and draining. He has to be watched all the time, he's such a 'random'. No one knows what he's going to do. Half the time it will be bullying, brutish stuff. Sometimes the dick thinks whatever he's doing is actually fun for everyone. He seems to have no fear and it's pretty obvious to anyone who isn't blind, that he's one can short of a six-pack. The staff let him get away with heaps. Now and again when they get sick of his crap behaviour, when he's really on the edge, they set him up and bang him in SNU. You can see it happening, the staff huddled together, the bravest putting out the challenge, and then they swarm like bees, have a scrap and he's gone. It appears to Jai that this only happens when they have no other choice or when certain staff members are on shift who aren't afraid of him.

It's one of the problems with this cursed place. Some staff are a lot better than others. Jai knows the shift patterns and who should be on but even so, you still never actually know who will turn up on the day until the shift starts. There are always lots of relievers. Nearly every shift has one and sometimes more. Most of them are all right. There's a couple he likes more than the regulars. But they aren't the same as the permanent staff. Jai has noticed some are 'try-hard' social workers. Some are chicken, so you can get away with stuff. Some don't do anything, just stand around like a spare dork at a party. Those don't last very long.

Also, all three teams are different. One team, the boys call them the 'staunch hit' team or SHIT for short. They don't put up with anything from the boys, not even a single instance of swearing. Funny that because plenty of staff swear, including some around the boys, especially when they're away from other staff, trying to be one of the bros. There are a couple of guys in the SHITs who know how to handle themselves physically, kung fu guys, and they step in as soon as there's any trouble and bang, someone's gone to SNU.

Another team is the opposite. Anything the boys do is tolerated and it's only when the 'shite hits the fan', that something is ever done. When they're on, breakfast and dinner times are usually chaotic, boys swearing at each other across tables, followed by threats back and forward, food flying about and useless staff pleading with them to stop. 'Stop you guys, please stop!' Jai thinks it can be a bit funny and entertaining, but also not good because that's when bad stuff is more likely to go down, like the biff! Jai had named this team the TWITS, Totally Weak Ignorant Tossers, but the name didn't stick with the other boys like the SHITS one did. Whatever, they're rubbish too, just for different reasons! He called the team on this afternoon the NESTERS, not either TWITS or SHITS, but it was a private joke and he never even tried that one with the boys. He thought it was pretty clever but no one would get it.

During dinner tonight Bentley was flicking food at Hatch Hitch. It wasn't a really big deal but he kept on doing it without anyone telling him to stop. Hatch, when he responded, was the one who got raked by the staff. Typical of Frank Thomas. What a hippie with his long plaited hair. He lets Bentley do what he likes. Hatch was pretty pissed off and he was vocal in telling Frank what was happening and to 'grow some balls!' The other staff must have heard it, everyone could, but they just seemed to put their heads down and inspect the food stains on the table cloths. Eventually the senior emerged from the office, stepped in and Bentley was sent to the 'time-out' room. But that only provided temporary relief, he pulled his head in. 'Sorry sir, sorry sir!' and was back after five minutes.

Bentley's in one of his moods. Now it's got worse at bedtime. He's being loud and won't shut up, always a bad sign. It isn't like he's being abusive, just being childish and silly like a naughty four-year-old. Jai's been around Bentley long enough to recognise the look in his eyes, 'Ground control to Bentley, Ground control to Bentley, come in Bentley where are you?' No connection with the looney space cadet! It's tiring and it'll keep going on and on until something happens.

Jai mutters to himself, 'Hurry up and blow it, we'll all be better off if the dickhead gets whacked into SNU. What's with the staff? They know it, we know it, just do it, man!'

Not all the boys are bothering to get into bed and the staff are getting grumpy because they aren't settling. They're pushing hard. Slowly things seem to be calming down. Maybe that's an end to it, Jai hopes but he's not holding his breath. Bentley won't close his damn mouth though, he's still yapping to the boys. Anyone can hear it, it isn't like he's whispering. Jai, who had previously been in Rata was moved to Rimu because beds were required for a group of older boys who came in after being caught in a stolen car together. He'd been happy with the move because the partitions offered some privacy and he was away from Bentley, and his nonsense. He didn't want to have anything to do with him, especially after the business at the Waimak.

Jai hears the day shift team leaving and the night staff come on. Wyatt wanders through the dorms. Mr Rogers is also on because he can hear his voice in the night staff office. Bloody hell, he sighs, the boys hate Mr Rogers, and Bentley hates him most of all.

Mr Rogers is doing the rounds. Bentley greets him in his usual way, sort of friendly-sounding but underneath it, he is trying to wind him up, get a bite.

'Hello, Mr Rogers, you on tonight? Oh good, just what we wanted, our favourite night time stalker. Will you read us a bedtime story? Please, please!' He has his little boy voice on.

Mr Rogers though doesn't take the bait. He smirks at Bentley and replies, 'You're wonderfully observant tonight. Great to see you too Breezer, my favourite little hoodlum. I'll give you a tip, go back to school and after a few years you'll be able to read your own bedtime story…every night.'

'That's' not very nice sir!' Bentley may not be too bright but he can recognise sarcasm when he hears it.

'No it isn't very nice, but, unfortunately, it's also true!'

He has another go at stirring the pot. 'I just love hearing your voice sir!'

'Much and all as I have a beautiful reading voice, it won't be being used tonight!' End of conversation.

As soon as Mr Rogers leaves the room, Bentley's straight out of bed and moving about, poking boys and giggling like a little girlie. Jai can hear it all from Rimu. Why have the staff gone, they know he's going to start again, Jai laments under his breath. He just wants to sleep. It's hard enough in Res at the best of times. Every sound the other boys make snoring, burps, farting, talking in their sleep, crying, you name it, you hear it. But it's even harder when someone is intent on being a dickhead.

Bentley is once again out of Rata. Jai puts his head under the blankets but he can still clearly hear the staff challenging him and the sound as he's running about from dorm to dorm. He hears someone from Rata say a frustrated 'piss off!' Then he hears Mr Rogers tell Bentley he's gonna stand at the door and watch until he's settled. That doesn't please Bentley who has a bit to say about him being a 'perve'.

All seems to be quiet. Jai drifts off. Next thing he feels someone rip off his blankets and he's being tipped out of bed. Now he's had a gutful. Whatever fear he may have experienced in the past does not have time to register. Overcome in a flash of rage he jumps up spontaneously, launches himself at Bentley and head butts him in the stomach sending him sprawling onto the floor. He's following it up with a boot but Bentley sees it coming and moves just in time. It's like nothing to Bentley though. He ignores the attack and he has a goofy grin on his face. By the time Jai is ready to deliver another kick, Bentley is already up and on the move, running out of the dorm. Jai picks up his mattress and angrily tosses it on the frame then sits back on it. God! he hates this bloody place, brainless dickheads, useless staff, dumb rules, aaaaaarrrgh!

Around him, boys are starting to move, and voices are getting louder. Things are winding up. Someone throws a book and it's all on. Now pillows are being ripped, their foam innards thrown, and bedclothes tossed on the floor. He's conscious there's a lot of noise going on everywhere and he can hear Bentley bellowing at the top of his voice that Mr Rogers wants to put him in SNU. He's sort of chanting it repetitively.

The whole place is pulsating now. The staff are still busy trying to settle things down, but Jai thinks no chance, they've lost it. Maybe someone is going to grab one of the staff and take his keys, easy to do. This fleeting thought is annihilated when the fire alarm goes off. What a deafening racket. Bloody hell! How stupid to have an alarm that is so easy to get at. Now they have to go to the gym, no rest for ages!

All the boys are swarming towards the stairwell. A few who have experienced this before are shouting to the others to evacuate. It all adds to the chaos. Jai hears crashing and banging, things being broken. He emerges from Rimu and stands in the hallway as the throng of boys pushes past heading into the stairwell. In the group in the stairwell, he sees Hatch Hitch and he has the black electric guitar. Jai doesn't know how he got it because he isn't a player but he sees he's waving it about like a weapon. Jai chases down the stairs, steps in front of him and shoves him in the face, while at the same time grabbing the guitar.

'What the fuck are you doing?' he shouts in Hatch's face. Hatch is rubbing his eye with his hand, where Jai must have accidentally poked it.

'Just having fun. Who cares man, it's not our stuff... F.T.W.' Hatch hollers to no one in particular.

'Not the guitar you egg! We'll never get another one if this one's broken!'

Jai holds the guitar above his head, away from the reach of the others as he is carried along by the melee down the stairs.

'What are you doing with that guitar Rehua?' The question comes out of nowhere and it's loud enough to be heard above the hubbub. It's Mr Rogers. He pushes a couple of kids aside and steps up to Jai.

'Give that to me! Have you been in the office? You know it's out of bounds to you lot. You're not allowed in there...ever... for any reason. I'll deal with you later!'

'I was just trying to save it sir' replied Jai, 'in case it was lost in the fire.'

'There is no fire. Some smart-arse just hit the alarm. There better not be any damage in the office, or anything else missing.' Mr Rogers is practically barking in his face.

Jai didn't say anything more. He catches a glimpse of Hatch grinning at him. I'll fix you later he thinks, and then we'll see how funny it is.

The boys are told to wait at the bottom of the stairs. Wyatt goes past him heading back to the dorms. But they don't wait for him to come back though, Mr Rogers takes them out of the building. Jai wonders what Wyatt is doing.

When he enters the gym there are only boys. Mr Rogers is still outside herding the stragglers along. Jai watches as Rubin Case, a 'mongie', smacks Tony around the head and says something to him. Jai knows why ... retribution. Tony was holding some dope for Rubin and it 'disappeared'. Needless to say, Rubin was not a happy camper and he told Tony to bring some in after his weekend leave. Tony didn't do it for whatever reason, and now Rubin was taking the available temporary absence of staff to remind him of his obligations. Tony was holding his head and crying when Mr Rogers enters the gym. Mr Rogers looks at him and says nothing.

The boys are buzzing about like a swarm of wasps. After the lull created by the evacuation, they seem to be winding up again. Mr Rogers holds the fort, standing by the door, waiting for the Fire Service.

A few minutes later Wyatt turns up and he has one of the boys with him, some kid Jai doesn't know, Danny someone or other. He seems to be upset and

Jai wonders if Wyatt has done something to him. Wyatt seems like an OK guy but you never know. He's a staff member in this hell hole so you can't really trust him.

Jai could've run when Mr Rogers was taking them over to the gym but he couldn't be bothered. Thirty boys could run in ten different directions and who could stop them. Not going to be me though he thinks, not tonight I can't be stuffed. At any rate, he's in his PJs, not a fashion item to be seen out and about in. He wonders who's done a runner, probably that dickhead Bentley. Mr Rogers does another headcount. Jai hears him confirm to Wyatt that Breezer's gone. Good riddance! He wishes he'd taken Chevy Woken with him, but whatever, he'll take what he gets. At least they'll all get some peace for a while.

The Fire Brigade arrives, then the coppers. The boys make plenty of noise towards the Police, snorting like pigs and giving them heaps. Then the dog comes through the door.

When Jai sees the dog he feels a bit of a chill. His mind flashes to a song Wyatt played one night called 'Police Dog Blues' and it was all about a nasty police dog that looked like it was itching to attack something. That's what this dog looks like, fierce and aggressive! He loved the tune and wanted to learn it as soon as he heard it. It was like an earworm that got into his head. The guitar has to be tuned differently from normal to play it. That was what intrigued Jai, he'd picked straight away, something sounded different. When he asked Wyatt about it he said he thought Jai might have an affinity with the song after experiencing some dog action when he was first admitted. Not funny! Wyatt missed the boat on that one. Love the tune, hate the dog… but hate the copper who set it on him more. The dog handler says 'talk' and the dog barks. It goes off! Short, sharp, staccato, like the rap of a snare drum. Jai unconsciously reaches for his thigh. His dog bite is long healed now, but not forgotten. Then everyone is quiet.

Jai is starting to feel cold in his PJs and he jumps up and down a couple of times and whacks his arms around his shoulders. The dog is watching him … so he stops. After what seems like ages, the Fire guys give the 'all-clear' and the boys are marched back upstairs and back to their beds. The Police dog bids them all good night with another bunch of noisy barks. The boys are tired after all the excitement and things quieten down quickly. Jai too, he's stuffed, all he wants is to sleep.

As he lies there he thinks, man, some of the boys looked like they'd totally lost it. He supposes it'd been a bit of a laugh though, entertaining in its own way.

He wouldn't want that to happen every night. He wonders what will happen over the guitar. He better not be banned from playing it because of something that jerk Hatch did. Who knows what Mr Rogers will do, he is such a prick and Jai doesn't want to talk to him, not now or ever. Thank god he hasn't bothered tonight but then he'd have his feet up by now having a wee kip. Jai drifts off.

The next night Wyatt comes into Jai's dorm before he goes to sleep.

'You still awake?' Jai ignores him. Wyatt ignores being ignored. 'I want to talk to you about the guitar. I just need to sort out what happened. Mr Rogers is pretty steamed up. It was in the office so someone must have gone in and taken it. More importantly, there was some damage done, books thrown on the floor and a hole in the wall. He reckons it was you because you had the guitar. What's the story?'

Jai hesitates, he doesn't want to be blamed for something he hasn't done. However, he also isn't going to nark on the little rat Hatch, no matter what he'd done. He'd dealt with him earlier today making sure that Hatch knew not to do anything with the guitar ever again. Wyatt is waiting for an answer.

'I didn't go into the office. I took the guitar off one of the boys because I thought he was going to break it. I wasn't going to let that happen. I'm not saying who before you ask, I don't nark. The main thing is it's still in one piece, and I can still play it tomorrow.'

'Ok' Wyatt replies, 'I didn't think you would damage it. People who love guitars don't damage them. I said so to Mr Rogers but I also said to him I would check it out with you. I'm taking your word for it. That's me, I'll take your word because a person's word is worth something. I'll sort it out with Mr Rogers, so don't worry about that.' He looks like he's thinking about something then he says, 'Just so you know if someone gives me their word I'm going to take it. But if they break it, well that's a different story and it will take a long time for me to believe them again... Goodnight Jai, sleep well.'

Jai lies there staring at the large patches of discolouration on the ceiling. It's hard not to see them even in the partial light coming through the vacant doorway. They look like a brown map of the world. On other nights they have made him dream of places he might go...sometime in his future. But not tonight.

Yes, he thinks, I gave my word and it's worth something. Most of the time no one believes me. He was glad Wyatt had, and without giving him a grilling that would actually show he hadn't. That was worth something too.

Part 5
Ten Months In

Chapter 27
Wyatt Is Mixing It Up on
Days and Nights

After my two days off I've agreed to do a set of morning shifts. I'm happy to take the opportunity although changing between night and day shifts, which is happening more frequently now, has physiological implications on my sleep patterns. But I want the experience, and frankly, I'm bored. While it can be challenging, very challenging at night, it doesn't happen often and, mostly when there is activity, it is over in an hour or so. I've set some limitations on when I'll do days however and will only do so when there is a good solid set of shifts to be had, and I get a two-day break before returning to nights. This proposal is mostly working, although like any good team member when there is a real cry for help I will always do my bit.

I arrive fifteen minutes early so I can catch up with my night staff colleagues. It's been a pretty quiet night so not much to report from them. They draw my attention to a new boy who came in a couple of days ago, just before I went off. Now I have time so I check out his file.

His name is Gerald Longstead although he demands that everyone call him Gerhart, and he doesn't respond to his real name to reinforce the point.

Despite not being in the formal system very long, Gerhart is well known to the Police. He emerged as a dangerous young man when he turned 16 years old. He's in residence because he was in a brawl in which a couple of Tokelauans fellows were badly injured. Calling it a brawl gives it more dignity than it deserved. It was a pack attack where the victims were significantly outnumbered. He is charged as a key player who used his Doc Martins liberally on a fallen and unmoving victim.

In his case notes, it says he's tight with a known gang of 'skinheads', white supremacists. He has swastikas tattooed on his upper arms and torso, an iron cross on his neck, 'White Rule' on his forearms, and 'Sieg Heil' across the knuckles of his hands. Not an exercise in subtlety that's for sure.

Gerhart is a big lad, about six feet tall and solid, big chest and arms from enthusiastically following his passion for working out. He's a human tank, confident in his physical prowess and he knows it and shows it. Now and again we have someone in residence who stands out because they are very articulate about the logic underpinning their criminal behaviour. Such is Gerhart. A couple of staff tried arguing with him during one of the group meetings when he chose to take his views public. All it did was give him a platform that he exploited to the max. It annoyed some of the browner boys big time and things got quite tense for a while. All very interesting. No doubt I will meet him shortly as he's in the main house.

In the final few moments before the other morning team members arrive, Ted and Mr Rogers share a bit of gossip. I'm covering for Ter, who was relieving for Gwynne, currently on annual leave. Ter has been suspended pending an employment investigation. The alleged incident happened a couple of days ago although it only came to light yesterday when a formal complaint was made. A boy is claiming he was assaulted while in the SNU. He was checked by a doctor but as it was already over a day since the alleged incident, any potential indicators had diminished. There were a few bruises found but it was hard to determine how recently they'd occurred. However there was another boy in SNU at the time and he corroborated part of the complaint saying he heard the two in a heated argument, swearing and grunting which sounded like people in a physical confrontation although he did not see the actual incident. The matter has to be investigated and because it's a serious allegation, it requires the staff member to be stood down.

Mr Rogers is pretty clear in his view, it's a waste of time. The only witness is unreliable, just a little weedy fellow who could easily have been intimidated into saying anything by the complainant, whom he described as a 'bully boy'. He says there was plenty of time to put the pressure on a witness given there was a twenty-four hour gap between the alleged incident and the complaint being made. Ted is more focused on the problems of working in isolation and how vulnerable it makes everyone, staff and boys alike. Neither thinks the investigation will take too long. Me, I take the view that if it happened then it needs to be investigated and I hope if there is no substance to it then it is over quickly. In the interim, I'm happy to be doing four mornings.

We're getting the boys out of bed. Reliever Wiremu Tomas, an older Māori man, a kaumatua and a respected elder for the institution, is in Rata, Abigail is in Kauri and Sarge is in Rimu. I am a 'floater', covering everybody. There's the usual noise coming from the boys as they are awoken, grumbling and telling the staff member to 'take a hike' or worse.

I arrive at the doorway to Rata, I see Wiremu is at Gerhart's bed asking him to get up. He doesn't move. Wiremu raises his voice and gives him a little shake, nothing out of the ordinary. Gerhart turns his head and when he sees who's attempting to rouse him, he snarls, 'Get your hands off me, you black bastard'.

Wiremu does not appear phased at all by this, responding in a calm voice. 'Come on Gerald let's get moving!' after which he turns his back and makes to move to the next bed where another reluctant riser is struggling to open his eyes and greet the day.

Gerhart springs from his bed, fixing Wiremu's back with a murderous stare. He's bigger than Wiremu by a good half a head. He shoves Wiremu hard in the back causing him to fall against the end of the adjacent bed. Wiremu grunts, obviously hurting. He takes a moment to get himself together. Blood is oozing from a cut on his head and he's looking slightly dazed. I move into the room. Boys are beginning to get up and I sense the collective agitation increasing.

As Wiremu staggers to his feet, Gerhart reaches under his mattress, grabs something and steps towards the rising elder, shouting 'Gerhart! Gerhart! You dumb fuck! I'll cut you, I'll cut you good! No stinking black fuck puts his hands on me!'

He extends his arm and it's clear he's holding something although it's hard to identify exactly what it is from where I stand. Wiremu, obviously concerned about what he can see reacts with a speed that belies his age. As Gerald steps towards him, he drops his shoulder and charges, knocking Gerhart off his feet. Gerhart reels and falls backwards crashing into his bed. Wiremu is leaning over the prone boy, his arm lifted, hand bunched in a fist. I cover the few steps from the door to Wiremu just catching his arm as he launches it towards Gerald's surprised-looking face. I can't prevent the blow completely. It lands on the side of Gerhart's head. Winded from the shoulder charge and stunned from the attack, the item in his hand comes loose and falls. Grabbing Wiremu by the shoulders I pull him upright and away. He's red in the face and shaking. Pointing his finger at Gerhart he says. 'Don't try that again Gerald. You skinheads are a gutless bunch.'

'That's assault you black cunt! Hey you!' nodding his head in my direction, his face contorted in rage, 'You're my witness, you saw it, he assaulted me!' he thunders, froth accumulating around the corners of his twisted mouth.

I ignore him, making sure I put my foot on the discarded weapon while also positioning myself between the two, a hand on each chest. Although all the fight has now gone out of him, Gerhart keeps up a torrent of abusive language. Sarge and Abigail have made their way into Rata by now. The noise level in the unit rises, often the way when a confrontation is in progress. Abigail steps over to Gerhart and says quietly while taking his arm, 'Come on Gerhart we need to go to SNU.' To my amazement he complies, walking off with Abigail still muttering under his breath. Sarge follows close behind.

I pick up the discarded item from the floor. It's a shard of metal, narrow like a stiletto, about as long as the palm of my hand, sharpened at one end with plastic tape wrapped around the other to make a handle. Another item for the already well-stocked 'Shanks Library' of improvised weapons which fills a cabinet in the administration building.

Wiremu still looks a bit shaky to me so I send him to the office to sit down. I attend to the boys who get on with their day once Gerhart exits the building. Since we don't have anyone located in SNU today, we will likely have to get a reliever because his admission has bumped up the numbers. Many of the relievers are Māori or Pacifica so the problems with Gerhart are expected to be ongoing. Turns out not to be an issue on this particular occasion as I am asked to take the role.

At midday, I get to sit in the office for a few minutes. John Land comes to see me and I am formally interviewed. My evidence is that Wiremu was assaulted and Gerhart threatened to hurt him, had the means to do so, and tried it on. Wiremu responded forcefully, true, but my intervention meant the matter did not get further out of hand. John tells me Wiremu has been given a couple of days to get checked out and recuperate. He decided not to lay a formal assault complaint against Gerhart. John says it was lucky I was there to be a witness. Gerhart made a complaint of assault against another staff member a couple of days ago and the matter is now the subject of an employment investigation. As far as he's concerned, this matter is closed. I don't say anything but I wonder if Ter, who is part Samoan, suffered similar abuse to Wiremu, maybe even an assault.

As I sit thinking about the morning's incident I decide to have a closer look at Gerhart's file. He has a faint olive tinge in his complexion and something about the structure of his face adds to my suspicion that he isn't the purest of the pure regarding his ethnicity. I hadn't noticed anything which might confirm one way or the other on my first reading, but it's only a small file so it doesn't take long to have a closer dig. In a request from his mother to the Department of Social Welfare, I find what I am looking for. She requested that Gerhart (she still called him Gerald) be released to attend the funeral of his grandfather, Mitchel Roads. To support the request, his mother sent in a copy of the funeral notice and there it was, Mitchel Hemi Roads. Our boy Gerhart has a little bit of Māori blood in him. Talk about denial! I close the file and toss it onto the desk.

Chapter 28
Wyatt Loses One

After the incident with Gerhart, I was asked to do several more clumps of day shifts. This is my last shift as cover for the reliever who, in turn, was covering for Rupert Frost, who's been off on sick leave for over four months. I was approached at the last minute because the reliever broke a finger during a restraint two days ago and is now off work too! Rupert was quite badly assaulted and spent two days in the hospital with a concussion. Since then he has produced medical certificate after medical certificate saying he is unfit to return. The general feeling amongst his colleagues is that he's lost his nerve. I can see how that happens. Since I've been at Stanmore I've witnessed serious attacks which have resulted in injury and heard or seen the effects of others. Not just involving staff either, but committed by boys on other boys as well.

I've now been here for what seems like forever and although I've become desensitised to many aspects of the work, not the violence ... and I hope I never do. Although I am confident I can handle myself in most situations, I often still feel vulnerable, although less so than when I started. The volatility and unpredictability of the environment create anxiety. With each new experience, my confidence grows. Despite this, I can't see a time when I won't need to be on top of my game day in and day out. I can't help wondering if I sometimes don't feel safe, how do the boys feel?

Mr Rogers has the view that the boys are like pack animals. If they get a sense you're weak, they'll menace you and possibly attack. That explains some of his brusque behaviour but it seems a pretty extreme perspective to me. Certainly, I've seen weak or inconsistent staff put under pressure. But I also know there had been many nights when the boys were upset, angry, or aggressive, and the night team have managed to get through somehow despite feeling, and no doubt showing, a degree of apprehension.

From my very first shift, I've consciously tried to take opportunities to make connections with the boys, encouraging a personal investment. The more they like or respect me, the more it increases the chance I will have a beneficial influence in difficult situations, and the less likely they are to do things that damage the relationship … like assaulting me.

I was involved in physically helping move a young man, Johnny Suzo, to the SNU. Johnny was in residence awaiting sentence in the adult court for a lengthy record of violent offences. He was a big sixteen-year-old, physically mature and around six feet tall. He assaulted another young person during the evening meal and raged around the dining room kicking over chairs and tables, throwing plates and making threats to staff. Two of us managed to tackle him. He continued to put up a solid fight. In the end, three of us were required to move him to SNU. The whole way we struggled. When physical interventions happen, the most dangerous times are getting hold of the boy in the first instance, and then the point of release from the restraint. Once we got Johnny to his cell we let him go facing the back wall, stepping back hastily as one is want to do in these situations. He was faster. He spun around and struck out with a closed fist, I was closest and directly in the firing line but he punched over my shoulder and hit my colleague Gwynne in the face and sent him reeling, the blood spilling from a split lip. Johnny did not attempt to leave the cell and we were able to extricate ourselves without further incident, carting our injured colleague with us. A few nights later I was speaking to him and asked why he hadn't hit me after all I was the easiest target. He told me 'Nah man, didn't want to hit you, you da blues man.' I'd had a few chats with him about his life, guitar playing, the blues, his interests, the sort of things I would have done with many of the boys. It was nothing special on my part, just showing him respect. It proved its worth as something he seemed to value. However, I am not under any illusion that the connections I make will save me from risk all of the time.

I've been tasked with working in SNU, something which has happened for the last two days because the numbers have been high. I am joined by a new reliever, Mateo Tau, who is learning the ropes. Ma is a big unit who has come from one of the local league clubs. He's heavily tattooed on his arms and on his upper legs, which are like tree trunks and exposed by his shorts. The blue colouring on his thighs is so dense it appears almost a solid block. From what I have seen so far he's quietly spoken, which can sometimes be a problem with relievers because it gives them no presence, but with him, I would describe his approach as 'economic'. He only speaks when he needs to. When he does bother to, it gets the desired results. I feel that we will be using him a lot in the future.

There's a reason we have beefed up security in SNU. For several weeks we've been experiencing ongoing issues, particularly at night, although not exclusively, such as uninvited people coming on the property, movements seen in the shadows on our nightly perimeter checks, young people leaping over the fence beside the SNU or lurking in the bushes at the back of the property. There's been the odd bang of something being thrown on the roof or against a window. Invariably by the time we got to check it out, there was nothing there or a glimpse of someone disappearing into the distance. At night we have a large and powerful torch but it's insufficient to identify detail at distance and while the front of the residence is well lit, the back is almost total darkness. There've been a couple of instances when I saw a young person at the window of one of the SNU cells. They hoofed it, leaping the fence next to the supermarket as soon as they saw me. I learned pretty quickly there was no point in chasing them, they would be gone before I even got to the fence. From time to time we'd hear banging on the roof of the SNU. Because most of the roof can be seen from the fire door on the second floor, I'd call up my colleague and get them to check it out. A futile exercise. Even when we knew someone was up there we couldn't catch them. There are two exit points and invariably the person or persons hear you coming, or maybe spot the torchlight, and use the most favourable one.

Something is going down. Generally when we raise our concerns with the day teams not much happens however additional incidents which have occurred in and around SNU during the day and intelligence that trouble is brewing, have contributed to a cautionary approach.

Currently, we have a boy in residence who has a high profile out on the street. There are rumours the street kids want to break him out. Those sorts of rumours are not uncommon however the volume of murmurings, in this case, warrants attention. Reese Cooney has been right through the care system; foster care, Hokio Beach and Kohitere. Since I've been at the residence he has already been in and out several times. He's well known to everyone, staff, boys, Police, and Courts. He's a likeable guy with an easy manner who gets along with everybody. His major problem is he just won't stay put anywhere he's placed. He just loves that street life!

His file tells a familiar tragic story. His father died from some unspecified illness when Reese was just one year old. His mother, unable to cope with the loss, descended into depression. The prescribed medication she received didn't do the trick and eventually, her use of supplements led to heavy substance abuse. She became a "poly druggy" using alcohol and pills, mainly barbiturates. Someone informed the Department of Social Welfare that Reese was being neglected and when the Department eventually intervened, they found two year old Reese filthy from head to foot with clothes caked in faeces, considerably under the average height for his age and about half his expected body weight. His little body was so thin all his ribs could be seen poking through his T-shirt. The investigating social workers reported the house was a tip and smelt of rotting food, clothes, furniture and dampness. There was no edible food in the fridge. The few bits it did contain resembled the fungus trays of a science project.

Reese was placed in temporary care with a foster family. He was the only child in the placement and the foster carers worked hard to get him back to being a healthy two year old. After six months he seemed to be coming right although he was still small for his age. During the intervening months, work was done with his mother to help her get past the addictions. It was unfruitful. Eventually, she had a total breakdown which resulted in her admission to psychiatric care. More permanent arrangements were made for Reese's care and the State took formal custody. Reese moved to a new placement, the second of many to follow.

Things progressed along for a couple of years without further notification of problems although Reese was an unsettled child, not sleeping well and listless. His placement broke down when the foster parents, who had their own children, decided they couldn't cope anymore. Reese was at school now. After a year or so it became apparent he was not engaged with education. It seemed he struggled to adjust to the regularity of school life. There wasn't a problem with Reese's intellectual capability, he just didn't take to structured learning. The other kids seemed to like him as did his teacher. He was very social and he loved to chat. At some point along the way the chat escalated and he began to distract others. It required a lot of teacher effort to manage his disruptive behaviour. He started getting excluded from class. By the age of seven, Reese was exercising his own choices about school attendance. Over the next few years, he'd been to most of the schools in the south of Christchurch. He didn't connect with any of them.

When he wasn't at school, which was often, he hung out in Christchurch Square. He was meeting other kids who were living partially or wholly on the street, most a lot older than him. He got into stealing food just to survive. He excelled at it and was generous. Reese discovered it was a way of ingratiating himself with other street waifs.

He started sniffing glue and other substances. In the file notes his social worker wrote how, during this time of considerable absences from foster home and school, Reese was found in The Square so out of it on glue that he had been taken to a State-run family home, a step up in the level of supervision from his existing care arrangements. He was just ten years old. In a matter of a few days, he was gone. At eleven years old he experienced his first stint of six months at Hokio Beach. A great deal of preparation went into a new placement for his return but it only lasted a few days. This time he wasn't found for four months. I saw a comment in his file from the Children's Court Judge asking whether the Department had been looking for him with their eyes shut. This attitude was prevalent among the Judiciary. It didn't only reference social workers but was also directed at the Police.

This long stint on the street showed how well Reese was able to remain undetected and how he'd integrated into the network of illicit doss houses the street people frequented. When he was finally caught his social worker believed there were signs he'd been abused. He was given a full physical examination. It appeared he had become sexually active. It was unclear whether this was by choice or if he had been assaulted. Social workers felt it would cast a significant shadow on his future if unaddressed. Reese did not want to talk about it, so he didn't, despite the efforts of skilled sexual abuse interviewers.

Reese is fifteen years old now and for the last three years, he spent all his 'captured' time in Hokio, Kohitere or Stanmore. No one has bothered counting how often he'd been in Stanmore. He's in and out like a yoyo. As soon as he has a chance, he's on the run.

Over the years he developed the skill of quickly engaging with adults and other kids. This contributed to Reese becoming a person of significance on the streets. Among the street people, adults and kids, his continual thumbing his nose at the system has given him additional standing. Police and social workers also know him so well he is on a 'first name' basis with many.

I met Reese for the first time when he returned from Kohitere and was transitioning through Stanmore en route to a placement in Rangiora. His social worker had created a very intensive, comprehensive programme describing it in a Court Report as 'the last and best shot there might be for a successful outcome'.

Reese wasn't enchanted with this carefully crafted plan because he absconded from Stanmore at the first chance he got.

He struck me as being in the 'likeable rogue' category. He wasn't interested in anything like sport or guitar, my major offerings, so he only bothered with me on a 'need to engage' basis. I'd spent time with him during the last few days which included many hours just talking with him. I found him to be moderately interested in a range of topics but with no passion for anything in particular…except street life. The SNU seemed to be the only way social workers could keep hold of him. His situation is additionally complicated by his continual absconding. He almost always takes off so quickly that the planned intervention doesn't have a chance to get established, for relationships to form, and for a platform of stability to be attained. Nothing ever seemed to be resolved for him legally either. A new offence would occur before the last one was processed or the plan would fall over before it started. I think no one knows what to do with him. As his latest report says, 'the solution is not obvious.' It's the social work merry go round although his caseworker isn't that merry about things. Reese doesn't seem to care one way or the other.

Another rumour floating around about him is this time in residence might be his last. He will likely be sent to Corrective Training when he turns sixteen in a couple of weeks. He's being held in the SNU until he's old enough to appear in the adult Court. He's already been there for over a month. The word got out to the street about his extended placement and probable sentence, and there has been a negative reaction among his supporters.

It isn't a surprise his friends got to know. An estimated two hundred young people from the greater Christchurch area are cycling through the hard end of the care system either on the streets, in residence, or some other form of care. Word about Reese could hardly have been contained despite it being a confidential matter. The boys always seemed to know a lot about each other. There isn't much in the residence that remains private, especially among the street kids.

Today Ma and I have a relatively problem-free shift. It was almost too good to be true as having five boys in such a confined area can exacerbate rather than reduce conflict. We are almost into shift changeover and I am looking forward to a couple of days off before I return to nights. The boys are in the gym so I take Ma into the office and start showing him some of the paperwork we need to complete before we go off. We're in the middle of this when we hear the distinct sound of glass shattering, the crash of pieces hitting the floor, followed closely by cheering from the boys. We rush into the gym. I see Jai Rehua getting up off the gym floor. He has minor bleeding from a few cuts on his legs. He's looking up towards the ceiling, I follow his gaze. In the corner of the gym ceiling, I see a space that once contained a skylight. Below it swings the climbing rope. Headcount. Reese is gone. I direct the boys back to their cells and leave Ma to manage this as I rush to the phone and call the office in the main residence. No reply. I call the senior's office. No reply. I call the manager's office.

'Mike Michelsen.' I finally get a response.

'Mike, Wyatt here from the SNU. We've just had a breakout. I can't get anyone in the office or any of the seniors. Someone needs to get out on the road quickly before he gets too far.' I already know it's too late, he'll be long gone but there's a process to follow. Somebody needs to make an effort on the slight off chance it might be successful. Mike doesn't say anything so I add 'It's Reese Cooney!'

'Bloody hell, Reese Cooney! The National Office crowd will be all over us like a rash now…and the press.'

'Mike, I appreciate the difficulties,'… actually… I don't! 'I need staff, a senior, someone, do you know where they are?'

'Ok, they're meeting in here, I'll get John.' Click.

I hang up and walk out into the SNU hall. Ma is standing there and all the unit doors are shut.

'Any probs?' I ask.

'Nah'

'I saw Jai has a few cuts. Were any of the other boys hurt?' I inquire.

'Superficial. I gave him a plaster. All the rest are fine.'

'Ok, we need to secure the place…' I don't finish my sentence. I am interrupted by the clank of the SNU door being flung open and the patter of running feet. The cavalry has finally arrived, too late and in the wrong place if they're going to have a sniff of catching our absconder.

Chapter 29
Not Again, Jai!

Jai awakes with a start. He hears someone swearing loudly somewhere in the foggy recesses of his mind. His eyelids are glued to his cheeks. He pries his eyes open. Squinting to adjust to the glare of the light pouring in from everywhere, he makes out the tell-tale charcoal writing 'Kill all KFs' burned onto the ceiling above his head. Fuck! Fuck! Fuck! Back in Stanmore. It takes a few moments to reach back into the recesses of his mind and recall how he got here.

It'd been one hell of a party, man, too much to drink though. Napoleon brandy, stolen by whatever his name was, he can't remember, and good weed too, some of the best he'd ever had, and he knows his weed. He'd been right out there in the cosmos. Why didn't he just lay back and listen to the sounds, even though he didn't like Led Zep who was being played endlessly on the turntable. The lead singer was too whinny for his tastes. Stupid, stupid, it'd driven him outside. He'd gone for a stroll with Eric, whom he'd bumped into at the party. They ended up smashing a window at the back of a clothing shop in Linwood. The alarm went off and, although he thought they'd been quick, he was picked up a couple of minutes later.

Why did he do it? It seemed like a fun thing at the time and some of the gear looked pretty neat. He'd fancied a couple of designer-looking T-shirts and a new jean jacket... that's right, it was purple, very cool. Oh man, dumb though, he thinks as the fog is lifting. Back in this hell hole!

His last stay in Res had been for nearly three months. At the time it seemed like forever. The judge agreed with Jai's lawyer, he'd been there too long and the judge talked about time served counting for something that's why he was discharged back to his mother. He accepted he'd be on a twenty-four seven curfew for the first two weeks as per his social work plan. 'An adjustment to reintegrating in to the community after being in residence for so long,' was what they called it. When he got home it was back to the same old same old with Mona. She was never there, or if she was, she was out of it on the piss or pills. More often than he cared for there was some loser hanging around he couldn't be bothered talking to. After a week, he couldn't stand it anymore. In the end, he just went out one night and didn't go back. He was always able to find places to stay and he hoped this time, as long as he kept his head down, no one would care. Then last night, not his first party night, but certainly the biggest, he'd gone to a house in Linwood.

When he arrived at the party he was surprised to see Eric. Long-time no see, in fact not since the shopping incident in Barrington Street. After being nabbed Eric was placed with his mother's sister, Ruby. He liked being there although he still came and went a bit. Ruby is a pretty good sort and Eric gets on well with her and her husband, Uncle Reggie. They don't have kids of their own so they have informally 'adopted' Eric. They even tolerate his occasional need to go back to the streets. The first time he did it he went back to their place after a couple of days and they just accepted it and got on with things without chewing his ear off. Eric is doing a catering course at a college in the city and Aunty Ruby and Uncle Reggie are very pleased about it. Maybe it's just that he's doing something, anything, positive. It's part-time but Eric loves it, cooking that is, not so much the discipline of having to study, but he's trying and so far it's working. Ruby and Reggie aren't averse to cooked goodies either, so things have been going well for all concerned.

It was Jai's suggestion though that they knock off the shop. It was just there begging for it to happen, and the insurance would cover everything. Afterwards, at the cop shop, Eric was lucky though because Aunt Ruby turned up, did her stuff, and took him home. The cops didn't even bother contacting Mona, a waste of time, they said. They rang the 'on call' social worker and Jai was taken back to Stanmore. He vaguely remembered now, he had been pretty out of it and abused the cops and the Stanmore dudes, probably why he's in the SNU.

He's been dragged from his semi-comatose state by shouting from somewhere outside his cell. Jai recognises the source, bloody Kedrick Lemon. You never know who will be in SNU when you come in overnight, but it could be worse. He's one of those guys who's a bit of a loudmouth although he's pretty harmless and doesn't give the boys or the staff much trouble. He's just tedious because he's always going on about some rule or other. He seems to know them all so he's got plenty to bellyache about. You know, he's got rights! Blah, blah

blah. Jai thinks I got rights too, and a headache, so right now I'd like him to shut up. He needs to get out of here, not out of Stanmore because that's not gonna happen quickly, but out of SNU.

There are two staff on this morning, Wyatt and some big Samoan dude who introduces himself as Ma. Jai hasn't met him before. He's a big muscly guy, like a bodybuilder. He comes to Jai's cell, fills the doorway, and just says 'Get up time... now.' And walks away. Jai senses he's best to do it without comment despite his instant irritation with the guy, his abrupt manner, the other noise in the unit, the colour of the walls...everything!

At breakfast, he meets the others. Kendrick, he'd already heard. Two of the others he doesn't know, John someone or other and Aaron Lamar, who speaks like a poncy git. He probably grew up with a spoon in his mouth, Jai thinks, I'd like to stick it in his ear. And there's Reese. Jai wouldn't say they're mates but they've had more than a nodding acquaintance over the last year. Reese seems like a good guy. Thank God! Someone to talk to.

After breakfast, he asks Wyatt if he is going to get out today. It's deflating to hear he won't be reviewed until tomorrow. When he asks why, he's told it's his third time in Stanmore and he has run before, so they want to be sure he's settled before they put him in the big house. He has a go at arguing but Wyatt holds up his hands, it's the senior's decision.

During the morning the boys are all together in the gym playing a bit of basketball. Wyatty is in the office and the big Samoan dude is standing by the door not doing anything. Must be new Jai thinks. He sits down on the floor and Reese comes and sits down next to him. They go through the usual questions, 'What are you in here for?' and 'When are you getting out?'

'I got picked up because the social worker reported me for not staying at my placement. I hadn't been there for a month or so. Horrible place and shitty people, too many rules and the guy, the father was a dick, always putting his hands on me, a smarmy creep, couldn't stand him. Bloody pastor too, fuckin' pedo more like it. As soon as there was nobody else in the house, jees ...I couldn't stand him.' Reese spits out his distaste.

'Were you with Pastor Rae? Everyone knows he's into the boys... pervert. If he tried it on me man, I'd kick him in the nuts, and then in the face. Bro, you should have told the Judge or the coppers or someone, your social worker.' Jai is surprised because it is well known on the streets that you don't want a placement with Pastor Rae. And Reese well, he's as street as you can get.

'Yeah, well who's going to take any notice of me? It was the bloody social worker who put me there and a Judge who agreed. I'd heard some stuff about the guy but at the time it seemed to be better than having to come back to Res. I was only there a couple of days before he sent the other three guys staying there on an outing and tried to get me to suck him off. It's funny you should say that about giving him one in the balls, cause that's exactly what I did when he pulled his wanger out. I got him a good one too. I should have kicked him in his fat ugly mug as well but I wasn't hanging about. He was shouting he's gonna report me for assault. The cops never said anything when they picked me up. Jees I laughed, you should have seen his face. His eyes just about popped out of his head, I thought he was going to explode.' He puffs out his cheeks, holds his breath until his face goes red and his eyes bulge, expels his lung full and then laughs.

'As far as this hell hole is concerned, I'm off this afternoon,' states Reese with real confidence.

'Lucky' replies Jai, 'looks like I'm here for another day at least. Who else is in the house, man?'

'I haven't made it upstairs yet, been in SNU forever, at least a month, but there are always boys coming in and out and the latest is that the Res is full up. The ones you might know, Chevy, Hatch Hitch, Bentley, J.T., that's who I know about. Don't matter to me cause I'll be gone. I'm leaving today and I'll be skipping the house bit.' He adds 'I don't think they were going to put me upstairs anyway because I'm going to Corrective Training, yeah man'.

'That's crap bro, Corrective Training is hardcore...J.T. eh? I haven't seen him forever,' says Jai.

'Yeah' continues Reese, 'He was in here for a couple of days but he's been discharged to the house. Got caught doing an armed robbery of a dairy. Indians, he said it was because he didn't like having 'wogs' in our country. He had a replica pistol and he thought it would do the job. He says it looked real, like a Luger. But he was wrong and one of the guys chased him out of the shop and down the street waving a cricket bat while someone else called the cops. He says he's going to C.T. too or prison this time, even if it was only a replica gun. At least that's what the cops told him when he was nabbed. He reckons he couldn't give a damn, he's got mates inside so he'll be looked after. He didn't say so but I think he's been prospecting for the Mongies, that's the word on the street.'

'Yeah, well it's what I heard too. He hasn't got his patch yet though. How are you getting out of here today?'

'Self-discharge! I'm not staying here. I got court in two weeks and the staff told me the senior, John Land, reckons I'll just run. Can't say he's wrong. Any rate I can't be bothered with those eggs like Chevy or Bentley, or most of the others. Who needs it? So I won't be going to the house. Once I get out I'm pretty sure no one's gonna bother looking for me and I can stay out of sight for months. I've done it heaps before and I'm all set up to do it again. So it's bye, bye from me'.

'A self-discharge from SNU?' Jai's a bit surprised. He knows Reese is considered a great escape artist, but always from the main house. SNU...? He pushes him again about what he means.

'Wait and see my man, wait and see! All will be revealed.' Reese taps his nose, unwilling to tell him any more even though he knows Jai will keep his mouth shut.

Lunchtime comes and goes. The afternoon programme starts up with the boys back in the gym. Jai is bored, there is only so much gym he wants to do. He's not feeling too lively anyway. The guitar that normally spent its time in SNU is down to three strings and isn't worth using. There are no new strings so he can't even fix it.

It's nearly shift change over time and the staff are in the office. Wyatt looks like he's showing the new guy how to do the books. Jai sits on the floor doing nothing. Reese is clambering up the climbing rope. Jai thinks that Reese is much fitter than he looks. It's not easy to get up that rope. He couldn't do it, not that he wants to. He drifts off in his mind thinking about how fit he was when he played football and rode his bike everywhere. It suddenly seems like such a long time ago.

The climbing rope is swinging in front of him, almost clipping him as it goes side to side. He's about to say something. He looks up just in time to see Reese, who's near the top swinging back and forward, back and forward. He keeps his mouth shut and watches. The next thing Reese swings towards the corner of the gym, kicking at the skylight as he does. Jai can see it has a big crack right across it. As Reese swings a second time he kicks out again and it splits with a loud crack, then the fractured bits dislodge. It's all Jai can do to get out of the way of the falling pieces. They crash to the gym floor and shatter, spraying glass everywhere. He feels little pieces hit him on his arms and legs. He checks to see if he is cut and sees blood on his left arm, but nothing much. He looks up, preparing to give Reese a couple of barrels for nearly killing him. Reese is gone… Self-discharge!

The other boys in the gym are hooting and shouting. Wyatt and Ma run into the gym.

'Everybody to their rooms', Wyatt is directing the traffic. The boys stand their ground including Jai.

'Move now!' Ma raises his voice just a little, but enough. 'Don't make me ask twice!'

OK, Jai thinks, not sure what Ma will do if he doesn't move but not wanting to find out. The others are moving too, probably for the same reason. Once they are in their rooms Wyatt tells them they will be staying there until the gym is fixed.

They spend the next three hours in their units. When they are eventually unlocked, they're put back into the gym. The broken glass is gone. The climbing rope is gone. And the hole where once there was a skylight is covered with a plastic sheet.

The rest of the day passes without incident although there is plenty of chatter about Reese's escape. Legend bro!

Chapter 30
SNU Ta Do

It's been two weeks since Reese's escape. SNU escapes are unheard of and it has caused a great deal of consternation. The incident triggered all sorts of enquiries as Mike Michelsen had feared. The General Manager of Social Welfare and the Minister have been asking questions. It created an atmosphere of tension and the situation became very uncomfortable for the staff at all levels. I wrote my report before I went off shift and showed Ma how to do his. Both Mr Rogers and Ted were asked to write about what they'd witnessed in the days and weeks before the escape. They were annoyed as they had been raising red flags about a potential issue for weeks and they felt these hadn't been taken seriously. As far as they were concerned the escape could have been thwarted. Maybe true, but I think their grumble was probably more about having to write additional lengthy missives when it was these that could have been prevented.

This was the first breakout from SNU since it was built back in the nineteen seventies so it has generally shown its fit for purpose. The fact that Reese was smart enough to orchestrate the breakout was something I secretly thought to be very clever, although I didn't say so to my colleagues. It had shown us a previously unidentified weakness. That's the way of things, the boys find ways to do illicit things and we respond to try and prevent them from happening again. It's another example of our symbiotic relationship.

I've enjoyed my various stints on days but it causes disruptions at home where, with Rose working full time, the childcare arrangements are disrupted. So it is good to be having a period back on nights so things can return to normal for a while. What's more, I have just had my 'weekend' two days off so I feel refreshed and ready to go.

I check the SNU on the way in. Five young people in tonight so two of the cells have an added mattress. Not a particularly good sign. High numbers in SNU possibly means the main residence will have been rumpty so I could be walking into fun and games upstairs.

I head upstairs. My cluster of shifts is with Mr Rogers. He isn't in yet, not surprising as he continues his silent protest about being handed shifts that are unsettled. While I wait for him to arrive I check out the files on the new admissions and take a look at all the recent incident reports. Two nights ago there was a fire lighting incident in SNU. Then there are a bunch of issues with 'wannabe' KPs. Also, new rumours have been circulating about a potential breakout from SNU and kids have been hanging around in the park again. The shadow of Reese's escape still looms large, paranoia is thriving. And I see there has been a problem with Jai who has been admitted to SNU. Definitely a range of issues that could flare up into something more.

The admission of two new boys can change the group dynamics, although so far there's no indication this is happening. They're keeping their heads down. Both are in Kauri, separated from the main group but they still need to be monitored closely. My Rogers will check them out first thing when he eventually gets here. He tells me he likes to 'connect' early but Ted reckons he just wants to know if they will be a nuisance, and maybe create a positive impression before they find out his nickname.

There's a new aspiring King Pin. He's doing all the usual stuff, being loud, challenging, bad-mouthing the staff, threats to other boys, and general bullying. It's unpleasant for everyone, disruptive, and can easily get out of hand. The unfortunate reality about KPs is that there's more harmony when everyone knows who's the head honcho. If, as occurs reasonably often, there are a couple in residence together, it only works if they find a way to coexist without undue friction.

Today's problem however involved three boys. One is a newish admission who, after a couple of days in SNU, has come into the open residence and is now finding his feet. Up against him is Chevy, not a real KP because he's not smart or supported by the boys, but he hasn't got the messages so he persists despite experiencing continual setbacks. The third player is Fish, a big boy with natural leadership qualities. He doesn't need to do much because he is known by everyone from his previous admissions. He is the sort of KP the staff don't mind because he's not an overt bully, is generally affable and likes to get on with his own business. But he also doesn't want to be bothered by the rank and file and makes sure everyone knows. Normally Chevy, who's often in residence at the same time as Fish, does not present a problem. But the new boy has changed things.

Roddy Patti is in Stanmore because of his involvement in an armed robbery. He is not physically big but he appears to be mature beyond his years. He has already expressed his disdain for being in the 'little boys' prison to anyone who cared to listen. After his admission, the group dynamics visibly changed. The staff know he's the catalyst although they haven't been able to nail down if he's doing anything more than the usual behaviours. Fish is not happy, it's upset his day. Over lunch, he had words with Roddy, quietly, but telling him to 'pull his head in.' Roddy had a few words with Chevy, who, wound up like a spring, challenged Fish to a fight and fronted him up before the staff could intervene. The fight didn't last long, and it did not go well for Chevy. As the antagonist, he ended up taking a hike to SNU. There was no apparent residual agitation from the KP related friction when I arrived. Fish and Roddy seem to have found a way to live together. It no doubt also helps that Chevy is gone for the night.

John Rheem and Aaron Pierce are two other boys currently in SNU. They were involved in a fire lighting episode. The incident was high profile hence there was a suite of incident reports to read, including one each from Ted and Wayne North. The event occurred a couple of nights ago when Ted was working with Mr Rogers. Ted was out doing the external checks at about half eleven. On exiting the administration block he walked along the side of the SNU, looking in the windows. As he glanced in the first window there was a flash of light illuminating two boys huddled in the corner. It was hard to tell exactly what they were doing although it was obvious that they were up to no good. There was another flash, clearly a lighter. He saw they were attempting to set a pile of something unidentifiable on fire. One of the boys was holding up a mattress which partly obscured their activities. He entered SNU and headed to the office and called Mr Rogers who was otherwise occupied upstairs. By this time there was smoke oozing out from under the door. From the smell, he assumed that the mattress was on fire and the resulting fumes were toxic.

I note that Ted couldn't find a fire extinguisher which is something that needs to be rectified. He had no choice anyway, he had to open the cell door. The wave of brown acrid smoke was so thick it nearly bowled him over. The boys didn't respond when he called to them but he was reluctant to enter the cell because there was a risk this was a trick to lure him in, possibly attack him and take his keys. Before he had to do anything the smoke set off the fire alarm and sprinklers in the cell. The concrete walls and floor meant there wasn't much that could burn and in a short time the fire was doused. As the smoke cleared he found a couple of sorry-looking boys, drenched to the skin sitting in the corner, along with a blackened still smouldering mattress from which a wisp of white smoke spiralled upwards towards the dripping ceiling. The alarm disturbed the other boys who, unhappy, started kicking their cell doors and making threats towards the firelighters.

Ted got everyone out of their cells and assembled in the SNU gym area.

What happened next proved to be the interesting bit for me. Fire procedures required all the boys to be evacuated from the building. That wasn't going to happen given he was on his own and had too many boys to safely supervise in an open area and also possibly the whole event was an orchestrated attempt to escape. Mr Rogers wasn't able to come down, he was managing the boys upstairs who had also been disturbed by the fire alarm.

The Fire Service and the Police duly arrived. The Fire Service chief was less than impressed that Ted hadn't fully evacuated. He threatened to report the failure to the manager. The senior, Wayne, came in. He backed Ted's decision, which I detect from the phrasing in his report, was much appreciated. He emphasised the obligation to keep both the community and the kids safe and supported Ted in using his common sense to do both. This didn't satisfy the Chief. He said the sprinkler system, while reasonably modern, had only been cobbled together so wasn't fit for purpose. He reluctantly acknowledged it did the job on the day when Wayne pointed this out. In his view, we'd been lucky and he intended to take the matter further. The Police offered to take the firelighters away but doing so was a waste of time as they would only come back the next day. Ted made them clean up the mess, the natural consequence of what they'd done. After reading the reports I couldn't help but think what is it about fires and young people? They seem to be a recurring theme! At least no one was hurt and Ted's approach was vindicated.

The last two SNU residents are Aaron Lamar and Jai Rehua. Aaron is a frequent flyer and is in for his third stint in residence this year after yet another absconding from his placement and more minor offending.

The final incident report I read is about Jai's admission to SNU. It appears that his behaviour had been deteriorating for a couple of days. While no one has been able to identify the exact reason, it was suspected to have originated from a call he had with Mona one evening. He wouldn't talk about whatever it was.

Yesterday when it came to bedtime he sat in the dining room and refused to move. Despite the team's best persuasive efforts, he wouldn't budge. When they attempted to move him he held onto the table and wouldn't let go. The scene was marginally comical with staff trying to drag him to SNU and Jai resolutely holding onto the table. The table however was too big to go through the exit door. Jai and the table managed to be separated at this point.

Plenty of activity going on.

So tonight Wayne North wants me downstairs in SNU. He thinks a presence in the building is required for security purposes. I confess I felt this was a bit of an overreaction. However, looking at the mountain of incident reports I get why he's being careful. I ask about bringing on a reliever but he says it can't be done as all the available relievers are working with the day teams but he believes we can cope. Of course, he says, if there is a problem we can always ring him!

I'm sitting in the SNU office now. It's so quiet you could hear a pin drop. This is the way it is in SNU. The normal sounds of kids snoring or shuffling about, so common in the dorm areas, are cloaked by the thick steel doors. I checked the inhabitants when I came on, they were asleep. I thought that perhaps Chevy would be a problem but he's doubled up with Kendrick whom I know doesn't like any nonsense … unless he's leading it. Jai is in the middle cell and he is the lucky one who is not doubled up. I feel I'm in for a long and boring night.

About midnight I hear noises coming from the roof. I ring the night staff office to get Mr Rogers to check it out from upstairs. He returns my call a few minutes later saying he can't see anything. In the interim I check the gym area, shining my trusty torch up towards the ceiling. The skylight broken in Reese's escape is, somewhat incredulously, yet to be repaired. I suppose there is a lack of urgency because without the rope there is no real way of getting up there. Still, it seems tardy and neglectful. In retrospect, this probably also contributed to Wayne's security concerns. The opaque covering seems to mask the beam and prevent it from illuminating anything outside. I detect nothing in the uncovered skylights. The noise has stopped. The power of the torch beam may be working its disincentivising magic. However, I decide it's prudent to go outside for a look around.

I can see there is activity in the park. It's hard to pin down individuals but the shadows are moving. Just for an instant, I see a form that could be Reese, about his height and build, partially concealed by a tree. I shine my torch in that direction but it's too far to be of any benefit although it looks like the figure is giving me the 'bird'. It wouldn't be like Reese to hang about Stanmore, after all, he spends much of his time running away from the place. It would be like him to give the place the finger, but then so would plenty of others.

Nothing further happens and the time drifts on. At about 3 am I'm struggling to stay awake. This morning was one of those mornings where, when I got home to sleep, a neighbour decided to chainsaw down a large tree in front of their property. Not unreasonable from his perspective, not helpful from mine. Something of the sort happens every week. The weekends are the worst but other times can be problematic as well, road works, trucks, a neighbourhood dog barking endlessly, kids on holidays, you name it, there are many things to prevent a good day's sleep. If I get four uninterrupted hours it's a bonus. If I get a total of six hours it's a rarity. Today I tried to go back to bed at five in the evening but the children, teatime, a noisy TV, it all got in the way, so here I am starting to have real trouble staying awake. I stand up and walk around, up and down the hall, about five metres, it's like being in a prison cell. I've been to the bathroom three times to wash my face, gone outside and stood on the doorstep and sucked in the cool evening air and felt the freshness of the night on the tips of my nose and ears. But still, as soon as I sit down in the office my head is nodding.

Suddenly I am jarred alive by a 'whump' coming from the gym. No matter how tired you are there's always a level of alertness sitting just under the surface of your consciousness. What the hell was that? I'm instantly alert and on my feet. The light from the hall is sufficient for me to make out a lump in the middle of the gym floor. At a glance, I can see it's not very big so I am intrigued rather than concerned. I go back to the office and switch on the lights before I go for a closer look. As I step through the gym door I smell it. It's a bag full of human excrement splattered on the floor. Someone went to a lot of trouble to do this, unpleasant trouble really because this does not smell like a healthy specimen. I look up and see the plastic covering over the broken skylight is gone. I'm gagging as I go to get the bucket and mop.

As I pass the office I let Mr Rogers know what happened. Things are quiet upstairs but he feels there isn't much he can do, which is correct! I can almost hear the laughter in his voice. I could have said bring your blanket and you can sleep down here, but I don't, no point.

I give the Police a call and let them know about the incident, maybe they've got a car in the area and will look around.

'That's shitty!' says the dispatcher. 'Some people just treat that place like shit! Ha! ha! 'Who would want to shit on Stanmore, it's a holiday camp for kids, haha!'

I am too tired to laugh but I can think of a few groups who have publicly dumped on Stanmore more than once, no point in saying anything about that either. The dispatcher, after his sojourn into frivolity, indicates they are a bit quiet tonight so they'll send someone out for a look around as soon as they can. I mention that it feels like it has to be an ex-client though. Who else has the motivation and also would know the layout in SNU? Boys have made threats about what they will do to the place if they get a chance and many are quite capable of following through. I'm not aware of any who have said they'll crap on it, but it could have happened. SNU is hated by the boys.

I clean up and get rid of the offending item. As I walk down the hall back to the office I see Jai Rehua at his cell window.

'What's going on sir?' he asks

'Don't call me sir. It's just a bit of nonsense going on outside. Nothing for you to worry about.' I reassure him. 'Why are you awake?'

'Baden's been at my window tonight, being an idiot, whispering things. I can't make out what the 'f' he's on about. He's whacked out and I told him to piss off. He's been back about three times, being a pain in the arse. But I think he's gone now.' Ah, that explains it!

Later I get a call from Mr Rogers. There are a couple of Police cars across the road and the Police are going through the park. They've brought a dog with them. One thing I have found with the Police, despite their sometimes negative talk about Stanmore, most often they provide the support we request. Can't fault them on it. I'm sure it'll be the last we see of the late-night park activities for a while.

For the rest of the night, I'm wide awake. It's like that, an incident gets all the adrenaline going. The pull of the darkest hour is past. I drag myself home and after seeing the kids off to school I get into bed. And someone nearby starts up their electric sander.

Chapter 31
Jai Gets a Night Visitor

Jai is in SNU and annoyed about it too. Lying in his bed after lights out he's thinking about the call he had with his mother a couple of nights ago. He'd rung her yet again to see if she could get it together enough to have him home. Unsurprisingly she was half cut. It blew him away when she casually mentioned that she had heard from Denny out of the blue. Can you believe it, after all these years? She said she'd told him to get lost. Ok, he could understand that, he's a loser and a deserter. But he still wanted to know more about him. What was he doing? Will he be in contact again? Will Jai see him? Does he know about Jai being in Stanmore? Where's he living? Mona either didn't know, hadn't asked, didn't care, or didn't want to say, he couldn't tell from her garbled responses. He slammed down the phone and Abigail who was helping with the phone calls that night asked if she could do something. But he didn't want her or any of them to even know what had happened, none of their freakin' business. He felt so mixed up afterwards but mainly he felt angry, enraged, at Mona for not asking or telling him what she knows, at Denny for not being interested in his son, for being in this hell hole where he can't do anything about any of it if he wanted to.

Today he'd asked John Land, the supervisor who was visiting the SNU before bedtime when he would be released from SNU. John said his caseworker Sarge would be on tomorrow and he would likely get out if Sarge recommended it. Pass the buck Jai thought, we all know John actually makes the decisions.

Jai drifts off into the place people go just before entering a deep sleep.

He is stirred from his slumber by a tapping on his window. He hoists himself up and walks over to have a look. It's Baden Jones. He hasn't seen Baden for ages. He knows him though because he'd met him before in Res. He's a bit of a dickhead. All he talks about is pills and girls. Jai didn't believe half of what he said because if it was true, the guy's the greatest Casanova since Casanova, and does it all when he's out of it on downers or uppers or whatever it is he takes.

'Hey Jai, it's good to see you my brother. Wanna break out?' Baden whispers.

'Bullshit man I ain't your bro. And I don't want to break out,' replies Jai.

Baden doesn't notice the slight. He continues, 'They haven't fixed the window in the gym. I went up and had a look, it's just got plastic on it.'

'Not gonna happen, they've taken away the rope... Someone's coming, I gotta get back to bed.' Jai ducked under the blanket as the red light in the cell gets brighter, a sign the staff are going to look in.

A shadow passes over the viewing window and shortly after the red light dims.

He's slumbering and he's lost track of time. A scratch at the window, then he hears Baden again, whispering.

'Jai, you awake? I'll bring a rope tomorrow and we'll lower it through the skylight, keep an eye out for it. It will be like the great escape, did you see that movie?' he says.

'Nah man never saw it, and I don't want to escape. It's not gonna happen. For a start, I'm locked in this cell, so how am I gonna get to the gym at night time? ...and it's not gonna happen during the day... the staff are twitchy after Reese's escape. They're already watching us like hawks. Anyway, I'm hoping tomorrow I'll be getting out of SNU and I'll be in the house.'

'Hey, what's the matter with you, don't you want to stick one to the man? I'll come down the rope and get the keys from the office. You'll be a hero, yeah get the fame! Jai the great escaper, from the secure unit!' He's slurring his words and Jai is getting irritated. Baden isn't listening, he's out of it and on top of that his plan is just plain dumb. Just as he's about to say something more the red light gets brighter. He scampers into bed just making it under the cover when he hears Wyatt's voice coming through his door, 'Everything all right in there Jai?'

He doesn't reply pretending he's asleep. A few seconds later the red light dims. He's having trouble sleeping now. Too many interruptions. He just wants to get some sleep and then in the morning go into the house. See who's about, play some guitar, do something to kill the time, kill the boredom. Maybe we'll go for a walk on the Port Hills or head to Taylor's Mistake for a swim.

After a while, his mind slows down and he drifts again into the netherworld. His sleep is fitful. Sometime later through his restlessness, he hears a voice again.

'Hey Jai, you awake? Want to have a laugh?' He doesn't, and he certainly isn't wanting to get up again, but he is concerned Wyatt will hear Baden who already sounds louder this time. He goes over to the window.

'Keep awake and listen out. I'm telling you it'll be funny as man. I'm gonna shit on the night staffer. It's that guy Wyatt, I saw him come out and look about a while ago. He's a prick who deserves to get a turd on his head. Make sure you tell the others it was me. I'll come back tomorrow night to check yous all out, and maybe do something else to put it on the night staff. Good times.'

'Baden, man, will you fuck off! I don't want to get caught talking to you. They'll only think I'm trying to escape. They're paranoid now, about escapers anyway. You've seen Wyatt, he's checking out every little noise. I want to get into the big house tomorrow and I don't want anything getting in the way.'

'Puck, puck, puck, you da chicken man, puck, puck, puck, you da chicken man!'

'Fuck off Baden! I'll dob you in if you don't fuck off!' Jai is urgent, shout whispering.

'All right, keep your hair on, I'm going bro! your loss, not mine.' And he's gone.

Jai gets back to his bed. He isn't asleep when a few minutes later the lights in the hall cast a yellow square on his wall and the red light inside increases. His stomach sinks. Wyatt is going to find Baden. If that happens who knows what the 'random' will say because he's got mush for brains. Jai might be considered an escape risk and then who knows how long he will end up in here. Bloody Baden, he doesn't even like the guy and he certainly doesn't want to take the rap for anything he's doing.

He gets up and goes to the window in his door. He can see Wyatt in the hall.

'What's going on sir?' he asks.

'Don't call me sir. Nothing for you to be worried about but I am just checking to see who's awake… And I see you are!' Wyatt doesn't look too bothered, just mildly annoyed.

Jai thinks he better say something. He doesn't want any grief from Wyatt and he doesn't care about Baden.

'Baden Jones was out there, at my window, he sounds out of it. He woke me up, but I told him to piss off!'

'Ok… thanks.' Wyatt moves off and he can hear doors being unlocked, opened and then locked again. He gets back into his bed. A few minutes later he hears a door again. Before long the red light filling his room is dulled down to a red tinge.

Jai lies there wide awake now. He starts thinking about the mess he's in. What's going to happen next and when? Nothing much has happened in the last few months. It feels like he's suspended in space, floating around unconnected like Major Tom the spaceman in Bowie's song. He hasn't been sitting doing nothing though, he has taken off a couple of times. Baden's plan though is the dumbest of all the dumb plans he's ever heard. Running hasn't helped him, he knows that, but he feels he's going to rot away in here. There are only so many walks and so much kayaking you can do. At least there's a bit of action out in the real world! Even school would be better, now there's a novel thought! And at least when he comes back from being on the run his social worker talks to him. Pity about the judge and the police, they also talk to him, just not quite so nice. Sometimes running feels like it's the only way to get anyone's attention.

The music is good though. He's still learning 'Shuffle Rag' in bits and pieces. He can do most of it now and Wyatt had said he will show him how to take some of the licks and use them in other tunes. And he does that picking style, claw hammer, yeah it's been good to learn and it works on some of the other tunes he knows. Claw hammer, a dumb name although he guesses the fingers are bent a bit like a claw and you do hammer the bass strings, but it's just fingerpicking with a fancy name. It's taken months to get this far, probably running hasn't helped the learning progress too much. He doesn't come across too many guitars in the doss houses he's hung out at. Ah well, he thinks, sometimes you just gotta go when and where the spirit takes you.

Old Wyatty boy, he's ok but he is still one of the staff guys so can't forget that. And he only showed Jai things when he was around during the day. He talks about music at night, it's interesting but Jai wants to learn and practice. He's brought the electric guitar into the dorm a few times because it doesn't make any noise if it's not plugged in but Wyatt wouldn't play it in Rata. He said it disturbs the boys. Bulldust man. Sometimes when the staff didn't take it, he has been able to practice at night, especially if Mr Rogers is on. But most often Wyatt or the 'Teddy Bear' grab it when they are patrolling. They say there's no point in leaving it upstairs at night because you're supposed to be sleeping. But there was a point. Lots of the other staff let him have it, not everyone, but enough. The believers were the easiest. Some of them are a bit vague about the rules or don't care. It's always worth a try, even if it only works once in a while.

If there's anything worth looking forward to in this place it's the nights when Wyatty plays. Jai's certain he'll play 'Shuffle Rag' now he knows he has an appreciative audience, and he'll play 'Police Dog Blues' too. He's pretty sure he gets a laugh out of playing that one. Sometimes after Wyatt has played and he's doing a check, Jai has let him know he was still awake and they talked about the blues and guitar playing. He's told Jai about other musicians worth a listen and he'd even brought in a tape of some blues guys which Jai put in his 'personals.' But Jai hadn't had anything to play it on. He'd forgotten to take it with him when he was discharged last time, and he wondered if it was still around somewhere. Wyatt played a few of the tunes for him that he'd put on the tape. He'd liked 'Vigilante Man', so cool, and played with a broken bottleneck, sliding it up and down the strings making the guitar weep and moan. His old man, for all his playing, wasn't someone who played bottleneck so that was something new he could try, maybe after he got 'Shuffle Rag' down. Although they're not going to let him have a broken bottleneck in this place. Another one is 'The House of the Rising Sun'. Everyone knows that one so it's good to play in the Res. Wyatt had written the names of the songs and the artists on the cover of the tape and he reckons you could get some of them from the library. Jai thinks that's a laugh because he only goes to the library when he's bored and wants to catch up with some of the bros. It's a winter hang out. Jai vows to himself next time he's in there he'll check the music out. Wyatty says they've got all the ones he likes and more. Worth a look at least.

Yeah, the music is good and it's the only thing worth doing when he's in Res. He begins to drift off to sleep. Thinking about the music always calms him.

Then Denny is there in his head. In the space of a heartbeat, he is awake again. Anger wells up inside him. Fucking loser!

Chapter 32
A Boy Is Distressed

Tonight I decided to do one more walk around the dorms before I go out and do the exterior security checks. I'm in Kauri opening the doors to the rooms as I 'sight the body'. When I open up Barty Roman's room I see him sitting on the bed with his arms wrapped around his knees. He's sobbing deeply. He's come in during the last week and he's someone I have met several times. I ask him what's going on in my best engaging manner. At first, he won't reply but I take my time, I am getting better at being patient and listening. Eventually, I manage to get out of him that he's going to Kohitere for the next three months and he doesn't want to. He's terrified, the most upset I've seen a young person at the residence. I try to put him at ease by pointing out that some boys believe bad things will happen when they come to Stanmore but now he's here now and he knows it's mostly just talk. All he says is this place sucks but Kohitere is worse. After that, he clams up completely and won't respond to me at all.

I go back to the office and tell Ted what's going on. He has no idea what to do but he asks me whether Barty is a risk to himself and whether we should move him to SNU. I can't see any advantage in doing that. I suggest keeping a close eye on him with regular monitoring. If he's awake and still upset next time I check, I'll have another go at finding out if there's something that I can do. While I am waiting I go through his file again. There is nothing that particularly stands out although I see he has previously been to Kohitere for a short period. In itself, this is a little unusual because, unless you are a local, boys tend to go there for longer periods. There could have been several reasons this happened although there is no indication why in the file. However it's there in black and white, he's going the day after tomorrow, first thing in the morning.

When I go back to his room I find Barty in the same position and the same state. I try again but this time all he will say is that he wants to talk to Abigail.

He says it over and over again like a mantra. I'm not getting anywhere. I offer to create an incident report outlining his fears and leave it with the diary for the day staff to follow up. No response just more sobbing and requests for Abigail.

I feel bad after this chat, concerned and powerless. In the end, I say to him that I will do my absolute best to get a message to Abigail so she can talk to him. I hate making the promise because I can't be sure that it will happen but I am caught in the moment.

Barty is a runaway and he spends a lot of time on the streets so I understand it might take a while to sort out a permanent and effective plan for him. But Kohitere seems like a stopgap, not a solution. In the end, he will come back to Christchurch and have to be integrated somehow, probably spending more time at Stanmore as he does so. However, it is his obvious terror that I cannot get out of my head. It seems to me that something must have happened last time he was at Kohitere to make him so upset. It doesn't take a rocket scientist to work out that the most likely cause is physical abuse of some kind.

His predicament gnaws away at me all night. I have often heard vague comments from boys about physical abuse, and occasionally, sexual abuse. Most of the talk is about getting the bash by staff, or how they turn a blind eye to bullying and assaults by boys. Sometimes you hear comments about alleged paedophilic behaviour but so far everything I have heard has been generic. Residences are mentioned but not specific people. Even when I've overheard a conversation between boys, like from outside a cell door when the boys are chatting at night, I've never heard names. I've discussed it with my night colleagues on the basis that there is no smoke without fire. Both can tell me of incidents they've heard about from other residences where a boy has done something to another boy, sexual violence, or where a staff member has been disciplined for abuse, and in one case, prosecuted. But they tell me these are rare, although they both assure me the rumours aren't.

I've made an undertaking to Barty now and I need to follow up on it. At shift changeover, I pass my concerns and promise on to the oncoming team. There are two relievers today as well as the two regulars. I talk to Ben Hogan whom I believe will follow things up. He says he will but he expects to be busy given the staffing situation. I try to impress on him how important I think this is and that Barty's reaction is way beyond anything I've seen before. He points out that Abigail is off on her two days break so he will have to get someone else to follow up. He will do his best. I don't feel remotely confident that he has understood the

236

gravity of the situation but I will have to leave it at that. I can't think of anything more I can do. I go home.

After a couple of hours of sleep, I am wide awake. Barty's plight is playing in my head like a stuck record. It's useless to continue trying to sleep so I get up. I decide to go back to Stanmore and see if anything has happened. When I get there I head into admin looking for a senior, anyone will do. But there is no one about. I see Mike Michelsen the manager coming out of his office so I collar him.

'Mike, sorry to interrupt your busy schedule but I need to talk to you.'

'Wyatt, shouldn't you be sleeping? You look like you need it. Must be important, you better come into the office.'

I am agitated. I stand hopping from foot to foot as Mike sits down behind his desk. Before he can settle in his chair, I'm making my case.

'Barty Romans was up most of the night. He is extremely upset, the worst I've seen since I've been here. He's due to go to Kohitere tomorrow and he's afraid, almost hysterical about not wanting to go. He wouldn't talk to me but he said he would to Abigail, and only her. She's off today and tomorrow but I think it is important that he doesn't go without talking to her.'

'I assume you passed this on to the day team.'

'I did but they're down a couple of permanent staff so, you know under pressure. I don't think they got how important this is.'

'Well… Barty wouldn't be the first boy to be unhappy about a residential transfer, I would hardly transfer anyone if I accepted that as a reason not to.'

'No, this is more than that. I think something must have happened to him. This was a real terror. Look, Mike, I don't know why but I feel that something isn't right here. Can someone ask Abigail if she will talk to him before he goes? It has to be today.'

'Well I'm reluctant to contact staff when they have their day off, but obviously, you feel very strongly about this so I will get John Land to get in touch with her and see if she is available. I can do any more than that.'

I thank him and leave feeling a little easier in myself. Even if Barty never knows, I've followed up in good faith.

Back on shift tonight I pass by Barty's room and pop in to see how he is. He is still very subdued but he does say that he hasn't seen Abagail but he has been told he is not going to Kohitere tomorrow.

I am relieved, at least something has happened.

Two days later, after the changeover, Abigail pulls me aside. She has talked with Barty. She cannot go into details because the matter is now in the hands of the Police and the Department. She can say that he made allegations and they are serious. He asked her to sit in on an evidential interview, which she did. She discloses that since she started at Stanmore there's only been one boy who's opened up to her about abuse, Barty. She is happy he felt he could. She tells me that many of the boys may have experienced sexual abuse sometime in their lives but they will rarely talk about it. Different for the girls in residence, they are more open and partly that's because it is such a common experience for them. Her feeling is there needs to be a culture of zero tolerance for any type of violence, physical or sexual, current or historic, and this has to be messaged and demonstrated to the boys over and over again so they believe it. And there needs to be real action when a disclosure is made. Only then will they feel ok to talk about it. But she also said an additional complexity is often boys feel it reflects on them negatively. They might be accused of being homosexual and this can lead to them being treated differently by staff and boys alike. There's also a perception they won't be believed, just as happens to many of the girls she has worked with. On top of that, there's a problem raising sexual abuse with male staff members. There's a trust barrier, especially if you think there may be hidden perpetrators in the ranks. Then if one of the staff has loose lips, the boy can get picked on or roasted in the group. All in all, no real safety in even bringing it up, in fact, it's all risk for the boys.

I feel so powerless and ill-equipped that I ask her what I can do if this sort of thing arises again. She's clear, 'Don't push, listen and offer support and do what you did, follow up a concern. It's best to do it with the young person's consent if you can, but if you can't, it's one of those situations that should never be ignored.'

I sigh, 'So much to be learned.' I feel the void, 'Thanks.' I turn to get on with my job.

'Don't thank me. You know Mike was impressed that you did something, coming in when you should have been sleeping, and didn't just let the matter go. He liked your intuition and your persistence. Yeh, he thinks you've got potential!'

That's nice, I think to myself but I have that familiar and pervasive feeling that the more I learn, the more I need to know. Two days later Barty is discharged to a family home on the Westcoast. I hear that he stays for a couple of days and then he's reported missing.

Part 6
Final Days

Chapter 33
Wyatt Has a Tough Night

I can tell from the moment I arrive that something is going down. It's in the air, almost suffocating. The buzz coming from the big boys' dorm greets me as I ascend the stairs. I sit down in the night staff office ready for handover. The first staff member to come in, Sarge, confirms it.

'It's been a strange old shift tonight. No major acting out by any of the boys but lots of whispering, lip, back chat, play fighting, you know silly stuff. Something's bubbling away. We had a new admission into the house from SNU today, J.T. He has been at home awaiting sentence from the District Court but he breached his bail. He's going to the big house this time, no more Boys' Homes for him. No point in keeping him in SNU though, because he will be here quite a long time before sentencing. That's John's view anyway and he's the boss. We think he may have been stirring things up but it's not obvious how. I pulled him aside to see if I could get a handle on it but it was a waste of time. The young people are in their beds so at this point we can ask no more... Oh... and I know you don't like it, but J.T. and Jai had the electric guitar up here tonight, it seemed to settle things down a bit. No doubt you'll collect it later on.'

More like buying peace, I think to myself feeling a bit grumpy. It's left to us to get it off them, and they're wound up. I'm developing a bit of cynicism but I can't be bothered to challenge the behaviour out loud.

Just as Sarge finishes, the rumble goes up a further notch. Mr Rogers has arrived. Somehow it seems more pronounced tonight, or maybe it is just my imagination playing tricks on me. He sits himself down. By now we've finished the handover but we have the highlights package again for his benefit. However this time Sarge adds, 'Oh and I should have mentioned, Jeremiah Hayes is back in the house tonight. He seems in a good frame of mind so I don't think he's contributing to the problems, but he can be a bit volatile so just watch him!'

This new information doesn't raise any alarm bells for me. I've known Jeremiah for some time as he's a frequent admission. He spent years in foster care after his mother deserted him. His care experience wasn't good. At the age of two, he was beaten by his foster father, badly enough to require hospitalisation. His social work report notes that from an early age he demonstrated signs of brain damage, possibly foetal alcohol syndrome. His behaviour was often uncontrollable. Trouble followed him into school. By the age of seven, he was sent to a special school for boys with physical and mental health issues. Eventually, he was medicated to manage his violence. By his eleventh birthday, he was the size of an adult and unmanageable without his meds. In the interim, he had become a runner and when he did so, the meds did not go with him. There were numerous incidents involving Police call-outs where foster carers, school staff or other kids were hurt.

Eventually, he entered the residential system, cycling between foster home trials and the various residences, Hokio Beach, Kohitere and Stanmore. At Stanmore, there's been a considerable number of incidents requiring physical interventions and he spends a fair bit of his time in SNU. I've been involved in a couple of these although they were at the minor end of the scale, nothing that I feel has created any personal animosity towards me.

I've talked with him a few times about things he's interested in like cars and AC/DC, and I've played basketball with him, one on one, when he was in SNU. We both enjoyed it. He's physically coordinated, and he's certainly big enough to be a ballplayer if he can just control his impulses and take a bit of direction. Both things at this point in his life, appear to be a bridge too far.

We take over the shift.

The hum does not abate quickly as it generally does. Now and then there's a raised voice, someone calling out, a snigger, a retort. I decide to employ my usually effective strategy of active patrolling, being highly visible and tracking the noise. I feel the need to step it up, partly because of the warnings, but also the sustained nature of the evident undercurrent. Mr Rogers is out and about too, doing his bit. He's getting the usual response, a bit of abuse, some name-calling. I admire the guy for his persistence but tonight it isn't helping settle things down.

It takes about an hour of non-stop patrolling from one end of the building to the other before everything becomes quiet and the boys finally appear settled. I head back to the office and tell Mr Rogers I'll go out and do the perimeter security checks. I've done the bulk of the 'active management' and want some air. No objection from Mr Rogers and no real surprise about that either.

The night is clear and beautiful. I can see the stars and a three-quarter moon illuminates the western sky. From the car park, I look up and down about a kilometre of Stanmore Road. Tranquillity reigns apart from a couple of young women wandering past the Working Men's Club, clearly in a merry state and having a laugh about the night's festivities. As they walk past I can hear every word of their conversation. Once they're gone I stand there for a couple of minutes enjoying the peacefulness. Nothing is happening in the park. And it's not yet midnight.

I'm outside the administration building when my feeling of serenity is interrupted by a muffled banging followed by raised voices. It's not often something happens inside SNU that can be heard out on the grounds. Probably tonight's stillness has helped. I immediately go to view the cells from their external windows. There are only two boys in tonight. I see them both standing at their doors, kicking and shouting out. I head inside and go to the first cell demanding to know what all the noise is about. The young fellow blames his colleague in the next cell for waking him up. He says he can't sleep now and needs a drink of water. I tell him to quieten down and get a drink from his basin tap if he needs one. I go next door and the same excuse is made.

This is a distraction.

I go into the office and ring upstairs. No reply. That's a bit odd, although Mr Rogers probably has his feet up, he will always get the phone if there's no one else to answer it. I assume he is out of the office. I need to get upstairs fast. The earlier brewing unrest may have been refermented. Fortunately, I have only been in the SNU for three or four minutes, not long in real-time but long enough in the world of residential distractions.

I exit SNU through the side door which brings me out next to the external stairwell leading to the second story fire exit. I bound up the steps two at a time. The door is still secure. However, I don't have any trouble making out shouting and banging coming from inside. It had previously been obscured by the racket from SNU, which has just started up again. Too bad, they're not going anywhere, kick away boys!

I go through the fire door, securing it after me. As soon as I enter the upstairs landing, I can tell this is a major incident. Boys are running up and down the hall in Kauri and in and out of rooms. There's hammering and crashing coming from

Rimu and Rata. There's no time to feel any emotion, it's a matter of marshalling resources and responding.

Hatch Hitch runs by as I'm about to step into Rimu and he looks at me, grinning from ear to ear. He's with some other guy I don't recognise. They seem to be going somewhere with a purpose. I have to shout to get above the commotion, demanding to know where they're going. They ignore me. I give a general direction to five or six boys who are now milling around near the fire door to get back to bed. I'm wasting my time! No one can get out the fire door, I locked and double-checked it so I leave them to it and head into Rimu.

I immediately recognise boys from Rata are also in there. It's so crowded I have to shove my way through the narrow space between the partitions to get to the office and locate Mr Rogers. The office door is open, the jamb is splintered. There's nobody in there. At a glance I see it has been rifled through, there are papers strewn everywhere, the chairs are upturned, and the log and record books are on the floor. The phone line has been ripped out of the wall and the phone lies in pieces on the floor by the desk. Maybe Wayne North, because he lives so nearby, will hear the hubbub and come over. Any additional body would be a help. But I don't hold my breath. I feel for now at least, we are on our own.

I step out and pull the door closed, kicking aside debris so I can. It won't latch so when I let go of the handle it immediately drifts slightly ajar.

I look into Rata. The dorm is deserted. A few of the boys are in the stairwell. Maybe Mr Rogers is down there but I can't hear his voice. I call to him, just in case, no reply. I leave them to whatever they're doing.

I go back into Rimu and then into the corridor heading to Kauri. There is a mass of boys still milling about the landing and fire door. I see the glass has been kicked and is shattered but it has not been breached, bulging, but held together by a fine mesh of wire. There's so much mayhem and noise going on I can barely hear my voice directing them to get back to their dorms.

Then the fire alarm goes off. It had been relocated into the office after an earlier 'collective disturbance' but the insecure nature of the door has made it easy to activate. Weirdly, the sound, while grating, is also a relief. At least now help will come… but when?

All hell breaks loose. If chaos can become more chaotic, it has! Thirty boys out of control, running about like lunatics…screaming, shouting, swearing, laughing, pushing and shoving each other. As I stand in the corridor I see Chevy get punched in the face. The perpetrator, Fish, sees me looking at him, grins and gives me a wave. I am about to say something when the ferocity of the din overtakes me. I hear screams of pain, sounds of rage, trashing and crashing. I am surrounded. Things are being thrown about, bits of bedding, clothing, wood ripped from somewhere, the crunch of "unbreakable glass" being pulverised. I see Bentley Breezer with what looks like the chair from the night staff office. He is smashing it against the reinforced glass next to the fire exit door at the end of the Kauri corridor. He turns when I shout at him to put it down and throws it against the wall. The legs puncture the wallboard and the chair remains jammed at forty-five degrees. He bolts past me screaming in my face and spraying a shower of saliva as he does so.

I'm well aware that anyone in the stairwell can't get past the doorway into the dining area until either Mr Rogers or I open it, so I don't worry about the increasing numbers of young people starting to go in that direction. Some of the more experienced guys are calling out to go to the stairwell. That's helpful! From the top of the stairs, I shout out to the boys below asking if Mr Rogers is there. I hear a couple of shouts of 'no' in response.

I make my way along the hall, the fire alarm continues to pulse and screech. The open night staff office door now has a large hole in it.

Where are you, Mr Rogers? He must be somewhere! I ignore all the activities of the boys and concentrate on my search. To get everybody safely out to the evacuation point in the gym will take both of us…and a minor miracle.

I call out his name, loud and urgent, but still nothing. I know it will be hard for him to hear over the sustained din. I head to the farthest reaches of the Kauri dorm and start a check more closely room by room, herding the odd straggler along ahead of me as I go. As I entered the second bedroom, I see Jason Taylor huddled in the corner by his bed. He is bleeding from his head and his T-shirt is splattered red. He must have been pushed over or attacked, something has happened, but there's nothing I can do about it at this moment so I shout at him to get up and move. It takes only a matter of seconds but I clear the junior dorm area and then move into Rimu, looking briefly into each partitioned alcove just in case I've missed something or someone.

By now all the young people are jammed like sardines on the stairs waiting for me to let them out. Still no sign of Mr Rogers. Only Rata left to check and I have already looked there a couple of times.

Now I'm anxious, where is he? A wild thought flits through my head that he has left the building. It's a possibility especially if things have got menacing or he has been personally threatened, maybe even hurt. But it would have to be serious. He's previously said the job wasn't worth his life or wellbeing. We've all thought about it but the risk is worse for Mr Rogers because so many of the boys hate him... and he knows it.

I'm in automatic mode, my mind directs itself away from thoughts of risk towards managing what is in front of me as best I can. So far it has been beneficial that there have been no signs of animosity directed towards me personally. I appear to be irrelevant to whatever is happening.

I re-enter Rata. I'm immediately aware this time there's a real fire in the far corner of the room. Flames are racing up a curtain and black smoke is cascading up the wall and across the ceiling. I run over grabbing a blanket as I go. In six strides I reach the far corner of the room and the bed nearest the fire. As I step around it I see him. Mr Rogers is lying on the floor. He's motionless, face down, blood covering the back of his head and matting his normally immaculate hair. There's a lot of blood, it covers the back of his shirt and has pooled on the floor. Beside him is the black electric guitar lying, bloodied, on its back. I glimpse what looks like matted hair on the pickguard. The guitar...we were supposed to retrieve it.

'Mr Rogers!... John! ...Mr Rogers!' I reach out and touch his back. No answer, no movement.

'John! We need to move, there's a fire.' I nudge him gently hoping it looks worse than it is but he doesn't respond. There's no time to check his vitals, we're too close to the fire so I grab his legs and start pulling him towards the door. As I do so I notice a streak of blood on the carpet which I am backtracking over. In that fleeting moment, I realise that someone dragged him behind the bed to conceal him from view.

The flames are spreading rapidly now. I can feel the intensity of the heat singing the hairs on my arms. There's blistering on Mr Roger's hand. I get him to the middle of the room and turn him over. It confirms my fears immediately. His face is a mess and there's a large wound on the side of his head. It's so stoved in I can see bits of bone and grey matter. He has no colour in his face. One eye is hard to pick out from the mess but the other is closed. It takes a few seconds to check the pulse in his neck ... nothing.

I want to get him out but I feel that if I keep dragging him on my own, even though he isn't a really big man, I'm not going to be quick enough to get us both out. I need help. The fire has now spread to the other curtains and thick black smoke is reaching out almost completely covering the ceiling. It's going to go up quickly. Thank god the fire alarm has already been set off. The sprinklers will surely kick in any second now. I drag him as far as the doorway of the dorm and shout out to the boys, 'Someone, anyone! Give me a hand, I need to get Mr Rogers out. He's badly injured, I can't move him. Rata's on fire and we, all of us, need to get the hell out of here.' I'm bellowing at the top of my voice.

I can only see a few of the boys because most are obscured by the L shaped stairwell. The noise from the boys, so evident a second before, stops. Now there's only the pulsing alarm and the crackle of the fire. Then a voice rises out from the jammed in masses, 'Get us the fuck out of here man!' It's Bentley.

Voices join in as Bentley leads a chant, 'Get us out! Get us out!' The tone is rapidly becoming more and more hysterical. I look up and see why. Smoke is pouring out of the Rata doorway and creeping along the ceiling. The boys can see it too. I can't delay any longer, we've got to move.

There's a whooshing sound as the sprinkler system goes off, followed instantly by a steamy hiss. I feel mild but instant relief! Hopefully, the water will slow or stop the spread of the fire. It might buy me time to get help and to get Mr Rogers out.

'Get out of the way!' I barge my way down the stairs to the fire door. It's hard work, many of the boys are openly panicking now. I shove them out of the way without ceremony or apology. I pick out two of the bigger boys, J.T. and Fish, 'You two get Mr Rogers and bring him downstairs, now! I'll open up the doors to get us out into the dining room, but he's coming with us. We all get out together!'

Neither boy responds. I wait, feeling the seconds tick by like heartbeats. Then J.T. says 'Fuck that KF, he can burn in hell.' The look of malevolence on his face chills me to the bone.

J.T. has spoken. I've got no time to argue the point. No boy will help now. Before I unlock the door and let the boys into the dining area I shout to the assembled cluster, 'You know the drill, wait by the backdoor! I let you out once I've got Mr Rogers. We'll assemble in the gym!'

The moment I open the door the leading boys elbow me out of the way and dash towards the rear of the building. I stay where I am to ensure all the boys in the stairwell are leaving. The first couple to arrive at the exit begin kicking at it. There's general panic. The situation is beyond boiling point. I catch a glimpse of Hatch who's managed to get to the front of the group and I see he's bent over doing something to the door handle. He has keys, I assume they're from Mr Rogers. Not much I can do except take note. I know they'll all be outside in a matter of seconds. I am a spectator to a potential mass escape, but I have other priorities!

I leave them to it and rush back up to Rata to have a last go at getting Mr Rogers out.

When I get to the upper landing I can see the sprinklers have dampened down the centre of the room, although they have by no means eliminated the fire. It has spread around the walls, particularly along the ceiling line where the sprays of water have not reached. The fire still looks robust and I suspect it has spread into the roof by now. The whole place could still go up any minute.

The doorjamb is on fire and flames grasp at me as I briefly take the scene in. I grab Mr Rogers and try to do a Fireman's lift so I can evacuate him. He's too heavy for me and I lose my balance and fall. I give up but I decide to drag him to the centre of the room where at least the sprinklers have mitigated the fire. Hopefully, the Fire Service and Police aren't too far away. I shield my face and run back down the stairs. The house is clear, with no young people in sight and the back door is wide open. I feel a cool draft on my face as the fire drags in oxygen to feed itself. I wonder how many boys have run away by now!

Chapter 34
Jai Gets Caught Up

Tonight's the night. Ever since J.T. arrived at the Res, all the boys knew what was going to happen. He told Jai not long after he was released from SNU and came into the main house, 'I'm off, bro. I'm not spending any more time in this 'try hard' kiddie's pokey. The judge is going to send me to prison for sure this time so I'm gonna have some fun before I go. And I need you with me. I want to go to your cousin Hermie's place.'

'Oh yeah' Jai says, not in the least enthusiastic but masking it as best he can. 'Why me? I'm getting out in a couple of days so I don't want to run, it'll just get me back in here and for longer next time.'

'The word on the street is that Hermie can get me down to Dunedin. I've got a good mate down there. We've got plans, yeah something big bro. I'll tell you about them later. Your cousin doesn't know me but he's got a good rep. If he can do the bisso for me then I need him so you're coming cause I need you!' It wasn't a request. Jai wasn't going to argue.

Everyone knows J.T. He's a vet, an experienced resident, a frequent escaper and a hard man.

He tells Jai more details about his plan during afternoon tea. He particularly wants to know who's on tonight. If it's Mr Rogers, it's going to be easier to execute.

His biggest risk is that he gets put back in the SNU for some reason. Fortunately, the SHITs team are not on this afternoon or it wouldn't take much because they don't like J.T. Since Reese's escape SNU security has been tighter than an airtight dope tin. And overall, the staff are generally more vigilant.

He cautiously sets about putting his plan in place. He needs others to play their part so lots of the boys in Res know what he's up to but they also know what could or would happen to them if they grassed. Jai can see him setting it up. It's the standard one, create a diversion, hit the fire alarm, and take off during evacuation. But J.T.'s not leaving much to chance. He has organised three distractions, one as soon as the night staffer goes outside to do their checks, one so he can get to the fire alarm now inconveniently relocated in the night staff office after the last riot, and one when everybody is evacuating and going to the assembly point in the gym.

He spent the last couple of days in the SNU before coming into the house, so he's already teed up those boys to act out when they hear something going on upstairs. Just a little extra diversion to distract the staff and keep them running in circles, or even better, maybe split them up. The SNU boys are up for it, anything to relieve the boredom, even better if it's late at night. They're going to stay awake and listen out. The fun always lasts longer at night.

Jai doesn't want to be involved. He's heard from his social worker and they're going to try him at home again. Only a few days to go and he's out. He's serious this time, he's going to keep out of the crap. He isn't going to do anything that might put his discharge at risk. He knows if he gets involved in any trouble at all, anything, it is certain to stop the placement. It'll show the Judge he's not settled, not changed, not ready to go back to the community, not reformed, just trying to put one over on him. But in his heart, he also knows he has no choice. He has to go with the flow, not doing so would have its repercussions. He just hopes not to get caught up in anything too serious. He feels more than a bit agitated. It was the way J.T. looked when he told him, determined with nothing to lose. It crosses his mind that he might be able to avoid running somehow once they get outside. Maybe, he can hang near the staff and they will stop him or just lose J.T. in the mayhem. Perhaps he can just return himself the night before Court and the Judge will look favourably on it. He'll have to see how things pan out.

During the after-dinner smoko, J.T. approaches Jai again.

'It's all on,' he whispers. 'That lazy bastard Mr Rogers is on. He'll be curled up by midnight and then when the other guy, the young guy Wyatt, goes out to have a look around, that's our best chance. I reckon I might be able to get Mr Rogers keys if he's asleep. If I do we'll get out the fire escape, it's the quickest way. If he's not asleep, or it looks too risky to try, then the fun's really gonna happen! Some of the boys are gonna start stirring it up in Rata. We've got to get him to come out of the office quick, so they're going to have a fight. All going well he won't lock the office up, especially if he has to act fast. Once he's out

I've got Hatch to hit the fire alarm. The main thing for you, just make sure you're ready!'

'Man, you know he'll lock the office, they always do,' Jai spots an obvious weakness.

'Then we're gonna go to plan 'C' and take damn the keys off him,' comes the confident reply. Jai feels a ping in his stomach.

So, the dye is cast, and whether he likes it or not, Jai is in. He has another desperate thought about how he can get out of it. Maybe he can get himself put in SNU, that would be the end of it for him although J.T would still go. But if J.T. found out, man, he'll 'get the bash' sometime in the future, and he'd get it good. The thought passes, better to wait and see he tells himself. Escape plans often don't happen… for lots of reasons.

Bedtime arrives. The day shift team leaves. The boys are twitchy in anticipation. The night staff are vigilant tonight, pacing about all the time like they know something's going down. Finally, things are quiet. He hears one of the night guys say to the other that it's time to do a perimeter check. Wyatty baby, so that's good he will be outside when the 'shit hits the fan'. He hears Mr Rogers say, 'You do it if you want to' and then footsteps on the wooden stairs. It will take about ten minutes for a check of the downstairs area and then Wyatt will go outside and could be away for at least twenty minutes, maybe more. All the boys know roughly how long these routines take. And Mr Rogers won't be doing any patrols so that's good.

About fifteen minutes later J.T. gives him the nod, it's on! J.T. gets out of bed and goes to the office door. 'I need to take a piss' he says through the door. Mr Rogers is not asleep yet.

'Get on with it' comes the reply, but he doesn't bother getting up. A couple of minutes later J.T. is back. He smiles at Jai and gives him the thumbs up. He whispers, 'He's awake, hasn't even got under the covers yet so it's plan B'

'Now boys!' J.T. says in a loud, urgent whisper. There's a general stirring in the dorm. Voices and movement, they've all been waiting. A few boys are out of their beds as are J.T. and Jai.

'Settle down, you lot,' comes a voice from the office. But J.T. calls out, 'I'll smash you, you bastard!' to no one in particular and stamps on the floor. Mr Rogers comes out of the office. He locks the door behind him and marches into Rata.

'I said settle down, it's time you lot were asleep. Get back in your beds and shut up!' J.T. who's in the corner farthest from the door is already up and dressed in his street clothes. He hisses, 'Fuck off K.F.'

Mr Rogers is standing in the doorway looking at him. The light from the hall illuminates his face and Jai can see he has a half-smile, half-smirk look on it. J.T. puts it on him again, 'Everyone knows you like the little boys. You sick fuck. You need a broom up your arse!' Even to Jai, this seemed pretty heavy. Mr Rogers thinks so too because his face screws up into a mask of anger. He strides over and confronts J.T.

'What did you say you little shit?' he growls.

'You heard me, bloody kiddie fiddler!' sneers J.T. 'Mr Rogers the fuckin Rogerer!'

Mr Rogers is enraged, he leans to within inches of J.T.s face. Jai can see the spit and venom as he does. 'You need to come with me to SNU sonny boy! You're disrupting the whole place and I'm not having it! On your bike!' Mr Rogers reaches out for J.T. and grabs him by the elbow. Jai thinks you have to give him credit for taking on J.T. by himself. Brave and foolish.

J.T. rips his arm free and in the same motion, he hits Mr Rogers hard with his elbow. Mr Rogers wobbles momentarily but he's pretty agile for an old dude. He's just about to regain his balance but before he can fully recover, J.T. steps into him and using all his weight and both his arms pushes Mr Rogers. This time he topples over, crashing into the bedside table, bouncing off it and falling onto the wooden floor. Blood appears on the side of his head where the impact has cut him. But he's quick and he still seems to have his wits about him. In an instant, he's got hold of J.T.s ankle and he tips him off his feet. When J.T. hits the floor Mr Roger grabs him in a headlock.

'That's assault you little shit, I'm gonna lay charges against you. You're done, you'll be in prison before the sun comes up, then you'll find out all about 'rogering' sonny boy.' He's spraying saliva everywhere as he shouts, oblivious to everything around him. He's lost it completely. J.T. is pushing off the bed with his feet trying to get traction and free himself, but Mr Rogers is holding on tight. The two of them are grappling on the floor like a 'Big Time Wrestling' show. Now Mr Rogers has managed to get on top of J.T. He has his forearm across J.T.s throat. J.T. is gagging and struggling to speak.

'Get... the... bastard... off... me, he is trying to kill me, I can't breathe, I... can't... breathe!' He's squirming around the floor arching his back trying to flip

Mr Rogers off but he's being held too tightly. Mr Rogers is stronger and more able than J.T. has anticipated.

Jai is aware the other boys in the dorm have been long gone, leaving them to it. They went the moment Mr Rogers stepped over to J.T. It's like they wanted to do their bit but make themselves scarce before anything else happened. They're running about the Rimu and Kauri as per the plan. Mayhem is alive and flourishing. Damage is being done. Some of the boys are screaming with excitement, caught up in the moment.

Jai is the only one left now apart from J.T. and Mr Rogers. J.T. is red in the face. He looks like he's gasping for air. Mr Rogers is talking to him, whispering in his ear. Jai can't make out all of what he is saying but he hears '… little shits think you can do what you want…assault… me… well…' His voice is stilted from his exertions.

'Get… him… off… get… him …off!… before he… fuckin… kills …me!' J.T. manages to rasp out, gulping for breath between the pleas. All the bravado is gone. Even in the gloom, Jai can see the panic in his eyes. Jai is momentarily paralysed. This shouldn't be happening! Staff don't attack the boys, it's fucked up, man… totally. He has to do something, anything, to stop Mr Rogers. He's going to kill J.T. Jai looks around desperately, what can he do? He sees the guitar by J.T.'s bed. He steps around the grappling pair and in two strides he has it by the neck. He's not thinking, just doing. It's like he's watching someone else's hands holding the guitar, swinging it, feeling the weight of the body as it drops, hearing a dull thud followed by a grunt and then blood, lots of it everywhere. Then it happens again… and again.

Everything is in slow motion. Mr Rogers pauses, he seems to be staring into the distance glassy-eyed, then he lets go and falls straight on top of J.T. He's still moving but in more of a twitching jerky motion. And he's making strange noises. J.T. scrambles out from under him.

'Thanks, man', he gasps, 'that KF was going to kill me. You saved my life bro.'

He gets up. There is blood on his face. He wipes it off with the sleeve of his T-shirt.

'Pull him behind the bed and grab his keys and let's get the hell out of here. The other guy will be coming back with all this noise going on!

Jai just stands there staring at Mr Rogers. He feels like a lead weight is tied around his ankles. He's aware he's still holding the guitar, he drops it like a hot brick.

'Fuck it, man, I'll get the keys, I need to get into the office… deal to the phone…see what I can find that might be useful. Come on! Come on! Come on!' J.T. slaps him on the face. 'Wake up man! Move him! Then get out to the fire escape door. The other guy most likely will come up that way. Delay him. And get some of the boys onto the stairwell in case he comes that way. We're in deep shit… so might as well go for it!' J.T. leans over Mr Rogers and grabs his keys which have slipped out of their pouch in the struggle. He deftly slips the large ring holding the bunch from the chain. He shoves Jai in the back and then he's gone.

It feels like it takes an age to drag Mr Rogers behind the bed. He's heavy even though he's skinny. A smear of blood follows them along the carpet. Jai knows he's badly hurt and he feels sick about it. But he was going to kill J.T. He rapidly repeats the thought over and over again in his head like a mantra, leaving no room for any others to grow. As soon as it's done, he heads to the door. It feels like he's running in waist-deep water. He pauses momentarily as he exits Rata, glancing back. Mr Rogers can't be seen.

J.T. is already coming out of the night staff office. 'I had to kick the fucking door in, too many keys and I didn't have time to try them all. Nothing in there worth anything, just some fags and a lighter. I fucked the phone so that won't be any use to anyone. Can't see us getting out through the doors now, it's too late. So keep stirring the others up, I'm going back in to check on the KF. I hope the bastard's dead. Then I'm gonna hit the alarm. If you see the other night staff guy coming, no matter what, slow him down!'

Jai just stands there. J.T. rushes past him and as he does he shouts. 'Get fuckin going!' And he heads back into Rata.

Jai finally moves. He runs into Rimu. It's a mess, stuff all over the floor, doors to wardrobes open or hanging loose, a haze of feathers from rendered pillows spinning around in the air driven by the constant flow of moving bodies. Some of the boys are jumping on beds, shouting or laughing hysterically. It seems as though half the boys from Rata are in there. He heads towards Kauri. As he enters the hall, he's aware that the fire escape door is being opened and he knows it's Wyatt coming back into the building. He doesn't want to deal with Wyatt. He turns around back towards Rimu passing Hatch Hitch and some other kid going the other way. They seem to be heading off with a purpose. He hears Wyatt shouting at Hatch.

Wyatt enters Rimu and shoves past, not seeming to see him, and disappears through the door. Jai just stands there being jostled by boys moving about him although he doesn't feel any of it. He sees it all and he hears it but it's like he's in a bubble, remote from everything going on, a spectator in a bizarre movie.

Then Wyatt is back going the other way pushing past him again. He's calling out for Mr Rogers. He can't have found him yet. Jai thinks some of the boys must have run back into Rata as well. No one can have seen him. Then the fire alarm bursts into life, filling the upstairs with a deafening Aarruggahh, Aarruggahh, Aarruggahh, relentless and pulsing. It drowns out most of the noise from the bedlam, but it adds to the frenzy and excites the agitation! Jai stands in the middle of Rimu screaming, 'Get out! Get out! Fire,! Fire!'

Chapter 35
Wyatt Barely Copes

As I head through the back door, I hear the fire trucks screaming in the distance. They'll be here in less than a minute. A sense of relief cascades over me. I run across the yard towards the gym. Good old Hatch must have obliged by opening it, surprising because I thought he would have taken off. A few boys are hanging around the door and a few are in the courtyard.

'Inside!' I'm urgent and directive, pushing aside a couple of boys, who are tardy in moving including Bentley. I'm momentarily surprised to see him. Once inside I shout at the top of my voice.

'Cool it guys! I want to do a headcount and make sure everyone is out.'

Everyone except Mr Rogers that is. In the front of my mind, I can still see his immobile and bloody body lying on the floor in Rata. Concentrate on the job at hand. Come on cops, Fire Service! I'm thinking, hurry up, hurry up, although I know in my heart it's almost certainly too late for him.

I notice that someone, presumably Hatch, must have opened the storeroom door containing all the sports gear. I see boys are going in and out. The group still seem highly agitated, talking loudly and excitedly, pushing, shoving laughing and hooting. Very few are moving as I requested, most are ignoring me I do my best to do a headcount. I get to twenty-three, way short of the correct number. I know it's not right but another count is pointless, there's far too much movement.

A couple of boys emerge from the storeroom. In their hands, they hold hockey sticks and they are waving them around. It's funny what crosses your mind at a time like this but my first thought is that I can't remember any occasions when the residents have played hockey. Why would we even have hockey sticks? I'm barely aware of the danger, too distracted to dwell on it. I'm having trouble getting my mind off Mr Rogers.

Then two boys with hockey sticks approach me. They stop four of five paces away.

'Yo man! That bastard Rogers got his good. You kid fuckers are all the same. Now you're gonna get yours!' The biggest of the two, Jeremiah, stares me in the eye for a second, then steps forward with the raised stick. Chevy, his offsider, stands his ground. He looks less assured.

'What are you on about? All you're doing is making things worse for yourselves so put down the sticks and get over by the wall so I can do a headcount.' I speak loud enough to rise above the general hubbub of boisterousness, sirens and fire alarms, but quietly enough so I think only they can hear. I'm beyond diplomacy, my tone is firm and my teeth are gritted.

Whatever rapport I believe I may have developed with Jeremiah over his time in residence is worth nothing. I'm about to get attacked. I feel emotional numbness, empty, I am cold. I won't be standing by and just taking whatever might be coming my way. I'll do whatever is necessary in the circumstances! I am tense like a wound-up spring. All of a sudden I'm very focused.

Before anything further happens, Jai Rehua, whom I was vaguely aware of in my peripheral vision, steps in front of Jerimiah and puts up his hand like a stop sign. Jeremiah pauses his advance.

'Cool it, bro, what the fuck are you doing? Not worth it man, if you're gonna piss off, just go! No one is going to stop you. No need to attack anyone, it'll just make things worse!'

Jeremiah is momentarily caught in a dilemma. I can see his brain attempting to process what's happening from the look in his eyes. He's caught between his rage and Jai. I know they've spent a bit of time together. He loves Jai's guitar playing and he's been frequently heard singing his praises to those who'll listen. He's like Jai's biggest groupie. I think if there's anybody who has some form of relationship with Jeremiah, it's Jai.

Just at this moment, a policeman walks in through the door of the gym. I hadn't heard their car arrive over the sound of the fire alarm, which continues pulsing through a speaker on the gym wall. They must have had a patrol car nearby to have responded so quickly. It's probably only about ten minutes since the alarm first went off. Whatever, they're here now and in the nick of time. The delay, just a few seconds, caused by Jai stepping up, probably prevented me from suffering a fate similar to Mr Rogers. Thank the stars Jerimiah isn't the quickest of thinkers!

'What's going on here?' the copper bellows in a commanding voice. Chevy, who is not noted for picking up anything subtle, seems to get the hopelessness of the situation and tosses his hockey stick away. He's only an 'also ran' anyway, just following the lead, but Jeremiah stands his ground.

'I'd think hard about what you're doing,' the policeman is looking him in the eye. 'Put down the weapon now!'

'Put it down Jeremiah I say calmly, 'it's over, let's not make things any worse than they are.' But Jeremiah is not registering. He's looking through me, I am nothing. He easily shoves Jai out of the way and steps closer, raising the hockey stick above his head, like a taiaha readying to deliver the killer blow.

In the time it takes me to blink he's on his back on the ground and there's a large Alsatian holding his arm and shaking it from side to side. He starts screaming at the top of his voice, 'Get it off me! Get the fucking thing off me.' The fire alarm suddenly ceases. The Fire Service has arrived. All other noise in the gym stops, except for the growling of the dog and Jeremiah's screams.

I am transfixed. A shadow walks past me and the dog handler stands over the boy and dog. He doesn't do anything immediately. He lets the dog, who has its teeth firmly sunk into Jeremiah's arm, continue to shake its head from left to right, doing its thing.

For a moment the world stands still. The boys are frozen. Only the dog and Jeramiah continue their frenzied encounter.

'Hey up!' is all the dog handler says. The dog lets go and sits down beside the prostrate boy, who grabs his newly released arm and begins sobbing loudly. Right now, I am reminded this is a little kid inside an adult body. I sigh in relief...and there's a tinge of sadness as well. What a mess!

'The dog team got here quickly,' the policeman comments to his handler colleague like nothing is happening.

'Yeah, we were over at the Workingman's club. Break-in, third this month.'

'Probably a lucky thing all round from the looks of it.'

I'm thinking about Mr Rogers. 'My colleague Mr Rogers, he's badly injured. I couldn't get him out. He's up on the second floor. He looked to be in a very bad way. Someone needs to do something quickly.' I'm talking fast, babbling, but I needed to get it out.

'Nothing we can do. The fire boys will get him. Let's just make sure this lot stays here. Jack, get Rory to have a chat with this lot. Let's make sure no one else gets any bright ideas!'

Jack, the dog handler responds with a command, 'Speak Rory speak!' The Alsatian barks half a dozen times in quick staccato succession. The boys, who had already moved on from the business with Jeremiah and started to become restless, some even making abusive comments at the Police, become instantly quiet. Their attention is now focused on the snarling canine whose head is bobbing from side to side, making each boy feel they are personally being watched.

'All right everybody, line up against the wall. I need to do a headcount and I want the keys back. Hatch, I saw you unlock the back door. And someone opened up the gym and the store cupboard so I know they're still here.' The boys begin moving towards the back wall. Hatch Hitch holds up his hand, he has the keys.

'They were already in the back door when I came downstairs sir,' he says. I can't be bothered to argue at this point, I take them off him. A glance around for J.T. tells me he isn't there. I go through the count. Amazingly he is the only one missing.

I let the police know. I keep my voice down so the boys can't hear me.

'One unaccounted for. His name is Justin Thomas, J.T... I think he might be responsible for the assault on Mr Rogers. I found him unconscious on the floor by J.T.s bed just after the fire started. The fire was spreading and I had the boys...' I stop myself from repeating the horrors. Inside I feel revulsion and I want to scream but I can't in front of the boys, no sign of weakness...ever.

'He can't have got far. I'll put out an 'all points' and we'll get him in no time. We know the little miscreant well. There is nowhere he can hide for long' says the copper.

A couple of firemen come into the gym all decked out in their gear.

'Everybody out?' is the first thing they ask me.

'No,' I reply. 'All the young people are out but my colleague didn't make it.' I give them a summary of what happened.

'The guys are already in the building' he responds. 'It won't be too hard to get to the second floor but a roof collapse is a potential worry. We'll do our best. Hopefully, the crappy sprinklers system will have done something. We need to get some water on the place too. Once the fire gets hold in the ceiling space it spreads like nothing you've ever seen. Good thing all the boys got out. Good effort there!' He turns to the policemen, 'Keep them here until we give the 'all clear.' Could take a while.' With that, he quickly departs the gym and I hear him shouting out commands to his colleagues outside.

I realise I finally have the opportunity to ring the on-call senior. I tell the policemen and he lets me know they will be staying till everything is sorted, along with Rory the dog. He sighs. 'It could be a long night for everybody. We'll be calling in help, including the appropriate investigators for such a serious incident. Not sure they can do much tonight but the scene will need to be preserved once the fire is out.'

I go to the SNU where there is a working phone, checking on the boys in the unit as I pass their cell doors. They are all awake and asking questions but there is no more door kicking. I don't answer, except to say 'Later'.

I call John Land who answers almost immediately. 'Hi John, I think you better come in...'

Chapter 36
The Aftermath

After about half an hour, the Police confirm Mr Rogers is dead. They believe the blows were sufficiently traumatic that he would have died instantly or within minutes at the most. They tell me there was nothing I could have done even if I'd gotten him out. I don't feel any better despite the news.

The Fire Service spends nearly two hours getting the fire under control and damping down hot spots. In the end, they are able to save the bottom level of the old house but the upstairs dorms and the flat area are damaged beyond repair, along with much of the roof. They remain at the residence for the rest of the night keeping an eye on the still smouldering second story.

The Police presence increases significantly now there is a crime scene to preserve and a death to investigate. They bring in a paddy wagon and the older boys are moved to the secure unit at Kingslea for the night. Jeremiah and Chevy, the hockey stick boys, get to spend the remainder of the night in the Police cells. They haven't ruled out Jeremiah as the potential perpetrator in the death of Mr Rogers. His profile, the fact he resided in Rata, and his aggressive behaviour in the gym, have all contributed to this view. He will be questioned as soon as they have someone free.

The remaining boys sleep in the gym for the rest of the night. We manage to get a few mattresses and enough blankets out of a downstairs storage area which fortunately suffered no damage at all. Some have to share the mattresses but it doesn't seem to matter to anyone. The night's excitement and events seem to have exhausted them and most are asleep quickly.

While the circumstances of Mr Roger's death have not been officially shared with the boys, they all knew he was seriously injured. Now they know that he's dead. We will need to get appropriate support services involved tomorrow. The on-call senior remains on the premises, and after ringing around for half an hour, he manages to find another senior colleague who comes in to help with the supervision.

I remain on the team although technically I should be sent home. The senior does not suggest this and I do not ask, I just get on with it. The busyness and uniqueness of the situation are a partial distraction from the horror of the events. My mind continues to race though and I know I will need some time to process what has happened. I certainly couldn't sleep!

The area upstairs is secured by the Police and Fire Service. I overhear the Police telling John Land they cannot separate out the boys tonight who might be witnesses to the events because there are just too many. In the morning they will want to speak to everybody who might know something. However, they do want to speak to me sooner rather than later, while events are still fresh in my mind.

When the boys are fully settled, I undertake a preliminary interview with the Police. I'm feeling pretty washed out. I recount what I can recall but I'm feeling cold and shaky. I did not witness many of the events and wasn't really in a position to identify who might have been the last person to see Mr Rogers alive. They ask me who might have a beef with him sufficient to result in an attack. I can't say. We've all experienced threats of assault, and serious harm to ourselves and our families, they are par for the course in this environment. Mr Rogers was far from popular but it is a long way from that to murdering him. However I say what we all know, these boys are unpredictable and in the wrong set of circumstances, anything is possible. The Police, the Courts, and anyone who deals with these kids know that boys from the residential system have gone on to murder people.

They have discovered from a few boys in Rata that Mr Rogers had a verbal altercation with J.T. but they all insist that they left the room as soon as the confrontation started. No one saw anything like an assault. A number of the boys reported that the guitar, now believed to be the possible murder weapon, had been removed by Mr Rogers. I can't help them any further on any of this because I was outside doing checks although I can confirm that the guitar was not removed before I went outside. I also confirm that the last time I saw it, it was not beside J.T.s bed but was on the other side of the dorm near Jai's. Not very helpful I'm afraid and the Police indicate they will want to interview me again later within the next twenty-four hours.

The body is eventually taken away. The fire and the water from the sprinkler have caused havoc with the crime scene and the Police indicate this will presen challenges for gathering their evidence. The police are clear, they are undertaking a murder enquiry.

The fire was contained to the upper story but that doesn't mean the residence will ever be used again. It is totalled, no longer habitable, and not repairable. In some ways, it's not as big a deal as it could be because the Department is preparing to move the boy's programme to the new site at Kingslea. Preparations are well advanced. The building designated for the boys is almost completed with only some external painting yet to be done. I'm sure the new residence will be made functional quickly by cobbling together some of the available resources and the hasty purchasing of bedding, furniture and other miscellaneous items. No doubt things will move with urgency now. Most of the stuff belonging to the kids was in the undamaged storerooms downstairs so it has survived. The same is true for many of the key documents which were in the downstairs office. The Daily Log and a few of the personal files that we had in the night staff room, along with our bits and pieces were all lost.

As six-thirty in the morning comes round, there are still Police on site although the Fire Service have just packed up and gone. The morning shift team starts to drift in for duty. John Land tells me to take a few days off and offers to get me psychological support if I feel I need it. I thank him for the offer. I will consider it but what I want most is to get the hell out of the place and hopefully, find some sleep.

As I walk the short journey home I appreciate the beautiful morning freshness. The sun is rising and it sparkles and dances on the Avon river as it streams by. Now that I have left the scene my mind is in turmoil. I'm questioning whether I want to work in the residential environment ever again. Since my first day in the role, now over twelve months ago, the night staff's safety concerns have frequently been raised with senior management. Yes, I know we are vulnerable, but up until now, it has all been a relatively abstract discussion point. I've experienced most things the environment has to offer but I never envisioned for a moment it could ever lead to this.

I've become immune to the threats, they are like the wallpaper, always there but after a few days, you don't notice anymore, only doing so in exceptional circumstances. I'd seen violence, even been attacked. But a death though? That's more than I signed on for. I know I'm not in a fit state to be thinking about this all but I can't turn my buzzing head off.

When I get home the usual morning mayhem in a house with three school-aged children is well underway. Noise, busyness, little squabbles, a commotion, but it's ordinary family chaos. I think how blessed I am to have the family I do.

Not so happy at all is my wife. I tell Rose what happened as the kids' whiz around oblivious to their father's trauma. Previously I've told her many, many hairy tails from my experiences in residence. I've always presented events, whether I was directly involved or not, as stories, yarns, and fascinating, revelations of different lives, perhaps even enjoying the mildly shocking nature these create for anyone who knows nothing of the real environment. Rose confirms that for her too, the stories have been remote like they are from another world. Even my staff colleagues have never fully registered as real people because she has never met them, never put a face to the names. Not so anymore, now everything is all too real.

She makes it abundantly clear she would be happier if I never go back to residential work. We will discuss it more later when the dust has settled and the clouds have rolled by a little. It all adds to the thoughts running around in my head as I finally get to bed. But I know it will be some time before I sleep despite my exhaustion.

After a few days off I feel agitated. A close examination reveals I'm wanting to get back to work. There are lots of things I don't like about the job but they tend to be about the Welfare System, the structures, and the politics, not so much about working directly with the boys. I'm hooked on the lives, the stories, the interactions, the potential, the drama, I want to keep being a part of it all despite what's happened. I feel an emotional pull towards the boys, and I think, despite everything, I can make a difference to some whose paths I will cross in the future. I'm pragmatic about how much any one person can achieve and I accept that I will have to live with failure, but the biggest failure, and the option that will certainly lead to failure, is not to try. I feel hope, and that above all else, is hugely important.

And I feel ambition. I know that given the chance I can make a difference, both in practice and in the ways things are done. I'm over sitting around being critical, it's a waste of time and energy, action is what counts. I know I can do things if the opportunity presents itself, however opportunity is more than luck, it is preparation and I need to get prepared. But first I need to talk it all through with Rose... when the time is right.

I have two further interviews with the Police. They are very open in their conversation with me. I must have been a potential suspect but it's plain they've ruled me out.

They nabbed J.T. two days after the events. However, they haven't decided whether to charge him with the murder or with arson at this time, although they told me they think he did both, possibly with Jai's help. They are the last two boys who are known to have been near Mr Rogers. Jeremiah has been ruled out as a possible suspect, many of the boys confirmed he'd been with Chevy in Kauri nearly the whole time. But the police had to acknowledge that the chaotic situation means that it is hard to track down who did what on the night and there were probably opportunities for other boys to have been responsible, albeit less likely.

J.T. and Jai, when interviewed, denied knowing anything. They were held separately with Jai being taken to the cells the night after the incident and interviewed. He was at Kingslea when the newly captured J.T. was interviewed. There were further interviews but the boys never came together or saw each other again.

Both boys claim the last time they saw Mr Rogers he was carrying the guitar into the night staff office. After that J.T. went to the stairwell and Jai went into Rimu. They agreed J.T. had an argument with Mr Rogers but said it was nothing, just the usual argument that happened every time they had the guitar upstairs. They denied any knowledge of how the fire started. Both boys said on that night the place was in a total state of chaos with boys running all over the place. They also made the point many of the boys didn't like Mr Rogers and everyone knew he was threatened on many occasions. He had also been assaulted previously. All of which was true. Their stories did not match one hundred per cent, but they were substantially consistent. Some of the boys also confirmed seeing Jai in Rimu and that he urged everyone to evacuate when the alarm went off.

The Police didn't believe either of them but had not been able to break their stories. I told them it was Hatch who had Mr Rogers's keys. They ruled him out too. When interviewed, lots of the boys said they touched the keys as they were passed to the person nearest the door. Hatch ended up with them because he was the one who knew which key would open the door, a challenge for most.

There was an additional complication for the Police. The evidence, in particular my evidence, identified the guitar as the probable murder weapon. Unfortunately, it was very near the source of the fire and away from the direct wash of the sprinklers. There wasn't anything left of it apart from a few bits of scared metal and the strings, so no forensic evidence of any worth. They agreed it was the likely murder weapon. Other potential causes were considered highly unlikely or ruled out at this point, such as Mr Rogers falling and hitting his head on the bed.

The Fire Service established the fire started with the curtains at the northern end of the dorm but couldn't find the actual implement that caused it. They suspected it was a lighter. Mr Roger's body had also experienced fire damage. The police were able to tell he had suffered severe 'blunt force trauma,' a nice way of saying he was struck several times and his skull and cheekbone had been fractured. They said it looked like he'd experienced a frenzied attack, at least three blows, almost like a crime of hate. They asked me if I thought Jai was capable of such a thing and I said to my knowledge there was no violence in his history, nor had he ever expressed any substantial negativity towards Mr Rogers, not within my hearing anyway.

Despite the questions about Jai, the Police were still pretty sure J.T. was the killer. They didn't feel the need to look too much further. They described him as a 'nasty piece of work who was always on the pathway to killing someone.' He had red marks on his neck, consistent with a fight or attempted strangulation but he claimed these were from a fight he had on the street shortly after he escaped, unwitnessed and the assailant unknown. The Police expressed their confidence they would eventually solve the case. And J.T. is going to prison. When the time comes, they'll know where to find him.

It takes a few days before John Roger's body is released by the coroner. I attend the funeral five days after his death. For the first time, I meet his daughters and his wife. I introduce myself before the service and express my condolences. I can feel their grief. There is a whole other part to a colleague's life we never see and only experience vicariously through the stories they share when you spend a lot of time together. That was how it was with Mr Rogers. He was much loved at home and I could tell he will be sorely missed. His wife, Bernie, bravely gets up to speak. They never for a moment envisioned the job would prove to be his end, despite his many tales of the difficult boys and challenging situations he faced. She says it was a random event, a risk of the job and John knew it and gladly took it on so he could help the boys. She holds no animosity towards the Department despite everything that has happened. She joked that John's chihuahuas were lost without him, off their food, and in mourning too.

Many of the big wigs from the Department attend the funeral and due respect is shown, and no doubt some relief is felt as well at Bernie's conciliatory statements. I sit at the back with Ted. We have an opportunity towards the end of the service to share our memories. Neither of us takes it up.

Rose and I finally make the time to talk about the job. After our initial shock, we get a perspective on what happened. I confirm I want to keep working in this area and view this as a random event. I make her a promise I will always put our family's interests first even if it means walking away from a risky situation in the future, or if appropriate, from the job altogether. In the end, I think she is persuaded because the residence offers a pathway to a professional career in the Department or within the broader welfare sector. Until now she didn't know about the conversation with my father many years ago that put me off being a social worker, but now she does. This is what I have wanted for a long time.

I have no qualifications however and recent events have reinforced a desperate need to improve my knowledge and skills. I feel a strong desire to get on with things, complete my degree, and become a social worker. John Land has made an open offer that I can move into the day shift at the next vacancy and the residence will help me start more formal training. I am going to take him up on this.

Chapter 37
Back on the Job

It's Monday night, nine forty-five p.m. as I arrive at Kingslea. The last and only time I've been here was for the big briefing. Then, I managed to see the car park and the marae. As I come on-site, I see a sprawling, brightly lit up campus resembling a small village. Multiple buildings are dotted all over the place, connected by a maze of roadways. I immediately wonder how perimeter checking works here, it would take half the night. No doubt I'll find out. I'm due at the nearest building so that's where I head. I will explore it all later when the circumstances allow.

Howard House, the new home of the boy's programme, is a two-story wooden building. As I walk in the door, which is unlocked, I'm greeted by a large open area with dining tables and a sizable living area surrounded by brand new, variously coloured couches and bean bags. I'm struck immediately by the smell of freshness, new paint, carpet, and furniture. There is a small kitchen just off the lounge. I can see an electric jug, a toaster and a large fridge. The major meals are prepared in a standalone facility elsewhere on campus. At the briefing I attended, the Department indicated they wanted to deinstitutionalise the system The first step is to create a home-like milieu for the children and young people This is the start, a change in the way the environment looks and feels Deinstitutionalisation is more than just changing the physical environment though, it encompasses practices and procedures, and it touches on attitudes and behaviour of both inhabitants and workers. Lots more change must be coming!

I, too, feel different. I'm on the verge of my own new beginning, a purposeful commitment to my future direction. My mind is swirling with these thoughts as I stride purposefully towards the reinforced glass wall and door at the far end of the room. Despite never having been here before, I know where I am going upstairs to the sleeping area. I go through a similar door at the top of the stairwell

The bedrooms open onto an 'L' shaped corridor and the night staff office is at the juncture, giving direct visibility of all the bedroom doors. All the boys have individual rooms so no more open dorms or partitioned areas. That's already a huge improvement I think to myself. Being able to see down both corridors is a second significant improvement on the old Stanmore arrangements. It's not quite business as it was, but it is also not so different that it isn't business as usual.

I'm about to see the boys for the first time since the events of the fire. Any anxiety I am feeling about returning is only the same as I always feel when starting any set of shifts. What boys will be in residence, what are the current group dynamics, and whom will I be working with?

I am particularly interested in seeing Jai if he is still here. I suspect he may know a bit more about the events that lead to John Roger's death than anyone else, apart from J.T. But J.T. is gone. Although he was caught a couple of days following the fire, when he appeared in Court the Judge remanded him directly to prison. I'm thinking about Jai because of the guitar, and his connection with the murder weapon.

Immediately, I settle into the new normal with a changeover briefing. Afterwards, Ted tells me how it's been for him in the intervening week since they all arrived at Howard House. He's been working with the reliever, Ter, who will stay as part of our team replacing John Rogers until a new staff member is recruited. I'll get to partner with him at the weekend. All good, at least he knows the ropes…and I know him.

Grief counselling was provided for the staff and the boys to help manage the loss of their previous home and the death of Mr Rogers. The feedback from the counsellors is the boys have moved on quickly, which they indicate is to be expected for this client group.

The impact on the staff is more significant. Ted felt it acutely because of his long association with Mr Rogers. The fire was something he'd long predicted, and the potential for loss of life in the event one occurred. He doesn't say as much, but I have the strong sense he wants to talk to me about it all again. I guess he may be planning to take possible follow up action, maybe he'll want to see his local MP as he's threatened to do so before over the issue. Now he has a real example to concentrate on. I'm not keen on that approach, I think we need to find our solutions from within the Service and I know that John's untimely death will mean an extensive review. I can contribute there. I also think he wants to pick my brains and see what I know. I expected it. I'm happy to talk about things but first I want to see the boys. I check on the whiteboard in the office and see a few names of those who were here last week, are gone. My eye falls on Jai's name. I ask Ted to fill me in on some of the regulars.

Howard House only has twenty beds and this has meant that a few of the older boys who were waiting for an adult court appearance have gone, Fish is one, sent to Corrective Training. Chevy's name has an 'M' by it, for 'missing' because he absconded within the first two days, running away on the walk over to the school which is some distance from the Boys Programme. It sounds to me like an ongoing opportunity for future runners. Reese was in an accident involving a stolen car and is in hospital … broken pelvis… so he won't be running anywhere for a while. The driver, unknown to us, was killed. Bentley is still in residence. Ted tells me with a grin that I'll be mildly amused about Hatch. An older cousin of his turned up after all these years, recently returned from living in Aussie for most of his life. He knew about the accident that killed Hatch's folks and made enquiries about his whereabouts from the Department of Social Welfare. He wanted Hatch to live with him. Social worker Goodley couldn't believe his luck and made the plans and got Hatch into court within a few days. Yesterday he was released into his cousin's care. He's now on a farm in Balclutha. Ain't life a funny thing!

Some good, some bad and some ugly, but I am up to date. I excuse myself. I just want to get out there and see the boys. Ted leaves me to it. He knows I need to find my feet in the new world before doing anything else.

I walk down the hall, looking briefly into each room and saying hello to the occupant. I am familiar with all the current crew. There's a new boy in the SNU, which is located downstairs and on the other side of the building. But I won't go there until later. Ted checked on him when doing his normal security rounds, he's settled. The boys show no sign of being interested in my return.

I traverse the long hallway, with six rooms on each side. I go round the bend to the remaining eight. In the end room on the left, I find Jai. He's sitting on his bed, not in it as he should be. I know he heard me coming and I feel he's waiting for me.

'Gidday Jai, I see you're still here. No discharge then? How are you settling in?' I inquire.

'Hi, Mr Blues man… Good…Yeah. No, the usual with mum, didn't come to court, any rate, the cops didn't want me out and about. This place … yeah it's ok. Heaps better than Stanmore. It's great to have our own rooms. Much easier

272

to deal with the eggs now, I just shut the door! Yeah man all good, all good...'
I'm working up to saying something but before I can, he adds, 'Oh, they have a couple of new guitars too and they're real quality compared to those crappy old banged up dungers we had before. Man, it's much easier to play tough tunes like 'Shuffle Rag' when you've got a better axe. And they've got a music room here so that guy John Land, yeah, he said there's going to be a music programme, you know they've got drums and a bass guitar. He said you are going to run it... choice...'

He pauses, possibly realising that I want to say something, and while I am interested in the news, I don't want to be diverted from what I want to say, the reasons I've sought him out. He opens the door, 'You been away?'

'Yeah, I had a few days to get over the fire and death of Mr Rogers. It was a pretty big thing...' Momentarily, the memory of trying to drag Mr Rogers out of the burning dorm comes rushing back. I guess it's going to happen for some time yet. 'It was a bad night. Nobody deserved what happened to him,' I pause for a moment as I experience a further burst of emotion. After swallowing I carry on.

'I wanted to see you and let you know how much I appreciate you stepping in when Jeramiah seemed hell-bent on using my head as a hockey ball. It could've been a difficult situation for me, and you stood up for me. Thanks, Jai, I appreciated it.' I mean it. Jai took a risk on my behalf and I feel it reflected the threads of a relationship, something for us to build on, especially if I am to move to day work permanently. He doesn't say anything, waiting before I move on.

My other concern is I don't want to see him caught up in the wash from what I believe to be J.T.'s murderous behaviour. There is one significant part of this whole sorry business that does not appear right to me, and I know it troubled the Police as well. The boys reported that when they last saw Mr Rogers, he was carrying the guitar out of Rata to the night staff office. But if so, how did it get back into Rata and why was it near J.T.s bed? That's not where we saw it when we came on for the night. Since both boys gave the same statement, either something else happened after Mr Rogers removed it, which seems unlikely given where it was found, or they are colluding on a fabricated story and both know something more than they're letting on. Jai doesn't seem likely to be a killer to me but I guess you could never say 'never', in the right circumstances... It's still far, far more likely that J.T. is responsible with his known propensity and history for violence. He could've easily intimidated Jai before he ran off, made sure they had a similar story after all there was a good few minutes where there was no staff about as the boys evacuated to the gym. I think this is a likely scenario and I can't help myself, I have to say something.

'I know you've been interviewed by the Police and I can't discuss the matter of Mr Roger's death with you because it's an ongoing investigation and any chats we might have could cause problems for the investigation. I certainly don't want to do anything that might prevent the Police from getting to the bottom of the matter'...I consider carefully my next comment... 'However I have to say, I wonder about that guitar. It all seems a bit odd to me. Guitars don't walk...'

Jai looks at me. His face is a mask. I carry on.

'What I can say is that J.T. is a piece of work and I wouldn't want to see you or anybody else for that matter, caught up in a serious investigation, possibly even taking more blame than they should, because of misplaced loyalty to him. That's all I wanted to say.'

Jai doesn't respond. I didn't think he would. He will never nark. He has his head down now so I can't see his face. I knew it was a risk to say something but I felt I needed to. After a moment of tension-filled silence, I make to leave the room, I have said my bit.

'It was a bad thing, yeah...really bad. But I'll tell you what I told the Police. J.T. can't have done it. He's all talk, hasn't got the balls. Sure, he's done some bad stuff but it's always when he's on the drugs or the piss. I don't know him very well but word on the street is he never really fronts up to anything. He's chicken shit, all blah...yeah blah blah blah. I guess something else must have happened.' A pause then he continues. 'And no worries about Jeremiah, we couldn't have the Bluesman hurt, no more guitar then.' He's looking up now and has a weary smile on his face.

I nod in acknowledgement. I guess I know my nickname now.

As I step out the door, Jai calls after me, 'Hey Mr Bluesman.' I turn in the doorway and look back. Now Jai is looking me in the eye. 'Mr Rogers... he wasn't a very nice guy... But he shouldn't be dead. Lots of things happen in this world that shouldn't have happened...but sometimes, they just do...'

I turn and walk away, ready to get back to my role.

Author's Note

This book is loosely based on my experiences as a night staffer working for the Department of Social Welfare in the late 1980s. The Christchurch Boys Home, colloquially called 'Stanmore Road' or 'The Stanmore Boys Home' was a real place offering placements for boys with problem behaviour from the greater Canterbury region in New Zealand. The actual date on which the home opened is unclear but it was during the 1940s. It closed in 1988 when the boys' residential programme was relocated to the Kingslea Site in the suburb of Shirley. The site already had a residential home for girls. The amalgamation happened as part of a suite of reforms to the residential care system which commenced in the mid-1980s and continued into the 2000s.

The location of the Boys' Home is accurate. The descriptions of buildings are only as good as my memory, contributed to by a few items I've managed to find including old photographs and plans.

The boys in residence were generally aged between twelve and sixteen years although at times boys as young as ten and as old as nineteen were placed there. The residential population was made up of boys held under the direction of the courts, state wards, those with mental health issues or intellectually challenged, and anyone else who could not be safely housed elsewhere. Placements were a crisis response and most often only lasted until safer arrangements could be made.

The Christchurch Boys Home operated a twenty-four-hour seven days a week programme. Three teams rotated through a roster to cover the day shifts and although the night staff did not work with those teams directly, they were loosely attached to one for administrative purposes. The night team were classed as 'domestic staff', which also included a cook, house matron, and gardener.

In 1987 the facility had around thirty permanent staff members. The staff group included a variety of ethnicities, ages and gender, as well as a diversity of attitudes and values. Staff numbers on any given shift varied over the years but generally, it was four or five working directly with the boys and a supervisor who was also a senior social worker. The residence also relied on a significant number of temporary staff, called relievers. There was almost always a reliever on shift and often there would be multiple at the same time.

Daily activities for the boys included schooling for all those under 16 years. In its last eighteen months, the programme for the older boys and non-school attendees was managed by three specialist coordinators. They also ran the weekend programme for all the boys.

The residence was a challenging environment, partly because of the mix of young people, but also because of the relentless nature of the work which required the staff to spend almost all their time on shift working directly with, and supervising, the boys. Meals were taken with the boys and breaks off the floor were a rarity. By far the majority of those I worked with were dedicated people, committed to doing their best for the boys in care.

This story is fictional. I have tried to create a picture of residential life and the residential community that captures some of what I experienced, both good and bad.

The staff profiles do not replicate any particular person. Any actual likeness to anyone who may have worked there is purely coincidental, except for Wyatt. I have partially based him on myself although this is mainly in his background. This is also true for the young people who form the characters in the book. The characters are composites based on the many young people whom I dealt with over the years I worked in residential or prison settings. Many of the young people had common histories and common issues but there were also significant diversities apparent in their cases. No specific young people have been used as the basis for any character in the book and any perceived likeness is purely coincidental.

Finally, the events described in the book are also made up. Some are based on the types of incidents and events that occurred in the residential system nationwide back in the 1980s. Some are built around the very real fears that night staffers experienced working in the conditions at the time. However, they are not specific to any real event or incident that occurred at the Christchurch Boys Home while I was there.

CPSIA information can be obtained
at www.ICGtesting.com
Printed in the USA
BVHW052113230623
666316BV00004B/91